Worlds

Published by Boann Books and Media LLC

NEW YORK

Worlds

by John Kearns

Published by Boann Books and Media LLC

For information:
Boann Books and Media LLC
70 La Salle Street, #19D
New York, NY 10027
www.boannbooksandmedia.com

Published by Boann Books and Media LLC

For information address:
Boann Books and Media LLC
70 La Salle Street, #19D
New York, NY 10027
www.boannbooksandmedia.com

ISBN: 978-1-79484-222-2

Printed in the United States of America

CONTENTS

1. Lust & Chastity

No hoax, insisted Laura. It's a miracle.

— I thought they just said it's not possible …

Paul Logan spoke to the crown of Laura's blonde head as she hid her face from the April showers and her hand fumbled with the keys. He glanced ahead at Charles's stumbling across Church Street.

— … that it's not old enough or something.

said you'd never get in the car with her again after last time never again take chances with your job your life for god's sake for a night out with this crazy barmaid yet here you go again as if bound to her not knowing this simple brit was in tow so drunk he might not wend long on this pilgrymage while on those perky breasts again she wears an oscillating fireworking heart which could be the wild longing of your own heart for something that might not be which could be just a dream but what would it mean and on holy thursday no less

— No, no, no. It's a miracle. These scientists were atheists, not religious at all, and they couldn't find any explanation for it. They studied it and said there is definitely a face on it and it could be God's.

muted consonants the words running together that accentless youngchickspeech no way to tell her origins

Her pretty hand swiped away some stray hairs from her face.

the jolt of the brown of her eyes against the backdrop of her yellow hair lovely in wet disarray her whiskey-brown kirghiz eyes above those cheekbones thrusting out like seacliffs on a headland

Streetlight glowed on the wet asphalt of Barclay Street, on the grey Roman stairs and columns of Saint Peter's Church, and on the dusty hood of the black jalopy toward which Laura led the way.

that little upturned nose the curving lips with the slight pout like rose petals i will kiss those lips again

That first rainy Thursday — it rained every Thursday lately — she didn't have a car. They were under the ferry terminal ramp when he gave her hand a little squeeze and it squeezed back. Paul Logan walked past the unclean pizzaplace window to the door held open by a string of frayed synthetic. The heat hit his body like a strong Atlantic wave. Paul ignored the smell of melting cheese and baking dough and sauce and ordered a bottle of Guinness and an Amstel for her. Outside the salt air was cool and tainted with gas fumes. A loose late-night crowd was scattered around the asphalt and among the rectangular columns. He walked past lone smokers and clumps of people looking through the cyclone fence between the terminal and the Coast Guard building. The rain had slowed down. The triple-decked orange and blue *MV John F. Kennedy* ghosted over the dark misty harbor.

Before the lapping cinereal water in the empty slip and against one of the white-painted columns leaned Laura, with her hands behind the small of her back. All her curves now appeared bolder. Her hips and thighs against the rectilinear backrest, her breasts rising out and up from her slim figure shaped a silhouette that made his heart jump. Her bangs clung to her forehead and her eyes were at halfmast: it was hard to tell if they were open as she crinkled the brown bag around the beer bottle. A breeze wafted the saltwater exhaust smell in from the harbor and set the ends of her hair waving. Above those sharply upturned cheekbones, her eyes, all at sea, squinted at him. She smiled, and leaning toward him dizzily, chuckled:

— Hi!

Her lips formed an oval that in another context would have been comical and she moved toward him as if submitting to some unseen force. It was almost a fall. It was nothing he could take credit for. And there followed a swift, flowing surge of a moment measureless, transporting, and transforming.

a thunderclap kiss that took us outside of time or stopped it the impatient commuters the shore of the bay l'onde si lasse the island's inchoate arteries no longer present the impossible manifested as actual

— It's totally a miracle. An official miracle. Crossing before Saint Peter's, Laura unlocked the passenger door. I thought it might be something you could write about.

she wore that tie-dye-heart the night we met shirt of many colors her own hearts energy flashed that expanding pattern now that selfsame heart radiates an idea portrait of the artist as a crucified man something dear to your heart supernatural but she let the limey in the front seat brits out

— You're right. That could be a cool poem. A good first line. "They've decided it's a miracle" … "It's an official miracle" …

Drops of rain constellating across his glasses, Paul squinted up at the weathered gold cross at the pinnacle of the old church. Laura pulled up the button of the back-seat door and Paul climbed in.

plaque for thomas dongan earl of limerick general in the armies of england and france irish patriot devoted catholic recall tourguides tale of john mccloskey who rowed across the east river every sunday to hear mass later the cardinal who dedicated saint pats upon this rock

It took a couple of attempts but Laura got the car started. It was one of the most beaten-up vehicles that Paul had ever seen. That it was a BMW made it seem haunted by luxury dearly departed.

For the sick of our parish, especially the old windshield wipers which have recently taken ill, let us pray to the Lord.

Lord, hear our prayer.

Remember, Lord, those who have died and have gone before us marked with the sign of our faith, especially those for whom we now pray.

The handles on three of the BMW's doors. Let us pray to the Lord.

Lord, hear our prayer.

The radio. Let us pray to the Lord.

Lord, hear our prayer.

The turn signals. Let us pray to the Lord.

Lord, hear our prayer.

May these, and all who sleep in Christ, find in your presence light, happiness, and peace. Through Christ our Lord. Amen.

The BMW inched past the stairs of Saint Peter's.

first time i made a visit make three wishes an involuntary word puffed out of me home

...

"All right, m*o bhuachaill*! If it's ghost stories you want to hear, well, *bi dho husht, a cuisle*, and list while I speak! Seamus Logan will go back to the beginning and tell you a story about how he left his own native home on a misty evening full of fairies and spirits. Come here and listen, Sarsfield *agradh*, and I will tell you a tale of how I walked the hills of Mayo, *Go saibhalah Dia Sinn*, from my home place of Bunowen to the wilds of lawless Connemara over mountains as trying to cross as this wild ocean that's tossing us about and how I did it all for my love, for my own, Mary, and she taken away from me by scheming parents, the Brogans, who cared nothing for the genuine love that was in us. I put on my Sunday clothes and, with me shotgun over me shoulder and a full powder flask hanging by me side, I set off, caring little for what might befall me.

"Through the lonely valleys, I could hear the voices of my family and the people of my townland.

"Seamus, don't give up your people or your home for a chimera! The wee girl never cared for anyone but herself. Sure, wasn't it just your imagination that brought you to believe that things were otherwise? Afterall, there's always some madness in love."

"Still, onward I trudged. And the mists among the hills began to form into faces. And the first face that formed in the mist was that of a man who looked like he was born before the Flood, such rivers of wrinkles his ancient visage had.

"And in his old man's wavering voice he sang out, 'Seeeaaamus! How can you leave without a faaaaaarthing in your pockets, abandoning all that you looooooove so dearly, all your friends and relaaaaaations and walk these looooooonely hills and vaaaaaalleys? How can you leave your house and laaaaaand, your ooooold ancestral hoooome?'

"I said not a word, for I knew it was only taunting they were. 'Twould take a cleverer trickster than that lot to fool Seamus Logan. I marched forward, presenting a stern face to the spirits in the mist.

"Then one of them in a young man's voice asked, 'Aren't you afraid?'

"And this goaded me into speech.

"'Ah, it's many and many a steep hill and low valley I have trod,' I answered, 'and many a lonely one. Yet, I never was afraid by night or by day of the living or the dead.'

"'Ach, but you've never wandered this far from your home before and never with no wish to go back! Any man would be afraid in this mist and fog and only a foolish boy would refuse to admit it! Out here with no food to eat and no dry money and no one to look after you ... Who? Who will look after you now, now that you've left your people behind?'

"'Who will look after me? Why, the devil can answer that question! I had a wee girl who promised to be my wife and she's gone off!'

"Then among the quick-drifting clouds a great length of hair fell from behind the head of the spirit. Before my eyes, he turned into the shade of an old woman much like my grandmother. It was a voice sweeter than ever you'd hear among the mortals. Sweet and high it rose among the competing voices of the bickering *Sidhe*.

"As Seamus began to sing, several of his 'tween-deck neighbors who were standing or seated either on chests or on their bunks turned to listen. Young Sarsfield opened his eyes wide and with his left elbow propped himself up on his straw-stuffed mattress.

"'*Strange news is come to town.*
Strange news is carried.
Strange news flies up and down
That my love is married.'

"And, she started laughing. An old and bitter-faced *bean sidhe* she was.

"'*Maise*, she didn't marry you, Seamus — did she now? Or you wouldn't be out walking the roads in your Sunday clothes alone of an evening like this?'

"Without pause, for all thought of keeping silence had left me now, I answered, and my speech filled with fierce determination.

"'On an evening not unlike this very one, I was walking the road back to my home from the shoemaker in the village of Moneen. And I heard a voice from Mary's door, cry, 'Seamus, come in. I want you.'

"Peering at her father's door, I saw Mary looking bright as day, though it was long toward evening. For she shone for me like no other. For wasn't it three years I was faithful to her, though we hardly had a moment alone together in all the time of our secret courtship.

"For 'twas her voice that called from the door and no mistaking it. 'Twas Mary herself, left alone in the house. Her family were at a wedding, said she. They had left her at home, so powerful afraid were they at all times that she would meet some young man and elope with him and not fulfill their wishes to arrange her marriage. Now here a young man had found Mary, *mo stor*, the treasure the Brogans had tried to hide away. They might as well have tried to hide the shining sun in their wee cottage.

"Sure, wasn't she grand to look at? Her eyes were such a deep blue they shone against the yellow curls of her hair and her lily-white skin. She wore a dark brown dress and there was a ruffle of white lace around her neck."

"'Now is our chance to declare our feelings,' said she. 'Do you love me?'

"'I surely do!' I answered.

"'As much as you love me,' Mary said. 'I love you ten times more. Be always at the ready, and when the time comes, I will fly to you! We will walk into the chapel and get married and sail away to the land of the setting sun. Let God take care of the rest!'

"'Still,' the bitter-face of the *Bean Sidhe* hissed. 'She went to the altar with a pockmarked brute fifty years old if he's a day!'

"''Twas her parents forced this slighting of me,' I raged. "'*Mara faisc* on the Brogans! For they always desired that it be to a rich man she get married. But, I do not forget her promise to me, broken as it may appear.'

"'Should we fail to survive,' said she, 'in this wild flight from our own, my spirit will follow you in all your travels and all your endeavors and when you leave this world, which is nothing but mist, I will be waiting for you on the white strand of *An Saol Eile*.'

"'So, let the sedge cut me!' I cried, and my voice echoed among the mountains and drumlins. 'Let the moors drown me! May the roadless, pathless wilderness lead me forever in circles. Sure it would be better than spending the rest of my days in Bunowen, frozen in the worst moment of me life. And, reminding myself of her promise always, whatever wanderings may come on land or on sea, each step away from my shame in Bunowen, brings me closer to eternity with her, when we will embrace each other always just as the mountains from time immemorial embrace the loughs and strands!

"And the spirits vanished back into the mist."

. . .

Perhaps you are alarmed, Father Gaire, knowing me as you do, to see me go on at such length over such questions which would have appeared so nonsensical to me in the past. Doubtless no less than a fortnight ago, I would have ridiculed a man who poured forth effort and ink to enumerate such unanswerable queries! Today I say, "Be careful what you mock — for you may become the object of your own ridicule!" Coincidences signposting visitations between this world and others?! Charlatans who claim to receive God's messages?! As a Jesuit priest and a teacher, of course I consider such notions absurd. I can hear your laughter as I write.

"Sarsfield Logan, you always chuckled at such heretical thinking!"

You should also be well aware of my desire to join in your laughter, which I would surely do if I did not find this predicament so distressing.

I have written to you previously of the extraordinary effect my recent labor on my journal has had on me, how it has produced in me not only a remarkable serenity but also a greater appreciation for the urban and natural worlds around me. Each night when I pick up my pen, it is like setting out on a journey with an unknown destination. In my last letter, I related to you how a fortnight ago a budding flower in Washington Square Park, once a matter of small concern to me, entranced me so that I felt compelled to pause in my perambulations to partake of its color, its aroma, and its softness against my fingers and how I could not even resist getting down on one knee, like some Druid in the forests of the Dark Ages or like Apollo adoring the laurel tree into which Daphne had petitioned her father to transform her. Likewise, I sometimes get entranced by faces I encounter on the streets of Greenwich Village — an old man concentrating all of his attention on his game of chess, a hardened, dirty-cheeked boy peddling newspapers, the sincere, distressed visages of young women protesting their working conditions.

There is one extraordinary example I can see as if she were standing before me. She was a young Jewess, *une petite pigeon*, hunched no doubt from all of the hours spent over a machine. Even if she had stood up straight, the top of her head would not have reached my arm pit. Her blouse fit her loosely except for her sleeves, and her skirt was dark and long. There was a frayed cloth wrapped around her index finger, an improvised bandage for what must have been an accident at work. Her strawberry curls seemed anxious to be free of her cap and her eyes gleamed with anger and hurt. As she spoke to the crowd in broken English and what I believe was Yiddish, she seemed the very image of both ferocious anger and vulnerable youth. However, I seem to have abandoned my point.

I thank you for the kind and comforting words of encouragement in your last letter, which remind me that the Faith I have followed all my life is leading me to praise the grandeur of God as reflected in His miraculous creation. Nevertheless, I fear the dreadful temptation to be wandering onto the crooked path of paganism has come to me again. Perhaps Father's greenhorn roots are poking out of the earth, revealing a latent tendency toward superstition in me. Father cannot be faulted for his primitive beliefs, though his Faith was unswerving as any I have seen. The only tuition he got was from a local hedge schoolmaster in Mayo. Despite the Greek and Roman classics, the Bible, and some Irish folk stories he had learned, he could not be disabused of the unfortunate bent toward superstition he seemed to have been born with. Perhaps he has passed these bogland tendencies onto me.

This time, however, it is not the path of transcendentalism but of enthusiasm that tempts me. For you see, of late, I cannot keep the thought from my mind that the nightly mental travels I undertake by means of my journal are leading me into encounters with a world of spirits. Heretical and illogical as I know this thought is, it returns to me again and again and I fear that I shall have to close the journal for good. For related to my work on it is a series of coincidences so strange and so seemingly united by a common theme that I cannot find any rational explanation for it. I feel like I have indeed transgressed somehow, in my thoughts at least, though I feel too uncomfortable to bring them up in Confession. In the name of Jesus Christ, Our Lord, I ask Almighty God to chase away these demons, these pagan thoughts from my mind, and show me the way back to enlightened path of faith in Holy Mother the Church.

For a couple of weeks, despite my concern for the poor mistreated girl, I did not fulfill my vow to investigate what happened to Esther Rosenfeld. Preparing and then marking the examinations for the middle of the term occupied my time and my mind. I did feel guilty about this, and, as I was proctoring examinations and marking the papers, I was often distracted by thoughts of that young woman so badly injured and wronged. The image of her being wheeled into Saint Vincent's Hospital — the bruises on her face and hands, the look in her eyes when she saw my Roman collar and decided to trust me in spite of it — kept returning to my mind.

One lovely day in March, a harbinger of the spring that had not quite come, the sun was pouring through my window and I could hear the Elevated train discharging numerous passengers setting out to enjoy a day strolling Fifth Avenue or Union Square. I found it exceptionally hard to concentrate and I realized that I was doing the students no justice evaluating their work while in such an agitated state. So out the door and down Fifth Avenue I went, making a beeline for that portal to Lower Manhattan, the Washington Square Arch.

For the first couple of blocks, I was not even sure why I was headed toward that monument in such a determined fashion. Then it came back to me that it was in Washington Square Park that I had run into the Triangle Shirtwaist Factory girls who knew Esther. Since it was likely that Esther was still laid up at home with her injuries, it seemed best to start my investigation by speaking with her friends. Somehow my legs had decided on this plan without consulting my preoccupied brain.

Washington Square Park was bustling as I expected. Fashionable ladies carrying parasols and wearing emerald earrings, strings of pearls, and great wide hats wandered about. An organ grinder crooned a song in Italian and a violin player, just far enough away, played music for long hairs. Both styles of music were somewhat hard to hear, however, because of the noise of automobiles, which replace more of our old faithful horses each day. Things change so quickly in this city; it's a wonder people have any time to consider what they are gaining or losing.

I leaned against the basin of the fountain. Now and then a gust of March wind blew some cooling drops of water on my neck. Despite this, I soon grew hot standing in my blacks out in the sun. Moreover, I saw no factory girls gamboling in the park.

I decided to look for a seat in the shade. Ambling past Garibaldi and along the lane of trees and eagle-crowned lamps, I noticed a young man's vacating a seat on a bench. The trees provided plenty of shade and I enjoyed the violinist's performance, which I was able to hear more clearly from my new location and to recognize as the second movement of Beethoven's *Sonata Pathetique.*

I watched the showy people strutting to and fro, the men in their shiny top hats and the women like well-nourished partridges in their expansive finery. It was amusing to observe their glancing at me in my Roman collar as I looked at them looking at one another. Ragged brown sparrows with stripes of darker brown on their folded wings hopped about in the grass. An old man fed bread crumbs to some pigeons. Squirrels kept their distance and, at times, were compelled to flee from dogs on fashionable leashes. I also noticed the large plain cross of the Judson Memorial Church high above the south side of the park, and I realized I had forgotten to bring my Daily Office. How distracted I had become in the last few weeks!

The violinist finished his piece and from the street I could hear some commotion, which sounded like political demonstrators or striking workers. I thought I could hear speakers stirring the anger of a crowd. I wondered if Esther's acquaintances were among them.

I left the park for Washington Place.

...

Janey Dougherty stood beside the door of the Horn and Hardart's searching the crowds on East Chestnut Street for Sarah. Her friend was very late, which was really unlike her. Janey's fingertips stroked the rough edges of the paperback *Jane Eyre* in her trenchcoat pocket: she didn't feel like reading. She took a deep breath of springtime. It made her want to daydream and people watch.

Across the street, Anne from the office hustled by in her winter coat — and a scarf, of all things. You'd think it was 40 below. A pockmarked-faced man meandered behind her, wearing a hat that looked like somebody had walked up and bopped it, "So, there! Dent in your hat!"

God! She remembered every detail. Almost every person who walked by during those minutes — and that's all they were, mere minutes — before he spoke to her.

A lady in a big Wanamaker's cloth-coat brushed by Janey, clutching the strap of her handbag like she was trying to wear it out. There was the guy from the drug store who was always trying to keep her there to talk under some lame pretext or other. A pack of teenage boys, boxes of cigarettes rolled up in the sleeves of their white t-shirts, strutted up Broad Street, trying to impress everyone with how tough they were. And, oh, how all of Center City trembled.

"Hello, Janey."

He moved right into her line of vision, eclipsing the kids. A total eclipse, one with the power to be felt a year later.

"Oh! Hello … Hello, Mr. Logan," she said nervously. "I … I'm supposed to m-meet a friend. But I don't know where she is. She must be running late."

"Well, I got stood up, too. I was supposed to have lunch with a client."

"Mr. Wheatley?"

"Yeah, that's the guy. Can't count on him. Anyway, I figured I'd treat myself to some real luxury at the Automat."

"Well, you made the right choice," she heard herself say. "One never knows whom one will meet at the Automat. And behind these little glass windows lay the finest delicacies of Center City."

Is that really the way it happened? Were you ever really that smooth?

"All for just a nickel?"

"A nickel and a heart willing to take a chance. Drop your nickel in the slot, open the window, and you just might find the greatest sandwich in the world!"

"Sounds like a bargain."

"That's what they all say."

Tell the truth, Janey. You wanted him to ask you. You had fantasized about just such a chance meeting, even a conversation about the weather on the elevator. He was so handsome: dark hair, blue eyes, thoughtful and noble-seeming brow. You knew he was getting married, had seen the grinning fiancée framed on his desk. But, you couldn't help yourself.

"The greatest sandwich in the world? Lucky thing I have two nickels. Maybe I can find a pair of them."

Then he paused and looked down at the street. It was adorable the way he was so unsure of himself sometimes.

"See your friend anywhere?"

"Sarah? No, and I have been waiting half an hour."

"I'm afraid we can't spare you from the office any longer. You're going to have to eat immediately."

"For the good of the company."

"For the good of the company, yes. Plus, I need some guidance. I don't wanna get stuck with some second-rate sandwich."

"Get one without mayo."

And his hand was on her elbow and she was no longer thinking about Sarah, though she pretended to take one last look.

After a moment, she met his eyes, fighting their gravitational pull. He moved toward the entrance to the Automat. She was in his orbit and floating toward the door.

He held it open for her. And she crossed the threshold.

...

A barmaid ther was of fair visage
Who drove both car and men of this viage.
Hir customers for draughtes did nat come first
But after drynkyng long most left with thirst.
A slepey youth ther was from Engelond
Who got to ryde up front ther with the blond.
With venerie this night hed have no chaunce
For with taverns sweete licour he could not daunce.
Enditing for her trew directiouns
Around the monuments, around the tombes,
A scribe ther was who labored by day.
Of historie hadde he ful much to say.
The secretes of the aunchient streetes he knew
The buildings and their buried builders, too.
And whan he met the barwench Laura the fre,
He offered for her wootful guide to be.
Som thoughte his goal to drynk 'til clock stryke three
But his passioun it was for venerie.
Poul's cock priketh him ful with corages
To goon on swich wantowne pilgrimages
Fre, ful blisful queynte for to seeke
To swynk no thoughte yeveth nor no rekke.
Certeyn of its own conclusiouns
It listeth not to resons interrogaciouns.

Laura hunched her shoulders and laughed, her head lolling drunkenly.

— Where are we going?

our captain is a giant child a monstered blonde brat but one you'd forgive anything

— The West Side Highway? Charles offered.

— I'm not takin' the West Side Highway. It sucks! she snapped. It totally sucks!

— How 'bout the FDR? Paul suggested.

— Yeah, the FDR!

keep riding to see where she takes this bateaux ivre recommend a course now and then but don't get out of this used car named desire and leave her to that silly giacometti stumbling man it's not all ludicrous sure she forgets your favorite beer but when you catch her attention she is interested in what you have to say and for some reason you'll never understand in you

She turned to Charles.

— How do I get to the FDR?

— I have no idea, he answered, the accent sounding like a put-on: *I haaaahhhhve neeyoooo ideeeeahh....*

The accent made Paul's stomach turn. 26+6=1. It was broad and long and could give an American the impression that its owner was uppercrusty, though clearly — over here on a temporary work visa to work as a cook in a restaurant — Chuckles was not.

from southern england way down by the cliffs of dover the bottom of the island like battery park hills over the sea any ancient druidical spiritual significance i wonder

— Turn right onto Church.

was in that new world coffee shop this afternoon fueling myself to write more procedures was that today

Getting Home To Hell's Kitchen

Getting home to Hell's Kitchen tonight involves:

- Determining and communicating the correct directions to Laura
- Getting rid of this Englishman
- Kissing Laura again and making a date with her
- Getting out of the car in Hell's Kitchen
- Walking Home

— Shit! I can't see where I'm goin'.

Laura flung her cursing wrist and hand at her windshield. The wipers had stopped about halfway up the arcs they had scythed through the dual fields of raindrops. The real rain had stopped but it would start up again.

Determining and Communicating the Correct Directions to Laura

Determining and communicating the correct directions to Laura entail:

- Finding the way to the FDR
- Taking the FDR to Midtown
- Getting from the FDR to Hell's Kitchen

Laura flicked the back of her hand at the windshield again.

her wrist flowed evenly and softly into a hand small pretty but not dainty flesh gobsmacking in its youth a hand the old men at the bar liked to take and kiss tir na nog

— That kid's got a good heart, one of them had told him. A real good heart.

my heart's quick wild striving certain only of its wanting and its beating not of sorting sense from quatsch

— Turn right onto Park Place, instructed Paul.

The light turned green. They began moving again, passing right by his office building. Paul imagined Myrna Rosenfeld lowering her glasses on her nose and glaring at his foolishness.

Broadway and Park Place. City Hall Park. Skyscraper supported with arching buttresses on Park Row. The old world of the newsboy.

— Turn right here on Broadway and go downtown, Paul continued.

Finally, I am getting my chance to show her around.

you know laura and charles what you see before you has been a public park since 1686 the first building was a poorhouse the current building arguably the finest piece of architecture in new york was completed in 1811 it has been the seat of local government since the site was also used as a public execution ground

The chapel and cemetery of St. Paul's. My namesake. Oldest church in Manhattan. For Prods. Conversion! Through its windows, Saint Elizabeth Anne Seton gazed at St. Peter's and said, "The grass is greener on the other side of the graveyard fence." Threshold to the Otherworld. Peter has the keys.

The light turned red over Fulton Street.

The tombstones, some blackened, some whitened, tilting left and right in the gloom, in the shifting soil and turf. Names no longer legible on most. An angel carved here. A cross engraved there. Slabs of stone laid in the dirt showing the cracks and erosion of centuries of rain and sun and pollution. As the quick world passes by on foot and cab and car and bus and onetrain … and higher up the people, blind to their last end, laboring — even now so late on this night of watching and waking — in Twin Towers of Babel. How many towers of babble on this island? Above, they are making deals with faraway lands — nothing to us on the street but an illuminated crossword puzzle. Below, tombstones with faded messages. And what do they know of us? Under the stones and slabs, are they aware? Do they chat with one another? Richard Montgomery gossiping — *Ababoona!* — with the minister's wife?

wreaths with green white and orange bunting still in front of the obelisks 1798 commemoration ô ma mémoire

In the busiest thoroughfare of the greatest city of America looming over the heads of pedestrians, drivers, and cyclists stand two obelisks, monuments of marble raised by grateful hands, for the dead: Thomas Addis Emmet and Robert M'neven, United Irishmen, Protestant Nationalists.

In the center of Western civilization, the home of republican liberty, approximately three and one half blocks from Laura's employer, called the Orange Crush Bar for whatever reason, on Murray Street …

> *where cunningham hanged sailors on chambers street in the wee hours of the night telling the cowardly neighbors to shutter their windows and shut their mouths oh i wish i could have been in the place of the wench who bloodied that devil's nose with a broom on evacuation day would that i had a broom to evacuate this car of the sassanach*

… and two and one half blocks from Paul's employer, Susskind Software, the stranger reads in glowing words, of the virtues and of the fame of the brother of Robert Emmet, bold Robert Emmet, rebel, scholar, and lover of Sarah Curran whose beauty brought about his doom. Those glowing words of praise are sculpted on the noble pillar erected to his memory on Broadway and covered by the shit of the freest pigeons to ever fluff their feathers. A firing-squad's shot away from where the Emmet monument stands, a memorial not less commanding in its proportions and appearance was erected to William James M'Nevin; and the American citizen, as he passes through the spacious streets — potholed and cracked and patched — of that city which the genius of liberty has rendered prosperous and great, and takes his eyes off of the ass of the girl in front of him, he is able to gaze proudly on these stately monuments, before which we place these wreaths festooned with tricolored bunting to commemorate the 200th anniversary of that high-minded non-sectarian rising and the burning love of freedom on both sides of the Atlantic.

> *high-minded ideals that degenerated into prods killing papes papes killing prods the roads the bridges wet with gore in which the horses slipped*

The devotion to freedom that the Old World punished and proscribed brought in the New World recognition and respect to these patriots from the gallant and the free. To their holy cause, honorable lives, and beloved memory, their sympathizing countrymen erected these monuments and cenotaphs, now dulled by exhaust and darkened by the dust of traffic rushing heedlessly en route to a regular slice.

> *Do mhiannaich se ardma/th*
> *Cum tir a breith*
> *Do thug se clu a's fuair se moladh*
> *An deig a bais.*

In Memory of:
THOMAS ADDIS EMMET,
Who exemplified in his conduct,
And adorned by his integrity,
The policy and principles of the
UNITED IRISHMEN –

A deathright his brother never got. Could write 26/32 of it now.

But where is the doorway to the Otherworld? Ask Nathan Hale posed like a dancer on the Broadway sidewalk.

— Sure, he'd tell you, a bus could run you down on Church Street but I regret that, unlike me, you will not know it's coming.

What is the way from one world to the other? From shore to Stygian shore? Where is the portal? Up on the platform. Under the Bridge of Sighs. Within the Tombs, shaped of ancient Egypt. Shade of Eastern ends. Staring stubborn doom. At multitudes unruly. Mulberry Bend. Its courtyard colored. Full of freckled faces. Hardened as Bowery brick and mortar. Let my people go.

They lead him forward. Hands tied. Priests and sacrificial victim. To the portal they erected. For the time being. For the time passing. For the time escaping. (Heavier for him than anything borne.) To stand on the portal. To drop.

An exemplary end. Purposeful, punitive. A rite of man, mandated, marked. The time chosen. The time arriving.

He kisses the cross. Blest portal of the Christ condemned. Asphyxiated at the Skull, giving weight to Seven Last Words.

"I only regret that I have but one life to lose for my country."

Grand and generous to lose the extra life he never had. About Laura's age. Grave words. Weighted enough to etch in granite.

"When my country takes her place among the nations of the world, then, and not 'til then, let my epitaph be written. I have done."

Magnanimous silent stone! Pass the fight with fools from Fenian dead to Fenian living. *Faugh a ballagh*! Fog of valor!

Time comes, trap falls. Through the portal he passes. Kicking like a kid newborn, held high. The rite complete, his soul departs and who but the most sensitive can see it?

— Fuck! It's stalling! Laura slammed her foot down on the clutch and slapped the stick shift into first. She twisted the key in the ignition and you'd think from the distortion of her body and the side of her face that she was trying to pull King Arthur's sword from its stone, to wrest the keys to the kingdom. But it worked. The ancient automobile started and began to move. And the weary horns behind it played but a few notes, a couple of sounds sampled from a traffic jam for a rap song.

The engine was running but the light turned red again.

— Shit!

...

One Saturday, having no teaching duties to keep me indoors I found myself strolling along Washington Place, beginning my Divine Office for the Minor Hours, when, like a pack of wild colts all finding their legs together, a gaggle of silly girls came stomping along the pavement, straight-arming and shouldering one another, joking in Italian and laughing uproariously. They appeared to be garment factory workers heading home, perhaps from the Triangle Shirtwaist Factory. I glanced from Psalm 119 to a bevy of pigeons circling over the bright Washington Square arch, and casting fleeting flocks of shadows on the ground each time they passed the sun. I praised God for the wonder of His creation, that he is able to make even these mundane little birds wheel so beautifully about in the sky, jockeying with dark-and-bright wings for position on the inside of their ethereal track. I remembered to pray for the repose of the poor forgotten souls buried in unmarked graves beneath where I walked, in land that also once suffered the shadow of the "Hangman's Elm."

The factory girls, so full of whatever shenanigans they found so funny — much like the boys (i.e., "adolescents") I teach at Xavier, who get similarly caught up in their tomfoolery — almost knocked me over. One called out to me, "*Buon Giorno, Padre!*" The rest of them doubled over laughing, causing them to stumble and to collide with one another, which set them to guffawing even harder. Seemingly drunk with mirth and high spirits, they rushed onward to Washington Square. They neither noticed nor acknowledged their stern countryman, Garibaldi, scowling down at them from his marble pedestal. I found it heartening the way they could be so gay after a day of what must have been miserable toil. "Humor to a man is like a feather pillow. It is filled with what is easy to get but gives great comfort." Another of Father's adages.

I meandered through Washington Square, delighted to observe a happy quartet of girls jumping rope and a mother walking hand in hand with her son. Near the arched portal to Manhattan's prime meridian, I had to take care to avoid the traffic—a double-decker omnibus with a bicycle hot on its heels — between myself and the fountain by which the Italian girls now carried on. One tall girl with blonde hair and aquiline features leaned against the fountain's basin, waved back to me and in accented English shouted, "Come here, Father!"

When they saw my approach, the factory girls shrieked and ran ahead.

Once I got beyond the Square, my ears were assaulted by the rumbling of the Elevated and the screeching of its wheels as it turned at Third Street. Though my eyes were on the *Divine Office*, I knew I was approaching Sixth Avenue.

I recalled a man I once saw sketching the Sixth Avenue El. I thought, "Why would anyone want to draw a space so unpleasant with cinders and sparks? Are there collectors who would want such a portrait hanging on their walls?" It also occurred to me that that artist might have done better to capture the expressions on the faces of the Triangle Shirtwaist strikers I had seen out in the bitter cold a few weeks before: the red-faced young women speechifying in foreign accents about the injustices they suffered daily, clouds of condensation puffing from their mouths too slowly for their outraged words. What a portrait could be painted or sculpted, like the statues in City Hall Park, of the young woman I watched harangue the crowd, her soft silhouette, her strawberry curls and determined expression, her crudely bandaged hand caught in a dramatic gesture! In a little while, this thought would appear prophetic.

As I was about to turn onto Sixth Avenue, I pondered whether, in honor of my high school *alma mater* and my middle name, I should stop into Saint Joseph's for a visit. I often do so when in this vicinity. However, when I did make the turn, I quickly forgot this notion. For, I saw what looked like another factory girl walking by herself under the tracks of the Elevated. She was coming toward me and appeared to be moving strangely. She was stumbling. Then, all at once, she fell headlong in the center of the avenue, disappearing from my sight behind the jammed-up traffic. Upon seeing this, the Italian girls, who were several doors ahead of me, let out a chorus of screams and aspirations. They froze in their tracks, all speaking at once in what sounded like distinct dialects. I recall making some ejaculation to them as well, but we were as uncomprehending of one another as the bricklayers of Babel.

The proper thing to do would be to get a policeman, but, there was none to be found. Not wanting to play the part of the Levite in the Lord's parable, I decided to attempt instead the role of the Samaritan. Though it might not be proper protocol, I did not wish to be found wanting in charity for the imperiled girl. I shoved my *Office* into my jacket pocket and rushed into the middle of the street, dodging between the slow-moving cars. As I arrived at the girl's side, she was still face down. However, she was moving her head and arms. Under her long skirt, her legs were beginning to stir. It appeared she was trying to get up.

"My child," I entreated. "Are you injured? What's happened to you?"

In answer came another chorus of screaming from the Italian girls. For they had followed me through the traffic. In the hubbub of expostulations and exhortations, curses and prayers, I heard a few groans from the poor fallen girl. She was struggling to get up again. I leaned down and took hold of her left forearm. She let out a shrill scream and flipped herself onto her back. Apparently, her arm was badly hurt.

But the sight that we now beheld removed our attention from her arms. The face I saw was familiar, yet distorted. I was fairly certain that she was one of the strikers I had seen outside the Triangle Shirtwaist Factory a couple of weeks ago. Like a modern, industrial Esther speaking up for her mistreated people, she had passionately exhorted the strikers to endure. But that impassioned face was now horribly changed. She had bruises on her cheeks, blood dripping from her nose, and a black eye. It seemed clear that these injuries were not the results of an accident. They were inflicted upon her deliberately. She had to have been set upon by some thugs. I would say that it was thieves who had attacked her but what could someone steal from the likes of her? Whatever the explanation, it was obvious that she needed medical attention. I looked around and still saw no sign of a policeman.

With the help of the girls who continued to send toward the bottom of the Elevated tracks their chorus of wailings, laments, and imprecations to the Lord, I got her on her feet and had her support herself on me with her sound left arm. The Holy Spirit came to me in that moment and I thank the Lord for it. I knew in a flash exactly what I should do: take her to Saint Vincent's.

She gave me a quizzical look when she saw the Roman collar, but was soon willing to accept that at least some sort of clergyman was helping her. She grew even more relaxed when she heard her coworkers repeating, "*Grazie, Padre*!" and "Thank you, Father!" Perhaps she thought they knew me. She was very brave and hardly groaned or complained as we made our way to the west side of Sixth Avenue and up to and across Waverly Place. The crowds on the sidewalk parted for us. Our little entourage must have been quite a sight, a bleeding girl leaning on a Catholic priest for support, leading a parade of expostulating garment factory girls. The men stared and a few women screamed. As we rounded the corner of Greenwich Avenue and headed west, a young man with ears sticking way out from the sides of his head dropped the crate of cabbage he was carrying and addressed me.

"Where're ya takin' her, Father? Goin' to Saint Vincent's?"

"That's right."

"I'll getcha some help. I'll run 'round the corner to the firehouse."

He sprinted ahead of us, while we continued our slow march. I was concerned to be heading through the neighborhood of the Jefferson Market. It was certainly not a place you would want to walk when you did not want to be jostled.

We made it past Christopher Street and, when we traversed the short block to West 10th, I heard the voice of the young man again.

"Father! Father! Over here!"

He was standing in front of the square, red mouth of the local firehouse. On the brick wall above the entryway I saw a sign reading, "18th Squad Company."

"Father! They got a stretcher for her! Over here!"

We limped over toward the firehouse and sat the poor girl on the stoop of the building next door.

In a moment, two firemen came out with a stretcher and a third tall one with a red mustache spoke to me. Later I found his name was McHugh.

"What happened, Father?"

"We saw her fall down in the middle of Sixth Avenue, under the El tracks. She looks-"

A flat, roofless motorized fire engine with the words HIGH PRESSURE F.D.N.Y. emblazoned on its side emerged from the maw of the firehouse. In the front were the driver and the siren operator. A few other firemen stood on the running boards.

"They're takin' her to Saint Vincent's," our young helper explained.

"Are you all right, miss? Can you speak?"

"She looks like she's been beaten," I offered. "She's not fully conscious and I don't know how much English she speaks."

The three firemen got her expertly onto the stretcher and lifted her onto the truck.

"All right. Thank you, Father. Thank you, girls."

"I'd like to accompany you, if that's all right."

"OK, but we have to make tracks. Donohoe," he said to the siren operator.

Donohoe joined the others on the running boards and I climbed into the seat he had vacated, praying silently. The girls called after me.

"They attackah her, Father!"

"Dey try toah make-ah her shut up!"

"*Lei è pazza*!"

"Tell *la Policia*!"

The engine pulled out onto Greenwich Street and the driver operated the siren with his left hand. Cars and carriages scattered to let us through.

I fingered my rosary beads and tried to concentrate on my prayers for the poor girl. So far, I had not heard her speak a word. However, I must admit it was exciting to be sitting atop the fire engine, weaving through other cars, swerving to avoid men who chose to ignore the pavements and walk in the street, dodging oncoming traffic when we had to pass a horse and carriage. In the center of the intersection of 7th Avenue, I at last saw a policeman, trying to direct traffic without a rein with which to control the rampant chaos. Donohoe kept the siren crying. I wonder what people thought of seeing a priest riding up there. Perhaps they surmised I was to perform *Extreme Unction*.

We arrived at the hospital post-haste and when the firemen took her stretcher down from the bed of the truck, the girl woke up and realized where she was going.

"No!" she said. "*Ikh bin Katholik nit*!"

"No worries, darlin'," one of the firemen said. "They will take good care of you here."

As they rushed her in to see the doctors, there were nuns in various types of habit proceeding this way and that. As she was being taken away from me, the girl looked up and in a gravelly voice said something like, "*A sheynem dank, Tateh*!" They tell me that it means, "Thank you, Father" in Yiddish.

For days afterward, I could not stop thinking about the defiant girl and wondering what had become of her. People called me "hero," but this displeased me. I was happy that the girl had received medical attention, but it is one thing to rescue someone and quite another to address the cause of the victim's plight.

It was only when the police came to the rectory to complete their report that I found out her name. I was stunned to learn that the street-corner prophetess was, in reality, called Esther. Esther Rosenfeld.

I informed them about the suspicions her coworkers and I shared about the cause of Miss Rosenfeld's injuries. They said they would look into it, but I did not put much store by their words. I will not give up, however. Providence placed her in my path. I must learn the truth.

...

She sat at her vanity and placed her hand upon her hairbrush. Her fingers were smooth and elegant. The jewel-encrusted brush was gold with red bristles. She picked it up, but Janey Dougherty did not want to comb her hair. In the mirror, her light blue eyes looked cold and hard: two gemstones that could not be broken. The physiognomy was, in a profound sense, disappointed, with a high forehead and crown that suggested sensitivity and not a little stubbornness. Disappointed and defiant beyond anger, she did not look as though she were going to cry: it was nothing like that. Still, there was a sadness beneath the hard look. Janey ran the brush thrice through the raven locks along one side of her head and put it back down. Only then did she think of the cause of that look in the mirror. Only then did she remember why she was sitting there alone, looking at a sullen face that was not to leave this house tonight. At that moment, she realized that a change had taken place within her and that a decision had been made to act. She would not listen. She would disobey, and it would not be a matter for Confession. Her mother's words lacked the force that always elicited her happy obedience. They did not ring true to her daughter. Janey believed her mother was wrong.

In her mind's eye, she could see the backs of the cars in the parking lot of the Woodland Diner, and they seemed to be winged vehicles. "Fins," they called them. She preferred to think of them as wings. Wings tucked behind the cars the way stately fat birds hold them.

She could see her sister there laughing at the boys' jokes, putting her hand on Ray Mahoney's shoulder as she lost her balance, pretending it was an accident when it really wasn't. Everyone knew it really wasn't, yet everyone pretended. Why?

"What're you askin' me that for?" the girls liked to say. "Jeez, what a question!"

No, they didn't like her and her questions and her quiet thinking life. Half of them hadn't read *Jane Eyre* for class. That was obvious. Though she had loved it! How she couldn't wait for Math class to be over so that she could hurry to Sister Patrick Andrew's English class and talk and hear all about it. But it was always a disappointment — wasn't it?

Hadn't her mother always said that her high school years were the best years of her life? Hadn't she said that the friends she made in high school were the friends she would have for life? She had indeed. But here Janey was, imprisoned by the woman who had prophesied all that.

No, they didn't like to sit and think and question things. The boys, especially, seemed to be all action, no thought. No one in that crowd had any curiosity about life in other times. They think Bill Haley started the world's clock.

Had she been born in the wrong time? This time clatters with haste and sweats with hurry. Inside the diner, the waitresses run their legs off. Hustle your bustle to get to the table. Get varicose veins fetching the people their food fast, fast, fast. Short-order cook. Fry it up and slap it on a plate.

The diner echoing with chatter, a constant hum. Drones in their chrome-plated hive. The greetings and departures. The deep voices of the men and boys murmuring. The girls: their high voices! Their squeals of laughter! Their cooing over the good or bad things happening: a cute design on a skirt, a spot of ketchup on a blouse. The thick clink of china as they stack the plates. The ring of the cash register and the rattle of its drawers. The cars starting outside. The gravelly growl of a motorcycle engine idling.

That's if you could hear above the music. The juke box had to be fed at all times. Hungrier for nickels than anyone there is hungry for chipped-dried beef or french fries with gravy. All the fuss over deciding what to play. The clacking of the song lists as they flip under the glass — hands reaching for the knob touching accidentally on purpose again.

Janey reacted too slowly to succeed at such games. When the moment exhorted her to act, she was as still as a deaf mute. And after all the commotion and phony arguing, the same old songs shake, rattle, roll, and love them tender as they did last night … and will tomorrow night … and the night after that …

She could hear all their spectral voices saying she was so weird and quiet.

"She can talk to Jane Eyre but not to us."

"It's like pullin' teeth talkin' to her."

"She doesn't even seem to try half the time. If she would just put herself out a little to make friends, it'd make a world of difference."

"I mean, smile, fer chrisssakes. It doesn't cost anything."

"And you know what else? She –ings. Ever notice that? 'I am go*ing* shopp*ing*.'"

Janey sighed over her clumsy ways. Dressed so pretty, such lovely hair and features, but such a dope, a klutz. She'd walk into the diner and be the first to spill ketchup on herself. Then no coquettish cooing would come from her, no stretching herself and her clothes and dabbing at the spot with a wet napkin, as if that little spot were the only spot in the world worth fixing your eyes upon. No, she would get hysterical, leave the diner in tears, race back home, and precipitate herself down onto that very bed in this very room. And Ray Mahoney would not follow her. No. He would just let her go, like the rest of them.

"How about the time I asked her who her favorite singer was? God! You'd think I was the bishop askin' her a question at Confirmation! She stuttered like a fool, hemmed and hawed, and then muttered something about what kind of music I meant ..."

Perhaps it was her fate to squander the offhanded chance, to never taste the seed within the moment's pomegranate. It was as though the instinct so natural in the vibrant others were removed stillborn from the womb of her soul. Five minutes after leaving the company of the witty girls or hours after it had been appropriate to make it, she would think of a sharp retort.

"So isn't it a shame," the high wraithlike voices pronounced. "That she's got the looks and her sister got all the personality?"

Janey ran the comb through the raven locks on the other side of her head.

"Yes, she is attractive," they would all agree.

"She takes care of her hair, and her clothes. She always looks natty."

"Yeah, she'd be a knockout if she weren't so weird."

"If she only had a little of what her sister has — right Li'? She'd be one of the most popular girls at West."

Her sister Lisa, the Leo — that's how Janey often thought of her, "Lisa, the Leo" —would have been out of the window and down the street by now. She certainly would not have imploded when faced with her mother's unfairness. Most likely, she would have charmed or cajoled her mother rather than going to pieces and raging through impotent tears. She would be on her way back by now bringing stories of boys and laughter and dark street adventures. But Janey was not like her sister, alas. Nevertheless, she thought, Lisa might never be aware of the profounder alterations taking place within her own psyche. Perhaps her sister could flit in and out of windows and in and out of her parents' favor like a butterfly, without ever suffering any filial dark night of the soul like Janey's.

However, the advantage that she, the more brooding one, had was that she knew herself. Though her self was like an ocean, she could feel the slightest change in its current or temperature, even at the deepest depths. But what was her self anyway? It was a stupid, awkward girl whom nobody liked and who couldn't think of a simple answer to a straightforward question at a diner. If only she could be someone else.

Deep down she knew, as her mother always said, that if she stuck to her studies and to being a good girl, they would all respect her, in the long run. I mean how did Jane Eyre win the respect of that Mr. Rochester? She did not bewitch his heart. He liked her because she was different! Loved her because she was different!

Feeling calmer, Janey surveyed the room reflected in the mirror. It soothed her to look at the curtains, the bed posts, the tiles of the parquet floors, the frills of the end of the bed spreads. But one fact remained to discomfit her in her moment of peaceful reflection: she had wanted to go out tonight, and she was still in this room.

The blurry colors of her dress and complexion and hair hovered ghostlike in the mirror. A tear ran down each cheek, unchecked by finger or hand or handkerchief. It brought to her mouth the salty dampness of just too much, too much to think about. Then the image in the mirror blurred beyond recognition. There was nothing her vision could grasp onto and call it hers or, rather, her.

The girls at the diner had probably turned her painful evening into a caricature, a cartoon with her mother as a wicked witch and herself as an innocent damsel helplessly doomed and comically waiting to be saved, whereas clearly no one would come. Not those boys, and certainly not Ray who would be laughing. Like the rest of them.

"Whatsa matter? Mommy won't let you come out and play?"

"But it's not fair. I wasn't allowed to go!"

No, no, no! Don't say that! Don't tell them that!

Enough of this. Dry your eyes and open the window. Free yourself. And head to the diner. And show them.

"I didn't know you had it in you, Janey. I really didn't know."

"So, how did you do it? How'd you get out of the house without anyone knowing?"

Mariellen leaning toward her from across the traditional table, the pink soft sweater fitting her so perfectly, as though her body and the garment had been made at one and the same time. Genuinely interested. Her straw in the fingers of her right hand, stirring the strawberry milkshake, and jabbing the bottom of her wide-based malted glass.

"Well, I sat thinking for a long time. And I knew that what my mother had said made no sense. I made the decision right away, actually, but for some reason I just kept sitting there thinking and thinking."

"Then I finally remembered what she had said and got angry. Who did she think she was? How could she expect me to sit here in my room all night? I'll be 18 next week. I'm not going to sit here for another minute. And just then I heard her going into the kitchen downstairs. So, I took off my shoes. I didn't want to be heard walking around on the roof!! Plus, these shoes weren't exactly made for climbing and jumping! And I climbed out the window and onto the roof. It was pretty easy really."

Ray elbowing her and muttering, "Good for you, Janey. You show 'er."

"Well, I checked the windows in the other houses and a few had lights on but I didn't see any people at all. So, I figured it was time to go. I had gone that far already and had even thrown my shoes to the ground. I really couldn't turn back then."

"But then," a silly little giggle escaped from Janey. "But then…"

"What? What?"

"Well, then, I had to slide down the flagpole."

"So? So what?"

"I kept thinking what if one of the neighbors, what if Timmy O'Dowd happens to walk by as I'm sliding down?"

Squeals. Genuine squeals came up from the table. Then some of the girls caught themselves and hunkered down over their straws, quieting themselves with their milkshakes, the boys pounding their palms on the table.

"I didn't know what to do for a minute. I almost just chanced it. But then, I thought to tuck the skirt between my legs. So I did that, wrapped my legs around the pole, slid down, and jumped."

Ray was looking downright proud.

"I didn't think you had it in you. Honestly, I didn't think you had it in you."

Listen to yourself, she said. The greatest years of your life spent with those lunkheads and that sniggering flock of magpies at the Woodland Diner. Hate to see what the worst ones'll be like. Friends for life?! You don't even like these people.

Janey looked at the closed window and then at the reflection in the mirror of her room and herself still in it. She vanished from the mirror and threw herself headlong on the bed and then there was nothing but wet, salty darkness and sobs.

. . .

Distracted by the intermittent tattoos of raindrops on the window, Seamus Logan, seated behind his oak roll-top desk at the 1604 Chestnut Street headquarters of the Logan Construction Company, leafed through some correspondence. His mind was not on business; his thoughts were all of the past.

Mary's parents disapproved of the love between Seamus and their daughter, and they always endeavored to keep the young people apart. So, in order to meet with Mary, Seamus became intimate with the narrowest, loneliest *botharins*, the bogs, and the rough pasture lands through which the fickle Bunowen River flowed: appearing full and rough after a rain and leaving nothing but rocky runs and the odd small pool when it was fine. He also knew well the times when her father and brothers would be moving to or from their fields. So, nervous was he at times that he caught himself worrying that one of the local animals might inform on him. But, strong as his fears might have been, his determination to see his beloved was stronger. He had visions of fighting the Brogans and vanquishing them all — and of Mary's arriving in time to witness his powerful devotion but to stop him before he did any serious harm. However, it never came to anything like that. Seamus and Mary avoided familial eyes and held their surreptitious meetings with neither incident nor noticeable suspicion.

But, there was one such meeting that always came to Seamus's mind as the years wore on. It took place on a showery day when they walked together among the most deserted *botharins* on the outskirts of Bunowen. Mary and Seamus talked happily of their future life together. On a few secluded stretches of road, they were even bold enough to hold hands. Might as well be hanged for a sheep as a lamb, they reasoned: just being found together would have condemned them. They even ran laughing hand-in-hand along the road when the frequent showers visited. Seamus remembered Mary's hair flying behind her as she ran and how her golden locks shone so bright against the low, dark clouds. With her hand at her forehead, she tried to shield her face from the drops. But, of course, this did no good. The wind was throwing the rain drops at them as if some matchmaking goddess employed the weather to bind the couple closer. All they could do was laugh. And laugh Mary did, and shriek, and giggle. And years later, Seamus Logan, could still hear, amid the drumming of the Philadelphia rain on the window, the merry sounds of the youthful beloved who had been taken from him by her parents.

On that long ago day, Seamus and Mary strolled along the Bunowen River, following its bank as it fell down to the strand. They stepped along the cliffside and stole between the rocks, down to the breakers, and around the dark cliff that now hid them fully from the eyes of the town. The winded couple fell on each other and embraced. In Seamus's sturdy calloused hands Mary's frame felt slight and delicate, but a fragile layer of precious flesh over rib rising and falling with subsiding mirth. She was a tiny bird in his arms who needed protection and care. Seamus brushed the wet hair from Mary's brow and cheek. Her face shone bright with amusement. Her locks hung bedraggled by rain. They kissed and Mary's lips were moist from the showers' drops and salty from her laughter's' tears. Presently Mary's breathing settled into a calmer rhythm and began responding to his caresses. In that moment, he could have picked her up and carried her three times over all of the roads of Ireland. And the passion enthralled not only his body but his soul, too.

Seamus put down his letters, stood up, and drifted toward the rainsnaked, drop-spotted bay window onto Chestnut. He remembered feeling on that day an intense need to give, even to suffer, for Mary, to deny himself and to attend to her, as if at that moment his soul existed for her rather than himself.

Mary returned Seamus's kiss, squeezed him, and moaned softly. This was not like the other occasions on which the ardor was mostly his or merely summoned up to suit the moment. No, this time the hour on the feminine clock, whose mechanisms Seamus could only guess at, had struck. She kissed as if all she wanted in the world was to kiss. Within the boundaries of the cliff walls and the formidable dark rocks being overcome by the tide, she abandoned herself to the showery hour. He could have fathered a dozen children by her.

Blindly, her hand roved over him, feeling the coolness where the wet shirt clung to his body. He caressed her back and sides and thrust his fingers into the damp thickness of her hair. She unfastened a couple of the buttons of his shirt and kissed his neck and chest. His hand brushed over her breast and then returned and squeezed it. Any restraint had flown away like the puffins who had taken shelter from the rain and from the intruding couple in the cliff's nooks. Her hand reached down to his trousers.

Seamus stepped back.

"Mary, we must not," he grunted.

"What?!"

"It's best to stop now or all will be lost."

"Is it not too late already?"

"'Tis, nearly."

"Nearly," and she took her hand away, looked down panting, then back up at him.

"We made a promise to one another, Mary, and Seamus Logan keeps his promises. I would not go back on the word I have given to you as you would not to me. And, surely, I don't want to dishonor you, *a cuisle mo chroi*, nor to see you dishonored in this world, the next, nor any other."

Before he had finished speaking, she had backed away from him and stood fixing her hair and her clothes. Silent and still, she stared out at the turbulent sea rolling toward the land, rushing shoreward heedless of the sharp rocks and casting spray high onto cliff walls. She looked so beautiful and yet so distant. Where had her thoughts taken her?

"I love you, Mary," Seamus offered.

Mary looked down at the darkened rocks below her feet for a moment before answering.

"I love you, too."

Then she gave him the look that puzzled him to this day. The gaze had some pride in it. That was plain. She was pleased by his strength and the concern he showed for her. But there was something else, as well, another aspect that wounded Seamus without warning or expectation. She looked back down at the roaring, hissing rocks.

"You're a rare specimen of a man, Seamus Logan," she said.

Was she happy that he was an unusual man? Or, did she find him strange?

"You are the loveliest creature on God's earth, Mary."

But what was the meaning of her change of expression? Was she disappointed? Did she question his passion for her? If he loved her as he had often declared, how could he resist her?

"I did it because I loved her," Seamus murmured to the rainy window and its burnished-brown frames. "I cared for her reputation and for the life together that we had planned. Anyone, any beast in the pasture, could have shown their love that other way."

Or had he been a noble-hearted fool? A high-minded *omadhaun* who missed the opportunity to demonstrate his passion to the love of his life? Considering the way the affair turned out, he often chided himself for his so-called strength and solicitousness. He had a chance and didn't merely ruin it: he rejected it. He could never tell other men that he had done this. They would laugh him out of the city of Philadelphia.

Seamus returned to his roll-top desk, sat down, and stared. How many opportunities had he taken advantage of in the New World? How many shrewd decisions had he made? And yet, on that long-ago day of two young people in love and happy and alone in the wild landscape of pounding surf and rocks and cliffs, an opportunity so natural and beautiful came to him and he complicated it with his thinking, his stubborn will, his concern for the opinions of the world. The woman he loved and all of the surrounding nature had sung, "yes" and he had said "no."

The walk back to Bunowen was not as merry as the way to the strand had been. Mary did get livelier as they proceeded but she was not the same for the rest of the afternoon.

Was she not concerned for her reputation? What had been on her mind? It was not long after that that her marriage banns were announced. Could she have known that she and Seamus could never be and decided to consummate their love before she betrayed him?

"Decided" sounded awfully strong word. It was more of a Seamus than a Mary word.

On his desk stood a photo of his wife, Nora, the mother of his children. There was a family portrait from when the kids were small, the baby looking so serious. There was another of young Sarsfield newly ordained in his Roman collar.

Seamus pushed some papers around until a police siren outside broke the spell. To live is to suffer, he thought. He rose, sighed, took his hat, and coat from the back of the door, and headed home.

...

EXT. SIDEWALK BEFORE VICTORIAN ROWHOUSE RESEMBLING A CASTLE. UNIVERSITY CITY, PHILADELPHIA — NIGHT

She slipped her tongue between her lips and between his and his tongue reached out to meet hers, and the warm, wet, moist, soft coarseness flicked against his and that's all there was to the world, that kiss. His lips brushed against hers, both of hers. Her lips were thin but her kiss was firm and ardent, a warm fruit plucked with the mouth. His lips moved away for an instant, then returned more forcefully, kissing, real-kissing, her lips. And they were soft and warm, both of them real-kissing against his, both of his answering both of hers. And she began to stir, stretching up just an inch or two higher and closer to him and everything was automatic as if they were doing this for the thousandth time and not the first, as if it had all been planned out and agreed upon before the party, before the cigarette on the front porch, before the laughs, before the walk, and before his arrival at her father's door.

INT. CROWDED HOUSE PARTY. TRADITIONAL IRISH MUSICIANS PLAYING. UNIVERSITY CITY, PHILADELPHIA — NIGHT

                         JANEY

          Lemonade sounds great, Mr. Logan.
          Thanks. That would be real gentlemanly
          of you.

                         JAMES

          Yeah, well don't' let it get around. It
          could ruin my reputation.

James hands her a glass of lemonade.

JANEY

It's hot as blazes in here.

JAMES

Why don't we step out on the porch?

JANEY

Sure. That might be just the thing.

EXT. ROWHOUSE FRONT PORCH, UNIVERSITY CITY, PHILADELPHIA — NIGHT

Sure, part of her felt like she shouldn't do it. She thought of the girl in the frame on his desk. His cousins certainly knew about that frail-looking blonde. She wouldn't be surprised if they knew the Philadelphia princess personally. But on the other hand, it was innocent enough. They were just coworkers cooling off from the heat of the party. Besides, *qui ne risque rien n'a rien.* Mostly she was flattered. It was he who was risking more. He was the one with the name, the cousins, the fiancée. She was just a girl from the neighborhood, a secretary. All she had to worry about was her reputation, which was indeed something to care about: Janey did not want clinging to her the word, "homewrecker." Still, she wanted to make her own decisions and let others think what they may.

The way they had been exchanging glances all night, she'd been waiting for him to try to get her alone. Her remark about being hot had been a nudge in that direction, what any good secretary would do for a boss.

JANEY

So, were you stood up again?

JAMES

No, just visiting some cousins and old
friends. How about you? Can you
recommend another good sandwich? How
are they around here?

JANEY

Quite tasty. You'll see.

JAMES

And hold the mayo.

No, that's not how it happened. It was awkward at first. The snappy dialog came later.

James held the door for her and Janey stepped out onto the porch. She paused with the porchlight behind her and let him go past. She imagined herself lit like a movie star: white light sifting through her fine brown hair, outlining her shoulder and hip, maybe even down to her ankle, the scene shot in black and white.

JANEY

What brings you to this party, Mr.
Logan?

JAMES

My mom was from the parish. My cousins,
the Dugans, live here.

JANEY

How 'bout that? Really? I didn't know
you were related to the Dugans. What a
small world! I went to school with
Paulie. So you came to see them?

JAMES

Yeah, not much going on in Ardmore on a
Saturday night. How 'bout yourself?
What brings you here, Miss Dougherty?

JANEY

I live up on Spruce Street.

JAMES

Smoke?

James took out his cigarette case and, porchlight catching the dark hairs on his hand, he drew two cigarettes from the case and snapped it shut. The case looked old, like something passed down through the generations. Janey's eyes zoomed in on the Gothic letters "JAL" engraved on it: James Logan of the Logan Construction Company. A for, "Aloysius"? With a cigarette in his mouth,

James searched his pockets for a lighter, lit her smoke and then his own, and inhaled. He slipped the case back into the inside pocket of his jacket.

Janey sauntered over toward the railing of the porch, placed her hands close together on it, and watched a dried brown leaf blow down the somnolent sidewalk.

A rollicking sea of fiddle, whistle, and concertina notes bounced through the open front windows and flowed out into the street. She turned around and half-sat on the railing, glancing down at the pointing toes of her saddle shoes, then taking the cigarette from her mouth and exhaling a stream of smoke.

                              JAMES

          John the General still has the troops
          going strong in there.

                              JANEY

          There's something special about hearing
          the music from out here. Like hearing
          hymns from outside church.

                              JAMES

          The Gospel accordion to Saint John.

                              JANEY

          Oh, that's very clever, Mr. Logan!

Janey touches his forearm.

                         JANEY (CONT'D)

          "The Gospel accordion to Saint John!"

He looked at her like there was something mysterious about her. Her bangs were still damp from the heat inside. She hoped he didn't notice.

                              JAMES

          Call me "James."

                              JANEY

          OK, James.

                         JAMES

          Funny we never ran into each other
          before.

                         JANEY

          Seems we can't stop running into each
          other now. Work, lunch, parties.
          What's next?

Janey puffs on her cigarette.

                    JANEY (CONT'D)

          Who knows?

The screen door slams. TOM DUGAN appears on the porch, filling
his pipe with tobacco.

Sprouts of gray hair stand in a semicircle around his bald spot
and he smiles at them with his round, kindly face.

                         JAMES

          Hey, Uncle Tommy, this is Janey, a girl
          from the office.

                       TOM DUGAN

               (With an Irish brogue)
          Sure, don't be introducin' me to me own
          neighbor.

                         JANEY

          Hi, Mr. Dugan.

Tom lights his pipe.

                       TOM DUGAN

          I've known Janey since she was in
          pigtails clatterin' down the pavement on
          her rollerskates with her cocker spaniel
          on a lead.

                         JAMES

          I would have liked to have seen that.
          Was she a troublemaker?

TOM DUGAN

Ach, no! Janey was a quiet one. Always
with her nose in a book or running off
to see a foreign filim. I'm sure she'll
be a good help to you in the office.
I'm thinkin' she was a wee bit more
studious than yerself.

JAMES

I hear nothing but good things about
her.

TOM DUGAN

That's grand. I won't ask her what she
hears about you.

Tom takes the steps to the street.

TOM DUGAN (CONT'D)

Good night, now.

JAMES

Good night.

JANEY

Good night, Mr. Dugan.

JAMES

Don't listen to him. Old Tommy loves to
destroy any of shred of respectability a
fella might have.

We hear the band inside strike up a new jig.

JANEY

Oooh, I like this tune!

JAMES

What is it?

                         JANEY

"The Connachtman's Rambles." Do you
like the music?

                         JAMES

No.

                         JANEY

Well that's a very blunt answer, James.

Janey laughed out loud. That gravitational pull again.

                         JANEY

You don't like it at all?

                         JAMES

Not a bit.

She laughed again and shook her head.

                         JANEY

Then what are you doing here?

                         JAMES

My cousins-

                         JANEY

Right. On your mother's side.

                         JAMES

The Dugans. That's right.

                         JANEY

Your mother's from the parish.

                         JAMES

She is.

                    JANEY

Nothing happening in Ardmore.

                    JAMES

Nothing.

                    JANEY

More fun in West Philly.

                    JAMES

Yeah. Let me walk you home.

                    JANEY

I'll get my purse.

EXT. SIDEWALK BEFORE VICTORIAN ROWHOUSE RESEMBLING A CASTLE — NIGHT

Unnwanted light falls from the third floor of the house, spilling
onto the street, pulling mouth from mouth and body from body.

                    JAMES

Maybe we can catch a movie sometime.

                    JANEY
OK. See ya in church.

Janey nods, smiling, and hurries inside. James steps loudly down
the pavement.

                    FADE OUT.

                    ...

Finding the Way to the FDR (cont'd)

1. Turn left.

2. Proceed through the Financial District to the South Street Seaport.

3. Take the **entrance** to the FDR, heading uptown.

— Take a left here to head to the Seaport.

Laura made a hasty left onto John Street.

doing as you tell her some sort of miracle anyway better direct her to my uptown toilet
before long john street bar and grill john ran faster to the empty tavern best in financial district take
her there for lunch pang of opportunity missed what does she remember of that hot ferry ride
paroxysm o ma memoire clear that i am but one of very many after her after it

On the big board, there are indications that multiple investors are tendering offers of big tips, jokes, rounds of shots, tattoos, jobs, pretending to like to dance, muscles, stories about the guys from Metallica as kids, gold watches, musicianship, tours around Tribeca, having a couple of poems published, power, reflexive kindness, and generosity all to lure one particular buyer who is long on looks but could be rolling the hedge forward for some delivery date more advantageous to her. Investors are shorting their assets to obtain a long position but remain uncertain about how much liquor and impressiveness it will take to become an insider for a session of vigorous trading — a highly sought-after opportunity on the Murray Street exchange. And the bids keep going up, up, up, up, up!

Paul met Laura on Friday the 13th. She was wearing that rainbow-colored tie-dye with the heart in the center of its chest. Too much to be believed, he knew, but there it had been: a colorburst heart dyed into the cotton that had stretched over her girlish tits, her Wonderbra proffering the vibrant symbol, for the hungry eyes of her customers.

— Whatsa matter? she said, tilting her head toward her right shoulder and bending down and sideways to wash the glasses: the curves of her torso, a glimpse of the small of her back as the shirt escaped from her jeans, the long blonde hair falling around her oval face, her fragile jaw, and dimpled chin. Didn't your friend like any of the bands?

— He had to catch a train to Westchester.

Over the din of the band smashing its way through *"Oye, Como Va,"* they'd traded remarks about the bands and her job and where she, too, lived in Westchester County. She had that young women's technique of raising the pitch of her voice with the volume of the music so that she could be heard.

john street methodist church founded by irish immigrants hearts strangely warmed thats
peter and john where are andrew and james first in the new world just as the prods were putting the
finishing touches on trinity church behind us hordes of pape newcomers came up this hill saying
don't be gettin' too full of yerselves now ghosts of the famished plodding on those cobblestones
suffer for your sins idolatrous stiff-necked paddies god prefers prayers in english to your latin and
irish gibberish

She kept leaving to talk to other customers and — *mirabile dictu* — coming back to Paul. She was more likely to reply than other young barmaids in the city. Her gestures were not as abrupt;

her poses held fewer angles and straight lines. Maybe that was why the walls of her castle did not appear so formidable to Paul, no mortar among her piled bricks.

and all the while the white heart in the center of her chest with multicolored outlines radiating from it simple curves red blue yellow slender at the bottom full at the top embrace me with your hybrid arms or cold with neither cusip nor currency nor index nor stock will my heart lie i pledge more power to your prepay elbow actual not budget actual i swear

Sellers are weighing reports with analytics that would seem to make it more attractive for the counterparties to enter negotiations about a potential contract, but remain bearish due to perceived market volatility. In late trading, the Englishman seems to be in a slump. His stock has declined several basis points. But the Irish-American has rallied despite a long day at work and hours of drinking. Delivery is unlikely at this point but a contract with the latter party would experience no roadblocks in regards to foreign exchange rates. The cash stream offered by his swap leg is considered quite liquid and the buyer is willing to accept collateral in exchange. Perhaps, after an examination of competing financial instruments, the counterparties can be induced to make a swap.

Seeing the one-way sign pointing uptown, Laura slowed the car at the intersection of John and Dutch Streets.

— No, Paul warned from the back seat. Don't turn here. We want to keep heading east.

— What?

— Keep going straight. Don't turn until the car is about to fall into the river.

— OK, Laura smiled.

But to whom does she grant shotgun ? A cook with no money, connections, talent nor discernible skill, neither flexible nor giving, who might not be allowed to stay in this country.

Laura usually worked at the Orange Crush oneday nights and Thursday days or someday nights and Wednesday days but tonight she was working for Fuchsia. And she liked it because it was more money and busier and the time went by faster. Why a New York bar would be named anything Orange was still beyond Paul.

At William Street, Paul pointed to an old building that was familiar to him.

— Hey, I usta proofread in that building.

yeah paul chicks dig proofreaders keep trying to impress her as she burrows further into your psyche starts with your eyes and ears soon shes in your veins seehear her bent over laughter feel the brush of skin smell her hair keep talking to her even when shes not around

— How do you like working in this neighborhood? Paul had ventured.

— I don't really know the neighborhood at all, she'd answered.

And his response had been natural, obvious.

— I could show you around.

The seller of a put option has the right to execute her option when the commodity of interest reaches its strike price. However, she has no obligation to sell. The details of when or whether the deal will be closed are entirely her prerogative. Of course, there will be occasions when it would be in her best interest to execute her option and disadvantageous for her to delay. For, if the deal is not closed during the option's specified window, buyers could look to trade elsewhere. If the option is not exercised, it expires until the next option is offered. No shares change hands and the money spent to purchase the option is lost.

The BMW glided past the narrow Gold Street and rolled by a Crunch gym and a Duane Reade, both dark, closed, and shuttered. The Financial District got so quiet after hours that it reminded Paul of the rolled-up sidewalks of Center City Philadelphia. Laura took her foot off of the gas pedal again at Cliff Street.

— No, no. Keep going … keep going …

Laura had said, "OK" to Paul's offer and told him to meet her at the bar at 7 on the following Thursday. That's when she got off work.

— Just tell Walter you're here to see me so you won't have to pay to get in.

She was so nonchalant about the whole thing that right after he left, Paul began wondering if this marvelous Friday the 13th conversation had ever taken place.

If an option contract is exercised, the writer is responsible for fulfilling the terms of the contract by delivering the shares to the appropriate party. As of yet, no tour of downtown streets has occurred. The Present Value of the tour may have been undervalued at the time of offer. However, the value of the offer when it was accepted has been Marked to Market and served as the beginning of ongoing trade negotiations.

As the car approached Pearl Street, Paul moved forward in his seat to talk to Laura.

— You know why this is called Pearl Street?

— They usta trade a lot of pearls around here?

— No, I read somewhere that the Indians used to pile all their oyster shells along here. It was so shiny they called it, "the place where the sun is born."

— "The place where the sun is born"? That's beautiful.

Charles started to stir, groaning and rubbing his eyes. Paul lowered his voice.

— It is. Makes sense, too. Sun rising over the East River … setting over the Hudson …

— As if New York is the whole world. This sounds like another poem.

Charles stopped groaning and sat up.

— Where are we?

— The sun's birthplace, replied Laura.

They passed Water Street and the ride got bumpier. The streets were paved with large ash-colored cobblestones, looking darker in the late-night gloom.

bricks and mortar in the cobblestones of new york's vieux carre there you go again with the whole sincere-and-cerebral routine as if it were just her mind you are interested in like with little carmen back in the bronx who took her black button eyes her pixie frame her short shapely brown legs and vanished like a dustspeck leaving you with her notebook full of poems and your guts uncoiling along the filthy hall floor but now hende poule perhaps if thou caughte hire by the queynte and helde hire harde by the haunchebones

Paul sat back and through drooping eyelids could see at the end of the next cobblestone block, the prow, foc'sle, and masts of the *Peking*.

— Well, here we are at the seaport, Laura. Now you can get ready to turn left.

— I used to wuhk at the South Street Seapawht, Charles interjected.

— Oh yeah? What were you – one of those mimes?

— No, I'm not bloody French.

— But you are a chef.

Laura guffawed.

Paul smiled.

caught in her electrical current keep this guerrilla campaign alive chase this dream not someone elses my dream through the reeling hardcore beer-soaked cacophony of her nights then vanish into the cawfee-in-a-bag-and-budder-bagel crowds of the daylit sidewalks pulse racing for weeks now a cuisle mo croi so much it gives me a headache hard to sleep relax or concentrate on anything that is not mundane busywork i step out on the susskind fire escape in the off chance of catching you sauntering along murray street and confirming its no hoax

...

A crowd of factory girls and onlookers stood before the Triangle Shirtwaist building by the intersection with Greene Street. I heard loud applause; a speaker had just finished. The audience murmured, restless for the next orator, anticipating something significant. They craned their necks to see the person being helped through the crowd, eager, and, perhaps a little fearful.

As I drew closer, it became clear that the strikers were supporting a girl of their own age and station, and that she was bandaged and limping. She turned around, and in the same instant in which I suspected it, I confirmed that it was true: it was Esther.

I was stunned. My wildest hope was that one of her coworkers might tell me how she was. Never did I expect to see her at the picket lines. Now, *comme c'est miraculeux*, she was standing in front of the strikers about to speak. And, speak she did — with a command of the crowd and of her message that made me envious! After all of my training in rhetoric, I could not hold the attention of a crowd in an elite classroom or glorious church the way this young girl did on a dirty, cobblestoned street, nor could I evoke the crowd's sympathies, stoke its wrath, nor reinforce its determination the way she did.

"People ask me why am I here? Who asks such a question? Only someone who does not know our lives. I am injured and should be in bed, they say. Would I be in bed if today factory was open? If so, there would be no pay! If today I came to do their work, they would not turn me away. But they have tried to turn me away from *our* work, *our* struggle. See how they have failed! See how they labored to make me stay home! Look at their fine work!"

Esther pointed to the bruises on her face and arms and to her bandages. The crowd roared, which added fuel to her fire.

"Such trouble they went to!"

She lifted up some of her bandages to show the wounds beneath.

"But from this work, no profit will they earn!"

Her comrades helped her down from the platform and I was so impressed with her speech that I went straight up to her. Some of the strikers looked at me suspiciously, thinking, perhaps, that I was going to urge them to work for a better life in the next world only.

But Esther called out, "*Tateh*!"

Then a few of the Italian girls waved to me. Esther and the others who knew me explained to the others in their native tongues that I was the priest who had helped Esther.

"Marvelous speech!" I exclaimed.

"Thank you! And thank you for helping me when I was hurt."

"Not at all. Not at all. How are you? I see that you are not completely healed."

"No, but I don't want them think they can stop me."

"I can see that. I was very moved by what you said."

"Thank you. To know more of our struggle, read this."

Esther handed me a pamphlet.

"I must go now."

Her friends were helping her along the street.

"Yes, you must get some rest. I'd like to read this and talk to you-"

She continued limping toward Broadway.

46

"Maybe I can help."

She stopped and turned to face me. She thought for a moment.

"You priest. You speak. You write ... Meet me here next week. Same time. When I am feeling better. We discuss how you start help us."

When I returned at the appointed time, everything was much as I had found it. Esther's bruises and scratches had started to heal, though she was still bandaged and limping. When she had finished giving her fellow strikers a stirring speech similar to the one I'd heard a week before, she came down from the platform without need of assistance.

"Another rousing speech," I told her.

"Thank you. You read pamphlet?"

"I did indeed. And, I believe you are right to fight for safer working conditions."

"And your church?"

"The Church's position is the same. The pope's encyclical *Rerum Novarum* or *Of the New Things* teaches that all laborers have a right to adequate worldly goods in order to live in frugal comfort, and priests have published in support of labor unions and that-"

She turned and spoke Yiddish to her friends. And started to head south on Mercer Street.

"Miss Rosenfeld, may I ask where you are going?"

"Home. I live East 4th Street."

"Would you like to sit down and talk? There is a comfortable, warm place on Broadway, where we could have a cup of coffee."

She gathered a frayed shawl around her shoulders and considered my suggestion. Instead of turning down Mercer, she accompanied me to Broadway. The sidewalks were overflowing with people. Streetcars and automobiles and pedestrians dodging around them clogged the macadam street winding downtown.

Fortunately, the tea parlor was directly across Broadway. We did not have far to navigate along the busy sidewalks of the Ladies' Mile, through those hordes of men with shiny top hats and affected canes, those flocks of women with dresses flowing out wider than the wingspans of their hen-like figures, and those stylish people descending from streetcars. The irony of discussing workers' rights surrounded by such well-heeled shoppers did not escape me. I imagine it was not lost on my intelligent, perceptive companion, either.

For a young woman who walked with a limp, Esther was quite nimble dodging the Broadway traffic.

If we got some strange looks on the street — and I saw one befuddled expression as I turned to admire the view of the Woolworth building, that cathedral of the religion that was making Esther a veritable slave — we certainly got more once we entered the fancy oriental tea parlor. As we proceeded across the black-and-white mosaic floor with arabesque patterns illuminated by soft-colored, unadorned stained-glass windows, the ladies in broad-brimmed hats stopped what they were doing. A few of them froze with their coffee cups midway between their saucers and their lips. Some eyes opened even wider when they saw me — in my blacks and Roman collar — come in behind her. Then the chatter became quite quick and avid.

The hostess seated us at a small round table away from the window and removed from the most crowded section. Esther got right down to business. She asked me what I thought of the pamphlet and wanted to know about my training in writing and speaking. I gave her a brief overview of the education of Jesuit priests. I told her that I work as a teacher and, therefore, write and deliver lessons along with the homilies I write and deliver at Sunday mass.

When the waitress came, Esther grew flustered. The dark-haired girl peered down at the Jewess with curious blue eyes. But, Esther had not looked at the menu and, was at a loss for words. I ordered two coffees and asked the girl to give us a few moments to look over the menu.

"Yes, Father," she said with a brogue. "Take your time, Father."

Watching the waitress depart, Esther explained to me that along with girls who were Jewish like herself, many of the girls in her factory were Catholic from Italy. So, in addition to my ability to write and speak, my being a priest would be a valuable asset to her cause. I could see that she thought of me as a powerful weapon to add to her arsenal. I said that I would be interested in providing assistance, when my duties and vows as a Jesuit priest permitted. I told her I had taken a vow of obedience, but I saw no reason why my superiors would object to my writing something for a pamphlet or helping out in some other way. Indeed, the Church has taught in *Rerum Novarum* that there is no intermediary more powerful than the Church (and here I lowered my voice) in drawing the rich and the working class together, by reminding each of its duties to the other. I explained that I have a special interest in the just treatment of immigrants, since my father had come here from across the sea in Ireland.

But then the Irish lass brought the coffee and I changed the subject.

"You must be hungry, Miss Rosenfeld."

"No, I have had my lunch."

"Maybe some dessert, then. You have been through some harrowing experiences. You could do with a little treat."

Somehow invoking my father's name had brought his indomitable generosity to my heart, as if he were speaking through me.

"No, thank you, Father."

"Some German Chocolate cake? It looks good. I saw someone eating it as we came in."

My tone of voice and gesture had caught the attention of the waitress.

"Miss, I'll have a slice of the German Chocolate cake. And, please bring us two forks."

"Straightaway, Father."

The waitress brought the cake and the two forks. As she gobbled up the sweet dessert, Esther was no longer the labor incendiarist. She was a contented girl. She smiled prettily, and even laughed, revealing dimples in her soft cheeks. And for a moment her cold eyes danced.

The cake quickly disappeared, though my fork never touched it.

…

Laura turned the wheel angrily, unable to turn onto the pedestrian cobblestones of the South Street Seaport's Fulton Street.

—No choice, declared Paul, but to turn around.

—Turn around?

—Yeah, make a U-turn on South.

the construction workers shoveling things around standing watching don't seem to care so busy seeming not to care they miss the hot drunk frustrated blonde behind the wheel probably getting overtime at their riverbank post as the sky turns from black to cerulean to blue and the fulton street fisherman bring in their catch putting their shovels down getting in the car are you crazy keep your eyes open

Out the window, Paul saw through slowblinking eyes the FDR stretching above them, lifted almost prankishly by devilish girders of steel.

the seaport the portal to this world celts always migrating westward through the caucasus turkey switzerland germany gaul spain britain scotland ireland aran then across the atlantics bowl of bitter tears 150 years ago a great continuation of the celtic migration

Among the throngs on the cobblestones by the dockside one evening so fair, wandering through the disembarked in rags whose sealegs stumble on unfamiliar terrain. No Ellis Island to welcome them. No Seaport mall for the clueless tourists to meander in. No giant tricolor hanging at MacMenamin's where the yuppies thoughtlessly imbibe. The air bears the fragrance of saltwater but there is no hint of gas fumes. Your nose can certainly tell you that the Fulton Fish Market is there! Even so, the newly arrived give off horrible odors! Pigs are snouting through the garbage scattered about the cobblestones. The clatter of wheels and crates, the cries of Yankee hawkers, hustling, rushing, the chaos of moving luggage and cargo … cargo carried from the Old World to the New …

Most of the new arrivals look exhausted, like salmon who have just made it upriver. They chatter all around me in Irish and in English.

Someone addresses me.

— *An bhfuil Gaeilge agat*?

– *An beaganin.*

I know how to say *un pocito* in many languages!

Wide-eyed, the crowds stare at me in my black leather jacket, dress shirt, and Dockers. Such nice clothes so clean and bright. Soft hands, quick easy movements in a gravity strange to them. Perhaps a little too much around the middle.

For despite the obvious differences they can see the Ireland in my face.

— You're as Irish as I am — aren't ya?! One of them says, looking me up and down.

Full of drink and not faltering, I shout to them:

— Embrace hope ye who enter here!

When they hear me speak, they are full of amazement at the strange accent that is on me.

One man is more eager than the others to address Irish words to me. He speaks English, too.

— *An Éirinneach tú*?

— *Ta me Meiriceánach.*

— *Cad is ainm duit*?

— *Pol Logan is ainm dom. Cad is ainm duit*?

— *Seamus Logan is ainm dom.*

— *Cad as duit?*

— *Is ó Contae Meigh Eo mé.*

— *Go sabhala Dia sinn*!

— Why are you so interested in me, young bilingual shade?

— I am your great-grandfather, Seamus Logan.

— I am your great grandson and I am the first of all of your American descendants to study Irish. And I am busy this year attending events commemorating the 200th anniversary of the rising of the United Irishmen.

— You are justly proud of your blood, says he. For we are a strong people who could take all that they would give, who would take what they would not give. From your clothes and appearance, the family must have been a success.

— You are my ancestor and give me confidence to speak. Suddenly, I feel that I am more than just myself but part of a great race on the move. And so great-grandfather, the future I will now lay out for you, ineffable things, which I probably shouldn't be telling you:

Day and night will you live in the stink of shit and piss and garbage. On summer days your wooden tenement will be like an oven. Crowds will sleep on the roofs in summer trying to get a wink of sleep to prepare them for the next day of backbreaking toil they'll be glad to have. On winter nights your home will be like a ship in the northern seas with icy winds piercing your walls, your floorboards, and your very bones. Extremes of cold and heat none of you knew at home, where even the poorest could go out to the bog to dig turf. Here you will have to pay for coal or send the kids out to scavenge for it. Some will be forced to burn doors, furniture, and bedding. And there will be drink. Plenty of drink. But what man who lived there would drink milk instead of whiskey?

One of the men with Seamus spoke up:

— Yes, our lives will be one big fight and ready we are for it! Every election will be a fight, too. Because what they understand here are numbers. And thank God we will have strength in numbers.

A dirty-looking Irishman who seemed more accustomed to his surroundings began shouting as if at all of the enemies of his life:

— Numbers, numbers is what ye understand and numbers is what ye will get, trying to come into our street with less than ten of ye at a time, numbers of lumps on your heads, numbers of pisspots dumped on your bloody booley uniforms, numbers of men to take back to the morgue with ye and out of this, less of a place to come to than another to get out of!

I turn to my great-grandfather:

— Seamus, you are a hearty man. And you are strong enough to take it … and survive … and succeed eventually. And you will lay brick and mortar, brick and mortar, building spires overlooking the harbor of New York and the ships rolling in and passing away. But in your heart's core, you will hear a call to set out for another city. The City of Brotherly Love will call to you and you will make a pilgrimage to that city's Southwark. There you will lay bricks on mortar and mortar on bricks until you build a company whose rowhouses will be as plentiful as the stars in the skies or the sands down the shore. And you will get married and you will leave behind the crowded, dirty, infested, noisy, dangerous city and make it to the suburbs! In St. Colman's of Ardmore at 11 Simpson Road right across from the Lower Merion Police Station, which may not be all that welcoming. And your marriage will bear fruit. You will have a son and he will be the pride of your loins for he will become a priest forever according to the order of Melchizedek, *sacerdos in aeternum*. But not just a priest — a Jesuit! *Ad Maiorem Dei Gloriam*! And he will be called Sarsfield for some oddball reason that no one will understand nor recall.

— Now that you have interpreted your vision of the future for me, Seamus says, I will foretell coming events for you. Ireland will become a great success. With an educated work force and favorable tax policies, the Land of Saints and Scholars will welcome major corporations to sojourn there. Even in the Six Counties, investments all will glimmer as peace comes lighting slow. Many Irishmen will make a voyage that is the reverse of mine, returning from New York over the wild ocean to their own native home where they will find cranes filling the sky from Galway to Dublin to Sligo to the outskirts of Tipperary Town. May you be as successful as they will be in those times!

Seamus continued in a softer tone:

— As for the companions with whom you travel this Holy Thursday, the lass will be difficult to win over to your side. She has a background which you do not suspect. But persistence and endurance may enable your day to come. The Englishman is of little consequence and yet he has youth and his speech has the power to charm.

— Seamus, one of his compatriots calls. That looks like a pub across the way. Will you not join us for a parting glass?

— No, Seamus answers. The first thing I must do upon these shores is give thanks to the Lord.

As the shade of Seamus wends its way up Pearl Street, it starts to fade. I call after him.

— I've heard that story before — that the first place you went was a church. But why didn't they talk about you more? Why were there no stories told about your passage? Because you never told? Because they never asked?

— I was too busy moving ahead. He stops walking and ceases fading for a moment. Paul! Listen and I will tell you why I named my son "Sarsfield." He was named after–

An English voice was calling his name.

— Paul! Paul! Wake up, mate!

And then Laura's voice.

— Wake him up! Is he awake? Is he awake? Where do I go now, Paul? Where do I go?

Finding the Way to the FDR (revised)

To get to the FDR:

1. Turn right on Wall Street.
2. Proceed to Broadway.
3. Take Broadway to the bottom of Manhattan.
4. Find the entrance to the FDR.

— Maybe you can take a right on Wall Street ...

— O.K., where's that?

— You just went by it.

— Thanks for letting me know.

— Sorry. I thought you knew where it was.

— No, I have no idea where I'm going. You gotta remember that.

They drove under the girders toward the lower jutting tip of Manhattan. A triple-decker Staten Island Ferry was floating in from the harbor. The patina face of the old Coast Guard ferry terminal stared, impassive.

— Turn right here, on Whitehall Street.

where the brits took over new amsterdam like this insipid limie who thinks hes taken over

. . .

In a day's time we went from seeing each other every day and having surreptitious lunches together three times a week to having no contact at all.

There was that one dark period, those awful days, weeks they seemed like, and perhaps were. What started it?

One lunchtime, I wandered down into the grey, wide lower church of Saint John the Evangelist to make a visit. I saw people in line for confession and joined them.

"Bless me, Father, for I have sinned. It's only been a few days since my last confession. Y'see, I usually go Saint Francis de Sales on Saturdays."

"Why did you come here?"

"I heard a call."

Then I poured out the story to him: that he was my boss, that he was engaged, that I loved him, and that he had gone away without a word. I was hardly interested in his advice or in any penance. It was just this outpouring that I needed. I think he told me to pray and have patience, not to encourage the man to be dishonest but to allow him to make his decision. I don't recall exactly. I do remember kneeling and saying some prayers for a while, the smell of the stale incense seeming an appropriate match for my foggy mind.

The talk in the office had gotten to James. It was not the same chatter that tormented me — from the secretaries and the sniggering mail room guys. He wasn't privy to most of that, thank God! It was the executive gossip that bothered him. His brother came to him and asked him about the rumors. He said he had overheard some remarks in the handball locker room and wanted to know if they were true. He told his brother half the truth. He said we had run into each other by chance at the Automat and that we had had lunch together a few times, that we were friends and nothing more. And this lying is what really bothered him: he is such an honest guy. He mentioned that he had found himself lying to people close to him — not only his fiancée but his family and friends, too — and that the guilt had really begun to trouble him.

Oh, but so much of this is guesswork! When he disappeared, I wracked my brain for reasons for his departure — any explanation but that someone else had taken over. For days, I went over every scrap of conversation I could remember. But to be more accurate, it was nights. I spent night after night playing and replaying the scenes in my mind until I could come up with a couple of reasonable explanations — those I described above.

Because when it happened, it made no sense. It was so sudden, so cold, that it hurt, especially during those first few days, worse than anything I'd experienced. I supposed I had been in love before but I had never felt anything this powerful, this painful. Indeed, the power of my love for him truly made itself known through this pain.

In those dark days I was unable to eat nor sleep. Music seemed to help, or make things worse. I'm not sure which. But, there were many hours in which I just needed to listen to music. I would fall asleep on the chair with the radio on and wake up with a sore neck in the middle of the night, the national anthem calling me to this strange attention. On other mornings, I would wake up in bed before my alarm and, as quickly as I would realize that I was in my own red room, the painful situation that had kept me from sleep would come back to my mind. And the blood would stop flowing in my veins. The scenes would start flashing through my mind again, and I would not be able to get back to sleep. This even happened on Saturday and Sunday, which made my mother start to question me. She knew that I liked to sleep in on weekends and, yet, there I was in the kitchen before she was, making a cup of tea with dark circles under my eyes, rubbing my sore neck.

The day I found out was the worst. I walked by his office several times and did not see him. There was no sign of his briefcase or overcoat, either. I was dying to ask his secretary, Miss Hauser, if he was ill but I didn't dare. Much as I tried to hide it, I'm sure she saw the longing, curious look in my eyes as I passed. But, with sheer feminine spite and executive-secretary condescension, Miss Hauser just stared at me with a cold smile, the cat who had eaten the canary. She refused to breathe a word to ease my anxiety. I am almost certain that she would not have told me where Mr. Logan was even if I had asked her in front of a group of clients. No, she seemed to enjoy my plight and her power to prolong it.

Later, I overheard some girls in the bathroom. One said she thought James was sick. The other said he was fine but that he had gone upstate for business. To Scranton, she thought, and that he wouldn't be back for a week. I felt like they were looking at me to see how I reacted but I would not give them the satisfaction. I just kept fixing my mascara, picturing a barren land with its nature ripped off to expose the bare earth and hoping the tears were not welling too obviously in my eyes.

I went back to my desk and pretended to be working. I looked at some forms and tried to type a letter. But the characters in my LCC steno pad grew blurry. I knew I was making mistakes. Still, I typed on. I did not want the girls to see me wiping tears from my eyes. Trying to seem natural, I made a few corrections with liquid paper. But, before long, the letter was too full of errors to be salvaged. I kept typing, anyway. They were not going to see me ripping the Logan letterhead out of the typewriter and throwing it away. The words were so blurred that I couldn't even read. By the end all I was typing was:

> Why did you leave without telling me?
> Why did you leave without telling me?
> Why did you leave without telling me?
> Why didn't you tell me?
> Why didn't you tell me?
> Why didn't you tell me?
>
> I stood at the station and could not board the train.
> I stood at the station and could not board the train.
> I stood at the station and could not board the train.
> I stood at the ticket window and could not pay the fare.
> I stood at the ticket window and could not pay the fare.
> I stood at the ticket window and could not pay the fare.

Each night as the El stopped at 30th Street, I would feel a pang in my stomach and my legs would ache to climb the stairs to 30th Street Station, before my mind was conscious of the station at which the El had arrived. One time I went so far as to get off the El. I stood on the platform and berated myself for being such a damned fool. Still, I couldn't prevent myself from heading upstairs. Every fluid in my body seemed to flow in the direction of Scranton. I priced the ticket, checked the schedule, but didn't dare follow through on my impulse. I called myself a fool again. I knew my mother would say I should never, ever be a lackey for a man like this. I did feel deeply ashamed that I had actually come this close to making a jackass out of myself. I wandered around 30th Street Station, as if in a dream. So many of my waking hours were like nightmares during those dark days. Except for the sound of my heels clicking on the marble floor I would have believed I was floating around that cavernous marble gateway to city after announced city. The real travelers, knowing exactly where they were going and bound and determined to get there, zigzagged in front of, behind, and alongside me. I drifted over to one ticket line that seemed to be for destinations upstate, but I kept wondering what James would think. How would he react were I to show up unexpectedly? Would he be happy to see me as he always seemed to be? Or would he be angry? If so, who would this angry James be? Not my James. Or, more to the point, really, her James. Besides, if he had wanted me to come with him, he would have invited me. He would have told me where he was going. And like the busy sounds reverberating around the station, the questions echoed in my head:

The ticket agent was asking how he could help me.

"Where're you goin', miss?"

"When's the next train to Scranton?" I heard myself ask.

"The 7:05 stops in Scranton. One way or round trip?"

"Round trip, I think? Um … I don't know …"

I heard a businessman behind me coughing. He picked up his briefcase as if it were high time he were stepping up to the counter.

"You don't know?! One way or round trip, hon'?"

"No, thanks. Thank you. Thank you, anyway."

And the agent looked at me as if I were crazy. And I wondered seriously if he might not be right.

I fled from the counter. What was wrong with me? I was terribly embarrassed by this brief encounter. But, really, my mind had been made up long before I got to the front of the line. What had convinced me not to go was the thought that James would be displeased, that image my mind had conjured of his face turning angry. If I could have convinced myself that James would have been happy with my surprise visit, I probably would have boarded the 7:05 headed upstate. The priest at Saint John's had counseled patience, and, perhaps, he was correct.

…

"It was the midnight dividing my last day of Bunowen and my first day of exile, when a shrill cry echoed from the ravines below and all around the ominous mountains over which I had trudged and was determined to traverse still, though it might mean my life.

"Not a moment's thought did I give for what to do. Up I sprang with a cold chill running down my spine and I raced, stumbling a bit along the rocky goat track, nor did I look behind me. I ran and I ran down the twisting paths neither my fear nor my downhill course letting me slow my pace. I don't know how much time passed. It seemed like hours but it might have been minutes. At last I reached Bundorragha, a well-sheltered village, which to all appearances was fast asleep. I slowed to a walk and caught my breath. The calmness and courage came back to me then, and when it did, Sarsfield, how I laughed! Sure, I might walk abroad day and night risking my life and limb in a strange countryside without a potato or a crust of bread on me and think nothing of it. But, let a woman scream in the night and I go running faster than Swifty O'Malley himself!

"I hushed myself and wandered down by the quay, for there was a harbor there and a great body of water. 'Twas Killary Bay. The moonlight shone on the bay but did not reveal to me the other side. I found a rowboat moored and unwatched by the quay.

"After all the twists and turns, the tormenting tricks of the *bean sidhe*, the misgivings and indecision, the bumps and scratches and bruises, it seemed the Lord had reserved the boat especially for me. It had been waiting there for me the whole time, a bit of kindness from heaven to soothe my pain-maddened heart. I blessed myself and asked the Lord's forgiveness for my borrowing the boat. I promised not to harm it nor to take anything not belonging to me. I just needed it to get to the other side.

"Placing the gun, powder, and bogoak walking stick I had found quietly near the bow, I unmoored the boat and rowed with great strength and steadiness across the dark bay, the dividing line between my old world and my new, flooding and ebbing between Mayo, my native home, and Connemara, my first place of exile. As I rowed, the past flowed away in my wake, just as it does now, lad, just as it does now. The flapping of bird wings came to me loudly over the water and I thought it was a Fury of home coming to fetch me back. There wasn't a human soul to be seen nor heard and yet I felt I was being followed. Except where the clouds drifted away from the stars above, the darkness was nearly perfect. I could see an odd candle in the windows of the town that faded steadily from my sight, but, sure, they seemed farther away than the stars. Darkness was taking the town. It seemed thicker than the water I was rowing. And every sound was magnified. Every creak of the oars in the oarlocks was the *sidhe* mocking my folly. Every bump of a wave against the boat was a ghost.

"A queer empty feeling was in my belly. I was sad to leave it all behind me. But, it was a relief to me as well … to see the past wash away with the ripples and the bubbles and they trailing away and vanishing in the moonlight … The taste of saltwater spray on my lips blessed me with forgetting and I felt lighter and lighter with each stroke I made. *Saoirse*!

"I was alone and tired and downhearted. I didn't know where I would lay my head nor how I would keep body and soul together but I was free. I was free of people's notion's about me and their expectations, free from worries about Mary … from the *botharins* on which I walked to meet her, the old cemetery where we embraced, the field from which I had picked wildflowers for her, the glen in which I had practiced a song to sing for her … free from the mocking or pitying eyes of Bunowen, and free of the weight of their cruelty. Having nothing but future, uncertain as it may be, I was free of the past.

"So, when I reached the other shore, I got out of the boat with a great sigh and took a brief rest. I had come to the land of which Swifty had told me. I moored the boat fore and aft, took my things, and walked toward the rugged hill of Derry-na-Clough. It seemed best to get out of sight quickly. For dawn was arriving. I climbed the hill, and, at the summit, I turned toward the south, and knelt down on the earth. I took some stones and laid them out in the shape of a cross, and said a prayer of thanksgiving to the Lord, as surely we will kneel and pray on the day when we reach the other side of this. Though we don't know what lies ahead of us, lad, we have seen the spires of Saint Colman's sink into the sea behind us and we left there for a reason. For tomorrow is another day and tomorrow we'll tell tales of these troubles just as I'm telling you the saga of my sad youth and we just pilgrims passing the time of the storm."

2. Gluttony & Temperance

A re we going to Brooklyn? What the fuck?! A high-pitched laugh came all the way from her diaphragm. It sounded like she was singing.

Paul looked past Laura's rain-drop-tousled, concentrating head and saw through the fogged-up windshield the towers of the Brooklyn Bridge.

Finding the Way from the Brooklyn Bridge to the FDR

1. Turn around and take the Brooklyn Bridge to Manhattan.
2. Take Park Row to Chinatown.
3. Take Mott Street through Chinatown and Little Italy to Houston Street.
4. Turn right on Houston Street.
5. Take Houston Street to the entrance to the FDR.

The suspension cables of the bridge came at his eyes like the quivering fingers of demented hands. High above the water and looking down. Like a Celtic sacred place. For these enormous standing stones, an immigrant blood sacrifice. The towers and span a graveyard of Irish workers. And the water down below. Dooncarton's stone circles, on the side of a hill above the sea. The whistling of the barbed wire in the seawind. Watch the cow dung as you climb. Round hills overlooking sea. Sacred to the ancestors. Valentia Island ogham stones and dolmens in the sheep's shitty field. Drumbeg stone circles, untouched. Right in the back yard. Fairy forts. Overlooking an inlet. The Rock of Cashel high on a hilltop over a valley stretching out with smaller hills humping down to the sea. Round towers of stones without mortar. Mad brick-and-mortar Manhattan, the island of hills, overlooking the sea.

Stopping after a visit to Ceide Fields, wandered off on your own down the muddy lane to relieve yourself. Returning, you thought of the ancestors, not these very ancient ones but the more recent ones who had lived in these ruined houses. And that is what the wind shrieked through the barbed wire, "Ruuuuuuuuuin!" "The last time you were home," your friend said, though you were not born here. And the ghostlike wind entoned, "Hooooooooooooome!" You imagined their lives: harvesting what they could from the sea, digging some potatoes in scattered patches on the hillside, tending the sheep up above. A life without luxury except the sea air, the taste of their own fresh food, and the occasional sunshine. But without an occasion for greed or sloth or gluttony or envy or many other sins for that matter. A life with hardly a temptation: what time did they have for sin? Surely, if anyone should get into heaven, it is these people. And you accepted it readily and without fear — one incarnation as real as the other in this country. Mary, Joseph, Saint John, and a Lamb! John with an opened book in his hand. Miracle. Yes, an official miracle. Or was the airport of the Knock built for a hoax?

On the other side, Laura found a place to make a U-turn. Through the web of stout wires the still-dark sideview skyline. From this suspension bridge of disbelief, the bluing of the night sky, backlighting wanly, the lonely yet familiar towers of Paul's Lower Manhattan world.

Strange Germanic tongue forcing the villagers — those more married to land of their fathers than they could ever be to their money —out of their hovels of homes to walk the roads with shoeless feet. Poverty, hunger, cruelty, humiliation. You knew it and felt it and heard them howling as the wind shrieked through the barbed wire. The indignant curses of young and old alike. You felt the boiling blood. The keening of the women for their children, for their husbands, for their toil and sweat, for their memories, and for the ancestors, the spirits who walked and the bodies that lay in that very earth, trying, if you don't mind, to rest in peace. *Ababoona*! Here, at this outpost, which seemed at the end of the world, a zone between here and there, land and sea, earth and sky, today and yesterday, This World and *An Saol Eile*.

> *... and twice farewell to my comrades all*
> *Who dwell on that sainted ground.*
> *If fame or fortune shall favour me*
> *Or I should have money in store,*
> *I'll go back and I'll wed the wee lassie I left*
> *On Paddy's green shamrock shore.*

The openings in the bridge's towers looked like Gothic church windows. Sky turning azure behind the lone-seeming spire of the Woolworth building, its broad and rather high base not visible.

Park Row. The open space in the sky above City Hall and the circle below Park Row: Police Plaza, the Municipal Building, the Woolworth Building, and the buttressed Park Row building. Piers and slips jutting out. Rooftop water towers squatting. Slovenly. Honorary guard of high-rise housing projects in formations flanking the bridge. Bracing sea air for our return to Manhattatinny: place of general intoxication. Conspicuous consumption.

saint andrews down there thats peter andrew and john now saints preserve us can you not keep watch with us one hour spirit is willing get her back on track

— You gotta take the exit for Park Row and loop around under the bridge …

— Where? Under the bridge?

— Over here on the right. Just get over … right after this cab …

But she didn't react quickly enough.

— Shit! Did I just miss it?

— It's all right. Don't worry about it. We'll just take the streets. Keep going straight.

Paul watched the exit ramp curlicue down and away from them like an ornament in an illuminated manuscript. He sat up straight and leaned forward.

— Keep going and take a right at the end of the bridge.

— I can't believe I keep missing these turns!

— It's no big deal. We'll just take Centre Street.

Laura turned right and drove uptown toward Chambers Street.

tweed courthouse all the tammany tiger fat cats lapping up the public funds a boon to construction companies too boondoggle to end all boondoggles

— Instead of heading past Police Headquarters we'll go through the courthouses.

— Cut out the middle man.

— Exactly.

They sat at a red light before the grand arches and columns of the Municipal Building's entrances. The green light flashed on.

— Is that African burial ground near here? asked Charles. I read about it in the *Times*. Are we going to go past it?

and gladly wolde he lerne, and gladly teche

— No. It's close but we won't go past it. It's a block or two to the west, near Reade Street. They were putting up some new federal building when they found all these African grave sites from the 17th and 18th centuries. People wanted it declared hallowed ground.

— I'm not really looking for a history lesson right now, guys. Paul, which way do I go?

— Better bear right here.

Laura's BMW entered the corridor of grey Greco-Roman courthouse buildings.

don't fall asleep

Paul leaned his head by the open window and stretched his hand out to try to touch the delicious New York City spring air.

keep watch i must i will irish construction graves behind us african graves to the west

The time is chosen and the time arrives.

And in rising air from shore to shore, the fiddle tells what even Irish words can't say … singing high and lonesome over the turf fire and the passing time, reeling like the restless sky, jigging like the shivering sea, piping away like wild geese on the wing … the bodhran rumbling like a far off storm approaching the cliff by the sea, attacking to drown with sound the roar of the surf and the crash of the waves on the rocks … from departed hand passed along to living hand … packed away with little else, carefully wrapped in ragged shroud and carried down to holds of the coffin ships ... until what land was lost is found again and the air can rise once more and flow, departed hand to living, generation to generation, rookery cellar to parish hall to railroad camp to Tin Pan Alley sheets, to liven land from sea to shining sea …

And the rhythms from the hands of the elders cannot be taken away though passed to hands in chains … the pulse from the palms and fingers falling on the djembe's edge, slapping rings and tones … notes chattering over the all-night fire like the castes of creatures in the teeming, initiation-rite forest … And the bass notes thump-thump-thumping with the flames flickering birth, life, death…birth, life, death …kept on, pounding, pounding maddening, maddening beats … Of *Suli* and *Dibon*, *Kuku* and *Liberte* … in their bound hearts below decks in the slave ships … buoying them through the rite, their passage … surging through the delta, up the Mississippi and its arteries, spreading electric on the winds, speaking to the body for those who could listen with the body … (But never will they know who will not feel) … until the slaves' rhythms freed the land of their bondage …

And the lively tunes rising from coffin ships and the free rhythms sprung from slave ships rocked and rolled … The departed hands passing on to living hands … The transmigration of soul … And everywhere the tune is played, it is the tune of the old hearth … And everywhere the rhythm is felt, it is the rhythm of the old fire … though we but gawk at those passing hands, like tourists on Saint Peter's Street, the Vieux Carre … peering through the time-filthed window of Preservation Hall … at the back of a drummer who keeps the beat of his band's muffled music … with the syncopated slap of his stick on the snare, the wavecrash of his cymbal, and the bass drum's body-speaking boomboom… boomboom… boomboom…

...

As James guided the station wagon south on Atlantic Avenue, Janey leaned her head against her cool window, gazed up at the streetlights hung with giant candy canes of evergreen leaves and twigs bound with red ribbons, and thought again about having more children. Christmas was just not the same without little ones around.

Kitty and Paul — she a snot-nosed seventh grader and he, looking like a man in his jacket and tie, a freshman at the Prep — had outgrown much of the Christmas excitement. Paul still enjoyed the Wanamaker's Light Show as a tradition, but now that he was a teenager with a deep voice she hardly recognized, he was big enough and ugly enough to take the Broad Street Subway there by himself. Janey did not like to think about that: she didn't like him on that subway. But now that the kids were older, they were not as much fun to spend time with and didn't keep her as busy. That they didn't need her as much as they had was a peripheral shadow she did not want to turn and face.

It was funny to be down the shore in the wintertime, let alone during the Christmas season, but James really wanted to see what all the fuss was about with the new casinos. So he booked rooms at Resorts International for Janey and him and their friends Dolores and Joey. Janey had no interest in gambling: she didn't understand throwing money out the window for nothing. At least when she overspent on shopping, she had bags of pretty things to bring home with her. But, when she learned the hotel was right by the beach and had views of the ocean, she agreed to go. She wondered what it would be like to see snow fall on the beach.

Last night, the Resorts' dinner was wholly forgettable. The casino's Roaring '20s theme, however, excited her. The Model T and Packard parked outside, the men in their old suits and hats, and the girls in their frilly, shiny flapper dresses opened the floodgates of Janey's imagination: rumble seats, hot music, exposed flesh, the flow of forbidden liquor, wild dances! But the hotel and casino, the restaurant and the boardwalk all had Christmas decorations up. And though it was clearly not an atmosphere for little people and they hardly saw a child, she had the same recurring desires. Janey wanted to have at least one more baby. "Time comes, baby comes," her grandmother used to say but who had the patience for that nowadays.

Tonight James insisted that they eat at Dock's, a Logan family favorite long before legalized gambling was a twinkle in the city fathers' eyes. Janey liked to joke that the owners were her cousins, though there was no relation that she knew of. She wondered if her mother who had arrived from Donegal in the '20s ever ate there. Janey wished she could ask her.

She hoped it would snow sometime this weekend! Jim O'Brien on ACTION News said it might, placing his frowning bad-guy clouds over South Jersey. And, it did seem cold enough. It would be romantic to be snug in the hotel room with snow falling through the cold sea air and covering the sand on the beach below them.

There were some days when she was not good for anything else ... when she felt not only the power but the will to excite desire ... when all she wanted was to don nice stockings and a short slinky skirt that swayed with her hips. On these days her walk drew more attention and she wanted to be out and about. She hated the ogling but had to admit there were times she liked the looks. Even men's stupid jokes made her laugh more. Given the opportunity, Janey would have joined the young people bumping to the disco beat and the moaning chanteuse. But there was no John Travolta to be found in this station wagon.

James pulled into Dock's parking lot. The valet seemed to recognize them. Janey smiled at the young man as she passed. He gave a discreet smile back.

On days like this one, that type of response gave Janey a little thrill, like when she could sense that a man has turned around to look at her behind. On other days their gawking and their clumsy attempts to conceal it were annoying: they were just leering, staring creeps.

Through Dock's front windows Janey could see candles and fir garlands and above the white awning a string of multi-colored lights. It seemed very Christmassy despite the salt air, the painting of a bare-chested Neptune over the door, and the company of merely adults.

What about James? What did he think about another baby?

He was non-committal. He was certainly not completely against it, though he had a couple of objections — about her age, the expense, the size of the house, the amount of energy and work it would require to take care of another little one. But why should he mind that? Most of the work of caring for the kids fell on her, anyway. And once it was a reality, once there was his child growing inside of her, he would come around as he did before, as they all do eventually.

James usually got romantic during the holidays, but not for the same reasons as she. His attentions had more to do with celebrations at the company. Surely, it would not be difficult to get him interested. But who knows? Instead of understanding him better over the years she found him harder and harder to fathom.

They walked under the cupola-shaped awning and James held the door open for everyone. The old dining room was bedecked with holly and garlands of evergreen and strings of lights around the permanent nautical decorations. On the walls were Christmas wreaths and tinsel. Any available shelf space was filled by red candles, figurines of angels, snowmen, choir boys, Santa, Mrs. Claus, and reindeer. Janey noticed that from two lintels there dangled clumps of plastic mistletoe.

At the coat check, she was proud to reveal her emerald-green dress with the shoulder pads and belted waist. She had dieted over the last few months in order to reduce. Though she was not satisfied with her results, she could see some improvement. Janey hoped that James had noticed, too. She had asked him what he thought when she was getting dressed, turning herself this way and that in the satin dress. She had put on her nicest bra and panties in case he did want to undress her later on. But he doesn't really do that or even watch her undressing anymore. He just takes off his own clothes matter-of-factly, not really looking at her until he is climbing into bed. Janey supposed that is the way it is with marriage. But it was not too late to change that. A getaway like this was the perfect way to spice things up.

A baby conceived in December would be born in August. That would mean giving birth in the hot weather. The hospital would be air conditioned, though. The baby would be a Leo, like her sister. Maybe she could name her, "Lisa." But wasn't Janey getting ahead of herself? A baby was conceived once without a man, but that was 2,000 years ago, and it was a miracle.

. . .

Though the home did not provide the ideal location for hosting such a large family, the Logans gathered for Thanksgiving at the old twin house on Simpson Road in Saint Colman's . Despite the success of her husband's construction company, Nora had always insisted on living "where the action is." After Moyamensing, Ardmore had been adjustment enough. Nora's daughter-in-law, Mariellen, couldn't count the number of times she had offered to host Thanksgiving in her Gladwyne mansion but the old woman's opposition remained steadfast.

Jimmy and Mariellen had tried to get Kitty not to cook but she proved as pliable as her mother. So, the women of the family countered with their own dishes: string bean casserole, au gratin potatoes, and apple pie. Along with her acclaimed stuffing, Kitty made turkey for everyone in the same pot her mother had always used. No one could talk her out of it.

Maybe Aunt Kitty just wanted to keep busy.

Mariellen sidestepped around the large table in the dining room to set Aunt Kitty's green and red glass goblets before the guests' seats. It wasn't Christmas yet but Nora had had always wanted them out as a harbinger of the season. Mariellen's daughter, young Nora, placed the knives and forks and spoons. Squeezing past them, Nora picked up the one of the goblets and squinted at the way the stem balled up in the middle.

"I've always liked these glasses," said she. "They look like they have knees."

Mariellen and Aunt Kitty laughed.

"You have quite the imagination there, Nora."

"She'll be graduating from Merion next year."

"Talking about graduation already?! I just can't believe it!"

Jimmy rushed in from the kitchen with his coat still on and started arranging some new bottles of liquor on the serving cart by the living room. The liquor bottles needed to be replaced much more often these days. He supposed that was to be expected. Sure, everyone was trying to act normal. They even made jokes and laughed. But if you looked closely you could see that they were paler, that their eyes did not have the same light.

"Hello? Hello? Happy Thanksgiving!" Father Sarsfield boomed from the front porch.

Jimmy grabbed his son, who was slouching toward the dining room, by a gangly arm.

"Mike," he whispered. "Go take Father Sarsfield's coat!"

The young man rolled his eyes and shuffled off toward the porch.

Jimmy called out to the women and girls in the dining room and kitchen. He threw a couple of ice cubes in a glass and reached for the bottle of Black & White.

"Sarsfield's here! Honey, Father Sarsfield's here!"

"Oh good, Sarsfield's here!"

"Sarsfield's here!"

"Sarsfield's here! I was startin' to wonder."

Jimmy hurried over to the armchair Father Sarsfield was just sinking into.

"Here you go, Sarsfield. Happy Thanksgiving — a week early, for some reason! Mike, where're you going? Siddown and talk with Father Sarsfield."

Mike plopped on the couch. Jimmy went to make a drink for himself.

"How are you, young man? How are things at the company?"

"Better than they have been the last few years."

"It seems like just yesterday you were at The Prep."

Jimmy returned with his scotch and soda and took a seat next to his son.

"Seems like yesterday to me, too," he chuckled.

"It's good to be back here," Sarsfield said. "Though I imagine it is hard having it here. It's our first Thanksgiving without Mother."

Leave it to Uncle Sarsfield, thought James, to bring up what no one wants to talk about.

"Yes, it is tough on everyone. Mariellen wanted to have it at our place, as she's been saying for years but-"

"This is what Mother would have wanted. Everyone under her roof as usual."

Mariellen and Kitty came smiling into the room.

"Hello, Sarsfield! How are you? Are you warm enough sittin' here?"

"I'm fine. Fine."

"I see Jimmy's gotten you your usual," Kitty said.

"The boys are taking good care of me."

"That was a good sermon this morning. You always say such a nice mass for us when you come back for a visit."

"It's always nice to be back. Though it is something to see how much younger some of the priests are. Most of them don't remember Father."

"True. It's hard to believe. I'm sure they have heard about him, though. The big stained-glass window in the back…"

"We're all getting older, Sarsfield," Kitty said. "There's no getting away from it."

"But it beats the alternative – right, Aunt Kitty?" Jimmy joked raised his glass.

"Well you boys enjoy your drinks and dinner will be ready in a few minutes."

"Mike, come with me and help your Aunt Kitty."

"But, Dad said-"

"Come with me-"

"Mike! You mother needs help. Go!"

A moment later, guided by Aunt Kitty, Mike carried a card table into the center of the room. He propped it up and galumphed back down the basement for some folding chairs.

"Sarsfield, are you going to be able to get around that? Mike, wait a minute, we need to let Father Sarsfield by first."

"I'll be fine. I'll be fine. We New Yorkers can squeeze through small spaces."

As Sarsfield lowered himself into his chair at the head of the table, the children came stomping up the basement stairs. On their way to the children's table, each one was made to stop at Father Sarsfield's chair and sing out, "Hi, Father Sarsfield!"

During the meal, the conversation did not flow as freely as it usually did — with the family members talking over one another. They chattered about the Prep, of course, followed by the latest news from the Logan Construction Company, despite Kitty's protests against work talk. Jimmy related an anecdote about meeting Mayor Lamberton, but Father Sarsfield did not know much about local politics and Kitty disapproved of that subject as well.

"The Eagles won today – huh, Father Sarsfield?" offered Jimmy.

"Yes, they beat Pittsburgh. I heard some of the game on the radio."

"Do you really root for the Giants, Father Sarsfield?" asked Mike.

"I talk about the Giants with my parishioners and students. It gives me something to chat about with the New Yorkers. But, as you know, I have always been more of a baseball man."

"The Phillies didn't give us much to cheer about this year."

"That's for sure."

"It's good to have Chuck Klein back ," said Sarsfield. "Even part time."

As the coffee started to percolate in the kitchen, a sense of relief wafted into the room with its aroma. Before dessert, however, they had to go through the annual ritual.

"Sarsfield, have a piece of pie."

"No, thank you, Kitty. I really need to head back to the rectory."

"Oh, have a piece of pie for once in your life," cried Mariellen.

"Why not offer him a fruit cup?" Nora sniggered and covered her mouth with her hand. "I think I saw some in the ice box."

"Sarsfield, which will it be apple or mince?"

"I don't want any pie. You know I don't eat dessert."

"But it's Thanksgiving. You can enjoy yourself a little."

"I have enjoyed myself a great deal but now it is time to go back to the rectory."

"How about some fruit-"

"Ssssh!"

Sarsfield started to raise himself from his chair.

"I must get back to the rectory. I will scandalize the young priests if they see an old fogey like me coming back too late. Thank you for a wonderful meal, as always."

"Nonsense. Jimmy'll drive you."

"Yes, I'll drive you, Father Sarsfield."

"I can walk. I have always been a walker."

"With all due respect, Father. It's out of the question. I'll give you a lift."

"Sarsfield," Kitty almost shouted. "Have some fruit cup. Sit here and enjoy it. Jimmy'll drive you back to the rectory."

Sarsfield agreed. Everyone applauded and Nora tried not to laugh too loudly. As soon as Sarsfield finished, he and Jimmy were out the front door.

"He's always had such strict habits," said Mariellen. "He'll never take anything for dessert."

"He knows how to push himself away from the table," added Nora. "We could all get better at that."

Kitty and Mariellen poured out more coffee, trying to finish up what was left in the pot.

"Mommy, I'm finished!"

The children's table had been restive for some time and was now impossible to ignore.

"I'm done, Mommy!"

"Can we be excused?"

The children were excused and as they scampered downstairs, Little James called out, "Let's play, 'Hide and Seek'!"

Mariellen shouted down the stairs, "Don't make a mess down there!"

A bang came from the front door. Leaving his coat on the front porch, Jimmy crossed the living room and stopped at the bar to make himself a drink.

"He's a tough one about dessert, boy," said Kitty. "He must be watching his figure."

"He was just going on about how stubborn you are, Aunt Kitty. Tryin' to force dessert on him."

"That's why he usually likes to leave without even saying 'goodbye.'"

"This time he couldn't get away with that!"

The Logans laughed and shook their heads.

"Sarsfield's abstemious, too. Two glasses of scotch, never a drop more even on Christmas. In all these years, I never saw him drink more than that."

"Too bad that doesn't run in the family!" chuckled Mariellen.

The basement was unusually quiet. The children must have been hiding.

"Things worked out nicely, I'd say," said Jimmy. "You might think we know what we're doing."

"At least we're keeping up the tradition like a normal Thanksgiving," Kitty said as she cleaned up the dessert plates. "But it's just not the same."

"Y'know, Sarsfield mentioned it as soon as he came in, 'This is our first Thanksgiving without Mother,' said he."

"He's not one for avoiding unpleasant topics. He likes to tackle things head on."

"Now if only the Eagles could learn to do that!"

"We didn't realize how lucky we were to have Mother host Christmas year after year," sighed Jimmy.

"Why do we always realize these things after people are gone?"

"Isn't that always the way?"

"It'll take time, I suppose. After a few years, it'll start to seem normal."

"Y'know, Mother was very disciplined. A strong-willed woman if there ever was one. I wonder if that's where Sarsfield got it."

"It could be. Mother never ate more than she needed," Kitty said. "With all the money she had, she was never ostentatious."

"She was always generous, though."

"Oh yes, she was downright extravagant when it came to her children and grandchildren! I meant she never spent money on fancy meals or things for herself."

"She enjoyed a good French restaurant from time to time but she was just as happy with a simple place."

"She had her spots. She was happy to go to her regular places. Fisher's … the Llanerch Diner … "

"She knew how to be happy with what she had."

"God bless her."

Jimmy raised his scotch. Playful screams could he heard from downstairs.

"Thanks, Kitty, for a wonderful dinner. Everything was delicious. We had a great time and it sound like the kids are having fun."

"Well, I'm glad. It's wonderful to have everyone here again for Thanksgiving," Kitty said, pausing by the kitchen doorway. "But, this year was different, of course.

She crossed the threshold and disappeared from view. Yet no one failed to hear her sniffling.

...

Finding the Way from Centre Street to the FDR

To find your way to the FDR from Centre Street:

1. Turn right on Worth Street.
2. Turn left on Park Row.
3. Turn left on Mott Street.
4. Turn right on Houston Street.
5. Take Houston Street to the FDR.

— Oyez! Oyez! Oyez! cried the court clerk. All persons having business before this Honorable Court of New York State are admonished to draw near and give their attention, for the Court is now sitting. Judge Laura presiding.

The door to Judge Laura's chambers opened and in she swept with her long blonde hair flowing freely across the shoulders of her black robe emblazoned with a heart radiating from the center of its chest, all of the colors of the rainbow.

— God save the United States, the State of New York, and this Honorable Court.

Curling a finger of hair behind her ear, Judge Laura turned to climb the stairs to her bench revealing in profile the elevation of her black robe at a slightly obtuse angle by the wonderbra she wore underneath. She took her seat and banged her gavel.

— This court shall come to order, she commanded, and asked for the first case on the docket.

The clerk, who can now be clearly identified as Walter, announced.

— Your Honor, the first case is the People vs. Paul Logan.

— And what, Judge Laura asked, is the charge?

Charles rose a little unsteadily on his feet, fixing the white wig that had almost fallen off and adjusting his long red robe.

— Mr. Logan is charged with misrepresenting his intentions. He has claimed to be interested in love when his actions show that he is truly interested in mass consumption of alcoholic beverages, particularly Guinness. It is hypocrisy, plain and simple. His so-called love has been perverted from the love of a beautiful young woman to the love of the next pint he can procure and quaff.

— Prosecution, you may make your opening statement.

— Your Honor, I know Mr. Logan has claimed to be a lover of some desperate ardor. However, we see little evidence of this. He claims that he goes to the Orange Crush Bar at 47 Murray Street on an errand of the heart and yet when he does go there he does nothing more than spend hours and hours drinking pints of black beer.

The lawyer for the defense, Paul Logan, representing himself, leapt to his feet.

— I object, your honor! Guinness is a stout, which is a type of ale.

— Sustained. Continue, Prosecutor.

— The People would like to point out that the Defense's foolish client has not even obtained the beloved's telephone number. Instead, he has repeatedly given her his business card in the vain hope that she might call or email him. This is not the behavior of a lover, even according to the loose and more egalitarian mores of 1998. Though he claims to be a poet, he has not presented her with a single verse. Unlike many lovers, he has not brought her any gifts to delight her. His words speak of a lover's intention but his actions are more in keeping with a man whose main desire is to consume and consume some more. Drink this pint, buy this bottle, accept free rounds of shots of which he knows not even the ingredients ... I submit to you, your Honor, that Paul Logan has been spending late evenings at or near the Orange Crush and neglecting his daytime job as a technical writer — whatever that might be — not out of love for a woman but in the desire to fill his belly with beer and-

— Objection.

— Prosecution will rephrase that.

— To fill his belly with stout and liquor.

— Thank you, your Honor.

The Prosecution would like to call to the stand, the alleged object of Mr. Logan's affections, your Honor, the beloved.

Laura rose and stepped down from behind the bench. Taking the required oath, she placed one hand over the copy, proffered by the bailiff, of *La Fanfarlo* by Charles Baudelaire, spread the fingers of her other hand over her heart beating boomboom boomboom, and pressed her palm over its radiating replica.

Charles paced back and forth before the witness stand.

— How long have you known the defendant? he began.

— About a month. He first came into the Orange Crush around Saint Patrick's Day.

— A well-known and predictable occasion for overconsumption of alcoholic beverages!

— Totally. But is that a question?

— In the time you have known him, has he made any declaration of love?

— No. But that would be pretty dudley-

— Please restrict to your responses to answers to the questions asked. He claims to be something of a poet. He has given readings-

— Objection, cried Paul. Defendant has written and published some poetry. A poet is one who writes poetry — even if not as often as he should. Therefore, by definition, this is not a claim but a fact.

From the witness stand, Laura ruled:

— Sustained. Totally. Prosecutor will rephrase.

— Very well. The defendant is something of a poet. He has stated that he has given readings and performed his own songs at open mics and "coffee houses." Yet, has he dedicated a single verse to your Honor, his beloved?

— He has not, Judge Laura replied.

— Lovers are known to give gifts. Has he bestowed a single gift upon his beloved?

— Other than many bottles of Amstel Light poured in pint glasses full of ice and some offers for expensive lunches, Judge Laura declared, the defendant has not.

— Nevertheless, a lover's propensity for giving gifts has not been much in evidence from Mr. Logan — has it?

— No, but I lent him the *Best Short Stories of 1998*. Does that help?

— No, it does not. No further questions, your Honor.

...

"My first morning in Connemara I wandered along the coast of Killary Harbor. I didn't want to stop in the town of Leenaun for fear that someone would accuse me of stealing the rowboat. I continued along what I later learned was the Clifden road past a village called Leenane. I had no destination. My purpose was to pass the time without arousing suspicion.

"I turned inland on a *botharin* and was shocked that my feet had led me to a town whose name beggared belief. It was called by no other name than, "Bunowen"! I had never known there was a Bunowen in Galway . There was even a Bunowen River! I had been running from Bunowen all night only to find my way to Bunowen! Was this more work of the fairies?

"Well, with the harbor to my back and some lovely mountains before me, I strolled along until I found a rock to sit on. In the distance was another village, this one abandoned. Behind the clutch of thatchless cabins I could see the potato ridges that had likely failed to feed the poor souls who had inhabited the *baile*. And snaking its way up and over the mountainside was a famine road to nowhere. The poor souls had had to work on the useless byway to show themselves deserving of a bit of food to keep them alive. I wondered how many had survived and what had happened to them. Surely, many of them must have left their homes as I had, and likely felt stronger regret at going. 'Twas a place with a sad history I had chosen to rest in on my first morning in Connemara but it was beautiful and peaceful. It suited me well enough for quiet was what I wanted and no trouble from anyone from this world or the other.

"'Let the sun rising over the ocean scatter the host of the *Sidhe*,' I whispered to myself. "And may the Lord grant Seamus Logan peace here in the light of day.

"'Sure last night,' I added. 'The palaver of spirit voices, the laughter and the murmuring, was the work of the fairies. And all that high-pitched singing and the keening of the women that was all fairy mischief, too.

"'Well, they did not get their way, those Furies sent by my family and friends. They could not dissuade Seamus Logan from the path he had chosen — even if they mock me by leading me to a place sharing a name with the one I had left. Mary has betrayed me. My home place has broken my heart. No force seen or unseen can make me go back. Nothing can change my mind once it is made up.'

"And I said an Our Father."

Seamus's steerage mate, Mick, stopped wrapping his fiddle and bow in the frayed sheet he kept them in and blessed himself.

"But, before I could finish my prayer, the wind shrieked through the empty windows (though few windows there were.) And a sudden swirl of dust arose in what had been the village's road. I drew in a wee puff of breath as my grandmother used and my hand reached out for my shotgun at the same instant. For the touch of my hand upon iron would keep them away.

"No form approached me and yet the howl of the wind through the windows was enough to drive me daft.

"'Surely, I am in a place of great suffering, and it a village with perhaps no survivors belonging to it atall,' I said.

"Then, before my eyes as the sunlight came over the heather-clad hilltop behind me, the abandoned village blossomed into life.

"Men, women, and children worked the fields and walked the roads. Families made their way home from mass. Everyone avoided the fairy fort on the hill beyond, for fear of being strayed. Women came back from the old well with buckets filled with water to boil for bathing and washing and cooking. One was the spit and image of Mary. And how I longed for her, forgetting, for the moment, the pain she had caused me! And the men in the *meitheal* haying in the sunshine, tossing it high, in a great rush to get it done. And didn't they dig fine potato hills and mountains of turf with their *sleans,* stacking it in pyramids for to keep out the dampness and the rains that would come? Fathers and sons in pairs stood apart from each other twisting the *sugan.* And I smiled to see them making the rope. They were that much like my own people back in Mayo's Bunowen."

Rosie, the old woman across from Seamus, nodded her head, appearing lost in a reverie about her own home place.

"But then I heard the wind swirling behind me and I knew the fairies were up to their devilish tricks again. I could not bear to look, but at the same time, I could not keep from looking. Men and boys were bringing in their animals from the slopes of the mountain, a green quiet hill, and the beauty of it made me full sad. For I knew what it was that was coming.

"When the children cried out in hunger and the women keened in sorrow and when the men called out in indignation and pain, it made me regret that I ever came to this village or was born in this sorrowful country at all, at all.

"A group of armed men in uniform approached the village. Grotesque and alien they appeared before this undulating, brilliant landscape. The stomping of their heavy boots on the gravel in the paths, the frightful rhythm of it, floated down the hill to assault my ears. The men moved in unison, their mechanical movements creating a sharper contrast between them and the people, and this place, even than their dress. They must have marched up from the glistening harbor for their awful morning's work. A local man trying to adopt an air of importance, doubtless the local sheriff, pointed out the particular hovel for these soldiers to call on. Lines of lean, cowed townspeople stood in stunned silence on either side of the road, gazing into the dust, suffering the soldiers to pass. The sheriff signaled for the soldiers to prepare for their work of desecration. They stood at attention. All of the villagers remained silent except the old *bean an ti*, a widow she must have been, who shrieked and cursed at the uniformed men and more vehemently at the local man directing them.

The commander of the soldiers read a proclamation from the court but the old woman took no notice. *Maise*, what did it mean to her, who had spent untold years at the hearth inside, rearing her children by it, cooking meals on it, talking with family and friends in its warmth? What could their foreign speech, mere accompanying prattle to their foreign dress, their foreign movements, and their foreign habit of mind have to say to her and hers?

A command was given and the soldiers turned to enter the humble dwelling. The woman screamed at the sheriff and tried to block the soldiers' way. But she was pushed back. The neighbor women came over to comfort her as the soldiers so bravely marched her beds, her bedding, and her utensils out the door. The women did their best to calm the old widow, and no one else made a row over this scene that was far too common for all who were present.

All too quickly the door was blocked up with stones and the soldiers, their outrage to hearth complete, strode away leaving the old woman sitting by her obstructed threshold covering her whole head with her shawl. A few of the neighbor women sat with her in silence. Sure, no sound came from the assembled villagers at all. They had all participated in this ritual too many times for any fight to remain in them. The ending had been as inevitable as the coming change of tide in the salty harbor below. And the same end would come to all of them, surely. Or the workhouse. Or worse.

"*Ochone*! But I turned back again and what I saw was all suffering, the tearing away of the loved ones from loved ones! And how they didn't want to go! They left and hated to leave! Just as ye hated to leave. And how those left behind hated to see them go! 'Twas the howls of the women I heard! The cruelty! Jesus, Mary, and Joseph! The pain of their *baile's* becoming barren! The keens of the women sharp as the *bean sidhe's* midnight shriek, chanting their verses for the dead and against their enemies, the indignant curses of young and old alike.

"And, God forgive me for saying so, but I then saw proud honest men reduced to stealing chickens for to feed their families and I saw stalwart people knocked down to the ground with hunger so that they crawled upon the earth like the creatures banished from our shore by Saint Patrick himself and they having nothing to eat but the grass until their mouths turned green from trying to soothe the maddening pain of the hunger that was on them. And there were worse enormities that these wretched people were reduced to that I cannot even say and could not bear to watch. And so, I turned away again and for a moment wished that I had never seen this village and that I could forget these visions of the shades of men who had done these deeds. But I reflected that everywhere it was the same with famine and suffering and destruction, with sundering of families and dying and it didn't matter at all where you were in the world. And though my head and my heart were filled to the brim with the sorrow of thwarted love, a great pity I felt for all of them. For, surely, if there is a something you gain from suffering yourself it is to feel sympathy with the sufferings of others.

"And I could feel their sorrows in my very heart and in my very bones! For they, unlike me, did not want to go! And they did not want to bury their loved ones in the great pit of the starved and the victims of the famine fever! And there, the dying, the living, and the dead lay on the same floor next to one another, nothing between them and the cold earth save the few miserable rags upon them, as if they were but taking a rest with one another, as in happier times after long work. And so many of them dying they turned half an acre of dirt and threw the bodies in without a coffin, one after another! And God rest their souls, every one of them.

"And I swore I'd never forget the land that I come from and what was done to it. Nor by whom. And you shouldn't either, me boy. It will help you understand why we have to suffer this long voyage in steerage. We can only go forward. For surely, there's nothing to go back to. Perhaps, having heard these tales, you will be able to pass them on to your own children someday. We can keep the people in all the poor suffering little townlands alive in the tales that we tell!"

"And so, lad. Remember this if you remember anything I'm telling you: know that whatever you have, no matter how precious and permanent you might think it is, it could all be gone tomorrow. I've seen it happen myself."

...

One of the happiest feelings in life rushed me out of the hotel room: a whole new city to explore! And the French Quarter no less! It was the week of the Catholic-school teachers' convention and she was at a special session for guidance counselors. The rest sat in meetings.

But I was free. To roam the cobblestone streets. To stroll along the narrow sidewalks lined with horsehead posts until my feet screamed complaints. To take whatever turns I wanted. To stop any place that caught my eye: voodoo shops on Saint Peter, antique stores on Royal, literary and historical sites around Jackson Square. Free like I wouldn't be back in the Bronx. To get lost, to get in trouble, to discover, to see my opportunities and take them, to file away in my mind the bars and restaurants for a kind of travel guide for degenerates. To sample the foods: God, it would take a week to try all the local foods. To drink as much beer as I wanted.

Until I had to meet them all for dinner.

I started out my day at the Cafe du Monde — with coffee and beignets. Do I want sugar on top? Yes! Yes, I want sugar on top! And, yes, give me another order of them!

Stopping by the little yellow house where Faulkner lived as a young man, I imagined him roaming the leisurely Nawlins streets, ruminating on his first novel. I took a brochure for their novel-writing contest. Maybe I'll enter it, if I ever finish a piece of writing long enough. Hard to imagine, truth be told.

Some of Faulkner's letters home were on display. Those Catholic school teachers at their convention would be surprised to learn how exotic he considered them. "Ma, these nuns go to church every day!"

Didn't go to mass but I did make a visit to Saint Louis Cathedral. Surprised at how Protestant-vanilla it looked with its white columns and flags and chandeliers. Like Saint Paul's Chapel near work. Suppose the papes didn't want to stand out too much in those days. But the paintings behind the altar and on the ceiling were impressive. And it was peaceful and quiet in the prayerful space. I finished a decade of the rosary and moved on.

I headed north and east along narrow Chartres Street, under the cast-iron balconies of Creole townhouses, past the squat buildings of tight red brick hotels with Gallic names like the Hotel Chateau and the Hotel Dumaine. Turning toward the Mississippi on Dumaine and then upriver again on Decatur, I strolled until I reached New Orleans's Little Italy. I passed Terranova's Grocery: a place that coincidentally shared a surname with my landlord and his bakery back in Little Italy of the Bronx. I found the Central Grocery and ordered a muffuletta. Might as well start with the place that invented them, I figured. They have quarter, half, and full-sized. Of course, I got the full-sized one. When would I be back here again? The soft bread from a round muffuletta loaf housed slices of salami, mortadella, mozzarella, ham, and provolone topped with marinated olive salad: diced olives with celery and bits of carrot and oregano and garlic and lots of olive oil.

The words themselves make you hungry.

Finding my way back to Jackson Square, I realized that most of my day had been consumed by eating. It was now time to drink.

I entered the Old Absinthe House where I saw that Walt Whitman and Oscar Wilde had tippled before me. I got a seat at the bar and had a local beer, Abita. It was no Guinness but it hit the spot. I liked the rundown atmosphere, the business cards tacked all over the walls. And the literary associations lent it some mystique.

I thought at first that I would have just one. But the first gulp hit my stomach like a soft caress. I could finish it quickly and have another one. So I caught the bartender's eye and ordered. While he was pouring, I downed my first Abita. The cold foamy beer filled my mouth, tickled the back of my throat, and went down easily despite the full stomach on me. I drank the second beer at a casual pace, looking at the spring Louisiana sun coating the filthy windows with light. How many years of dust coated that window? I wondered. But the next moment I started to feel anxious. There was plenty more to see and more beer to drink elsewhere. Also, my glass of beer was getting lighter: a new one would have to be found. I tried to reflect on the literary luminaries who had visited this place but I kept feeling the pressure of time.

So I gulped down what remained of my second beer, left a tip for the bartender, waved, and left. I figured I would probably be back there with her later, anyway.

At three o'clock live music began to pour onto Bourbon Street from the bars: I could hear rock and ragtime and blues nearby. I didn't know which one to choose.

Then I had a vision. Across the street, on the sidewalk, under the neon signs, the filigreed cast-iron balconies, and the colorful flowers stood a gamine in a white-and-red trucker's cap. Her light brown hair fell past her bare midriff to the unfilled loops of her roughly scissored cutoffs. Her legs strayed for insouciant sunburnt-pink miles before reaching her pom-pom socks and platform sneakers. And, her slender arms were stretched out toward a tap and a cup! On the street! Beer prices were listed on the wall behind her. She filled a Styrofoam cup for a guy who paid her and walked off. Was she some kind of a vendor voodoo priestess who had transformed her hot dogs into beer? Was this love at first sight? I was over in front of her in a flash.

— Are people allowed to drink on the street here?

— They sure are. Her electric-blue eyes shone in amusement. You can roam all over the Quarter with a beer in your hand.

I bought a beer from her, making a little small talk about the weather. She responded naturally and easily. She was accustomed to tourists but softer than a Manhattanite.

I started walking along Bourbon Street again, dazzled by the smorgasbord of music. With the beer in my hand, I didn't have to choose a particular style: I could listen to them all!

First, I stopped at a jazz bar and listened to a ragtime number. Next door there was a Cajun-zydeco band with a guy playing a washboard hanging from his shoulders. I sidled over and stood by the door for a tune or two. A hawker tried to lure me inside, telling me there was no cover charge. But, I had no need to sit down nor to step out of the beautiful spring sun.

My reverie interrupted, I chugged the rest of my beer as I sauntered back to the black-magic beer-tap girl.

— You're getting the hang of it, she said.

— It's pretty easy to get used to.

— You'll be like a Big Easy native before you know it!

I wandered a few doors down to hear what other types of music were on offer. A screaming guitar stopped me. A muscular young black guy in sunglasses was wailing away on a blues solo. I stayed for a couple Muddy Waters covers, then moseyed farther on. I found a male beer vendor. Not as appealing as my genie with the light brown hair, but convenient.

This was the life. Music and beer in the open air with the old ramshackle buildings leaning on each other with elegant decrepitude. It was like France and Spain in a climate that was almost Italian. Even Ireland was represented in the distant sign for Paddy O'Brien's.

Wherever the Catholic sun doth shine,
There is always laughter and good red wine.

And Hurricanes, too, I guess. Not to mention beer after beer finding its way to my belly stuffed with local delicacies. I was feeling pretty good by the time I headed back to the hotel to change for the Catholic-schoolteacher's dinner at Arnaud's. I didn't want to leave but reassured myself that I would be back for more fun — with company.

As expected, Arnaud's with its tall green plants, its paneled walls hung with painted portraits —probably of the three previous generations who had owned the place— and its mahogany-framed windows looking out onto the Rue Bienville was stuffier than my afternoon street party. The Classic Creole Cuisine, however, delighted my taste buds. Before my meal, I had a Manhattan, sharp as you wanted it to be without being harsh. I sipped it carefully, though: I didn't want to be too unsteady at this official function.

I started with the Turtle Soup. The guy next to me told me it was one of their famous dishes. He said turtle meat has the flavors of seven meats: hints of pork, chicken, beef, shrimp, veal, fish, and goat. (Eat dinner with a bunch of teachers and that's the kind of conversation you get!) I'm not sure if I identified all seven but the soup had a combination of flavors that can make your cheeks pucker and your throat burn. The broth was rich, like a superior version of the gumbo I had tried near Jackson Square the day before. Every mouthful was out of this world. Just when I thought it could not be any more delicious, the waiter offered me a shot of sherry, like they do with snapper soup in Philadelphia. I said, "Why not?" (That could have been the motto for my day.) It didn't really need more flavor but who am I to mess with tradition?

She wouldn't try any. She was afraid because of her shellfish allergies. She also avoided most of the other soups, the shrimp, and the whole selection of oysters. She settled on a chicken gumbo, which wasn't bad.

Me? Like my father and mother, I could have eaten the whole section of the menu labeled, "SHELLFISH"! But people who had been to Arnaud's before kept pushing the Pontchartrain. It was a local name and it had its own song:

> *And at each social gathering a flowin' glass I'll drain*
> *And I'll drink a health to me Creole girl by the Lakes of Pontchartrain*

So, yes, a Pontchartrain and another Manhattan, too, when you get a chance.

After that, it would be back to beer for sure.

The Pontchartrain was a filet of fish gently sautéed and presented on the plate with Louisiana crabmeat piled on top and rich-looking sauce flowing over its sides. It seems the French-Americans, like their cousins across the sea, know how to make eating an experience for more senses that just taste. The fish alone would have been a savory adventure: light and soft and moist on the tongue with a delightful but not too strong flavor. But there was also that crabmeat! I ate a few pieces by themselves. I also scooped up forkfuls of fish and crab and sauce and crammed them all in my mouth at once. I had never had a meal like this one before.

Of course, she wouldn't even touch it because of the crabmeat. I think she got some chicken dish.

— Chicken again?! I remember joking with her.

But I don't think she laughed. She was not having as great a time as I was. Though it was hard not to be brought down a little, I tried not to let her affect my mood.

Laissez les bon temps rouler!

Cheerfully, I filled her in about all that I had discovered — the Absinthe House, the beer on the street, all the different styles of live music in the afternoon! Incredible as this meal was, I was looking forward to shedding the society of these teachers, nuns, counselors, and principals and getting back to the *Rue Bourbon*!

But when we did escape, she had a couple of new acquaintances in tow: one plain-jane teacher from Maryland and a Dean of Students from some high school in Ohio. Bill and Judy. I kid you not. They wanted to stop at the first place they saw. I tried to tell them that there were many options and that the best thing to do was buy beers on the street and sample all of the music. But what value did my advice have when compared to some young elementary school teacher's judgment that a tourist trap looked "cute"? So, we stepped inside, were overcharged for 8-ounce glasses of beer, and heard some Hendrix covers. The guitarist sounded good but I could listen to classic rock on K-Rock or WNEW back in New York.

I eventually rousted them out of there. The teacher and dean did not last long. I was relieved to see them head back to the hotel. My afternoon thirst for adventure — and beer — came back full force. I dragged her down the street to the Cajun-zydeco place I had enjoyed. Now there was a lively crowd and the band was giving people a chance to play the washboard with the shoulder harness.

An effervescent cocoa-skinned girl with frizzy pigtails was welcomed to the stage. She had bright eyes, an infectious smile, and a devil-may-care attitude. I wished I were inside with her, instead of in her majesty's heavy dull presence. The accordion player helped her place the washboard over the sleeveless orange t-shirt that fell over her slight figure. Lithe and sexy before, she now resembled a tall lissom robot from a 1960s sitcom. I was laughing and so was the crowd inside. However, it took the young woman no time to learn to scrape the washboard along with the band. And, she made funny faces and wisecracked with her friends as they cheered her on. I was loving it, and about ready for another beer!

I couldn't believe it when I heard her yawn. I turned to find her covering her mouth.

— I want to go back to the hotel after this one, said she.

— So soon? We just got out here. There are plenty of other bars. I'm almost finished this one. Let's have one more.

— I got to get up early tomorrow.

— I know. I know. But this is Nawlins! You gotta experience this. We can sleep when we get home. One more beer and we'll check out some more places ...

— I'll have to see it another time. I'm tired. I have to get up in the morning.

— Another time?! Who knows when we'll be back here again?! What other time?!

— Plus, I really don't want any more beer. My stomach is so full.

I couldn't tell you what it was so full from. She avoided even reading half the menu.

— Ah, c'mon, one more!

I started toward a blonde beer vendor who was good looking but not as young and sweet as my afternoon friend.

— If you order another beer, I'm leaving without you!

— Ah, go ahead! I said as I collected my change. You wouldn't know a good time if it jumped up and bit you in the ass!

Then there was shouting and arguing and I did some cursing and off she stormed, the very image of an ill-tempered schoolmarm.

And I was alone again with a long street full of bars and clubs to explore, lots of music to listen to, and a full beer in my hand.

And I got another one for good measure, drinking it amid the blinking white lights spelling DESIRE.

I woke up the next morning with my clothes on and a half a cup of beer on the nightstand. Alone.

She had stormed off again, apparently.

...

Dear Father Gaire:

Since my recent industriousness with regard to my journal began, I have come across startling reminders of men who were influential in my discovering my vocation and my becoming the man I am today. I am sure you will make light of these coincidences, dismissing them as products of an overactive and enthusiastic imagination, but these experiences have made an indelible impact on me.

A few days ago, I read in the newspaper that a Xavier alumnus, a fellow by the name of James Walker, had announced his candidacy for Assemblyman of the Fifth District. (The "Young Man's Candidate," they are calling him. I pray that he will do some good for this district and its people.) Delighted that one of our alumni had decided to enter public service and puffed up with school pride, I set out from Xavier to a baseball game our boys were playing in Hudson Park. I have always considered baseball a thinking man's sport, as you know, and have had a passion for it since the days of my youth in Philadelphia.

Though the temperature was chilly, the spring afternoon was bright and cheerful enough to encourage one to wander off from his intended route and to linger now and then to admire some object of manmade or natural beauty. And, thus, I enjoyed my walk of ten or twelve blocks to the park. Even when I arrived at my destination, I did not go straight to the diamond. Instead, I circumambulated the park via its perimeter walkway, which enabled me to admire its sunken garden, lagoon, and gazebo. I paused to examine a monument, placed in the park in 1898, to some firemen who had perished, God rest their souls, in 1834 and said a decade of the rosary for them. Near the corner of Hudson and Leroy, a familiar odor came to my nostrils and stopped me in my tracks. I looked down at the pavement and smiled to realize that the gingko berries scattered there were just as malodorous as their West Philadelphia cousins.

Attracted by the crack of bat against ball and the cheers of the small crowd, I hastened over to the ball field. Happy to see that Xavier had the lead over All Hallows High School, a new school up in Harlem run by the Christian Brothers, I stood near the cement bleachers behind the Xavier dugout. However, my enjoyment of the game was somewhat diminished by the conduct of a crowd of young ruffians seated nearby. They were making rude jokes to a man, several years their senior, and yelling remarks at the umpire, which I found completely uncalled for. Indeed, I was surprised to see them sitting near the Xavier dugout. Their rowdiness and disrespect was such that I had them pegged as Christian Brothers' boys.

I did my best to tolerate the uncouth young men. It was in a bohemian district I was perambulating, after all. I reminded myself that I needed to be patient with my fellow children of God and that it wasn't for the disapprobation and condemnation of others that I had become a priest. Moreover, the young men did hold the older gentleman in some esteem. Yet their rowdiness and ill-mannered jesting continued unabated. I said another decade of the rosary and tried to calm down. But, it was difficult. I noticed they were passing around a flask, perhaps more than one, and consuming quite a great deal out of it. Rude and intoxicated at a high school baseball game?! After a couple of more minutes and a few more rude remarks, a great anger started to come over me. I could not countenance the obtuse-seeming tolerance the older man had for their wearisome humor. Indeed, he seemed to be getting some sort of enjoyment from it. I started to move away from the bleachers to put some distance between these ruffians and myself. They were not only distracting me from the game but also disturbing the buoyant mood in which I had set out for this park.

Then I noticed that three of the young men sitting down in front were taking their leave of the rowdy company. It seemed strange for them to leave a game that they had so keenly supported only moments before. But, taking their seats would get me farther away from some of their more annoying companions. I wondered if it wouldn't be better to just stand and watch the game. Yet, my legs were tired and I felt I had to reinvigorate myself for the walk home.

The group grew more subdued after the three had departed. This made my respite more pleasant than I had expected. Plus, the game was well played and the score was close. Xavier was up by a run but All Hallows had a man on second with only one out. I started to succumb to the drama of the game and to feel more at my ease.

Moreover, my curiosity was aroused by the frequent allusions to our native city, which I could discern in the conversation of those around me. (At first, I thought I was imagining things, that it was the smell of the gingko trees that had filled my mind with thoughts of home.) However, as I listened more closely, I noticed that the older man especially seemed to repeat the name, "Philadelphia" quite often, and, in an accent that reminded me of my youth. Likewise, my ears pricked up when I heard street names like "Market," "Walnut," and "Broad" woven into his conversation. This brought back memories of my days in the City of Brotherly Love before I received my vocation, before the seminary, before Xavier, before this great city began ringing in my ears with its expansion, activity, and ambition, as well as the cries of its poor.

However, I did not want to broach the subject of our common native city right away. I was bashful in this exuberant company of seeming drunkards and I was still smarting from the rudeness I had seen on display. I enjoy a strong drink on occasion but watching these fellows imbibe made me never want to touch another drop. Nevertheless, the excitement of the game did lead me into some intercourse with them.

A high fly ball arced through the cottony clouds and our right fielder, Collins, sprinted in to make an impressive running catch. More impressive still was the presence of mind he had to throw the ball to third without a moment's hesitation to get the runner who had tagged up at second. The right fielder throw reached the third baseman's glove on one hop, getting the runner out, and retiring the side. I cheered and clapped my hands, turning around to see the excitement of the Xavier rooters behind me.

"Double play!" the older gentleman said to me. "Did you see that catch, Father?"

"I did. And how about that throw?!"

"Flawless!"

"A very alert play!"

As All Hallows took the field and warmed up, I turned again to the older gentleman.

"Excuse me, sir," I began. "I could not help but overhear several allusions to places in Philadelphia. Do you mind telling me if you hail from the City of Brotherly Love?"

It turned out that my surmise had been correct, and a most pleasant conversation ensued. Truly, he must have wanted the company of a man of his generation, for he took to my conversation as the thirsty desert traveler must take to the first container of water brought to him in the oasis. The gentleman told me he is a widower who had spent his entire life in Philadelphia; he had drawn many sketches of the streets and buildings there. Having begun drawing seriously in high school, he had always made his living as an illustrator.

The gentleman was visiting his son who had followed in his father's footsteps by earning his keep through drawing but, being ambitious of a painting career, had moved to New York City. Having seen the energetic way his son had taken to and been inspired by his adopted city (as indeed so many have before him), the gentleman said that he had begun to feel nostalgic for his early days as an illustrator. I understood exactly what he meant. Though he talked little of his homeland, Father often spoke about his carefree days in New York City.

"Don't arrange any sightseeing or special entertainments for my benefit," the gentleman had urged his son. "Get a group of your comrades together and bring me along as your peer."

So they had had a couple of mugs of beer in a local saloon habituated by young artists and come out to watch the ball game — with a few full flasks of whiskey. He offered me a sip from one he said had thus far remained untouched. I declined.

The talk then turned to my background and career. I naturally dwelt upon my time in the seminary and further studies and the posts to which I have been assigned. He said he had been educated by the Jesuits himself. But my interlocutor, being from my native city, wished to delve further into the past, asking what high school I attended.

"I went to Saint Joseph's Preparatory School," I informed him.

"Aha!" he cried. "I went to the very same school. Are you sure you won't have a drink with me now?"

"It is a remarkable coincidence, but, no, thank you. I usually allow myself only a scotch before dinner."

A remarkable coincidence it was, indeed, especially considering the contempt with which I had regarded him but a matter of minutes before! He went on to tell me that during the course of his education, which had begun at Saint Francis de Sales parochial school in West Philadelphia, proceeded through the marble halls of Saint Joseph's Preparatory School, and culminated in the cap and gown he eventually wore at Saint Joseph's University, that there had been one teacher, one crucial individual he had encountered who had changed the course of his life, influencing his choice of career — and even his son's! It was the man who had urged him to pursue art as his livelihood, and that man had taught him at Saint Joseph's Preparatory School.

"Why, this is yet another remarkable coincidence," said I. "In all my years of schooling there is just one teacher whom I have always thought of as having had more influence on me than all others. He was the man who first kindled the fire of my vocation within me and, indeed, urged me to pursue the life which I lead — and that gentleman I met at Saint Joseph's Preparatory School."

My former schoolmate and sudden crony agreed that this was extraordinary. He told me that his uncle, now advanced in years, once taught at our common *alma mater*. It was a time that his uncle had often recalled with relish. Yet, there was some disappointment that the priest's time there was so short.

Well, I never would have suspected, at my first seeing this man behaving in so unseemly a way, that he would have come from a family so distinguished as to have Jesuit in it — and his uncle no less! I was filled with amazement and had to find out the identity of this priest.

"We always called him Uncle Mick but you would have known him as Father Michael McGillicuddy."

The heart almost stopped within me. The noise of the crowd and the city fell silent. The drifting clouds of smoke and the movement of the spectators appeared to freeze and the pitched ball to suspend itself between the mound and the plate. My blood rushed through my veins as if I were under some kind of threat.

"My friend," I continued, and I meant it now. "You don't know how accurate your words truly are. For I did know your uncle as Father Michael McGillicuddy! And he is the influential teacher of whom I spoke!"

There followed a strange silence and stillness while he allowed the meaning of my words to sink in. Then he suddenly put out his hand and shook mine vigorously.

"What's your name, pal?"

"Sarsfield Logan."

"Nice to meet you, Father Logan."

He handed me the untouched flask. I clinked it against his, took a small draft, and handed it back to him. Caught up in the jovial moment, I forgot my earlier concerns about his bibulousness.

"Logan?" he queried. "You wouldn't be related to the construction Logans by any chance — would you?"

"I am, indeed. My father, James, founded the company in the last century, after he had come over from Ireland. But as you can see I have followed a different vocation."

We had a jovial time reminiscing. He wrote down his and Father McGillicuddy's addresses and I promised to begin correspondence with his uncle and him. I wrote to Mr. McGillicuddy a few times and I enjoyed exchanging missives with Father McGillicuddy for a certain period but, as often happens with old but distant acquaintances, our correspondence burned brightly for a time and eventually faded and extinguished itself.

...

— Defense, Judge Laura intoned, pausing for a sip from her pint of Amstel Light on the rocks, you may make your opening statement.

— Defense will show that Paul Logan's true interest is indeed love and not mass consumption. First, he suffers from ongoing and chronic palpitations of the heart and finds it difficult to concentrate on his work when he thinks of his beloved, which he does constantly. Second, if I may remind the Court, the defendant's first visit to the Orange Crush Bar did not end in drunkenness but in a friendly exchange with the beloved and an arrangement to show her the dynamic cobblestoned streets of Tribeca.

— Objection, shouted Charles, adjusting his wig as he came to his feet. And what would he show her there? Only more bars!

— Overruled. Defense, please continue.

— He did not need to get her phone number since a definite appointment had been made, including arrangements assuring that when my client came into the bar to pick her up, he would not have to pay the cover charge for the live band contracted to play that evening. Third, when he kept his appointment that night, making a good faith effort to fulfill his end of the oral contract to provide a tour of Tribeca, it was the beloved who urged him to remain in the bar, despite his frequent protestations, until both of them and several comrades had had their fill of alcoholic beverages. This same scenario has played out on multiple occasions throughout the spring of 1998. The defendant has repeatedly sought to take his beloved out, only to be kept inside the Orange Crush. Just recently, he has offered to take her out for an expensive lunch.

— I object! This is but an excuse for more consumption! Charles interjected. Stuffing himself with fancy sushi! What does that have to do with love?!

— Overruled. Prosecutor will allow the defense to make its opening statement. Please continue, Paul.

— The Defense concedes that the defendant has not made any oral or written declarations of love in poetry or prose. However, it is important to keep in mind that my client is a somewhat reticent man of Northern European, Celtic stock. Moreover, because he is somewhat older than the beloved and, until recently, had been in a lengthy relationship with a fellow faculty member of Saint Philomena's high school, he is unfamiliar with the romantic culture of this decade, and, has decided, understandably, and, if I might suggest, wisely, to err on the side of caution and not making any overt declarations of his feelings.

— As far as poetry is concerned, the defendant has been out late at night and working during the day which has been detrimental to his poetic output. He promises to make this up to her at some future date. Also, the differences in their levels of education and their short acquaintance have, once again, caused my client to be circumspect and have inhibited him from taking such an obviously revelatory step as the composition and presentation of a work of, perhaps, unwanted love poetry.

— Prosecution moves that Defense stop hedging and get to his point!

— Prosecution mentioned the lack of gifts brought to the beloved. Well, I would like to submit into evidence Exhibit A, a book on Celtic calligraphy and ornament, *Ready-to-Use Celtic Designs: 96 Different Royalty-Free Designs Printed One Side*, complete with instructions on how to assemble various colorful parts into portraits of large initial letters or dazzling carpet pages. The defendant used one of his heart-palpitating lunch hours to walk several blocks up Broadway to The Irish Book Shop to purchase this gift for her. Indeed, he has watched and waited with this book in his bag throughout this very night — and I hesitate to bring this up as it may ruin his plan — but, knock on wood, my client will surprise his beloved with it before he gets out of the ramshackle BMW. It is a type of gift for Easter, but one whose thoughtfulness and specificity in matching her interests indicate true affection on his part.

— In conclusion, I would submit to you the very obvious fact that the beloved works in a bar. It seems clear that the consumption of potables is a natural, and, it would seem, inevitable part of an evening spent at her place of employment. To no avail the defendant has repeatedly asked your Honor to leave the premises of her employer and to explore the streets and riverrun horizons of the picturesque environs as she herself stated are unfamiliar to her. Hunger is not his motivation for asking the beloved to lunch: the defendant is willing to prove this by hunger strike. Smash the H-Blocks! He has never entered the Orange Crush Bar simply to slake his thirst, which is, along with his capacity, indeed prodigious. Instead, he has always come to spend time with his beloved. I ask you, "What is a lover to do when the beloved seems perfectly contented to remain among the denizens of the Orange Crush long after her shift has ended?" The answer, I'm sure you'll agree, is that a lover, if he is true, must remain in the proximity of his beloved. Otherwise he cannot hope for success or happiness.

— To enter into the record, the Defense Counsel began, the passionate half an hour my client and the beloved spent on the lower deck of the Motor Vessel (MV) John F. Kennedy, I call my first witness, Lady Liberty.

Lady Liberty glided up to the witness stand. She had some trouble placing her left hand on the bible, as it was already holding a heavy stone tablet. However, her right arm, perpetually raised, presented no difficulty.

— Did you see the defendant, Paul asked, and his beloved on the lower deck of the Kennedy ferryboat several weeks ago?

— Yes, I did. Zis was a very memorable occasion. It was quite a steamy spectacle for someone used to nothing but bored commuters and gawking tourists.

— Would you describe the two as lovers?

— Objection! Defense is asking the witness to indulge in conjecture.

— Sustained. Continue, Counsel.

— What were they doing when you saw them?

— Zey had zeir arms around each ozer and were kissing quite passionately.

Charles stood again.

— Objection, your Honor! How can the memory of a statue be so vivid about two of the tens of thousands of people who pass by her each day? I suspect she has been coached as to what to say.

— Overruled. The witness has totally taken an oath to tell the truth.

—As I say, zis was a very memorable encounter. Zis piece of land on which I am imprisoned, zis, as you say, "Liberty Island," can be cold and lonely. Perhaps someone of your impassive nation would not appreciate zis, but a sight zis amorous, it catches a lonely girl's eye and can make her, how do you say, *verte de jalousie.*

Judge Laura sighed and shouted impatiently.

— Please continue with the questioning, Counselor.

— Were they kissing on the lips?

— Yes.

— Were they using their tongues?

— *Mais oui.* As a Frenchwoman, I discerned zis right away.

— Was there any fondling or caressing of erogenous zones?

— Only slightly tentative caresses. For zis was a public place in the New World and not — *quel dommage* — in Paris. For you see, it is not only the immigrants who pass me who long for their homelands.

— I understand that, muttered Charles.

— Would you describe the pair's behavior as that of people who consider themselves "just friends"?

— *Certainement pas.*

— Objection! This is opinion, not fact.

— Overruled!

— No further questions, your Honor.

...

Dock's piano player was performing, "Let It Snow," one of Janey's favorites, especially the way Johnny Mathis sang it. The swarthy young waiter pulled out the table so that she and Dolores could take their seats on the banquette. As Janey nodded her thanks, his eyes met hers for an instant, and she saw the start of a smile.

She wondered if James could see that other men were finding her attractive. Would it make him jealous? Would he want to take her himself, to prove to himself and to her that she belonged to him? What a strange animal business! People were no better than beasts – weren't they? Hey, if that's what it takes. Makes the world go round and brings new babies into it.

James used to be a beast. Janey once longed for the day when he would leave her alone. She needed her sleep, especially when the kids were little. James often said that women don't know what it is like to be in this sort of state all the time. Janey found it hard enough for a couple of days per month.

Janey was not as young as she once was but she was not yet 40. She could still have a baby. But what about taking care if it? Would she be able to function without sleep and with all that constant care and worry? Would she be able to chase after a toddler when she was in her 40s? She thought so. These days she had energy she didn't know what to do with. Plus, James made enough money to hire someone to help her.

From her seat, Janey could see how profuse with Christmas decorations the restaurant walls were. Dock's had held nothing back! It was the same everywhere they went. All around Ardmore, Havertown, Drexel Hill, Philadelphia, and now Atlantic City there were colorful flashing trees in the windows and nativity scenes, Santas, elves, reindeer, and sleighs on the lawns. It was on TV, too: all the Christmas specials, Donny and Marie, John Denver, Bing Crosby, Rudolph, Frosty, and the Grinch. And this year, Charlie Brown's needy wisp of a tree, made her ache to dress a toddler in a cute Christmas outfit.

A frumpy, drab-dressed matron was wobbling back to her table from the upstairs ladies' room when into the dining room sauntered a striking red-headed sylph, no more than 18 and not wearing a bra. These young girls! Still, Janey's eyes watched her weave through the close-set tables. A scarlet dress hung from her wide, ivory shoulders on spaghetti straps and was cinched with a sash around a waist she could have fit in a necklace. As she sashayed past a luxuriant Christmas wreath, her thick, wavy hair got stuck in its fir twigs. She teetered on her black high heels for just an instant. Then, with a smile, the girl swatted her errant lock with the back of her hand, and strode on.

James and Joey had their backs to the young redhead and did not see her. Janey saw from their reactions that many of the other men did — some of them old enough to be her father. Dirty old men! With a twinkle in his eye, the piano player watched her saunter away. He tried to hide his amusement when the wreath grabbed her by the hair.

Doubtless, the young thing felt the room's masculine eyes upon her. The attention must have felt new to her, or at least novel enough for her to court it. She'll learn to regret it, though. Unwanted attention gets old fast. Janey hated it when men made comments on the street or when the Center City construction workers (even LCC guys, despite Old Man Logan's reprimands) shout rude remarks, making the narrow Philly streets reverberate with their base desires. What was the matter with them?

The charming olive-skinned waiter came over and took the drink orders. Janey loved the tailored tux and bow tie he wore. James asked for a Manhattan, straight up with rocks on the side, and succeeded in getting his old buddy, Joey, to join him. Dolores had a gin and tonic and Janey went for a Harvey Wallbanger.

"I always wanted to try one," said she. "It has such a funny name!"

When the waiter brought the drinks, the piano player plinked the chords for, "I'll Be Home for Christmas." Taking a long sip from his cocktail and then raising his glass, James said it reminded him of being in the service. He took another drink. He heard it in Germany at Christmastime. No song had made him more homesick, he said.

Janey began to feel that James was slipping away. Perhaps he would get too drunk and forget all about her. But maybe the drinks would loosen him up and make him more fun and spontaneous. It sometimes did.

James ordered oysters and Joey made obvious, crude jokes. But Janey didn't object tonight. Maybe Joey would put ideas into her husband's head.

She had to get James back to the room early. Maybe the best way was to get him to make it happen. When James was slurping his oysters, the piano player started playing "Winter Wonderland" and Janey toed James's shin under the table. He smiled at her but continued the story he was telling.

Fingers crossed James would figure out what was on her mind and steer the evening so that they could get back to their room and be alone. After all, he must want that, too. How often did they get a weekend without the kids? And wasn't he the one who had arranged it all?

James told her that sometimes when he is sitting in a train station or in a restaurant, he wonders why people are watching ball games or rushing to work or shopping. Why aren't they all making love? Janey was not familiar with desire as all-encompassing as that. She could drop anything to go shopping.

"What are you going to get?" Janey asked her husband.

"I know I am being predictable," James apologized, swirling the ice in his drink. "But I think I'll get Dock's Seafood Fry."

"C'mon! Try something a little different," Janey teased. "Spice things up. After all, variety is the spice of life."

"It's hard to pass up this variety. I get shrimp, flounder, a crab cake, and fries."

The handsome waiter returned with his pad and pen. Janey imagined he spent a lot of time on his hair, fighting over the mirror with the women in the house.

"I'll have the crab cakes," said Dolores.

"Madam?"

"May I have the lobster tail, please?"

"Hmmph!" James said. "Variety is the spice of life, huh?"

"I knew what I wanted when I left the house," Janey declared shutting the menu and pursing her lips.

James laughed and shook his head.

The waiter turned toward Joey.

"I'll have the New York sirloin, medium rare."

"Real smart," snapped Dolores. "We travel all the way down the shore to a famous seafood restaurant by the Atlantic Ocean, and what does the big oaf order? A steak!"

Janey smiled and shook her head at the supposed offense. But she thought, if the man wants to have a steak, let him have a steak. The place is known for that, too. Live and let live.

"The steaks are good here," said James.

"Yeah, but he should have some seafood! I mean, we're a stone's throw from the beach."

"All right. All right. I'll have the Beef and Reef. That way I can have filet mignon, lobster tail, and some peace and quiet."

Joe really was a sweet guy, Janey thought.

"And you, sir?"

James ordered his usual.

The waiter left, and, Dolores, dabbing horseradish on an oyster cracker she had pulled from the tall glass jar, remarked, "I gotta stop eatin' these. I won't be able to eat my dinner."

"Oh, God, that reminds me!" cried Janey, throwing her chin in the air and smiling. "Did I ever tell you the story about the oyster crackers at Fisher's when I was expecting Paul?"

"No, I don't think so."

Janey looked at Joey.

"You never heard this one either?!"

"No, no! What? What happened?"

Janey arched her back against the banquette and continued.

"Well, I went to see Dr. Hunt for a checkup and had arranged to meet James at Fisher's afterwards. You know Fisher's up on Broad Street?"

"Yeah, sure, the old seafood place," Joey said.

"It was easier to meet there than to come all the way into the office in Center City. Do you remember that, James?"

She bopped her shoulder into James's.

"How could I forget?"

"So I get there a little early and the old waiters at Fisher's recognize me. My family went there a lot and the Logan family are all regulars, too. So he seats me at a table. I love those red-leather chairs with the heart shapes cut out of the back. Even several months pregnant I felt comfortable in one of them. Well, right there in front of me on the old wooden table is a big bowl of oyster crackers and heaps of horseradish. I have one with a little horseradish and then another with a little more ... and before you know it, I'm going to town."

Leaning out over the table, Janey slapped James's hand.

"You know how I am with horseradish — l love it! — I could eat spoonfuls of it right out of the jar!"

"She can't have a roast beef sandwich," added James. "Without it."

"Luckily, the waiter gave me a glass of water or I mighta died. I couldn't control myself. Before long my eyes start to tear up. But I just keep goin': oyster cracker after oyster cracker with forkfuls of horseradish. A couple minutes later, tears are running down my cheeks."

"Just then the *maitre'd* shows James to our table and he turns white as a ghost."

Janey was overcome with laughter and leaned forward onto the table.

"What happened?" says he. "Did you get a bad report? Is there something wrong? Is something wrong with the baby?"

"I start cryin' laughin'! The poor guy didn't know what was wrong with me! And I couldn't explain to him 'cause I was laughing too hard. Remember that, James?!"

"I think we laughed all through that dinner," he said.

Janey lifted her Harvey Wallbanger and clinked it against James's rocks glass. James laughed at the silly memory and signaled for the waiter to bring him another Manhattan.

Joey chuckled and shook his head. Dolores smiled but did not say much. She did not share in Janey's mood and certainly not in her ambitions for the evening. So far she seemed to take every opportunity to converse only with Janey or to make snide remarks about her husband.

A busboy propped open a tray stand. Their svelte server placed their entrees on it and distributed them among the diners.

Janey dug right into her lobster tail. Each chunk tasted delicious, especially when she first placed them dripping with butter on her tongue.

She joked with Joey, "Wanna try some of my lobster tail?"

"Hey, maybe yours is better than mine!" Joey laughed.

The foursome shared lobster and crab cakes and shrimp and steak with one another. But, unfortunately, Dolores's attitude did not improve. Throughout the meal, Dolores snapped at her husband for any reason or for none at all. She even corrected his pronunciation and grammar a few times, which came across as cruel. Joey was not the best educated or polished man around but he was a hell of a nice guy and had always been a true and loyal friend to James and to the company. There was no call to belittle him like that. Aside from firing back in self-defense now and then, Joey took it all good naturedly, as he usually did.

Janey did not know the details but it was clear Joey and Dolores were having problems. She felt bad for both Dolores and Joey, but she was miffed that Dolores's hostility toward her husband was getting in the way of her plans.

The cute waiter reappeared and Joey ordered cheesecake. Dolores and Janey decided to share a piece of German Chocolate cake. They were already so full someone would have to roll them out of there. They all asked for coffee, except for James who wanted one more Manhattan.

When they got back to Resorts, Joey said, "Yo, James! You know this place is open 24 hours? And they give us free beers while we gamble. Whaddaya say?"

"Oh, James, didn't we have enough of the casino last night and today?" Janey interjected. "I was hoping for a quiet night tonight."

"Yeah, but we've never gambled on the east coast before," said James.

"And when can we ever drink in a place for 24 hours?" asked Joey.

As they strolled across the casino parking lot, James murmured in Janey's ear, "Joey really wants to go. I can't leave him by himself."

So Janey calmed down.

While the men played the one-armed bandits, Janey sat with Dolores looking out at the boardwalk and sipping a chardonnay. Dolores complained about Joey and their marriage. Janey sympathized but it was beginning to wear on her nerves. Finally, she told Dolores she had a headache. Dolores gave her an aspirin. They said "goodnight" to the boys and headed upstairs.

Janey lay awake waiting for James, with the aspirin on the nightstand. She was wearing her pink negligee. She had read a page or two of *Trinity* but it had been hard to her mind on it.

When James came in, he talked about how Joey had needed to blow off stream.

"Can you believe the way Dolores would not get off of his back?"

"It was sad," she agreed.

Clearly, they had lost at the slots or he would have led with news of his winnings.

That glass of chardonnay made Janey have to pee. When she returned from the bathroom, James had fallen asleep, his poorly buttoned pajama top exposing a small lawn of black and grey chest hair. His mouth hung open and he was already snoring — a clear sign he had drunk too much.

And, sure enough, when she went to the window to close the curtain, she saw that it was snowing. Snow down the shore! But the ocean had few waves. It appeared flat and black with white scribbles of foam here and there, like shapeless Santa Claus whiskers discarded after a long night's party. Snowflakes vanished as they touched the dark Atlantic and evaporated as they hit the sand. Despite all the snow flying in the air, nothing was accumulating on the ground. Nothing was sticking.

...

wide blocks of houses for the poor hard efficient uniform upright rectangles in rows childrens cries echo in the stickball streets jumpropes twirling fistfights jeff caps illfitting trousers jackets holes at their joints the manhattan bridge head and blue shoulders high barely looking down on tiny ancient order of hibernians street where squats in the middle of the block unnoticed saint james church kingpatron of nova eborac patron of my father and fathers fathers where at five-hundred years of age the aoh a carraig an aifrinn upon its shoulders gave miraculous birth to a new world son faith of our fathers keeping the fire lit living still collect all four thats peter andrew james and john street methodist

Finding the Way from Chinatown to the FDR

Finding the way to the FDR from Chinatown entails:

- Directing Laura through Chinatown
- Crossing Canal Street
- Passing through Little Italy to Houston Street
- Taking Houston Street to the FDR

Laura's car climbed the hill alongside Police Headquarters. Paul looked to his left at the stars and green stripes of the NYPD flag. The Irish had to put their mark on everything. Something to prove. And they proved it, committing the crimes and arresting the criminals both.

remember the smith high school boys who had guns in their backpacks outside philomenas waiting for those little grey skirts locked inside that shoebox all day tough scared kids on south bronx streets did they even know who al smith was

To direct Laura through Chinatown:

1. Proceed to Chatham Square
2. Turn left onto Mott Street
3. Take Mott Street across Canal Street

dont want to get her lost again in these twisting narrow streets dont want these inscrutable blocks dragoning up to and through the crioch of canal to cockblock you celestial dragons chasing pearls among the clouds fruitful as your chase maybe moreso do dragons fly among the rain clouds

A triangular park came toward them. They could see the back of a tall pedestaled statue.

— Who's that, laughed Laura — Confucius?!

— Yeah, I think it might be, answered Paul. Confucius say, "Turn left!"

Laura laughed. Rain spattered on the windshield, large drops obscuring their view.

— Check out the name of this place — "Dim Sum Go Go"!

— Seriously. You need to take a left here.

— Here?!

— Yeah, Mott Street. By the Citibank and Dr. Tooth. Right after Dragon Restaurant.

— I thought the sign said "Moth Street" for a second, Charles drawled.

no chaz the sign says england get out of front seat give it back thief mystery of small dark passages hidden doorways streets like outdoor hallways with restaurants on either side secret ways strange to live in this neighborhood what went on in these 150-year-old cramped dwellings always wanted to buy a chinese playboy from one of those stands so many chinese people they must be doing something interesting behind those walls of old dirty brick and mortar

Appetizer

Fried Wonton	Buffalo Wings
Wot fun number	Chicken Feet
Barmaid's Tofu	General Tso's Kissin'
Crab Rangoon	Ear Lobe
Goo Goo Eye Fan	Poo Lup Top
Scallion Beefcake	Han Hook Bra

Westchester Wanton   Philly Spring Roll

— Wait a minute, Laura cried. I can't turn here! This is a one-way street!

— Sorry. Keep going. Make a U-turn and we'll go up Mulberry.

— Where are you telling me to go?

— I don't know these one-way streets. I don't drive around here. I always walk.

— Do you want to get us home, Paul, or are you desperate for Chinese food?

at least i am here for a reason chuck perfidious dog in the manger go back to sleep in your own country i am famished by the way

— Shit! I hate this rain!

It was coming down harder, in smaller drops. Laura was now on Worth Street, headed back toward the courthouses.

in my travel guide for degenerates could recommend chinese late night food peking duck house wo hop shanghai café hop sing 100 mott big wong king hop kee new wonton garden the trashstrewn streets see the cabbage leaves in the gutter the chinese newspapers on the sidewalk

— Sometimes when my friends and I go out after work, we come here late at night. Great stuff when you've been drinking.

— No, you have to have curry, mate. Indian food! That's what we always do in the UK.

Starters

Samosa	Pakora
Cappa Feelah	Chapati
Bhel Pooni	Cunna Lingam
Mahagashtrian Fish Gravy	Mulligatawny Soup
Lipsan Nipples	Opam Lukhi
Aloo Papri Chaat	Heevant Megawntu
Kulcha Sutra	Aloo Hoti

— Take a right here, just before the park.

Laura drove slowly up the confining start of Mulberry Street. On the right she passed a Lutheran church and two funeral homes with awnings covered in Chinese characters. On the left stretched quiet Columbus Park.

— What's with all these funeral homes? Laura wondered aloud.

— Indian food is great, Paul said to Charles, but Chinese works — believe me! The cool thing is a lot of these Chinatown places are open all night. I like to go to Woo Hop's. You gotta love it! 24 hours a day!

The BMW swerved and almost rear-ended a parked car.

— You're gonna kill us all! Paul cracked.

— My driving's not that bad! I'm not used to these narrow streets!

her bad rhymes with fad not a new yorker wet menus stuck to the sidewalk trash starting to float in the gutters fishy oil probably flowing in that stream too orange plastic bags with chinese characters on them welcome to chinese restaurant wrappers try your nice chinese food with chopsticks the traditional and typical of chinese glonous history and cultual lives of those guys chopping fish all day american dream women in the sweatshops upstairs

House Specialty Entree

Tandoori Chacha	Dal Makhani
Shaag Paneer	Aloo Woopi
Vajayjay	Baqar Kunni
Punani Saffron	Vaj Madras
Palak Paneer	Hell's Kitchen Phulka
Lickah Appam	Wunda Tatas
Poon Poli	Papidan Condom

— Chicken tikka masala is the best!

— I like tandoori chicken. Chicken jalfrezi....

— I love the naan!

— Oooh! Aloo paratha! With potatoes inside!

— Will you guys knock it off? You're making me hungry!

An old Chinese man and a little dog clearly confused about why they had had to leave their dry, warm apartment walked out into the middle of Mulberry Street. Laura hit the brakes.

— Where did this old dude come from?

Then the dog turned and started to bark at the BMW.

— Hey, I just saved your life, you little shit! What are you barking at me for?

— He wants you to save him from being put on a Chinese menu!

— Or into some curry dish!

— What curry goes well with small dog?

— Madras is very spicy, said Charles. Could cover up that canine taste.

— Vindaloo might be better. It's the spiciest, Paul responded. And the funniest word!

As they reached a stop sign, Paul looked up the incline of Mosco Street.

— I can't believe it, Paul exclaimed. The dumpling place is open! I've never seen it open at night. I've only stopped there for lunch.

Above the doorway of the only lit place on the tiny Mosco Street, Roman letters spelled out, "Fried Dumplings."

— I could eat a Chinese menu, said Charles.

— Are they good? asked Laura.

— Good?! They're delicious!

— Let's get some!

— Pull over here. I can jump out.

— I'll go, too, offered Charles.

every silver lining has a cloud

— What about me? This place seems pretty scary.

— Just sit here. Maybe pull two of your wheels up onto the sidewalk. No one will bother you.

PORK

Moo Goo Gai Clam	Happy Joy Fun Combo
Philly Please Shake	*Triple Delight
Kum Pao Chicken	She Too Young
Four Seasons	Sweat and Shudder Pork

*Not available on Thursdays.

Laura eased the car past the intersection and over to the right side of the street. She had no problem pulling up onto the sidewalk, empty except for the wet bags, newspapers, and wrappers stuck to it.

— What about the cops?

— They're all at Wo Hop's.

late nights at wo hops waiter with beaten blue jacket water in a squat glass like you'd have as a kid at a diner his finger in it as he puts it on the table scallion pancake appetizer the crunchy noodles you have to ask for them there with the mustard so hot going right up your nose wash it down with the tea turned cold in the thick ceramic cup with the red stripe around its lip fits right in your fist egg roll crunch vegetable taste inside bite too soon burn the roof of your mouth but you hardly notice wonton soup with the wide plastic blue and white spoon poultry broth hot and sour soup big scoops throat-tightening heat

...

"One more ghost story for you, Sarsfield, since you seem to enjoy them so much. This one I experienced myself and what I saw and heard haunts me to this day.

"As I roved out from my home in Bunowen, I never rested until I reached Connemara. I had turned my back on Croagh Patrick, the beautiful holy mountain I had seen daily rising up to its pinnacle like a pyramid no man could create, but shall see no more. Likewise, I had left behind the Bunowen River, where I could pluck trout from hiding places I knew as well as they and throw their slippery hides onto the banks. Through the loneliness of the Tawnymacken bog, I quick-marched all the way, finding nothing but small little streams and the rough clumps of hills rising like monsters from the bogland. In the cool fresh air raw and moist as if wet by the dew of the coming morning, I passed Cregganacopple and Cregganbaun, to Derryheeagh and Derryheigh and Glenkeen, all of these place names etched upon my mind like the carvings of the raindrops on the slabs of limestone along my path.

"While the sun stayed up on that long summer day, I was cheered by the tight yellow bunches of flowers they call celandine and by the gentle, purple heather holding its head above the wild swaying grasses. But, when it turned dark, the surroundings turned sinister. The wee hills and mounds of earth metamorphosed into the shapes of ghouls and the stones and rocks and lichen shells under my feet made fearful cries. Branches of bog oak, '*giusach*,' the old people call it, mysterious enough by day, were transformed by the night into a dog's *rigor mortised* remains, a mummy, or a twisted creature of the Otherworld.

"The landscape was barren and I had grown so used to its emptiness in the dark that when I saw a hawthorne tree with its branches blowing in the wind, I thought it was a great ghost. Picking up a bogoak branch, I ran and ran looking everywhere for a place to hide. But I could find nothing. There was nowhere to even shelter from the rain except the odd stone cowshed shrinking from the wind moaning through the mountain gaps. Soon I got ahold of myself and realized there was nothing for it but to keep going.

"Keeping the stout branch as a walking stick, I followed a small brook that chattered away to keep me company. Eventually it grew louder and I took this to be a good sign. It told me I would soon be approaching the bay. Before long, the brook turned into a stream and the stream led me to a mountain pass they call, 'Doolough' for the darkness of the lakewater it conceals. But, as I was to find out, that was not the only darkness abiding in that locality. Some moonlight fell on the lake and helped me to see a wee bit. At the crest of a glen I found a flat patch of land surrounded by rocks, looking down on a wee goatpath and over the lake. I later found that this place is named, 'The Stroppabue.' I sat myself down in that place and peered at the narrow path, at the *Dubh Loch*, and at the three dark mountains that seemed to stand guard before Killary Bay. For a feeling it came over me — carried perhaps by the hint of salt in the moist air — that I had not many steps to take in the County of Mayo before saying 'goodbye' to it forevermore.

"I wasn't there long when the mists began to gather. Slowly, the distant shadows of mountains, the lough's far shore, and the stream that had led me to the Stroppabue began to fade from my sight. And, I began to shiver. Bit by bit my surroundings were obscured until all sight of them was annihilated by the burgeoning fog, and by my heavy eyelids urging me on to sleep.

"But my eyes opened wide when I heard strange sounds in the ravine — grunting, groaning, and heavy unshod footfalls. What creatures were below? The whole mountain pass had been empty a moment before. Where had they come from? Were they climbing up to me?

"Through the mists, I perceived people struggling along the road. Their eyes were bulging from their sockets and their skin coated with some brownish ooze shone in the moonlight. It would not be right to describe them as people walking the roads for surely there was not enough flesh on their bones for them to be called people and surely the tracks they were walking occupied not enough earth to be called roads. They were going up the ravine and back down again toward the lough and, I'm relieved to say, showing no interest in my astonished soul. They seemed intent on some sort of work. But what work could they be doing in a place that seemed so rarely trod by human feet?

"Then up from the ravine arose a chant, a droning, unearthly song.

"'We haunt this mountain pass
For this is where we walked
To find relief and rest
Where there was none,
For this is where we looked,
To find some hope, some chance,
Where there was none,
For here we spent our lives
To buy our deaths.'

"Leaning on my walking stick, I struggled to my feet and stepped back, almost tripping over a large stone behind me. The walking skeletons stopped moving and looked up.

"'Who's there?' I said in a voice just above a whisper, 'Who's there?'"

"No answer came from the ravine, except the echo of my own question.

"Then I remembered myself. My fortitude came back to me. I stood straight and tall, with my chest heaving out and declaimed my answer to the echo.

"'I am Seamus Logan of Bunowen, in the barony of Murrisk, in the County of Mayo, the plain of the yew tree, home of Ireland's holiest mountain, Saint Patrick's Reek and the fortress of Granuaile, and, heartsick as I am, I have left my native home to find a new life in Connemara. And I have taken a seat in this spot to rest from my weary travels, meaning no harm to any creature in this world or *An Saol Eile*.'

"Up from the ravine again arose the otherworldly dirge.'

"'We haunt this mountain pass
For this is where we walked
To find relief and rest
Where there was none,
For this is where we looked,
To find some hope, some chance,
Where there was none,
For here we spent our lives
To buy our deaths.'

"'Whom did not give you relief — the people of Mayo, *go saibhalagh Dia sinn*? For the natives hereabouts are renowned for their generosity and kindness to strangers.'

"From the darkness of the glen came an echoing chant:

"'Captain Primrose … Colonel Hogrove … Mister Carroll … Captain Primrose … Colonel Hogrove …. Mister Carroll …'

"'Men of venom taking their privileges here where all venomous creatures were long ago banished,' I replied, my anger feeding my courage. 'Who are these men? What did they do?'

"'Those villains are no more. Nor are we. 'Twas the time of the Great Hunger and the workhouses were bursting with the hungry and the sick. We had to obtain tickets for outdoor relief from the Westport Union. So, on a cold morning at the end of March, we walked to Louisburgh, there to find if we were seen fit for the help we so sorely needed. But, the relieving officer, Mr. Carroll, informed us that Captain Primrose and Colonel Hogrove had removed themselves to Delphi Lodge, and that he himself did not have his books ready. He told us that if we wanted outdoor relief to follow him down to Delphi, saying we must be at Delphi Lodge by seven in the morning or be stricken from the rolls. We rested during the night before the houses in Louisburgh and when the morning came, we found many dead. The four hundred of us who remained in your world, sighed, looked to heaven, and set out on foot for Delphi.'

"''Twas well named. For it foretold many fates.'

"'So we set out from Louisburgh, passed this lough, and followed the Bundorragha River through a landscape of forbidding low trees and sharp jutting rocks, a land inhospitable. We trudged miles in these rags to the wildest region of Ireland where no man lives to this day. Men, women, and children stumbling as if drunk over a landscape of menace, bursting into tears over the smallest obstacle, desperate to live for another day, another hour, another breath ...

"'The hunger and the cold and the fatigue were heavy upon us surely,' lamented the ghost. 'But the thought that men could behave this way toward other men was an even greater burden to us who would split our last potato four ways, and a fifth if a stranger were to come along the road.

"'We arrived at Delphi by seven but no one came to our aid. Wet and hungry beyond words, we sat beneath the pine trees on the well-tended green lawn and waited. Some poor souls expired while we waited, though others, near death themselves, sat up with hopeful attention. For we were powerful anxious to hear word of our deliverance. It wasn't until noon that the devils came out, and only to tell us our arduous journey had been in vain. They could do nothing for us, said they.'

"'So it was the same goat paths back through the Doolough pass through the rivers again and all the way back to Louisburgh, a difficult enough walk for a healthy well fed man.

"'And many fell down and died along the banks of the *Dubh Loch*. 'Died from starvation and cold,' the doctors pronounced, though we who were educated only in a hedge school could have given the same *post mortem*, and more.'"

"Seamus, for the love of God, why choose a tale such as this of all the stories to tell in the world?" objected old Tom. "All it will do is upset the boy!"

"And give him bad dreams!" added Rosie.

"And disgraceful memories of the land he left behind him!" said young Kevin.

"Go ahead and forget everything, if you want!" Seamus shot back. "Leave it all behind you! I know who is responsible and I will remember! The boy should know it, too! And as long as I have breath in my body, I will continue to tell the tale, so that others remember, too!"

"Leave him alone to tell his morbid stories," Tom muttered. "The man is starting to lose his senses, I'm thinking."

"'Your tale fills my spent heart with rage," I said to the shades. "For how can a man turn away the hungry traveler from his door? Could they not spare 50, 20, 10, even one of your number?'

"The shades simply shook their heads.

"Now, Sarsfield, the first spirit continued:

"'Between Louisburgh and Delphi Lodge, corpses were as numerous as sheaves of corn in an autumn field. And many of us, though starving we were, volunteered to trek these paths and give the dead something of a burial, where there is land enough here in this barren pass. Some bodies lay on the side of the road for days, left there for the dogs and the ravens. Some were thrown into a mountain slough with a few sods of turf to cover them — about as helpful to them in death as their scanty rags had been to them in life.

"'When we reached this very spot, Stroppabue, tremendous squalls came and like giants from the days of Fionn mac Cumhaill, took up men, women, and children weak from the hunger the walking, the cold, and the wet and tossed them into the ravine and into the lake. Piercing hailstones came down upon us like a plague from the Most High meant for the hard-hearted pharaohs in their warm homes. Some of our people tried to climb the Stroppa but lost their grip and fell. Those who fell into the lake never recovered.

"'And it was here doing this work with my companions that I lost my own life. And so we walk the Stroppabue in our rags to this day as a reminder to our people and to the masters of our people.'

"This is a crime I will never forget!" I answered the ghosts. "Men unable to care for a country's living or dead have proven themselves unfit to govern. And their crimes of the Great Hunger shall be their undoing in this land!"

...

And Paul and Charles were out of the car and jogging uphill, hungry, toward the harsh white light. Red Chinese characters ran along both sides of the dumpling shop window.

at the top of the slope transfiguration church built from the same rubble as saint pauls chapel before the italians the chinese busiest irish catholic church in the world weddings baptisms funerals weddings baptism funerals their ghosts drew me to pells dinty

A dog started barking. Paul pulled his cap down over his brow to block the rain and looked around the cramped, old streets and back toward the long slender park. It was deserted. No dog to be seen. But, within the narrow walls of brick and mortar, he could certainly hear its bark — angry and loud.

— Not a very welcoming mutt — is he?

— No dumplings for him, said Paul.

The two men trotted onto the yellow-lipped stair and entered through the door and the slit-plastic curtain of the dumpling shop. Inside, Paul scanned the brief menu above the counter.

wonder if they have brits out why the hell is he here oh but charlie'll appreciate this

— Check it out! They're only five for a dollar!

— Help you? The old woman sung from behind the counter.

Charles rubbed his palms together.

— Let's get a little bit of everything.

— Yeah, we'll have three orders of fried dumplings, answered Paul, and two orders of fried pork buns.

— Might as well get three of each, mate. With these prices.

specially if someone else is paeyin for 'em eh wot

— Why not?

— 15 fried dumpling. 15 pork bun. Something else?

— No, that's all. Thanks.

The old woman turned and shouted in Cantonese at a young guy standing by the fryer. It sounded to Paul like angry baby talk. The young guy in the blue smock and white paper cap with a red border around it gave a surly look to the floor, but obeyed.

The dumplings glunk-glunked into the wok. The fryer started hissing. Wherever he was, that dog was still making clear his displeasure. Then his barking was drowned out by the spitting and sputtering of the dumplings, as the young man shoved them around with a wooden spatula. Charles's and Paul's stomachs rolled and flipped like acrobats. Their hunger, which had been narcotized by a night of beer and shots, was now awake, sitting up, and making fervent demands.

NOODLE

Lo Mein	Longevity
Chow Quim	Mai Bone
Shanghai Style	Pat Thigh
Keepon My Fun	Chow Mine

Paul paced over to the steel counter and high stools where people customers could stay and eat. Charles followed him.

— You know those sauces they have on the tables of Indian restaurants — that sour green sauce, the brown sweet sauce, and the little onions or radishes or whatever? I never understood exactly what they are there for.

— They are to help people adjust the spiciness to their taste, I suppose.

ya s'pose do yeh now well blimey that's smashin in't it

— I don't know. I just put them on everything — even those oniony yellow wafers they give you. I don't care.

The frying pockets of flour filled the small storefront with the aroma of pork and onions and chopped bok choy, cabbage, soy sauce, rice wine, and sesame oil. The hunger of both the Englishman and the Irish-American gurgled at the tops of their stomachs and then fell deep down inside them. It would not be ignored.

nice if they had a bathroom here but no such luck will be all right til hells kitchen

Paul and Charles stared at the wooden spatula. On several of the dumplings appeared black ovals of burnt dough. They could almost feel and hear the crunch of their teeth squeezing into the charred wrapping.

SEAFOOD

Shrimp with Head	Philadelphia Roll
Mamaroneck Fuck	No Come Too Soon
Shaved Young Cunt	Shrimp with Garlic Sauce
Shrimp Tool	Hot and Spicy Trim

— Six dollar, cried the counter lady.

Charles handed her bills with Abraham Lincoln and George Washington on them.

— Thanks, Charles.

plates of piled meat rice covered with swaths of brown greasy sauce broken up by clear bubbles black bean sauce dark oyster sauce sesame beef with seeds on it steam rising the same pile reforming in your stomach szechuan specialties the spicy chicken red peppers burning your tongue seafood some people get a whole fish comes out on the table with the head still on it scallions vinegar you can even get lobster for a cheap price with a gingery sauce brown clam sauce one time got me sick but so good you can see a mouse squeezing itself into a hole in threshold to the kitchen but you don't care just feed me

The two looked expectantly but the quick-cooking dumplings were not quite ready yet. No change was coming. There was nothing to do but watch the young guy scoop the dumplings from the wok into paper bags.

But Paul turned away.

Laura's car was still sitting halfway up on the sidewalk, her hazard lights throbbing in the dark, like his competing pangs.

Finally, the guy in the dirty apron handed the dumplings to Charles.

— These smell fantastic, he cried, as they ran from the restaurant to Laura's car.

— I thought you forgot about me, Laura said.

— We didn't forget you. You've just turned into a giant dumpling in our minds.

— Like in the cartoons! Haha! "Hey, stop looking at me like that!"

— But you look so scrumptious, my dear! Paul smiled.

— I don't know what is in each bag. Just pass them around.

— Thanks. I feel like bitin' right through the bags, said Paul. Take this and eat it.

Laura turned sideways toward the bags between herself and Charles. She flipped her hair over her right shoulder and bit into one of the dumplings.

— Mmmm, mmmm … so good.

—Yeah, these are great. That's why I take the ten-minute walk up here for lunch.

Then the conversation ceased. Inside the car there were only the sounds of chewing, smacking lips, and crinkling bags and wrappers. Outside the car the rain finger-drummed on the roof and tires whsshed along Mott Street. Then that dog started barking again. The windshield was covered with rain drops and the windows started steaming up.

— I'm gettin' full already, cried Laura as she chewed on a pork bun.

— Gotta finish 'em all, Paul replied.

— No worries there, mate. These things don't stand a chance.

like the zulus iroquois other tribes your brave ancestors massacred eh

They were running out of napkins and licking their fingers.

— How many more left? asked Paul.

— Two pork buns and three dumplings.

—One dumpling each. C'mon, Laura.

—I can't. I'm so full.

—One more dumpling! C'mon, you can do it. Then Charles and I will finish the buns.

— Maybe I can give it to that dog.

— C'mon, Laura. It's got your name on it.

She forced the dumpling down and Charles and Paul did the same with their dumplings and buns. Then they all lay back panting and grunting. Wrappers and napkins and bags lay strewn about their laps on the seats of the car.

— That was so good but now I'm gonna explode.

— Were they good? I don't even know if I tasted them.

After a few moments, they gathered up the trash and put it in the bags.

— There's a trash can on the corner. Let me out.

Paul put the garbage in the can and stood looking up at the misting rain drifting under the Chinese-lantern streetlight.

good place for a murder as mom-mom used to say deserted now should i drag charles out of the front seat feed him to that five points guard dog in the old days there would be plenty of people to murder or be murdered on mulberry bend the tombs waiting for them all cops would only come here in groups of ten we in our full-stomach suburban car just passing through

3. Envy & Kindness

Janey stepped carefully, straightening her back so that her head stayed right behind the head of the girl in front of her. She wanted to adjust her veil. It kept slipping, she felt. But, she didn't want to unfold her hands or appear vain in front of Sister and all the parents and families. Flashbulbs popped on either side of the procession as it made its way through the crowds. She saw lots of faces she knew — faces she'd seen around Saint Francis De Sales for six years. When she spied her parents, Janey gave them a shy smile but kept her posture erect and her hands folded. She didn't clasp her hands the way her dad did when he went to receive communion. She folded them like the Virgin Mary does in all the statues. The brim of her dad's hat sheltered the big camera he held in front of his face. She hoped he got a good photograph of her. Lisa would be coming behind her and she was sure to smile big for the camera. She was always looking for special treatment — and usually getting it. They might make even make more than the usual fuss over her because she was an eighth grader and this was her last May Procession.

Janey glimpsed the sidewalk of South Farragut Street beyond the lines of people. As she made the turn, the fragrances of honeysuckle and of the white fallen leaves of magnolia trees displaced the odor of incense. She preferred all of the above to those stinky gingko berries. The setting sun lay its warm rays on her right cheek. She was almost free. But she didn't want to feel that way; it was a sin.

Then, in the sun's rays, amid all of the smiling parents and grandparents and babies, she saw a young man in a blue suitjacket with gleaming gold buttons. She averted her eyes but could not help but notice the shine on his smart, black, wing-tipped shoes. She hadn't seen him around before. He looked a little older — and since he was watching the procession, he was clearly not a Francis de Sales student. Her breath caught in her throat for a moment. A high school boy!

Janey lifted her eyes. He was looking at her. She returned his gaze for an electric second — he smiled at her — but then looked back down again. It almost made her forget where she was and what she was doing. Why did he focus on her? There were many other girls, line after line of them, dressed identically and walking in identical postures.

Who was he? How could she find out?

After the procession was over and she was dismissed, Janey doubled back to find her parents and Lisa. Though she tried her best to appear casual and to talk normally with her family, her neighbors, and friends, she kept twisting her head this way and that to see if she could spot that high school boy. She played with her nextdoor neighbor's toddler, Frankie, who looked so cute in his little red overalls, but her voice sounded way too loud to her. She tried to quiet down, but couldn't help herself. Frankie would make a funny face or noise and she would go into hysterics.

The high school boy was talking to one of the eighth-grade girls. Maybe the girl was a friend of Lisa's. Janey told her parents she was going to find Lisa and headed in the boy's direction, approaching at angles like a bird of prey homing in on a mouse. She identified the girl as Marianne Gallagher, an eighth grader she knew only to see.

She milled around for a while finding nothing exciting. Getting impatient, Janey lunged around a cluster of gabbing adults and nearly bumped foreheads with her sister.

"What's the matter with you?" Lisa said. "You got ants in your pants?"

As Janey was trying to explain herself, fix her veil, and smooth her dress, Marianne Gallagher called out, "Hey, Dougherty!"

Marianne waved Lisa over and gossiped with her about the procession, the teachers, a boy who sang a real clinker during the hymns, and some girl who dropped her rosary beads and was forbidden to go back for them. Janey took little interest in the conversation, remaining on the periphery. She just wanted to meet the boy.

Finally, Marianne introduced them. His name was Michael Herman and his little brother had been in the procession with the third graders. His grandmother had died recently and his mother wanted to keep the house in the family. So, they had just moved into the parish from Havertown. He was finishing his freshman year at the Prep and the trip from Francis De Sales would be a little shorter for him. He said he had passed by the neighborhood many times — as he was studying on the El: the Prep gave a lot of homework but he really loved the school. Lisa and Janey talked to him about the neighborhood and Clark Park and how fun it was on the streets where they lived.

As he conversed with Lisa and Janey, his gaze went back and forth between them. But Janey thought she saw a special twinkle in his eyes when they met hers. They suddenly opened wider, she thought, and the first sproutings of a smile could be seen at the corners of his lips. She was jolted with the same sort of charge as when he had gazed at her during the procession. She felt as though a fireplace had been ignited within her and you could not help but feel its warmth.

Mike spoke of trivial things — exams, baseball, the summer job he would be starting with Western Union. It didn't matter much to Janey what he said. She toyed with the ends of her hair and fixed her veil as it dislodged itself from her curls. She dreamt of sitting on a bench in Clark Park with him in his Western Union outfit, the old trees like ancient deities smiling down blessings on their love. Lisa did a lot of chattering, too, but Janey paid even less attention to that.

After much too short a period, their parents called Janey and Lisa to introduce them to some old friends and their awkward offspring. Janey wondered if she would see the boy again. She thought it likely that she would not.

Then one afternoon there was a knock at the door. Lisa was up in their room, already changed and singing along to some obnoxious 45. Janey was still in her hideous uniform. She looked through the peephole. And, there, standing on the front porch, was Mike. She almost screamed. What could she do?! There was no time to go upstairs and change. He was waiting on the other side of the door. He might have even noticed her eye in the peephole. She ran the fingers of both of her hands through her hair, smoothed the plaid skirt as best as she could, and pulled the door open.

"Oh, hi!" she said, curling her hair over an ear. "So nice to see you, Mike."

"Nice to see you, too," Mike replied.

His eyes darted around the painted floorboards of the porch.

Then he asked, "Is Lisa home?"

"No, she's not," Janey said, bringing the door closer to her as if to block the noise from the girls' bedroom. But Lisa's record had come to an end.

"She went out afterschool … somewhere … I don't know where."

Mike smiled as if he had finished something difficult. He turned sideways.

"Well, tell her I came by."

Janey's mouth opened but she could not make a reply.

Did he just ask me to be his messenger?!

She closed the door with hardly a sound and stood frozen in that spot. The whole house, the whole street was quiet except for the creaking of Lisa's feet above. Janey lost track of how long she remained there, her nose but inches from the door.

Another song jangled out of the record player upstairs, and Lisa tooted the repetitive lyrics of the chorus.

But Janey did not move: she would become a boulder blocking the doorway.

...

Dear Rector O'Keefe:

Having heard much of the Italian University being established near Greenwich Village, I ventured over to visit the institution and to spend some time with the Sisters of Reparation who have, in the middle of this bustling city and within mere shouting distance of some of its overflowing slums, forsaken the fallen world outside of 51 Charlton Street, dedicating themselves instead to praying for it around the clock. I thought it would be the least I could do to offer them some blessings and perhaps administer the sacraments of Penance or Holy Communion. However, my visit left quite a strong impression on me, one which inspires me to write to you, dear Rector, to propose some cooperation between Xavier High School and the "Italian University."

When one ventures near the aforesaid address, one quickly becomes acquainted with the legendary personage of Miss Annie Leary. One could more easily avoid hearing the name, "Athena" near the Parthenon than that of Miss Leary in the vicinity of the Italian University. The women from her institution eagerly show visitors the new clothes that they have made from the gingham and calico given to them by "Miss Annie" so that they can be presentable when they go to work. The urchins smile and ask, "Are you here to see Miss Annie, Padre?" Their dirty faces brighten with expectation and hope at the notion that you might be a friend of their great benefactor.

Miss Leary is well known in the upper echelons of society as well. Evidently, she lives uptown at Fifth Avenue and 84th Street. The sisters informed me that Enrico Caruso, the great tenor, performed at a benefit for the University and that Pope Pius himself sent a blessing on the occasion of the institution's opening.

On the day that I visited the Italian University, I was disappointed to learn that Miss Annie was not present, but I was not as crestfallen as everyone else who kept telling me that she had gone to an important luncheon uptown. Fortunately for me, the lovely young Miss Cardella was willing to show me around the two Charlton Street buildings that comprise the University.

To take care of the children while the mothers work, Miss Leary has dedicated 53 Charlton Street, next door to the cloister of the Sisters of Charity, as a place where small children can play and recreate under watchful and caring eyes. I saw the little Italian children making castles in the sandboxes, swinging on swings, riding on a seesaw, and climbing on the monkey bars. My enthusiastic young tour guide explained to me that in the summertime, "Miss Annie" is so thoughtful that she has the play areas covered with a tent so that the children are not cavorting in the sun's heat.

At Miss Leary's Christopher Columbus Art Institute, I found many children of the neighborhood's Italian immigrants engaged in painting and drawing and thought perhaps some of them might be imbued with the artistic genius of their race. Could there be among them a new Giotto or Raphael preparing to arise from these mean streets? It seems absurd to imagine, but the Lord works in mysterious ways. He can raise up a prophet or a genius from the unlikeliest of places. Indeed, He has generally done so.

Moreover, this quarter of the city has no shortage of those laboring with brush, pencil, or charcoal (often with unfathomable choices of subject). It is only fitting for these young New Yorkers to do the same, though one might imagine that their mothers and fathers would prefer that they spend their time on pursuits more remunerative. I took a stroll around the classroom and many of the young pupils competed with one another to show me their work. (It was clear that these classrooms don't often get visits from priests.) Though most of the works did concern themselves with biblical themes, alas, I discovered no budding Michelangelos in my brief examination of the children's *opi*.

Nevertheless, so impressed was I with my visit and tour that I went back a second time to have an interview with Miss Annie Leary.

Miss Leary was a regal and elegant woman. Though she was not particularly tall, she projected a large presence. The wide figure she cut and the skirts and abundance of drapery attached to them, together with her outsized personality, made her appear larger than life. Despite her imposing figure, there was something about her that was, at the same time, quite approachable. I think it was her eyes. They draw one toward her and, once one gets close, they reveal the kindliness of her face, which communicates her genuine interest in what one has to say. Despite her patrician air, she seems truly to like people. Moreover, she is quite democratic in her affections. She showed interest in everyone who stopped to converse with her.

We sat together in a cozy drawing room she had near the first-floor chapel at No. 51 Charlton Street. It had a large crucifix over the fireplace and, displayed prominently atop a high table and lace doily, was a gilt-edged illustrated bible and a set of rosary beads. It appeared that what I had heard is true: Miss Leary is very devout.

I learned that she is a first generation American, born of Irish parents. Her father made his fortune selling hats to the well to do. I told her that my father, although very successful as well, had chosen a line of work less refined and more exposed to the elements. I was gratified to hear that she had heard of the Logan Construction Company, founded by my father, possibly through some of the friends she has on the Upper East Side and on the Main Line.

I expressed to her how I admire her charity and her great devotion to the poor. She would hear none of it. She said she saw people in need and was thankful to God that she had the opportunity and the wherewithal to assist him. Again, I was struck both by her upper-class charm and her perfect–seeming sincerity and pragmatism.

So, I told her about my work at Xavier and how my expertise in French and Latin did not do me much good in the streets around her school. I wondered aloud how a school full of college preparatory students and an Italian University might combine forces. For I surmised that that was the reason she had granted me the interview.

She expressed great concern about the Italian children and their difficulty in getting a good high school education. Their poor English-language skills, she explained, often prevented them from succeeding with the demanding curriculum of a school such as Xavier. Of course, she said that the tuition cost was prohibitive for most of them as well. I wondered aloud if somehow I could get my school to offer some worthy children's scholarship based on their achievements in the art classes at her University. She thought that would be wonderful and it is for this reason that I write to you, Rector, to use your influence to somehow make this possible.

I also had the less ambitious idea of having some of our boys come over to the University and tutor the children in English, help them with their themes, read some simple poetry or short stories with them, and generally help bring their academic skills up to the level required of a college preparatory school.

Though we might come from different backgrounds and races and have had different advantages in life, we are fellow Catholics, who generally all have an immigrant past. I believe we should work together.

I told my superior, Father Flemming, about Miss Annie's university and the work that is being done there. I suggested that perhaps the Jesuits could join in helping teach the poor children who struggle fewer than twenty blocks from our residence. He suggested that I put this proposal in writing to you.

This lone 73-year-old socialite with the cooperation and spiritual support of the Sisters of Reparation has achieved so much that she should be lauded to a greater degree than her humility would accept. Yet, she needs our help. And the very help she needs is the very strength that we have — our academic achievements and scholarship. Perhaps we can accept some of these Italian boys with some financial assistance into our school and have our volunteers help start to flow a steady stream of intelligent, well prepared young men from the Italian slums to the halls of Xavier High School.

Yours in Christ,

Reverend Sarsfield Logan, S.J.

Dearest Father Logan,

We have given your proposal careful reflection and prayer. Our mission at Xavier is to educate young men to be good Catholics and to be prepared for professions such as the law, medicine, or business. Your concern for the poor of the Italian slums in Greenwich Village is certainly quite admirable. However, we are not an art school. In fact, as you are no doubt aware, our own art facilities and time for instruction in such fields is quite limited. At this time, neither Xavier High School nor the Society of Jesus can see our way toward offering a scholarship based on achievement in the fine arts. We suggest that Miss Leary look to an institution whose goals and facilities are more in line with her students' abilities and ambitions.

We are quite willing, however, to encourage the boys of Xavier to volunteer to help with the reading skills of the pupils at the Italian University, as long as the extra work does not interfere with the progress of their own studies. We think this interchange will bring marvelous benefits for the development of the academic and spiritual lives of both tutors and pupils. I am sure this is not that answer that you had wanted to hear. However, it is the only one we can offer at this time.

Yours in Christ,

Rector Joseph O'Keefe

...

Vinny De Angelis ambled with a slight limp up sleepy Mulberry Street. His legs and back hurt from standing. Though he'd changed into shorts and a t-shirt after he'd closed up, he still smelled like the Ristorante Pontelandolfo.

Umberto's Clam House. Still open and lit up. "The Heart of Little Italy." Funny they called it that before there was a Big Italy. All those waves of people who had come over here at the end of the last century and done shit jobs doled out to them by their fellow countrymen — from *Abruzzi* or *Calabria* or *Sicilia*. It was only over here that they were called Italians. Some dreamers were trying to create it and many *paesani* with no recourse but the real world had to run from them. Vinny remembered a story his *Nonno* used to tell him.

Colonel Gaetano Negri's unification troops arrived at Pontelandolfo at dawn. Forget your loyalty to the king. We want loyalty to a new republic. This to *Pontelandolfesi* who had been tending sheep on these same hills, finding grass for them between these same sunbleached stones since before their Roman Empire and before their SPQR. What changed for them through the ages, except winter's becoming spring or wet weather turning dry? Landolpho, a local hero, even died defending the *ponte* over the *Fiume L'Alenta* against the Romans. That painting of him on tiles at the restaurant, looking like some ancient mosaic. *Stemma della città di Pontelandolfo.* Too bad he wasn't around in the eighteen hundreds.

Colonel Negri, the butcher of Pontelandolfo and Casalduni, ordered his troops to shoot the men and boys, bayonet the groveling women. They raped any girls they could catch. Concetta Biondi hid from the predators in a wine cellar, refusing to be violated. They shot her and her blood mixed with the wine on the floor. If you don't want to be part of my dream, go down to the Underworld or over to the New World. Turn Old Saint Pat's parish into Little Italy.

Vinny already felt the tickle in the back of his throat and the texture and taste of his first Bud Light. But he needed to make a stop first. He turned right on Grand Street and headed toward the Chinese guy open all night on the Bowery.

This poor guy, who knows what he's been through? Wonder if he's running this little coffee stand to pay off some outrageous vig to one of those snakeheads. Story on NPR a while back. Might be one of those guys on the ship run aground in the freezing cold water off Rockaway Beach. Clinton let some of them Golden Venture guys out of jail last year.

— Hello, Sir.

— Howyadoin', guy? Can I get a cup of cawfee with two sugars and just a little bit of milk? Just a little bit.

— Coffee, two sugar?

— Yeah, two sugars and just a little ...

Vinny tilted an invisible, miniature pitcher of milk with only the slightest movement of his wrist.

— Just a little bit.

The coffee guy scooped in the two sugars and, conscious of Vinny's watchful eye, added only a few drops of milk.

Ten of 'em drowned trying to reach the shore. Helluva thing to die so close to their goal. Couple hundred of them packed in the hold of a ship with rats and bugs for 112 days. From Thailand to Kenya and around the Cape of Good Hope, puking up the one bowl of rice and peanuts they got a day. Paying 3,000 bucks for this luxury cruise and owing some snakehead don 30,000 more once they get here.   I guess if you gotta why, you can put up wit' any how.

— It's the way she likes it. Whaddaya gonna do?

— I know. I know. Woman picky. Holding it around its rim, he lowered the coffee cup into a waiting brown bag and slid it toward Vinny. One dollar.

But these people stick together. They get help from family and friends already here. They pool their money. Sometimes they even lend a guy money to pay the snakehead. Better to owe your family or friends than those cold-hearted bastards. And they all go into business together. No wonder they are outflanking Little Italy on three sides. Walk a block east of Mulberry during the day, you'd swear you're in China.

Vinny paid and walked out.

Still, helluva thing to go through. Wonder if he'd tell me about it if I aksed him.

He strolled back to Mulberry Street and, having fulfilled this final duty, limped a little more quickly uptown.

Guy's probably Korean, anyway.

— I have to pee, Laura announced.

Half a block above Kenmare Street, she had pulled over by a fire hydrant and, just like that, thrown it into Park.

— So, you're stopping here? Paul objected. It's just a couple blocks to Houston.

The door opened. Traffic noise. Trashtruck squeaks and bangs. Sighs, grunts, muttering. Laura's blue-jeaned legs stood her up in the middle of Mulberry, an inch or two of the flesh around her waist appearing as her grey shirt rode up on her. The hood of her blue sweatjacket fell around her neck before the back of her hand flipped it up again.

jumps out in the middle of little italy as if it were a parking lot in mamaroneck

Paul looked out at the high fence of the locked-up playground, at the Chinese Tui-Na place with a map of the touch points of the human body protruding from its gated storefront, the cell phone place. Good Luck Haircut.

— Where're you gonna go?

— In the bar.

She pointed at a filthy tattered awning with sharks on it at the corner of Spring and Mulberry. The Spring Lounge.

— Paul, can you sit up here, she asked, pointing to the driver's seat, in case the cops come?

— Uh … all right.

Bending over Paul as he sat looking through the windshield with its immobilized wiper at the five-storey buildings and the tangle of fire escapes, she demonstrated.

her shoulder practically hitting me in the face strange clothed lapdance only a little rougher hair fragrant but still damp her breasts almost touching the tops of my thighs can't look pay attention

A black banner with white letters and a tomato in a chef's hat offered PIZZA BY THE SLICE.

— You have to hit it. Hit it! she was saying, referring to the stick shift, which was nothing but a headless chrome post.

She backed out of the car and paused for a second.

her cleavage deep and so close love that when you can see the veins sometimes see that in a strange woman on the subway or the gym and feel intimate with her

— I'll be right back! Look out for cops! and she was jogging across the street.

not a great ass not bad either was about to suggest she try pomodoro pizza because the bar might not then again if you were a bartender would you block her way to the loo or anywhere else if she appeared in your doorway in the middle of a showery april night she was used to miracles she expected them and they never failed to happen

Off she trotted toward the awning and then under it and along the wall to the front door. A heavy-set man in a t-shirt and shorts, with close-cropped hair, black on top and grey on the sides, was limping toward the bar with a small brown bag in his hand. He stopped dead in his tracks. With a comical smirk, he stepped grandly forward, opened the door, and held it for Laura. She waltzed right in as if she were the Persephone the place had awaited all winter.

objects in mirror are closer than they appear the hazard light indicators blinking tic toc ... tic toc ... tic toc ... tic toc ...she'll come ... right back ... she'll come ... right back ... gotta be responsible for this jalopy and drunken brit taking chances again hanging out like a teenager looking out for cops at the pleasure of her majesty her crown of blonde her 36-24-34 mantle too great a risk ya think heading forward without looking back no wish to become a pillar of salt

Above the angling street of tenements, half the Empire State Building's pinnacle could be seen. Its lights were still on. But, Paul kept an eye on the rearview mirror, grateful not to see any cops. An occasional car whisshhed by. A cab with a lit Available light quickened his pulse for a second. But, for the most part, Mulberry Street seemed desolate; no municipal enforcement of law needed. Suddenly, two cars in front of them, the red brake lights of an old grey Toyota flashed on and the headlights shone on the back of a VW Jetta. The Toyota was backing up and pulling out of its parking spot. Where had the driver come from?

do it yes take another chance take the spot this close to houston and the elusive fdr so what but what the hell let's exhaust the city that never sleeps

— Charles, check it out! A parking spot right there!

In the rearview mirror, a car was heading up Mulberry toward Spring Street.

— A spot of luck I suppose.

— Luck we can't waste. C'mon. Let's surprise her.

— Right. I need to shake the snake as well.

The car passed them, stopped at Spring, and drove off into the shadows.

No other cars were coming. Hitting the chrome post as he had been instructed, Paul put it into drive. He pulled alongside the auto in front of him, having some difficulty shifting into reverse. There was still nothing coming. He backed into the spot. But he didn't get the angle right. He had to fight with the stick shift a third time, pull out of the spot, and back in again. Fortunately, the rear-view mirror showed neither cops nor approaching cars. He did better on his second attempt but had to hit the chrome post several times in order to move up and back, to right the car inch by inch.

The two men got out and crossed the street.

— Wonder if Laura will have a laugh over this, Charles said.

— Get her an Amstel on the rocks and she'll be just fine.

Charles and Paul entered the Spring Lounge and drifted across the floorboards toward the horseshoe bar. A trio of stuffed sharks seemed to circle the bar, the low blocky tables and stools, and the jukebox.

we're gonna need a bigger boat charlie

A big great white arched its back over the entrance to the tiny back room, where half a hammerhead hung on the far wall. Another great white swam with a rubber hand sticking out of his mouth above the mirror and the handful of customers who sat facing it. The guy with the brown paper bag was one of them.

Evidently, Laura was still in the bathroom.

cervisiam non habent

Paul cast his eyes this way and that for the bartender.

— She'll be back in a minute, the brown-paper-bag man offered.

who brings coffee to a bar

Bogie played poker in a picture taped to the bar mirror. Photos of regulars and bartenders in zany poses were slapped up nearby. Cagney and Sinatra looked on from opposite sides of a paneled column.

A familiar bass line with a jerky hesitation between the first and second notes meandered through the jukebox speaker. Laura came out of the bathroom, spotted them, and smiled. Before the singer could ask where the sexy thing was from, Laura cried:

— Oh! Did you see this movie?

And was out dancing between the column and the knee-high stools.

— When they were in line for welfare?

Paul hesitated. Charles never moved. A skinny guy in his 40s with a thin beard and mustache appeared out of nowhere, howling and clapping his hands. Laura stood among the scratched and beaten benches and tables in the middle of the room, arms out in front of her and her elbows bent. She moved her shoulders up and down and bounced.

check out skinny beard guy the quick acting predator who had picked up the scent of drunken pussy gotta learn to be that quick smell blood in the water and spring

When Laura turned her squinty, slanting eyes at Paul, this time he did not delay. He bounded over to her, feeling as if her were stepping out on a tightrope. Soon his eyes were inches from her high cheeks, her half-mast eyes, and her red, mad-wide smile. And he danced and sang with her, shouting where did she come from and how did she know he needed her? Lunacy. But who would pass up the chance? The song ended, the skinny beard guy drifted away, and Laura and Paul joined Charles at the bar.

— Still no bartender? Paul asked.

— She's coming, reassured coffee-to-a-bar man.

central casting send us a neighborhood guy yeah hes perfect

Out on Mulberry Street, a wet and hunched-over figure fumbled with the sash of her clear, shiny raincoat. A rainbonnet covered her hair. She looked like an old lady — except for the tight pink pants. She stepped inside, shuffled a few steps toward the bar, and stopped. Through the raincoat sleeves could be seen a series of dark tattoos on the amber skin of her arms. Hands under her chin, she undid the rainbonnet, lifted it carefully off, and shook free a mane of jet-black hair. It fell from her round head and curled around her neck and shoulder as in a tired casual embrace. Then the raincoat came off. And, the old lady became a sexy girl from a rock video: a big-haired, Asian Elvira Mistress of Dark with bombshell tits encased in a silvery reflective halter top.

and an exposed midriff of course we are living in the age of the exposed midriff

She threw her discarded garments on a ledge by the end of the bar and leaned her bare tattooed arms on the curved counter.

taut round hips peachy ass in pink spandex great body yeah not a lot of scars

Charles gazed at the bartender's cleavage and raised his eyes approvingly toward Paul. Paul threw a new big-head Jackson twenty on the bar and ordered a bottle of Bud, a pint of Guinness, and an Amstel Light with a pint glass full of ice.

— Looks like we got a latenight party here, the bartender said. Dancin' up a storm! I saw you guys through the window and thought it was a miracle. Except Giuliani has outlawed miracles.

She placed their drinks in front of them. Her eyes smiled as Laura poured the Amstel Light over the ice in her glass.

— By the way, Laura asked Paul, where's my car?

Everyone laughed and Paul searched his pockets for the keys. Vinny pushed the brown bag across the bar.

— Here's your cawfee.

— Thanks, sweetie! The bartender purred. She took out the discus-thrower cup, tore open the lid, and tasted it. Mmm. Just right.

—I have to watch that guy, remind him every night. He always wants to put too much milk in.

— Well, this is perfect. Thanks, Vinny.

and his name is vinny are you shittin me

She took a dollar from the tip jar to give to Vinny who held up his hands and said:

— No, no! Fuhgeddaboudit!

Paul removed the car keys from his pants pocket and handed them to Laura. Vinny turned to them.

— I told ya she'd be back.

Paul got a sick feeling in his stomach, but he responded:

— You weren't lyin'!

— We don't get much dancin' in here. You guys are all right. I'm Vinny.

He put out his hand and Paul shook it.

— My name's Paul. This is Laura …

Vinny smirked at Charles who was swaying forward and back.

— … and that's Charles.

— He seems to be dancin' to his own music.

— He's had a few.

— We all have, Laura added.

— I got some catchin' up to do. I just got off work.

— Are you a bartender? asked Laura.

— No, I work in a restaurant down the street, "The Ponteandolfo."

— Oh, Charles works in a restaurant, too. He's a cook.

— He's studying to be a chef, said Laura.

— Oh, yeah? Charles, where do you work?

— American Restaurant.

— Well, I didn't think it was a British restaurant. Be outta business in a week — right? I'm just kiddin'. You're English — right?

— We do have some fine chefs in Britain.

not good enough to tempt the hunger strikers

— Don't mind him, cracked Paul. He thinks he still has an empire.

— We do! We still have Canada!

— Until it melts.

...

There was no snow at all. The wind was blowing some leaves down Simpson Road as if it were still November. Some neighbors had already hung their Christmas lights; the Hallorans even had their tree up. But it was time to stop looking out the window. What is there to look at, anyway? Tommy Devlin, Dot's boy, was ambling down the street, with his eyes fixed on the sidewalk. Trying not to break his mother's back? wondered Janey. She really had to get going. Tommy stopped and bent down. He picked up a candy wrapper and stood there jerking his head around like some strange bird. Janey realized Tommy was looking for Candy the Elf. The nuns at St. Colman's told all the children to pick up candy wrappers as they walked, and that the wrappers would form a trail, which would lead to Candy himself.

Good way to get them to clean up after themselves, Janey thought. Still, there was something underhanded and twisted about the whole thing. Thinking of nuns, Janey shivered. Even their clever stratagems contained dashes of meanness and bitterness.

But she couldn't dilly dally looking out the window. She had to get Kitty's hair ready and make sure Paul's shirt was ironed and his suit was not a mass of wrinkles. They'd have to get to the Ardmore station by 4:15 and buy their tickets. Or they could buy them on the train but that would cost extra money. Oh, and she had to get herself ready, too!

Maybe it would have been better to have taken the 3:15 or at least the 3:45. That way they could have given themselves more time and not have been so rushed. But there was nothing Janey could do about it now. As long as they made the 4:15, they'd be fine.

She found Paul in his room, looking out the window, still in his underwear!

"Young man, I told you to start getting ready. What are you doing?"

"Tommy Fitzgerald is picking up wrappers!"

"We need to catch the train so we can have time to stop into Daddy's office before the light show."

"I want to go find Candy! What if Tommy finds him first?"

"We have no time for Candy the Elf right now! You're still in your underwear and I told you to get dressed 20 minutes ago! Besides, I'm sure Tommy would rather be going In Town to see Santa, instead of looking for one of his elves. Now, come on!"

Such an imagination! You never knew what he was thinking about.

Paul slumped back to his bed and started putting his legs into his itchy pants.

It was strange to change from his school clothes into even dressier clothes. Usually, Paul put his play clothes on at this time of the day.

"Don't walk hunched over like that. You'll get curvature of the spine."

Janey stood over him to make sure he didn't get distracted again. She helped him button the top button of his dress shirt and clipped his tie on for him.

"Now I have to go help your sister. Keep yourself nice and neat until I get back. We want the people at Daddy's company to see what a handsome gentleman you are."

Kitty had managed to get her dress on over her head but it was all cockeyed. And her hair was a complete mess. Janey combed it with the little girl's favorite Mrs. Beasley brush.

Kitty wore a cranberry coat with a matching pointy hat. Paul said she looked like Little Red Riding Hood. Or she could have been Peter Pan if she were a boy.

She did look cute in her little red coat and hat. But, something was wrong.

"Kitty, there's a leaf on the back of your coat."

Janey loaded both kids in the front seat of the car. She had no desire to hear them fighting over who got to sit up front — as if it mattered for a two-minute ride! She did manage to make the 4:15, though she had to kill a couple of Chinese. As they boarded the train, Kitty and Paul fought over the window seat.

"Paul Logan, is it too much to show a bit of kindness to your little sister? She's three years younger and a lot smaller than you are. And it is Christmastime!"

Paul stayed put, taking out his *Highlights* magazine. He found his place in the story he had been reading and without taking his eyes off of the page, slid his behind away from the window. Kitty bounded into the seat and, watching the houses and trees go by, cuddled and rocked "Floppy," her stuffed bunny rabbit. Janey wasn't crazy about the idea of carting the bunny all around Town but it fit easily into Janey's purse, and if it would keep her quiet …

At Suburban Station, Janey shepherded the kids through the hustle and bustle. People were rushing in all directions for their trains.

"Stay together! Hold Mommy's hand!"

She found everything so busy and crowded that she was surprised at herself. It seemed that she and James had switched roles. Janey was the girl from West Philly, after all, and James was the suburban boy.

She stopped to let the kids watch the ice skaters underground near City Hall before heading up to the street and to the offices of Logan Construction Company, a walk Janey knew by heart.

On Chestnut Street, she paused again and sighed in front of the fast-food joint that used to be Horn and Hardart's. They were starting to disappear.

"Why are you stopping there, Mommy?" Kitty wanted to know.

"Nothing. Your father and I used to eat lunch there a long time ago."

"At Burger King?" Paul asked.

"No, it was a restaurant back then."

Young people didn't even know what they were anymore, the Automats.

The lobby of the office brought back a flood of memories: the granite pattern of the floor tile, the security guard's desk, the Roman-numeraled dials above the elevators, even the Christmas tree with its gold tinsel and uniform red balls hanging from its branches. It was all so much the way she had remembered it that as she looked at each familiar thing and found it in its familiar place, it was as though she were looking at her memory of it rather than the actual object.

When the elevator arrived, Kitty and Paul immediately quarreled over who got to push the button. When they reached the 11th floor, Florence was waiting for her elevator down. Of course, she found the kids absolutely adorable and all their misbehavior completely charming. They are always cute if they are someone else's and you don't have to take care of them 24 hours a day.

Florence made unimaginative small talk with the children. There but for the grace of God go I, Janey thought. Paul and Kitty were polite, though they seemed confused by this lady in a long black coat that smelled of peppermint, with pointy glasses like a cartoon librarian's, who acted so friendly to them.

Janey wondered what it would be like to just keep working and not have to worry about kids. Something to be said for it, she imagined, to be a single woman working in the office, time and money to herself, decisions made by herself, for herself.

Florence fingered a folded up rainbonnet in her hands. She had just taken it out of her purse, which was still opened, when the elevator doors opened. But what good would it do for her in this weather? Janey supposed that she wanted to protect that well-sprayed head of hair.

Janey had once felt a connection to old Florence, both of them having grown up in West Philly. Florence was from Transfiguration, where she still lived and remained ready to extol her parish's virtues at the slightest opportunity.

Florence kept repeating about how cold it was. And the crowds. All those people out seeing the Christmas lights, that was too much for her. Thank God, said she, that she lived so close to the El. She could be on her own front porch in 15 minutes.

What temperature did she want it to be to go look at the Christmas light show — 107? Old coot talking herself into being satisfied with her life. If she is in such a hurry to get home, why didn't she go? Instead, she liked to play doggie in the manger, and keep them from getting in to see James. Dried up old prune. I think somebody is "J-e-."

Nevertheless, Florence made a fuss over the kids, which always brought a smile to Janey's face, no matter the circumstances nor the source. She gave them each a peppermint candy, cooing, "Merry Christmas!"

Finally, they heard the "ting" of an electric bell. Florence's elevator opened.

"Well, have a good time! I hope Santa is good to you, kids! Merry Christmas!"

"Merry Christmas, Florence! Take care! Kitty, Paul, say, 'Merry Christmas!' to Florence! Bye bye!"

"Merry Christmas!"

"Merry Christmas!"

When they entered the offices of Logan Construction Company, everyone was excited to see the kids. Even the executives and the girls bundled up and rushing toward the elevators stopped to greet them and marvel at how the kids had grown. The welcome made Janey's worries seem silly. Long gone were the days of the scandal over the office romance and the broken engagement. People reacted, Janey thought, as if a couple of the Kennedys had popped into the office.

The women purred and squealed over the children — even a few new ones she did not know so well. Janey couldn't get over how young their faces looked. Such smooth complexions! And, Glory be to God, those tight sweaters and skirts couldn't help but make them look shapely. They must turn many an executive's head. As Janey once did … As Janey once did …

She was trying to reduce and had lost a couple of pounds but try looking like that when you have two kids, sweethearts.

They must wear girdles.

James heard the commotion and came out from his office.

"Daddy!" cried Kitty and ran over to him and gave him a big hug. Paul followed Kitty looking around at the desks and the furniture and the switchboard before he also hugged James.

James leaned over to Janey for a quick kiss.

"Should we take a walk around the office? Do we have time?"

"OK, but quickly. There's not much time if we want to catch the 5:30 show."

As the Logan family strolled over to Wanamaker's, Kitty and Paul debated about whether the Wanamaker's Santa is the real one.

Amused by the children, James settled the matter.

"The real Santa Claus comes to Philadelphia on Thanksgiving at the end of the Gimbels parade — remember? When he climbs up the fireman's ladder? Then he leaves his helpers here so he can go build toys in the North Pole."

They got a spot in the center of the Grand Court right near the eagle. James lifted Kitty up and sat her right between the talons of the giant bird's left claw, her short legs dangling and her heels bopping the granite base. Paul furrowed his brow for a second and then, discovering that he could move around, decided he liked it better where he was. Other parents glared at them because they had gotten a good spot and because James had secured the last perch above the crowd for his daughter.

While the Logan family waited, they looked around John Wanamaker's Grand Court, an enormous hall with columns and arches in every direction. There were miniature trees decorated with tinsel and white lights and bows and Christmas balls — on top of the displays for gloves and perfume and handbags, watches, wallets, and fancy pens. Janey loved the merchandise and cast longing eyes toward the women milling around, examining this item or that, the way she used to when she worked down here. She knew she had no time to shop this evening, however. She was here for the show.

The display began one storey above them and stretched two stories higher, to the ornate ceiling of the nearly 100-year-old building. Purse-sized snowflakes fell in rows from the top of the display to the bottom and a giant tree turned color after color.

"Kids, which is your favorite color?" asked Janey.

"Blue!" cried Paul hopping up so that he could be heard better.

"I never heard of a blue tree!" declaimed Kitty.

"It's a magic tree! So it can be any color. And it's right there in front of you, stupid!"

"Paul James Logan! Santa Claus and his helpers are watching you right now!"

Kitty leaned down and shouted between her feet.

"I hope he heard you, stupidhead!"

"Kitty! Paul! It's Christmastime! You should *not* talk to each other like that."

"Santa knows she is a bad girl and won't bring her anything. Just coal!"

James grabbed Paul by the shoulder and moved him away from the eagle. It hurt.

"Stop it," his father whispered. "Stop it, right now!"

Kitty and Paul were always spoiling for a fight, even now when Janey and James were going out of their way to do something nice for them.

They all silently waited for the show to begin. Paul read the block letters that stated, "Next show: 5:30" and the happy script under the giant tree that wished everyone, "Merry Christmas." The murmur of adult voices, the prattle of children, and the clacks of shoppers' footsteps, clear when you stood near their sources, turned diffuse in the spacious hall.

Suddenly, all the lights in the Christmas tree and the strings of falling snowflakes went out. And the Grand Court of Wanamaker's grew bright.

Before anything happened on the screen people started to clap.

"It's gonna start!" Paul cried

"It's gonna start, Paul!" Kitty shouted.

Janey smiled. They were cute when they got along.

The people quieted down as the whole Grand Court went dark. And, with the strumming of harp strings and a majestic fanfare, the tree lit up again and the fountains began dancing, their jets of water changing color in the air. John Facenda's voice baritoned off of the walls, welcoming all to what John Wanamaker proudly presented:

"The annual Christmas pageant of lights!"

"Is that Santa's voice, Mommy?"

"No, that's John Facenda. He used to do the news on TV."

"A brilliant holiday spectacular depicting the color, warmth, and joy of the yuletide season … starring the breathtaking Magic Christmas tree!"

Then it was time for the story of the Nutcracker. A little girl found a nutcracker under her tree on Christmas morning. Against the backdrop of Tchaikovsky's mysterious tiptoeing notes, the toy soldier cracked nuts made of yellow light with his flapping jaw. The pieces fell like the colored snowflakes all the way to the bottom of the screen. But he wasn't an ordinary nutcracker: he was a nutcracker that came to life!

Winged fairies in ballet shoes appeared in blue, yellow, and white and the strings waltzed the music around the spacious hall.

"Look, Kitty! The dance of the sugar plum fairies!"

"My favorite!"

Kitty clapped her little mittened hands. Paul watched her display of joy and smiled to himself. Janey thought maybe all the trouble she had had getting them ready and bringing them In Town was not so annoying after all.

Janey reached up to Kitty.

"Let me hold those mittens for you, hon'."

"With a wave of her wand the sugar plum fairy takes us to the enchanted clock shop!" John Facenda's voice intoned.

A colorful clock appeared high up on the left. Its pendulum swung in time to the music and its two perpendicular hands, likewise, moved around its face to the song's rhythm. With each beat, a cuckoo bird, too, opened its beak and pantomimed a call. Another clock appeared lower down, and others materialized all around the giant display. Paul bent his knees and straightened up to the beat of the song, joining the pendulums and the clock hands and the cuckoos' beaks. The music sounded like the clocks could march away, but they didn't.

When the song stopped, the clocks disappeared and snowflakes began to fall in straight lines from one side of the screen to the other. Sometimes they seemed to fly upward the way real snowflakes sometimes do, especially in the city.

Janey remembered watching them from the office window before she was married. The canyons of buildings created upward currents of air that kept the snowflakes above the ground, helping them avoid their fate for just a little longer. In the background was an instrumental song she recognized, beginning with a quick fanfare and gliding into a lovely waltz. It was "Alpine Sleigh Ride." She had the album at home: *Music for a Merry Christmas* with a svelte and jaunty snowman on the cover.

Next, a chorus of jazzy women's voices chanted:

Dasher! Dancer!
Comet! Cupid!

To Paul, the performers seemed to be right behind the screen, singing and playing, just like the organ at the Phillies game seemed to be right under the AstroTurf of the infield. After all of Santa's reindeer were named, Rudolph finally appeared, fully grown with a wide rack of yellow horns and a rhythmically flashing red nose. At first Rudolph wanted to play in the reindeer games, like everyone else — Paul always pictured the reindeer games in the Saint Colman's schoolyard — but the other reindeer were mean.

Why were they so mean to him just because his nose was different?

Kitty bobbed up and down in her seat.

"Rudolph!" she cried. "My favorite!"

"Your favorite?!" snarled Paul. "How many favorites do you have?"

"Paul," commanded James. "Leave her alone."

Then one foggy Christmas Eve ...

A happy Santa wearing a thick white beard and bright red suit and hat appeared with his arms spread wide.

A little girl shouted, "Santa!"

Paul turned around. It was not Kitty.

Won't you guide my sleigh tonight?

The nose that had made him weird turned out to be a special gift! Paul wondered if the other reindeer were ever mad that Rudolph, the one they always picked on, got to be the leader.

But they all loved him, the song said.

As the collection of lightbulbs imitated Rudolph's leading Santa's sleigh across the sky into history, James took Janey by the hand and squeezed it. It was something he hadn't done in public in a very long time — so long in fact that it startled her: for a split second, Janey thought it was some stranger. But she was reassured by the feel of his palm against hers, by the familiar hair of his hand in her fingers.

A more modern-sounding song began with a bouncy bass line and fell into a steady, swinging rhythm. Candy canes and toy soldiers danced jerkily upon the screen to "Jingle Bell Rock," as interspersed toy drums hammered out the beat.

As the song faded out, Santa's Express Train stretched itself all the way across the top of the exhibition. It was way up by the ceiling! They had to tilt their heads far back, making their necks ache, to see it.

"Want me to lift you up, Paul?" James asked.

"No, thanks, Dad. I'm OK. I can see."

James and Janey smiled at each other. Their son had always been independent.

As the Santa Express flickered cheerfully through a winter wonderland, Santa himself rang the bell from the back of the engine.

"A choo choo train, Kitty," Janey said. "Like the one we rode to see Daddy."

"The Santa Express goes to the North Pole — right?" Paul asked.

"Yes, that's where he makes all the toys," explained James.

"For the good girls and boys," Janey added.

Snowmen lit into being in pairs, growing closer and closer together as they ascended toward the ceiling. They made a Christmas tree shape!

There must have been some magic
In that old silk hat they found.

Paul thought it would be neat to have a magic hat. He wondered if in the summertime you could bring it down the shore, make a sand man, and bring him to life. But you couldn't keep both a snowman and a sandman alive with just one hat. What could he do? Maybe he could take the hat from Frosty when the weather got warm. The sandman could use it during the summertime and Frosty could have it back for the winter.

Was the magic hat real or was it just a story?

The weather must have gotten warmer for Frosty. The lights outlining the Frosties' shapes started to fade. They were melting!

All the Frosties on the giant screen waved both of their arms. It was funny the way their forearms flashed up and down, up and down.

John Facenda's voice filled the hall with his deep and heartfelt, "Goodbye, Frosty! Goodbye!"

A chorus of children's voices, much higher pitched than the announcer's echoed, "Goodbye … Goodbye … Goodbye" their voices fading with the lights … Janey hummed along with the tune of "So Long, Farewell" supporting the children's singing.

That part always made Paul sad. He didn't like to think that Frosty was gone.

But the song said he would be back on Christmas Day. And Paul remembered that Christmas hadn't even come yet — and that it hadn't really started to get cold yet. Frosty would not have to go away for real for a while. Paul hoped it would snow soon.

"John Wanamaker wishes you and your family the happiest holiday ever!"

As "O Tannenbaum" played, the Grand Finale lit up the whole three-storey display. All of the characters from the various tales flashed back to life — enchanted clocks, nutcrackers, reindeer, sugar plum ballet dancers, toy soldiers and drums, the Santa Express, Rudolph, and some candy canes and snowflakes! The Magic Christmas Tree blinked color after color. And the dancing water fountains reflected pink and green and blue and red … Even though they had seen it every year, Kitty and Paul clapped and cheered — especially when all the Frosties beamed white, black, and orange back onto the screen. He wasn't really gone after all!

The exulting recorded orchestra fell silent and the clapping died down. Now echoing around the hall were the shuffle of shoes upon the marble floor, the high-pitched chatter of children, and lower-toned chitchat of adults. Here and there a child's shriek or a parent's command could be discerned. It seemed to come as a surprise to the audience to find themselves in the middle of a department store. Gradually, the Grand Court began to empty, people making room for the next audience for the next show, conversing about what they had seen and what to do next.

"Let's go upstairs to see Santa," Janey said.

Santa at Wanamaker's resided on a hidden throne, only to be reached via a journey along a holiday lane, a big line with red ropes on one side and barriers covered in green felt on the other. As you waited in line, you saw pictures of other kids with other Santas of other years, smiling babies and boys and girls, each photo bearing a big number telling how many miles it was to the north pole and an illustrated elf nailing up a scroll reading, "SANTA and ME." And once you got near the front of the line you'd see some big lights and a camera on a tall tripod, and there was Santa.

While Kitty sat on Santa's lap and had her picture taken, Paul reviewed his mental list of what to ask for. The most important item on the list was a guitar like Danny had on *The Partridge Family*, one he could use for his band. He also wanted a G.I. Joe with Kung Fu grip. Some of his friends already had that.

He sat on Santa's warm lap and the big white beard tickled his cheek. He remembered everything. At least, he thought he did. Either way, anything forgotten would be covered by "and lots of surprises."

The photographer flashed a picture and the afterflash blinded Paul for a couple of seconds. When he was able to again make out the tripod, the camera, the lights, the green felt barriers, and the people waiting in line, he saw that his mother was placing Kitty on Santa's other knee.

"Mom!" he objected. "She already talked to Santa! Why is she back?!"

"I'd like to get a picture with the two of you in it. You look so cute!"

"I only want a picture taken by myself — not with her!"

"Be a good boy now, Paul. Remember, you're sitting on Santa's lap."

Paul stopped arguing but when the photographer went to snap the picture, he didn't smile. He knew that Santa couldn't see his face.

...

Seamus left his compatriots on South Street and watched them slapping one another's backs and stumbling on their sealegs on the unfamiliar terrain. Wide-eyed and subject to a different gravity than the more powerful force compelling their fellow pedestrians to rush about, they stepped carefully across the busy street. For, the traffic appeared to have no patience for these aliens.

Seamus leaned against a lamp post that looked like something taken off of a ship. It surprised him that people were not sick and tired of the sea and its accouterments, as he was, now they had reached land. It looked like a sailor would be able to scamper on the lamp post's staggered spikes right up to the top in no time, especially as it would remain much stiller than a ship's shrouds. Perhaps men did climb up there to light the lamp under its conical cover. Seamus smiled to see that his comrades did finally make it across the street safely. He said a prayer for them, asking the Lord to let their entire stay in this new world turn out the same: that despite challenges, difficulties, and dangers, they would make it to the place awaiting them unscathed.

Seamus was getting jostled. He saw several unsmiling wizened faces and heard grumbling that he thought was addressed to him. Most of the traffic was coming down the street toward him and he realized he was in the way. He discerned that there were two distinct streams of traffic on the pavement: one moving down on his left and the other heading up on his right. Seamus thought it best to move over to the right side. So he picked up his portmanteau and gingerly crossed both streams and leaned himself up against the brick wall of a building.

He felt dazed from everything that he saw and heard and smelled. He could not believe the number of people around him. He had never seen so many in his entire life – even if he added up all of the people he had ever seen — and here they were in one place. He could only compare these crowds to flocks of sheep brought to Clifden on market day or schools of mackerel that came in close to the shore in such numbers you could practically walk out to sea upon their backs. If the Lord wanted to cast a net down here to catch men, he would surely catch enough to fill it. The people seemed so hurried and yet so expert in hurrying through these narrow streets. He wished he were like them. He longed for the day that he too would be at home in this type of place, though he felt it was a long way off. They paraded by him in all shapes and sizes and varieties of dress, speaking languages from all over the world. It was like the end of the workday at the Tower of Babel job site.

Seamus heard some Irish brogues in the crowds, too. At first, he thought they were relations of his shipmates come to meet them. But he soon realized his mistake. His fellow passengers to whom they acted so friendly did not appear to know them at all. The smiles of those Irishmen waiting on the dock were too practiced altogether, their palaver too well rehearsed. Seamus kept his distance from them and observed their actions. He did not trust them, though he saw others go willingly along with their suggestions. A few of them tried to lure him in but he would not even reply to them.

Seamus awaited his chance and stepped into the flow of foot traffic. Masts of ships loomed up and down South Street and the noise from the loading and unloading of cargo and from the fish and vegetable mongers filled the concrete, brick, and stone defile. He followed the people in front of him as if he were waiting in a swift-moving queue. He crossed a few narrow streets, trying not to step in the puddles or on the discarded vegetables and hunks of bread surrounded by filthy birds. He even saw some pigs rooting around in the streets. He smiled. They were cleaning up the slops strewn everywhere in this land renowned for its abundance.

Seamus well knew that he was in close proximity to the sea but the stench that was growing in his nostrils with his every step was far worse than any he had encountered at home. It reminded him of the salty seaweed smell of Killary Harbour at low tide but magnified many, many times. As he crossed Fulton Street, the large man in a pea coat who had been in front of him, a stevedore by the looks of him, turned to go up that broad street and Seamus discovered the origin of the odor. There was a monstrous beehive of a fishmarket with people and horses and carts and handtrucks and crates moving in all directions. Men were loading crates of fish onto the backs of carts. Others brought fish into the market under the awning that covered the whole pavement. A couple of men delivered blocks of ice about half the size that they were themselves. The multitudinous comings and goings and the ease and expertise with which the men worked at tasks so unknown to Seamus amazed his eyes but the stink of the fish so overpowered his nose that he felt he would soon be unable to breathe if he did not cross to the other side of the insistent street.

Seamus wandered up Pearl Street.

Having seen the difficulty that his comrades had had traversing that time-pressed avenue, Seamus focused his entire attention on getting himself, his portmanteau, and his walking stick safely to the other side of South Street.

It still stank like fish.

Keeping his head down, Seamus walked to the next street as quickly as the others around him did and turned left. On his way up the wee hill, Seamus muttered to himself.

"*Maise*, I now understand why it is these Yanks hurry so!"

He found himself on a narrow street of solid houses made of brick with thin layers of mortar. Many of the houses had storefronts whose windows were surrounded by wood beams ornately carved and painted white. This street was far less crowded than South Street, and, though the smell was not greatly diminished, Seamus breathed more easily. He did not know where he was going and did not want to ask for directions. The people hereabouts did not seem to take kindly to strangers. One drunken man stumbled and nearly fell down in front of him, cursing all the while. There were some cheap and unsavory looking hotels about. As much as he wanted to be settled, at least for the night, and to lay down the burden of his portmanteau, he felt that none of these places was the one meant for him. He was happy to follow the call he felt to find a church. Besides, he wanted to be farther away from the sea and the sad memories of his crossing.

Standing before a butcher shop, he hardly noticed the variety and abundance of meat on the hooks, so filled with sad rememberings was his mind. He passed a candle maker, a tailor, a cobbler, and a blacksmith. The cobblestones in the street reminded him of the larger towns of home, like Clifden and Galway and lifted his spirits a bit. They brought a bit of the Old World into the New for him, as he imagined they did for others.

At the top of the hill, Seamus came to the crossroads of Beekman and Pearl Streets. He turned right to get away from the fish market and because Pearl Street reminded him of oysters and Galway.

He reached the Brooklyn Bridge building site and heard the accents of home. Men were working with bricks and hods, joining two great cities, as he had read. Was this presumptuous of the builders, erecting a pair of arrogant towers taller than all others?

Then miraculously the name on the street signs changed to James Street. His name in English! He followed.

In the middle of the block, stood a building like a small Greek temple with a domed cupola. The facade's inscription declaimed from the fieldstone: "*D.O.M. S. JACOBO DEO OPTIMO MAXIMO*"

Seamus stepped closer and found another inscription, this one on the façade.

THIS IS NO OTHER BUT
THE HOUSE OF GOD AND
THE GATE OF HEAVEN

He would stop here.

Seamus pushed the door open. He felt the cool air and scented the faint remnants of incense as his eyes adjusted to the dimness of the sanctuary. A cluster of women with kerchiefs on their heads knelt in the pews on the Blessed Mother's side. Another was to the left of the altar lighting a candle. A gaunt old man in a ragged jacket sat alone on Saint Joseph's side fighting to keep his head up and his eyes open. A woman was sweeping the back of the church.

Seamus walked down the middle of the center aisle, looking right and left, searching not just for an empty pew but for the right one. He did not want to be too far from the altar nor to have to carry the portmanteau to the front and back again. Not quite halfway up the aisle on his right, Seamus found a pew with its kneeler down, as if waiting for him. He genuflected, put his portmanteau and stick on the seat, and knelt.

Seamus pulled the beads from his pocket and said a decade of the rosary in thanksgiving for his safe journey to the New World. Behind him the sound of straw against marble signaled the progress of the cleaning lady. As he prayed, Seamus could not help examining the artwork of his first church in America. The altar was triple arched, like the three-leafed shamrock of Saint Patrick. Above the altar there were paintings. One showed Christ by the lake of Gennesaret exhorting His first apostles, Peter, Andrew, James, and John, to discard their nets and become fishers of men. How strange it was, Seamus thought, that he had used that analogy when he had first gotten off of the ship. It was uncanny, too, that the church he found would be named for his own patron saint. And, there was a ship in another painting above the altar quite similar to the one from which he had lately disembarked. He supposed it was not strange that such a nautical and piscatory images would be used here so close to the harbor. But, the last thing he wanted to look at was a ship! He had seen enough of ropes, chains, sea chests, sails, ship's wheels, blocks and tackles, shrouds, and masts during his passage. He was even sick of the smell of the sea now that he saw how it could swallow the dead so much faster than could the land. Seamus offered a second decade of the rosary for his shipmates who made it safely and for young Sarsfield who had not.

The steady scraping of the straw from the cleaning lady's broom across the marble floor had come closer to him. She must have been working her way to the front of the church. Seamus prayed one more decade of the rosary for his future in this new country and the three wishes he had just made:

1. Some useful work to take up
2. A place to call my own
3. A bride to share it with

When he finished, he started to get to his feet, stretching and letting escape from his mouth an aspiration he had learned in Connemara:

"*Gabhaigí buíochas le Dia na bhflaitheas!*"

The strawbroom scraping stopped right behind him.

"*An bhfuil Gaeilge agat?*" the cleaning lady whispered.

"*Tá, cúpla focal.*"

The cleaning lady had a kerchief on her head like the women praying and there was reddish hair peeking out from under it. Her face was wrinkled especially around the eyes and Seamus noticed a black wart on her chin. A friendly light shone in her eyes.

She looked at Seamus's portmanteau and asked, "Are you just landed?"

"This is the first place I've stopped."

"Come with me to the back of the church."

Seamus picked up his portmanteau and stick and followed the lady up the center aisle. She was short and wobbled back and forth in her frayed dress and worn jumper. She stopped by the holy water.

"Where are you from?" she asked.

"The County Mayo. "

"That's where I am from – from Killala! How about yourself?"

"Ballina," Seamus said.

"What's your name?"

"My name is James … James Logan."

"I'm Jane McElroy."

"Very pleased to meet you."

"And you're just after landing?"

"Just arrived today."

"Have you a place to stay?"

"No, I have a friend in the construction trade I mean to contact …"

"Well, you can stay at my place. I run a boarding house just 'round the corner. C'mere 'til I show you where it is."

She led him through the vestibule and started to open the door until he put his hand above her head and opened it for her. Seamus liked Jane immediately.

"You just go around that corner to the right. You'll see a sign for McElroy's Boarding House. It's not Buckingham Palace but sure it's clean and respectable and I know you could use a rest after your long journey."

"Indeed I could, and I'm glad my pilgrimage to the New World has brought me here to your kindness and hospitality."

He tipped his cap to her and started on his way.

"My husband knows where men can get work, if they are not afraid of it."

"I'm never been afraid of hard work, nor of anything else in this world."

"Save the brave words," Jane said with a smile. "For when you know what you're gettin' into."

…

Carrying his guitar, amp, and book bag, Paul Logan reached the top of the staircase of the Campion Student Center at Saint Joseph's University and went right to the stage. He checked in with the bespectacled, dumpy-looking brunette with the clipboard. Paul was determined that every detail for his performance at the Student Coffee House be just right. The settings on his amplifier were adjusted precisely. He had dreamed about all of this in his room at home, and practiced everything. It was time to show his new school and its students — these complacent alligator-shirt wearing nimrods — his electric music and poetry, even if they didn't understand, as his parents certainly didn't. It was time to bring back color and rebelliousness — wasn't it? To revive the spirits of these deadened people! He had imagined his performance would be bold, dramatic, and better than all the others.

Paul placed his amplifier and his electric guitar on the stage in front of the microphone stand. He plugged the amp into the power strip, as the clipboard girl had instructed. Making sure the red light of the amplifier was not lit and that the power switch was depressed toward "OFF" — it would have been horrible to cause screeching feedback and make everyone put their hands over their ears — he inserted one end of the cord into the amplifier and the other into his guitar. Turning the guitar down low, Paul switched the amp on. He strummed a chord or two; it sounded okay. He withdrew a guitar tuner from the compartment beneath the red plush interior of his guitar case. He had tuned the strings at home. Still, he gave them a quick check.

He needed a beer. But there was one thing to do first.

Paul took his book bag into a men's room stall. He took off his winter coat and polo shirt and removed from his bag his multi-colored dashiki. It was mostly blue and yellow with a kaleidoscope of white, red, black, and orange. He didn't know what the significance of the dashiki was. To Paul, it looked Indian but occasionally he'd seen black people walking around Philadelphia in them: it might have been African. Around its neck and sleeves were colorful patterns within patterns. Did they have some kind of meaning that Paul didn't know about? Maybe they were like the decorative designs in the *Book of Kells*, a bunch of craziness with animals and snakes and disembodied heads but when you stepped back, it all added up to a Greek letter or two. But, there was nothing representational in the design — just colors and shapes. It was like a mosaic, or maybe like Somerset Maugham's Persian rug, an arabesque pattern beautiful but meaningless. He lifted it over his head. As he got his arms in the sleeves, some dude banged through the loud unsteady door. It was time to get out of there. He put his winter coat over the dashiki and pulled it up so that it could not be seen.

Paul took a seat close to the stage. He wanted to be near the action. He removed a can of Old Milwaukee from his bag, pulled off its poptop, and took a slug. He dug the recent edition of the *Crimson and Gray* literary magazine from his book bag and made sure the *Daily News* scrap was still marking his poem. He put the beer and the literary magazine down on the table and stood. Students were entering, chatting, deciding where to sit. Trying to appear casual, he removed his winter coat to reveal the many-hued dashiki, which unfurled to his thighs, and sat back down.

Someone groaned. He pretended not to notice. It came from somewhere in the back of the room, he thought. Paul continued to go about his business. He looked over his published poem and reviewed the lyrics to his songs. His ears and cheeks grew hot.

In his daydreams, Paul had imagined walking boldly and colorfully onto the stage to dazzle the audience with something they had never expected nor seen. But now he felt foolish. Here he sat in the front of everyone wearing a flimsy dashiki in the middle of winter. And he didn't even know what country the motley thing was from. He looked up at the familiar but blank faces. He felt like a silly ant in one of their labs, the only myrmidon of many colors crawling through the farm's tunnels and around its hill.

As he took another gulp of his beer, Paul glanced back to see the place where the sound of disapproval might have come from. He saw some of the fraternity guys sitting way in the back. Could it have come from them — the guys who had recently initiated him into their brotherhood? He doubted it. His own brothers in the fraternity turning against him just because of a colorful shirt? They liked their old-fashioned rock 'n' roll, blues, and rockabilly. But he didn't think they would be so close-minded about clothes, especially since they talked about the 60s so much.

The clipboard girl stepped up to the microphone and introduced the first act, a singer named Alice something.

An attractive but heavy-set brunette strapped on her acoustic guitar and hustled up to the mic. She strummed a few times and spoke softly. Paul didn't pay much attention. Before his performance, all the other acts were a tiresome blur. The girl sang a version of Joni Mitchell's "Both Sides Now" in a lovely, soprano voice. It was very good and the crowd enjoyed it. She could certainly sing better than Paul. But the originality of his performance would make everyone forget her. Slowing her tempo as she neared her conclusion, she added a trill to the last line, which was quite effective. Paul applauded.

He went over how he would introduce his songs.

— This is a song I wrote about a girl I hung out with one night drinking beer in a park. I really liked her. She was a beautiful blonde with brown eyes and a lot of spirit, he could hear himself saying. A few months later, I found out that she had tried to kill herself. Don't worry. She has recovered, and, from what I hear, moved out to California. This is called "I Understand You" and it's dedicated to Stephanie.

After Alice left the stage, the mistress of ceremonies introduced another acoustic guitar player. He had a pimply face and curly head and was called Steve somebody. Steve sat down, adjusted the microphone, and began to play. His skill was more advanced than Paul's; he switched easily and cleanly from open chords to barre chords and back. But the song he sang was another cover, Bob Dylan's "I Shall Be Released." Paul's would all be originals. Steve did play an original song next, a folkie-sounding number about nuclear weapons and how war is tough on the poor.

— How insightful, thought Paul.

Paul was introduced and took the stage. The fraternity brothers in the back applauded and hooted and hollered. The dashiki caused self-consciousness to wash over him again. His vision of conquering this Coffee House appeared wild and silly.

— Here comes the big dreamer! Paul muttered.

How could he have thought that this was a good idea, that these Ronald-Reagan Hawk-Hill people would appreciate his strange clothes and act? But, there was no going back now. The guitar strap went over his head and he stepped up to the mic.

He rushed through his introduction to "I Understand You," forgetting to say that the girl had recovered and moved to California.

He started strumming and the sound rolled over him like a wave down the shore. He saw all of the faces looking up at him, curious, interested, at least. He started singing the words of the song, "You might not understand me/But I understand you." But, he couldn't hear himself. What was happening? He glanced behind him at the electrical cords and the pile of amps. He kept singing. There was really nothing he could do.

chapped your behind

— See? God punished you, Mom would say.

He persevered to the concluding chord.

There was some applause but not what he expected. Maybe the audience was able to hear and understand the words, but the vocal must have sounded like shit.

He moved on to his second song, "Childhood." Slow and mysterious, it had weird ringing ninth chords played one by one, and Paul was able to his voice between them. But it sounded strange, like hearing your voice on a tape recorder: that's not me. When he reached the chorus's more spirited strumming, the vocal disappeared again.

It was hard to tell what people were making of his little act. Wake the dead, indeed! Still cadaverous after all these years.

And just to make sure everyone remained shrouded in mortality, Paul stopped strumming for the centerpiece of the song, the poem recitation. He picked up the recent edition of the *Crimson and Gray* and read the poem from it. Someone definitely groaned then. This time it was clear that it had come from way in the back — from one of his "brotherhood, scholarship, and charity" buddies.

Well, they were just betraying their ignorance.

His parents were against him — and had tried to prevent his bringing the guitar and amp to school. His own fraternity brothers were kicking him to the curb. But he didn't care. He would be the outcast on stage, the misfit, the rejected one.

When he finished there was some decent applause and some smiles from the crowd. After he came down from the stage, one guy shook his hand and said, "Good job." Another guy came up and said he liked the way he had worked in the poem from the literary magazine. So, at least there was some appreciation for what he had done. But nothing like what he had dreamed.

The last act to take to the stage was a tall skinny guy with curly blonde hair. He looked like an 80s version of Peter Frampton, but more bohemian. As Paul put his guitar and literary magazine down and popped open a beer, the skinny guy and his short friend mounted the stage and sang with impressive harmonies.

The audience cheered and applauded in the middle of the songs. Paul couldn't understand it. Sure, they sounded a little like Crosby, Stills, and Nash but there was nothing groundbreaking about their act. He had given the crowd moving songs about suicide attempts and the end of childhood. Yet, they had hardly paid attention.

The duo then went into a familiar song about a house with two cats in the yard. It sounded like something written for a commercial. Now the crowd began to sing along.

Paul turned around and glared at the mob behind him. What was happening? This trite stuff — admittedly well executed, but, come on! — this treacle is what people admired?! At the Jesuit university of the fourth largest city in the United States?!

Paul had an anxious feeling in his stomach, like he had just asked a girl out and been rejected. He didn't mind that people didn't like his dashiki or Morrisonian poetry recitations, but this whole-hearted embrace of music that was so mediocre, that was nothing but simply ... pretty ... made him sick to his stomach. He seethed. Bitterness oozed into his throat and mouth. He wanted to lash out at all of them. They were all against him. They had all gotten together to ruin his dreams, to crush his faith and his hope. Paul wanted to grab his guitar and fill the whole student lounge with feedback. He wanted to storm out. But he had to wait until his fellow artists finished. He suffered the loud applause, the "Yeahs!" and "Woohoos!", glaring at the girls' jumping and jiggling.

Then he realized the worst part of it all. *She* hadn't come. The girl he liked at the time and wanted to impress.

And who was *she*? What was her name? Kathy? Maggie? Mary? He couldn't remember.

...

After they knocked off work, the lads, as usual, headed straight from the building site to Boyle's at 8th and Washington to drink mugs of foamy lager. Lined along the long bar stood an array of foremen, bricklayers, stone masons, laborers, and a few apprentices. It was only those in the building trade in the bar at this time of the day. They were all Irish, too, and the lilt of their accents came as a relief to Seamus's ears. You were starting to hear more Italian than anything else on the streets of Moyamensing these days.

Admiring the afternoon sun streaming in through the high streaked windows, Seamus felt happy that he had listened to Dennis and come to Philadelphia. He could throw up the 16-by-31-foot brick houses so popular here when he was drunk or hungover or asleep. And, with all of the Irish muscle around —the power that was transforming the landscape more than any other — they could fill the Delaware Valley with rows and rows of houses. And, they were sold as quickly as the muscle could build them: no land needed to be bought, only rented with long leases at low prices. "Ground rent," they called it. A bricklayer Seamus worked with just bought one for $300. Unlike land-famished Manhattan, the City of Philadelphia had 130 square miles (rather than 22) within its limits. People who had lost their homes in the Old World could find a home here. And Seamus could provide it for them.

Sometimes as he carried his hod up the ladder, he thought of the caved-in thatches and the empty windows seeming to cry out in horror over what had happened to their inhabitants … those abandoned villages he had seen in Mayo and Connemara. He thought that all of those poor souls who had lost their homes could have new homes here of solid brick from which no Bloodyback could evict them.

"When are you going to walk down the aisle for me, Mary? You know that I love you."

Boyle's daughter, Mary, a buxom, rosy-cheeked girl with a dimple in her chin was the only woman who ever came into the bar. She would load trays of food into the dumbwaiter behind the counter, hoist them to the upstairs diners, and hurry out again. The lads liked to tease her. But Mary gave as good as she got.

"Mary, when will you marry me?"

"Soon's I get your wife's permission, I'll get measured for the dress."

Seamus liked the young lass, too. He enjoyed her quick wit so much that he wasn't even troubled by her given name. That all felt like ages ago, anyway. And, sure there were so many lasses named Mary he could hardly get his feathers ruffled each time he encountered one.

But what also helped the memory of his heartbreak fade was his interest in a new girl. She was named, "Nora McLaughlin" and she came from nowhere near Mayo. She hailed from all the way down in Cork.

"You wouldn't be sparkin' Mary, now — would you James?" said Dennis. "Your heart belongs to Nora now, I'd say."

"His eyes only see one woman, so they do."

"Takes no notice of Mary atall."

Seamus had met Nora at one of the dances in the basement under Saint Paul's, the brick church over at 10th and Christian. They had danced a few numbers and chatted over punch on the sidelines. It had surprised Seamus how easy it was. The conversation was all flow and no ebb. He thought her an extraordinary girl. She had wit and beauty and was nobody's fool. She made it clear that she was well able to look after herself.

Seamus and Nora met at the same dance a week later. Before long, they were meeting for dinner at one of the new Italian restaurants in the neighborhood. Of course, people began to talk. It was all fun for Seamus, even the needling. He had never been part of an item like this, never part of a romance that could be discussed openly.

"This is my round, gents," he said, and slapped some coins on the counter. "Boyle, let's have a few more mugs of beer!"

"That Nora must be a handful, though, James," Dennis said. "I've got to hand it to you."

"She's quite independent. A strong-willed woman if there ever was one. But I don't mind. It's a bit challenging to deal with her at times but I admire her spunk."

"But a lifetime of challenges? I don't know. Is that what you want?"

"A lifetime —is it?! Sure, I've only known the lass a couple of weeks. Who's talking about a lifetime?!"

"A lass like that won't wait long. She'd have no patience for a man's dithering. She's the type who knows what she wants and is ready to take the next step, like."

"Well, so am I, Dennis. Seamus Logan keeps moving forward. I came from Ireland to New York, and thanks to you, I found greener pastures here in Philadelphia. I didn't dither. I packed my portmanteau and bought myself a train ticket."

"But not before you punched yer man in the face!"

"True," Seamus laughed and swallowed half a mug of beer. "That is true, indeed. So, … you see what I mean. Nora's not the only one. When I know what to do, I take quick action. Just ask the foreman with the broken nose."

Seamus saw Nora to the dance at Saint Paul's again that Saturday. They had the usual lovely time but Dennis's words reverberated in Seamus's head whenever Nora had a distracted look on her face or wasn't enjoying herself. She did act a little more stand-offish than usual. She didn't laugh as much at his jokes. Or was it just his imagination? She did say she was tired. She had had a long week. Maybe that was all it was. But it was so hard to know. He wished women came with a manual.

There was one moment when he came out of the jacks to find her laughing at a crack made by some lad by the punch bowl. Nora returned to conversation with Seamus straightaway but she had appeared slightly flustered when Seamus returned. Had he caught her at something? Or was she just enjoying an amusing remark? She did like a good laugh. Her sense of humor was one of the traits he liked best about her.

What was that lad's name anyway?

Someone told him it was Shannon. Danny Shannon.

The following Wednesday as Seamus was making his way to Nora's boarding house on Carpenter Street, he spotted Shannon coming the other way. Seamus nodded to ol' Danny Boy, but there was no warmth in his greeting.

What was he doing on Nora's street?

That night Nora even mentioned Shannon's name a couple of times. She repeated this funny remark that he had made and that one. Seamus frowned when he heard the name but she continued with her story nonetheless.

Was she interested in this other fellow? Could she be thinking of Shannon instead of Seamus?

At the end of the evening, Nora kissed Seamus warmly on the dark South Philadelphia street. Seamus felt that he really did love her. She was clever, strong, fun to be with, and self-reliant. She would not remain on the market for long. Nor was she one to wait patiently for an offer. Nora would accept the man who would take bold action, not some timid fellow. She would be a true and worthy partner for Seamus and all of his plans to rise in the building business. He would not be a bricklayer all of his life. Seamus felt that Nora sensed this. Nora, likewise, would not remain a domestic forever. No, she was not made for running of the homes of others. She was made to run her own. And Seamus would provide it for her.

On Monday after knocking off work at the building site, Seamus walked up 8th Street to Walnut, where he crossed the threshold of the first jeweler he found.

…

Leaving Wanamaker's, Paul wanted to be first out the door behind his mother but somehow Kitty sneaked in front of him. She was always ruining things. She had a knack for messing up his plans without even knowing what they were.

They were on the way to his favorite part of the Christmas visit to Center City —Lit Brothers Enchanted Colonial Village. Paul liked the Wanamaker's Light Show a lot. He had seen it every year for as long as he could remember. It was a tradition for him — and for his family — and he always looked forward to it. But the Light Show had really become Kitty's favorite. She was at the age at which she could really enjoy it.

Paul noticed a movie theatre across the street but it didn't look like a nice one. There were no movie posters that Paul could see, only blurry pictures behind glass of ladies, one with blonde hair, one with brown, one Chinese …

Paul's dad bopped him on the shoulder.

— This is Market Street, Paul, he said. Did you know that the streets on Center City were named after trees — Chestnut, Walnut, Spruce, Pine …?

— Like a Christmas tree! said Kitty, though Dad wasn't talking to her. She was always trying to butt in, ever since she first came home from the hospital, screaming like a banshee and stinking up the car with her dirty diaper.

— And you know who gave them that name?

— Who?

— Look behind you! And way up in the air. See the statue way up on top? That's William Penn. He named all the streets, the City of Philadelphia, and even this state — Pennsylvania. Get it? Penn-sylvania.

— He must have liked trees.

— I think he did. He wanted a nice city for the people — with lots of grass and trees and fresh air.

— What happened? wondered Kitty.

— Not everything works out the way you plan it, sweetheart, their father chuckled.

A couple of different Santa Clauses rang their bells on Market Street, collecting money for the Salvation Army. Janey pointed them out and told the kids that Santa's helpers were in Philadelphia to collect money for the poor. Paul imagined that the money fell into a hole at the bottom of the bucket and through a tube to underground elves ready to deliver it to people in need. None of those Santas was the real one. He must have been busy in the North Pole. But he might be around — seeing you when you are sleeping, knowing when you are bad and good.

A blind man passed them tapping his cane on the sidewalk. Tap tap tap tap.

Paul wondered if he would get any enjoyment from the light show. You needed eyes for most of it. But he might like the music.

As they crossed 12th Street, his mom pointed down the block.

— There's St. John the Evangelist Church, where Daddy goes to mass sometimes.

— When he can't make it to Saint Colman's? Paul asked.

— Exactly.

Squeezed into a narrow city street, it looked different from their church. And, there was no schoolyard.

— Did you go there, too, Mommy?

— Yes, I did, she answered and she kept staring at it and staring at it. A long time ago.

— You used to work at Daddy's office, too — right?

— That's right. Mommy worked there before she got married.

— You were a secretary like those other ladies.

— That's right.

— Now you take care of us.

— Yes, I got a promotion!

Janey leaned on James's shoulder and they both smiled.

At 11th Street, there was a trolley running on tracks in a cobblestoned street. The trolley was green with a white roof and it rang a bell to let people know it was coming. It made a strange humming noise just before it started moving. There was a wire sticking up like Alfafa's hair from its roof. It was attached to another electric wire above it and gave off cool sparks!

Paul thought if some kid tied his old sneakers together and threw them up on that wire, the sparks would set the sneakers on fire. And the whole street would smell like stinky feet!

Kitty kept stopping in front of the store windows to look at the lights, the little Christmas trees, the mechanical elves, and the moving Santas.

— C'mon, Kitty, Paul heard his mother saying again and again. Stay with us.

But Paul never looked back.

— Did you ever ride the trolley, Dad?

— Yeah, I used to. There aren't as many as there used to be. Everything's gettin' modern these days. Y'know, sometimes my friends and I used to jump on the back and get a free ride.

— James! his wife exclaimed. Don't teach him that!

— It was a long time ago. It was a different world. When people used to leave their doors unlocked. Besides, it was a long way to get to Shibe Park to see the Phillies.

They saw some horses and buggies clopping down the streets, the heavier, faster cars acting like bullies trying to get around them.

Kitty held her nose.

— Ohh! Smelly!

Paul thought it was cool to think about going back to the days of riding horses, and fighting with swords.

They had to stop at a red light to let cars go by.

— There's Lit's! his mom exclaimed, pointing to a large Victorian structure that stretched its columns and archways the length of a whole city block. Not much farther!

— Where the Enchanted Village is! cried Paul.

— That's right, said James. Up on the second floor.

— Did Lit's used to be a castle? Paul asked.

— No, it's always been a department store, his dad said. Lit's is made up of 33 buildings.

— All put together into one store?!

— How did they do it?

— I don't know. It was done a long time ago by some very smart men.

— The people back then were smart — weren't they?

— Yes, they were, Paul. Yes, they were.

— Like your granddad — and his dad, added Mom.

Paul looked around, counting parts that could have been different buildings.

— C'mon, hon', Janey said. It's time to go in.

They took the escalator up to the Enchanted Colonial Village. The lines of dressy parents and children serpentined through white fences — stopping in front of the displays of near-life-sized mannequins with motors inside them. The mannequins repeated the same movements over and over. That was so everyone would see the same thing no matter when they came. And there were so many things to see. It was like a whole town full of people and their jobs, but from a long time ago. Mechanical mannequins fixed watches, sewed pants, carved meat, sold pets, made glass by blowing through a tube, and ate a Christmas dinner at a long, crowded table while women and girls prepared more food in the kitchen. The Logan family saw a cobbler making shoes and Kitty jumped up and down at the sight of the Wig Maker's Shop. The little school room had a gentle-looking teacher with bifocals on her nose and old desks and ink wells. It was so different from Saint Colman's! But, still school.

It was funny to watch the mannequins. It was like someone had put a spell on them to be stuck forever in one place, performing one task. Kitty giggled at her father's imitation of the motions of the candlemaker and the blank expression on his tilted face.

Paul imagined the blacksmith putting down his hammer, lifting his feet up from where they were fastened to the floor, and walking past the open-mouthed families into the shopping areas of Lit Brothers' Department Store. How shocked he would be to see all the modern gadgets for sale:

electric razors, curling irons, heated plastic hair curlers for the ladies, little clocks people can wear on their wrists, and toys that could zoom or walk on their own! He would hear the announcements over the loudspeaker and not know where the voice was coming from. A staircase moving by itself? Magic!

— Lordy! he might say, like Tom Sawyer.

But they might not have said that in colonial days.

And then if he went out into the street he wouldn't believe how much has changed. He'd be scared by all the cars on Market Street. Cars?! What are cars? He wouldn't even know what to call them. To him they would be dangerous creatures with bright eyes and round black feet.

The street names would be familiar — Market, Chestnut, Walnut and the ones with numbers 15th, 16th, 17th. But everything else would be so different — the tall buildings and the street lights and the traffic lights. The El roaring under the sidewalk? He might think it's a monster and then duck into the doorway of a store with TVs in the window. People inside a box moving and talking, all in black and white? Even black-and-white furniture and black-and-white houses? What is this witchcraft? The horses and buggies would be familiar to him and might calm him down. Phew! At least, he could have some work he knew how to do — making horseshoes!

The whole display was supposed to be like the Olde City of Philadelphia. Paul's dad said that it was like history come to life — the streets and shops and people all back to life the way they were in olden times.

Like Frosty? Like the nutcracker? What if you could really make the past come back to life, instead of just pretending?

A group of chubby, rosy-cheeked men in the Village Tavern held metal mugs and pantomimed singing a song. Paul's father pretended to toast with them.

— Hey, cheers! God rest ye, merry gentleman! Dad cried to the mannequins.

— Hey, Dad, are these robots? Paul asked.

— I guess you might call them that, Paul. They can move around like people. But, they can't go get your dinner for you like on *The Jetsons*. It's amazing what they can do nowadays, though — huh?

— Yeah, it's so cool. I wonder when people will be able to make real robots.

— Who knows? You never know what they will come out with next.

Janey asked the kids what they thought. Would they like to eat that bread? Skate on that pond? Watch the doggies box and wrestle in the pet shop? Paul nodded his head but was too full of his own imaginings to have much to say. Kitty said "no" to most of the things, though she might eat some cake if the bakery made it.

Paul looked up from his reverie to see his mother bent down and murmuring something about "Santa" and "a lot of trouble" to Kitty who stared straight ahead at the butcher shop and pouted. The expression on her face was so different from what it had been during the light show, when the Sugar Plum Fairies were dancing and Rudolph's red nose was going blink blink blink … or when she called the escalator handrails fat snakes on their way up eight flights to the Wanamaker's toy department … or when she pointed down at the dolls, the Barbies, and the games through the metal-mesh window in the dented grey monorail depending from the ceiling … that it made him feel sad.

Kitty was his sister. And she was not having fun. He liked the other Kitty better, the Kitty with the happy face who Mom and Dad asked Paul to take care of on the monorail, the joyful Kitty, who had been so excited to look down from the ROCKET EXPRESS car at the sprawling electric-train layout and find Mom and Dad shopping.

Kitty was small. She liked to wear mittens. And sometimes she got leaves and twigs stuck in her wavy hair or on the back of her coat. She was so little. And she was his sister. He remembered her all the way back to when she was a baby and she used to cry when she was supposed to be sleeping. She was Kitty. She was his little sister. And she was cute. And … and he … If anyone ever did anything to harm a hair on her head, he'd be held for murder.

The Logans stopped in front of some murals of real Philadelphia landmarks.

— That building is called Christ Church, Paul's dad said.

Pointing to a second one, he asked:

— Do you know what *that* building is called?

Paul knew the answer but he said nothing to his father. Instead, he stuck his nose into Kitty's wavy hair and whispered.

— Independence Hall! she exclaimed.

— Very good, Kitty! his dad said, looking at both of his children. That's very good.

…

Mrs. Daly sent a boy to Father Sarsfield Logan's classroom with a Palmer-method message stating that Rector O'Keefe wanted to see him in his office.

Opening the door to the Rector O'Keefe's office, Sarsfield felt the familiar closeness of the room, an atmosphere which he frankly had never liked. If he spent as much time in it as the rector, he would always be covered in sweat. Sarsfield smelled the same pipe smoke that always hung in the air and saw the same shelves packed so neatly that you might wonder if the books were ever read. The rector sat behind his desk as usual in his wing-backed chair. It was all so familiar and yet Sarsfield's instinct told him something was different. He entered the room with a sense of trepidation.

Then he saw why.

Seated in a chair to Sarsfield's right was a young man in blacks and a Roman collar. Was this a visitor? Was he the new priest they had been expecting?

"There you are, Sarsfield," the elder Jesuit called. "Come on in!"

"Thank you, Frank."

"Sarsfield, there's someone I would like you to meet. This is Father Stanley Primrose. He's come to join our community and our faculty. Father Primrose, I'd like you to meet Father Sarsfield Logan, one of the senior members of our faculty and indeed one of its leaders."

"A pleasure to meet you, Father Primrose."

"Nice to meet you, Father Logan."

"Siddown, Sarsfield, I think you and Father Primrose will find that you have a lot in common."

Father Primrose had fair skin and a full head of reddish hair, neatly parted on the side. But what kind of name was, "Primrose"? It didn't sound like a Catholic name. "Stanley Primrose?" It conjured the image of an old fossil wearing a waistcoat, taking high tea, and making condescending remarks about Papists.

"Welcome to Xavier, Father Primrose. Where're you from?"

"Thank you, Father. I'm from Poughkeepsie. About 50 miles north of here."

"Well, that's the first thing we have in common. I come from outside of New York City as well — from Philadelphia."

"Haha, here's the second thing. I did my theology at Saint Joseph's College."

"Did you really? How 'bout that? I graduated from Saint Joseph's Prep before entering the order."

"I used to eat lunch with Brother Clancy who had just transferred from the Prep."

"Oh yeah? Brother Clancy? How is he?"

"He's great. Gettin' a little older but still full of energy."

"That's not surprising but it's still good to hear … Good to hear ..."

"I knew you two would have a lot to talk about," Rector O'Keefe cried.

He appeared very happy to see that the two priests were hitting it off.

O'Keefe dropped a book of matches and in a single motion Primrose bent over and swept them it up. The motion would have caused Sarsfield a couple of adjustments in his seat, a few pains in his arm and back, and several grunts.

Sarsfield's sense of foreboding which had been submerged for a few minutes under the friendliness of his new community member began to rise to the surface again. What was the import of this meeting? Why was it necessary for Sarsfield to be introduced to Primrose alone?

Primrose had a nice way about him and they truly did have some things in common. But he looked more like one of the students than a faculty member. His cheeks and eyes had no wrinkles and he lacked Sarsfield's paunch. Primrose's eyes shone with enthusiasm; it was clear the cleric was eager to take on his new assignment. But Sarsfield could not help feeling alienated from Primrose. He resented his slim figure. And, his hair that looked like his mother had combed it.

His mother must be very proud. His mother must be still alive.

The conversation had flagged.

"So, Father Primrose, what subject will you be teaching here?"

"Father Rector has asked me to teach French."

"French? Well, that is yet another thing we have in common."

A few Sundays later, Sarsfield departed from his bedroom window's view of rooftop water towers and brick-and-mortar walls, creaked down the stairs of the rectory, and proceeded across the street to the steep stone stairs of Saint Francis Xavier Church. Under the triple arches and behind the elegant columns stood Father Primrose still in his vestments from the previous mass. He was surrounded by a few ladies of the parish. Sarsfield chalked this up to Primrose's being new. For two weeks after that Father Logan told himself that Primrose's delicacy had brought out the maternal instinct of the ladies. But today it was clear that the crowd comprised both women and men — as well as girls and boys. Sarsfield could no longer deny it. In a short time, Father Primrose had become quite popular with the Xavier parishioners.

"Hi, Father Logan!"

Father Primrose gave him a gleaming white smile.

Father Logan nodded and shuffled into the vestibule of the church.

The students liked Father Primrose as well. Sarsfield had noticed this from the lad's first week on the faculty. The boys would call out to Primrose in French in the hallways and joke and laugh with him. Perhaps they, too, thought he looked more like a student than a teacher. Sarsfield assured himself that their enthusiasm would wane as the school year wore on and the new teacher's novelty wore off.

As football season turned into basketball, Sarsfield started spying Primrose at games. His first-year French students would urge Primrose to sit with them. Once, even some of Sarsfield's boys waved Primrose over to join them in their section of the bleachers. Xavier won that night over Fordham Prep but Sarsfield did not relish the victory. His hips and knees hurt worse than ever as he climbed the stairs to his room.

Sarsfield took solace in his classes and tried not to think much about the new priest and his popularity. But Primrose would spring into his room when Sarsfield, after completing another tired lesson, was still packing up his things. His big smile, warm greeting, and boundless *joi de vivre* soured Sarsfield's stomach. He knew the rector would want Primrose to teach Sarsfield's favorite class: French Literature. *The Romance of the Rose*. *Candide*. It was as inevitable as all else approaching the old Jesuit.

And one day it happened.

Mrs. Daly sent a boy to Sarsfield's classroom with a Palmer-method message stating that Rector O'Keefe wanted to see him in his office.

...

Only a quarter of Paul's Guinness remained in his glass. Asian Elvira raised her eyebrows at him and Paul nodded.

oh she's good

— So, you work at the restaurant, too? she asked Laura.

— No, I'm a bartender.

— Oh yeah? Where?

— At the Orange Crush near Wall Street.

— That's a rock place — right? I know some guys who have played there.

Laura introduced herself.

The bartender replied:

— My name is Verve.

— That's a lot to live up to, cracked Laura.

Nodding, Paul walked away to the men's room, leaving behind their girl chatter, high-pitched, soft, and free-flowing. On a splintering wooden sign between the bathroom doors were the words:

Lasciate ogni speranza, voi ch'intrate.
Abandon all hope, ye who enter here.

Paul stepped inside the tiny brick-and-mortar room. In front of him was a wooden shelf where guys could put their beers. They knew what they were doing when they built this john. Now if they would only fix this door. He washed his hands in the unsteady sink and returned to the bar.

On a column holding up the tin ceiling hung a black-and-white still, labeled in white capital letters: FELLINI - LA DOLCE VITA. It showed Marcello's leading Sylvia out of the dormant *Fontana di Trevi* by the hand, a Triton's and hippocamp's looking surprised to see them go, and Sylvia's dawdling Orpheus-gaze.

Above Cagney was John Wayne.

— That's a cool tattoo, he heard Laura say. What does it mean?

— "May the roar of the beasts of prey," Verve recited as she pointed to the characters on her arm, "become the mantra of compassion."

— Is that Hindi? Paul asked.

— Tibetan, Verve replied, from the *Tibetan Book of the Dead*.

— Wow! That's cool, Paul said.

— I've thought about getting a tattoo lots of times, Laura added, but I was never sure what to get or where to put it. I was thinking maybe like something small …

As she drifted into tattoo talk with Verve, Paul stared at the back of Laura's head. How can the back of a head be attractive? And yet there it was. Her full arm elbowed the bar, her fingertips on the pint glass. He was glad she was not tattooed. She had hung her sweatjacket on the back of a stool. Paul's eyes traced the silhouette of her denim hip and side, the small of her back swathed in grey cotton cresting up to her shoulder blade.

lauras doubleprotruding tiedye heart radiating energy electrifying your hearts humming burning spring awakening april showeres bringing flowres of sir topaz last time was with kathy but different when it works happens to two of you this one has the absence ache the allday quickbeat in the heart carmen really the last time nights on the rooftop tar soft under your feet green lights of the george washington bridge winking at you more planes waiting in line to land at laguardia than stars in the sky parsing your every philomenas word and hers first thought in the morning last lust at night

But this Orange Crush is just as powerful. Laura could stand in the rain across the street by the mural of a tomato in a chef's hat or she could wade in the fountain in Washington Square with the arch looming over her and Garibaldi eyeballing her sideways, working hard to unsheathe something …

LAURA

Paolo! Come here!

PAUL abandons his full pint of Guinness.

                    Verve

      That was rude of you, Paul.

                    Paul

      I don't know what could've come over me.

                    Verve:

      Lack of discipline.

                    Paul

      Possibly.

Rain had begun to fall again. His feet were still wet from a puddle he had stepped in somewhere along the way, probably on little Mosco Street.

Verve held an ice-filled pint glass in front of her flat abdomen and the nozzle of an upturned vodka bottle in front of her face. The clear liquor fell right at the cleavage of her breasts as they bulged brown against the unhappy constraints of her silver top.

— So, Paul, Vinny called. What do you do?

— I'm a technical writer … for Susskind Software.

Vinny knitted his salt-and-pepper brows.

— Paul says he has a real job in an office but I think he's makin' it all up.

Paul smiled. She had made this joke before. This time he replied:

— I am.

— Paul's a poet, too, and a drummer, said Laura. He writes songs and poetry.

— How about yourself? Paul asked.

— Me? responded Vinny. I show outta-towners to their tables in my grandfather's restaurant.

Paul and Laura laughed and took gulps from their pint glasses.

Verve was racing back and forth behind the bar, mumbling to herself. When she refilled the pints, she struck a casual-bored pose, her weight on her right foot, her hip thrust out, impatient for enough beer to fall from the tap.

Tino Martinez was being interviewed on TV.

— Opening day tomorrow, Paul offered.

— Yeah, Vinny said. Oakland As.

— They used to be the Philadelphia As. So I maybe I should root for them.

— You from Philly?

— Yeah, I grew up there. I live here now, though.

— Lived in this neighborhood my whole life, Vinny averred. Went to Old St. Pat's up the street. Born in Manhattan. Live in Manhattan. Prob'ly die in Manhattan.

up the street in 1844 one thousand nativists marched but philly native dagger john said if they touched a single church hed make new york a second moscow three thousand armed irishmen awaited them outside old saint pat's numbers is what they understand numbers is what they got

— We're lucky to have baseball. Y'know where my grandmother is from in Italy, you know what they do for fun? They roll cheese! I swear to God. *"La ruzzola del formaggio,"* they call it. They take a big cheese and roll it around town. They bet on it and everything. I'm not kiddin' ya.

— Sounds like road bowling in Ireland. They do the same thing but throwing a stone down a country road.

— Countries that don't have baseball, ya gotta feel sorry for 'em.

Verve perfumed past. The two men fell silent as she turned toward the old cash register and balanced herself on her high heels, straightening both pink legs. They could see the shelves of cheap liquor though the bottle-shaped space between Verve's thighs and buttocks. She pounded some keys, slipped cash into the drawer, and slammed it shut.

— Ever hear of Pontelandolfo's? Vinny asked. It's our family business. We got a good lunch special over there during the week. You oughta take her there, he recommended, thrusting his chin toward Laura. The *Penne Tricolore* in Arrabbiata sauce? Maybe a little *sausice*? Delicious!

— That's a good idea.

Vinny turned to watch as Verve flounced from behind the bar to the jukebox.

ecce homo puppy dog eyes pursuing her everywhere puppylike sniffing where she is where she was can put you off your feed fetching her coffee just a little milk for a small pat on the head maybe a mirror behind the bar maybe another sitting next to you

Verve inserted a couple of singles into the jukebox and punched in some numbers.

— This song's for Bobby, she shouted, pointing to an older man who looked nothing like a "Bobby." He was an egg-shaped guy with a big belly under a dark tie and white shirt with turned-up cuffs. His head was a smaller egg, bald with grey-flecked sideburns, dark-rimmed glasses, long chin, and a jowly mouth with a cynical expression.

His eyes trailing Verve back to her post, Vinny slapped Bobby in the back.

— Gimme a fuckin' break! is all the egg-shaped man said.

The song blasted from the jukebox. With a control she had behind the bar, Verve turned it up louder and dancewalked left and right. She was singing every word of the song and trying to get others to join in.

— Sing! she shouted to Laura and Paul and Charles. Come on! Sing, Vinny!

The request was impossible to resist. And, once she had the customers singing loud enough, she turned the sound off so that only the customers' voices could be heard. Then she turned the sound up again.

When the crowd got a little quieter, she shouted:

— Keep going! Keep going! Try to keep up with the record!

Verve adjusted the sound whenever she felt like it — for only a word, a line, a chorus, a verse — and the customers never knew when. She crouched down to sneak over to the control. She made faces. Her rope of black hair swung this way and that. She rose to her full height and crouched again. Once people started to catch on, Verve faked going for the control.

— She's goin' for it! Vinny shouted a few times. But, he was only right once.

It was hard to sing and laugh at the same time but Paul and Laura did the best they could. Charles was laughing and joining in on the chorus.

The crowd lost the song and caught up with it again but before long was doing pretty well at the game. It was easy to sing loud when the jukebox was blaring. It sounded funny to hear the crazy bar voices when the jukebox fell silent. The game was so simple and so hilarious that he wondered — with all the time he had spent in bars — how he had not seen it played before. The song came to an end, leaving in its wake the sounds of laughter and bated breath.

Charles's hand slapped the bar. He had caught himself falling asleep standing up.

— Better get your friend home, Vinny smiled. He's a little wobbly.

Charles suddenly lurched away from the bar and stumbled toward the door.

— Looks like he's goin' somewhere, Vinny said.

Laura polished off her Amstel on ice and put her sweatjacket back on. Seeing Laura heading for the door, Paul told Verve:

— That was hilarious!

He shook hands with Vinny and Bobby. As he raised his hand to waive to her, Verve leaned her shiny, silver tits on the bar and, grabbing his cheeks in her hands, kissed him "smack" on the mouth.

He was chuckling and his head was spinning as he made his way out onto the wet streets of Little Italy. Had she done that because she liked him or because she was putting him on? It was not the bartender he had hoped to kiss but it was something. And it was a good laugh. Oh, well. Freedom's just another word for nothin' left to lose.

Vinny's chin was nearly scraping the bar. But Verve just lifted her discus-thrower cup and took a petite sip of coffee. Mouth still open, Vinny's head tracked Paul as he hustled out under the portrait of Laurel and Hardy and chased Laura around the corner. Staring agape, Vinny watched Laura and Paul hunchback between parked cars and across the street. They loaded Charles into the back of a BMW, jumped in the front, and drove off toward Houston Street.

4. Pride & Humility

In the shadow of the toney oaks and maples of Philadelphia's Rittenhouse Square, Jimmy Logan escorted his wife, Mariellen, and mother, Nora, toward the entrance of the Catholic Philopatrian Literary Institute. The two Mrs. Logans chatted quietly but Jimmy remained silent, a yard behind them. The doorway was festooned with stone ornamentation and flanked by two Corinthian columns supporting a Romanesque arch. Above the arch a lion rampant guarded each side of an orb of iron grillwork. Quick-stepping in front of the two ladies, Jimmy opened the door and held it for them. Inside was a narrow hall with mosaics on the floor lit by a brilliant chandelier like a fecund bulb about to burst with myriad diamond seeds.

As the string quartet performed, the men — some in tuxedoes, others in finely-tailored suits, and still more in worn, dark suit jackets — circulated in the Grand Ballroom, drinking whiskey and beer. Jimmy thought the piece by Beethoven. Women made up a smaller portion of the crowd but Jimmy's eyes and ears were drawn toward them. How could he help it with all the finery they had on display, their hats veiling parts of their faces, their parasols, their loud heels, and their high-pitched laughter? A few children scampered about but they were given a short rein.

Jimmy got his mother and his wife some refreshments and a scotch for himself. The women fluttered off to join a chirping circle and Jimmy was content to let them go. It pleased him that they knew enough to keep their distance from him. They understood what it meant when he grew silent and withdrawn. For mother and wife knew very well that Jimmy liked to talk. It was not that Jimmy was not proud of his father or the company: quite the contrary. He would get into the spirit of the celebration soon enough. He just needed to let this cloud of anger and unsociability pass.

Jimmy drifted around admiring the gilded, marbled room. Several doors led from the grand ballroom, each with carved laurel leaves draped over its threshold and each with a pediment above it. A few men stopped him to offer their congratulations. He gave them a nod and a quick smile but very few words. He cast his eyes upward at the recessed ceiling of gold and white, like a constellation of suns now and then allowing a chandelier with candelabra to descend from it.

In the center of the far wall was a marble fireplace etched with grapes and grape leaves and a relief of tipsy-seeming cherubs drinking wine and pulling a stubborn horse who appeared to have had too much to drink himself. A cherubic satyr playing a tambourine brought up the rear. Jimmy made a study of it as he sipped his drink.

A young guy passed in front of the fireplace and greeted Jimmy, "Hello, Mr. Logan, and congratulations!"

Jimmy saluted the man but said only, "Thank you very much."

On each side of the fireplace was carved a Classical wine pitcher and a Bacchus head smiling below it. Jimmy observed the attendees' settling down into their seats for the ceremony and thought the relief a bit Dionysian for this restrained gathering.

At the podium before the rows of chairs with a center aisle, Dennis Ryan, Jimmy's father's vice president tried to tamp down the conversations around the room, especially the baritone murmuring back by the bar. Jimmy stayed on his feet, near his mother and his wife in the front row. Although he was an officer of the company and wore a tuxedo as the men on the dais did, Jimmy would keep his mother company while his father took his rightful place at center stage. As the room grew quieter, Jimmy still lingered, looking back at the fellows at the bar. The scotch and lovely surroundings had started to bring out his natural garrulity. But, that was his father up there on the dais, and family is family. He took his seat.

"Over a quarter century ago," Dennis began. "Our founder, James Logan, departed from his beloved Erin, the land it grieved him sore to leave behind, and came here to the City of Brotherly Love to make a new life for himself. True, he was not the first immigrant to sojourn in our Quaker City. Indeed, newcomers from Europe and Asia and Africa have lived here for generations. However, his was no ordinary arrival on our shores. For his arrival here, like that of Aeneas on the shores of Latium, was destiny. Yes, it was James Logan's fate to help transform this foal of a city to the expansive, sure-footed metropolis it is today. Mr. Logan has spent a quarter century erecting house upon brick house, row upon brick row, block upon brick block until his handiwork can be found from Moyamensing to Bridesburg, from East Falls to Port Richmond. And the homes he has built have not been for the princes of this world but for the ordinary people who only want to work and raise their families in decency and security. Indeed, the city of Philadelphia has more home owners than other cities of somewhat greater fame and notoriety, and as a result has greater health, fewer pitiable scenes of dire poverty, and greater stability than other cities in the Eastern Seaboard. It's for this reason, I'm proud to say that I was the very man who encouraged James to come here to Philadelphia out of those slums of New York's Lower East Side.

"Hear! Hear!" called Seamus, and the crowd burst into applause.

"There has been a great deal of hard honest work between that day and this, but allow me to point out something crucial — that the success of Logan Construction Company," continued Dennis. "Is due not only to the hard work of James Logan but to the sharpness of his business mind: his brains and circumspection! He has seen and avoided pitfalls that other men would have fallen into."

Applause filled the Grand Ballroom again.

"Not only has James Logan's construction benefitted the working man who lives in his homes but it has also been a boon to the men who built them. Because Mr. Logan has been such a friend and benefactor to his employees, the Logan Construction Company has been able to avoid the unfortunate scenes of violence and labor agitation that much of our city saw earlier this year. Our employees are the envy of the workers in the Delaware Valley!"

The men cheered and clapped, especially the rowdies back by the bar.

"Of course, James Logan's life has not been all business and profit. His work for the Roman Catholic Church, for the Faith he holds so dear, is well known. It is fitting to point out here in this building where the idea for a Catholic school system, one parallel to and yet more effective than the public system that had so poorly served the children of our coreligionists, was first discussed, that Seamus Logan has labored mightily to build schools in which Catholic children can be educated according to their Faith. He even says it was God, and not me, who told him to come to Philadelphia!

"I want to recognize James's beautiful wife, Nora, the true and only love of his life. We congratulate her as well. For it is well known that behind every great man, there stands a strong woman. And in this case a strong woman from Rebel Cork."

More cheers erupted from the rowdies.

"And before I bring the man himself up to the podium, I have one more remark to make. I want to commend his parents back in the Emerald Isle for the grand thing they did when they christened him James. For didn't William Penn himself, the founder of this great city and the Commonwealth of Pennsylvania —who, as it happens, also lived in Ireland before coming to the New World — keep beside him as a reliable comrade and loyal friend another man by the name of 'James Logan'? So what better man with what better name to come here and found a new enterprise that is today 25 years old?! Ladies and gentleman, I give you the founder and president of the Logan Construction Company, my friend, Mr. James Logan!"

Nodding to his left and right at his associates and pointing at Dennis and laughing about some inside joke, Seamus Logan made his way to the podium and waited for the hearty applause to die down.

"Twenty-five years — is it? Sure, it's hard to believe!"

The applause rose again and echoed through the ornate hall.

"As I look out at this great assembly of people," Seamus said. "Associates and friends and their families in this beautiful institution where I read as a young man, it is truly hard for me to believe that 25 years have passed and so much has occurred since the day I decided to go into business for myself as a contractor. I came here to the city of Philadelphia as a young man with a dream of owning my own business and it has no doubt come true. I left my home in the County of Mayo to seek opportunity in the New World ... I sailed away from the land of Ireland, the Old World, for which my heart still yearns ... the land of my beloved faithful people .... who taught me the Faith and what it means to put in a hard day's work, though for nowhere near the rewards we receive here ... the people for whose freedom we still dream ... as the colonists in this city dreamed of their freedom from tyranny ... *maise* from the same tyrant ... here in Philadelphia where a group of men in the July heat wrote and signed a document that changed the entire world. But that dream's day will come, as surely as our dreams have come true today."

Cheers and cries of, "hear, hear" burst from the back of the room.

"Nevertheless, at the Logan Construction Company, we are not dreamers. We are builders. And in a quarter century, what have we built? Let us reflect upon it. I believe that brick by brick and house by house we have not only built streets and neighborhoods and contributed to the growth of a great city, but also we have constructed a portrait — a portrait of teamwork, of a company that is really a family extended from the one at its nucleus. Ultimately, all of the bricks and mortar we have laid, the houses and schools we have built, and the churches we have assisted in erecting draw a portrait of ourselves. In my native County of Mayo (God help us!), the old folks have a saying in Gaelic, '*Molann an obair an fear* - The work praises the man.'

"Let us hope ... let us *pray* ... that our twenty-five years of labor have painted a portrait of us that is pleasing to Our Lord and which we can look upon with a sense of satisfaction and good conscience. Looking back at all of the trials through which we have passed and the successes we have earned and gazing out at the colleagues and friends and relations with whom I have worked, I attest that it as a beautiful portrait."

Some rake with too much free beer in him muttered, "And Mr. Logan saw all the things that he had made, and they were very good."

Jimmy looked around. There was no way to tell who it was.

As Seamus spoke, looking out at those assembled there, his face grew bright and cheerful. However, there were a few instances when, in the midst of this happiness, his face went blank. Seamus did not frown exactly, but his smile receded and he appeared to forget what he was about to say. These were mere momentary lapses, however, noticed only by the most attentive and sensitive. Each time his characteristic gift of the gab rescued him and he plunged back into his topic.

"And it is my profound hope and prayer that our next twenty-five years will be just as successful and transformative of this city, of those who work for us, and of those for whom we work as those we have seen. I have no reason to believe that the decades of the 1910s and those that follow should not see the same expansion as have occurred in our first decades.

"In this grand assemblage I am proud to see my beloved wife who has been a helpmate to me all of these years, and to see my son, his beautiful bride, and my younger daughters. My wife and I would have loved to have seen our eldest son, Revered Sarsfield Logan, S.J., at this celebration but we take great pride in our son's commitment to the Society of Jesus and his duties at St. Francis Xavier High School in New York. Indeed, if any parent can glow with more pride than Nora and I do over Sarsfield and our other children, I'd like to meet him.

"As much as I would have loved to have had my eldest son's attendance, I recognize that his priestly duties take precedence and I am willing to sacrifice my son's presence *Ad Maiorem Dei Gloriam* – For the Greater Glory of God."

The audience chuckled but Jimmy knitted his brow. Father Foley came up to the podium to say the Grace Before Meals and loose the crowd upon the buffet. But all Jimmy could think about was his brother and the excuses sent through the U.S. Mail.

Dearest Father,

I am writing to you from the very busy and sweltering Saint Francis Xavier High School in New York, where final examinations are in progress and the boys are at once becoming serious about their final tests of the year and giving nervous vent to their desire for tomfoolery, to send you my heartiest congratulations on the twenty-fifth anniversary of the Logan Construction Company. It is truly an anniversary worth celebrating. You have earned it by the sweat of your brow and the exertions of your intelligent mind. We are all proud of your achievement and marvel at how far you have come since the days when you had only a few helpers.

It is for this reason that I am deeply sorry to say that I will not be in attendance at the grand celebration of the quadranscentennial celebration at the Catholic Philopatrian Literary Society. I have two reasons to explain my absence. Firstly, as I mentioned, the celebration is being held when Xavier is having its final exams. This is a very busy time of the year as I need to prepare my exams in French and Latin, proctor the exams, and, most demandingly, mark the examinations and calculate the students' grades. It is one of only two times of the year in which piles of marking and grading must be completed under the cloud of a deadline. Much as I would love to, it would be quite difficult to leave my post and travel to Philadelphia and back on a crucial weekend to join in the celebration. It would simply mean too much time away from the work I am asked by my superiors and called by God to do. Secondly, speaking of my vocation to the priesthood, much as I share in the pride of what you have accomplished, I am troubled by the idea of indulging in a public celebration in front of crowds and newspapermen. It seems to contravene my efforts at practicing humility in my daily life. It is a great temptation to me to join in the celebration in pride of my father's and my family's accomplishments and for a lay person there would and should be no hesitation to take part. However, since joining the Society of Jesus, I have endeavored — in addition to the required vows of poverty, chastity, and obedience — to mortify any manifestations of pride within me. For it is a weed that thrives in the garden of my soul.

Please give my love to mother and to Jimmy and the girls. Congratulations on a truly noteworthy achievement and enjoy the celebration.

> Yours in Christ, I am your beloved son,
> Sarsfield

His mother had shown Jimmy the letter when he had come to pick her up. But when Jimmy finished reading it, he hissed into his wife's shocked ear, "Humility, my eye! Sure. Why should he show up? It's not his achievement. It's only his father's."

...

The hour is so late it could be called early morning. I have endeavored to sleep for a few hours and have had no success. I can hear every horse's hoof on the street and every car engine. It surprises me how frequently the El train arrives in the wee hours. Usually I am quite able to block these sounds out.

But the noises outside on the street are just a symptom of the problem. For the truth is my blood is boiling tonight. I am very angry at the superiors whom I have taken a vow to obey. This I must admit and stop distracting myself with other causes of my sleeplessness. My anger has brought grotesque and sinful visions before my eyes — visions of petulance, rudeness, revenge, and even violence. I have had similar experiences in the past dealing with anger. No matter how peaceful I feel during my preparations for bed, once my head is placed on the pillow, visions of fiery rage appear before my mind's eye.

As I tossed and turned in my bed, I realized that the solution would be writing in my journal. In this journal, as it is meant for my eyes alone, I can express myself — even the shameful and dark parts of myself — as I can nowhere else. So, I have taken up my pen to record the impulses of which I am ashamed and, thereby, purge myself of them.

Whence has this anger sprung?

Through walking the streets in the neighborhood in which Saint Francis Xavier is situated, I have learned about the immigrant communities in the vicinity. I have met some of the newer immigrants who, like my father, the well-respected man who fought himself to the top of the ladder with a hod, came here to build for themselves and their families a better life, and yet, are finding progress stubborn and slow. One young Jewess, Esther Rosenberg, a fiery leader of strikers at a shirtwaist factory, has become a friend and comrade. Through my acquaintance with Miss Rosenberg, I have become more sympathetic to the plight of those who live around me, foreign as the people might seem much of the time. There is something about putting a friendly face on a member of a group you have considered alien to yourself that makes that group less strange. And so I have come to feel a certain bond not only with young Esther and her striking workers but with her compatriots and coreligionists. I smile when I hear people speak Yiddish and I feel as if I am an initiate, one who can understand what they are thinking and feeling, though I know only a handful of the words they speak. There are times when I almost expect them to be able to recognize my sympathy for them upon seeing my face, but, of course how could they?

My experience visiting the Italian University on Varick Street has had a similar effect on me. After my getting to know the young Italian students and their teachers, the children have become transformed in my mind from dirty-faced, foreign-speaking urchins in black socks and short pants to individuals with names. Now when I see children on the streets of Greenwich Village, I think, "This one reminds me of Anthony, and that one looks like Anna Maria." As a result, I could no longer turn a blind eye to their plight. My father could have been like them. Indeed, he spent his early years in America in squalid conditions working as an immigrant laborer in this very city. Did Our Lord turn away from the lepers and the blind and deaf who crossed His path saying that this was not His mission? Certainly not. Even when He told His Mother His "hour is not yet come," He acceded to the love of neighbor urged and demonstrated by His Blessed Mother, the Virgin Mary. Furthermore, learning the story of Miss Annie Leary, a woman with a background not unlike my own — how she saw the plight of these new immigrants and took action, considerably admirable action, has fed my spiritual growth and expanded my ability to care for others. Stories in the newspapers about Mother Katherine Drexel, a debutante from my native Philadelphia who gave her great wealth to found the Sisters of the Blessed Sacrament and to establish schools for poor colored and Indian children have bolstered this growth and expansion within me. I have come to believe that Our Lord is present in that Italian University, guiding the hands of those Neapolitan students as they learn to write and draw and that He walks, too, on the shirtwaist factory picket lines alongside their older sisters and their Jewish neighbors.

This writing has calmed me, as I hoped it would. My heart still pounds with resentment but without the passion it had while I was in bed. Outside, the birds attending some ornithic convocation in a thick-leaved linden tree are chirping about the sunrise. It is not yet bright but I suppose the birds sense the coming day more than I.

Inspired by the lives of two admirable women and filled with a zeal I had not experienced in years, I decided to act. I sent a proposal to my superiors asking that we find some way to get our more privileged boys to assist the newer immigrants and the Italian University. I laid out my argument carefully and sketched what I thought was a compelling portrait of Annie Leary. But the rector rejected most of my proposal. From my point of view, he seems to have replied in the narrowest of ways, in a fashion that required no sympathy nor spirit of innovation. His answer was to keep things as they are. I should call his response, "*Rerum Antiquorum*!" Did he even discern what I had gone through and what I was proposing? I'd say not. This is what has kept me awake most of the night.

Lying in bed, I imagined myself going over the rector's head to *his* superior. I could hear the whole conversation in my mind as if I were watching a play. And, I could see the humiliated and angry look on the rector's face when he found out that his selfishness and short sightedness had been exposed for what it is. But I thought that was taking things too far and would end up reflecting poorly on me.

I envisaged several scenes in which I could ridicule him in front of the faculty and the community. In my mind, I wrote and rewrote the jibes and insults I would fling at him, trying to make them as sharp as can be. But, again, I thought I might make a spectacle of myself and reflect poorly on my cause. I thought this was no way to act, and, surely, no way to demonstrate that my ideas are worthy, my reasoning superior.

However, I have taken a vow of obedience. Surely, the Lord requires me to continue to obey my superiors. But why would He put such men above me? Why could He not open their hearts to see that they did not always have to follow their accustomed courses, that there might be new people to help and new ways to help them? I feel that my spirit and heart have grown and yet theirs have been stunted. God forgive me for writing that, or even thinking it, but I must confess that I am prideful enough to entertain this thought on a recurring basis.

Maybe it would be better not to do anything overt. I could sit at faculty meetings and community meals and glare at the rector with steam coming out of my ears. It is hard to imagine being civil to him after this. I could give only one-word answers to his queries. He would know the cause of my anger.

Let him find someone else to take extra proctoring assignments or to say the early mass when one of the other men is sick! He would feel it when my hand is not raised to volunteer as it usually, perhaps too often, is. I have been too biddable and now I am being taken for granted.

But was it for personal credit and glory that I joined the Society? No, our motto is, "*Ad Maiorem Dei Gloriam*"! It was for service that I became a priest and a Jesuit. Nevertheless, I begin by wanting to help, proceed to imagine that my spirit and heart have grown larger than my superiors', and end by threatening to withhold my assistance. Surely, pride has overwhelmed by defenses! It must be repulsed. Perhaps this is the Lord's way of teaching me humility. What is more humbling than to have to take orders from someone you feel is inferior to you?

I have long ago given up the right to determine my own fate and what courses of action I might follow. I have given myself up to the Lord. I must live in accordance with what He wants, for He can only desire the good. Indeed, He is the Good. I am but one tendril in an infinite, universal garden grown of God and His Beloved Son. These disdainful feelings and imaginings are merely temptations, admittedly strong temptations, which are the natural result of the sinful condition of this fallen world. I have taken a vow of obedience to my superiors in the Society of Jesus. And that vow is for life.

As the dawn's light spreads across the sky behind the buildings and the El, a calm is spreading over me as well. Perhaps the exertion of writing has spent my rage's energy or perhaps seeing my own thoughts recorded on paper has brought me to my senses. But all of the anger now and the visions of revenge and petulance have dissipated. As the outlines of the buildings and trees and stoops become clearer and clearer, so these vengeful ideas appear sillier and sillier.

Nevertheless, I would not be human if I did not find it galling that I, who have given so much and am asking but for an opportunity to give even more, am denied. I have half a mind to simply defy him! I could get out of bed and head over to the Italian University and execute exactly what I had proposed — to help these poor children. I could even refrain from wearing my blacks as I generally do so that people would not know I am a Jesuit or even a priest.

Maybe I will write my father to ask him to donate money. If he can pay for that giant stained-glass window in Saint Colman's, he can buy something for the poor immigrants who got off of the boat after him — or has he forgotten that except on Saint Patrick's Day? I have done everything Father has wanted me to do. (It's a good thing I am happy as a priest because I really didn't have much choice.) So, he could do something for me. He could build a Logan wing of the Italian University and I can stand with my family name above the door and have my picture taken — and smile. And he would know what I am smiling about.

And He would, too.

He knows everything that is in your heart, sleepless night or no sleepless night. The Lord called you to be a priest and you have answered that call. That includes drinking from the chalice you would rather have pass from you.

But when I think of the years of study and service I have given to the Society of Jesus, I am still filled with anger. I discover a means of service in which we can help the very community in which we live and my ideas are rejected with only a pretense of serious consideration. I look at the red brick walls outside my window and I want to smash them. Are we but money changers in the temple? The sun begins to expose the water towers on the buildings. I want to open them up and let the water pour all over the grounds of the Xavier Rectory.

God forgive me and I hope that if anyone reads this someday that he understands that I record this here in order to exorcise it from my system with no intention of acting it out in the light of day. But I could imagine arguing with the rector and getting so frustrated with his poor reasoning and his arbitrary decisions that I punched the bully and coward in the face. I can feel my knuckles squashing his nose and see his blood spurting onto his cheeks. Saint Ignatius, as an *agere contra*, would probably have me sit next to him at dinner to combat my prideful tendencies, or invite him home for Thanksgiving.

After pacing my room. I have just reread this morning's entry and I am appalled at the ideas I have put onto paper. How dare I presume to know that the Lord is in that Italian University, that I alone perceive what is best for the Jewish and Italian immigrants of this quarter, and that my superiors understand less than I? I had the temerity to compare my ambitions to the mercy the Lord showed to lepers and myself to the great-souled Miss Annie?! How have I let this hubris take possession of me?

To mortify my tendency toward pride, I will pray the rosary — particularly the Joyful Mysteries. I love to contemplate how Mary, the young Jewess with no experience of men and little experience of the world, was visited by the Angel Gabriel. Not only did she accept this extraordinary visit in her quiet chamber much like this one, where she was alone, as I am, and perhaps praying, as I should be, but also she accepted the shocking words of the angel. He told her she would have a Son and despite some small objection raised by her powers of logic, she was pious enough to answer the Angel Gabriel with the words, "Be it done unto me according to your word."

I must remember this. It is not my will that decides but the Lord's through His messengers, the superiors He has placed over me, no matter how unreasonable they appear. Truly, obedience often is the most difficult of the vows I have to keep. It must be the rebellious, ambitious blood I have inherited from Father. However, my proposal has been rejected for a reason. It is not for me to understand as it was not for me to decide. It is for me to accept, as Our Lady did. As Our Lord said, "Thy will be done"!

I put down my pen to take up my rosary beads.

...

"Along with all the fugitives and assorted strangers they welcome, the people of Connemara harbor many strange and curious beliefs," Seamus Logan offered.

The storyteller paused and looked around at his neighbors in the steerage compartment. Was there a spark of interest in his subject? It was hard to tell.

"I'm not certain how many had the effect that was claimed," he continued. "But the people clung to them as strongly as they did to the practice of their religion."

Seamus's eyes roved over the emigrants lying on straw-filled mattresses or sitting on chests of scratched and scuffed wood. The steerage neighbors had been entertaining one another for some days now, and most of their best stories had been told.

"For one thing, there were many things you'd see in ordinary life that the people considered to be great omens of change — for either good or ill. No one knew which, only that there would be a great change."

"What were they?" asked Sarsfield, opening his eyes a slit but remaining supine.

"If you saw frogs changing color or heard the curlew's call or spotted some swallows flying low, that could mean things would not remain the same for long. Also, if you saw falling soot or felt midges biting in the summer."

"Midges biting?" said young Kevin. "Sure, there'd be great changes occurring every day of summer in my home place."

His remark caused chuckles all around.

"That one always did seem strange to me," Seamus smiled.

He gazed at the floor trying to recall more superstitions.

"There were a few I learned when I was a child that I thought of as I walked the roads from Bunowen to Connemara. One evening I heard a cuckoo call on the right side of the road and my heart grew light thinking that I had good luck ahead of me and all the bad luck behind me. For I knew it was fortunate when you heard the cuckoo on the right side only."

"The landing of magpies is the same," said old lady Rosie. "It's good luck if two of them land to your right. But, if three magpies land to your left, they bring bad luck."

"I never heard that one, Rosie. I spied several magpies along my way but took no notice of how many there were or what side of me they were on."

"I suppose the sides of things is very important to the Other World," added Mick the fiddle player. "I was always told it was bad luck to place a bed facing the door."

"'Tis silly of them to pay so much attention to what we are doing," said old grouchy Tom.

Tom's comment imposed a stillness on the group and Seamus again lost his train of thought. He looked over at Mick who had put his fiddle aside, giving it a rest after a number of jigs and reels. The boat creaked as it rocked this way and that. Hard heels struck the wood above as the quality strolled the deck.

Seamus's young companion had closed his eyes and had little color in his cheeks.

"You're looking poorly, Sarsfield *og*. Are you any better atall?"

"The same. Only a little tired."

"Well, if we were standing on the firm but lawless land of Connemara instead of floating on these rolling waves, I would have loads of remedies for you."

Seamus could hear the voices of his former landlady and the other women of the village chattering about how to care for various maladies.

"Is your throat sore?"

"A wee bit."

"Well, people in Connemara put a stocking filled with hot potatoes on a sore throat. Have you ever tried that?"

"Never," Sarsfield chortled, then coughed. His eyes were opened wide now.

"If you had boils, we could apply kelp from the Killary Harbor to them — boiled in milk! How would you like that?!"

"Not a bit!"

"And, for a fever, they'd take you to the seashore and keep you there until the tide came in. The outgoing tide would carry away the infection and the fever."

"Sounds like it would be cold!" said Sarsfield, shivering.

"The lad is talkin' some sense now!" interjected grumpy Tom. "The waves takin' away his fever, no less. A boy with a fever would catch his death in the cold sea water."

"Well, that's what the people who lived by the sea in Connemara believed and my own people in Bunowen as well. And they lived long and healthy lives, God bless them."

"Indeed, they did," said Rosie. "People who followed the old ways were always well protected. Turning against the old ways is a terrible risk. Terrible risk entirely."

"It is, Rosie. It surely is. The people around Killary Harbour had ways of staying safe at sea as well," said Seamus. "Since we are on a boat, Sarsfield *a gradh*, I'll tell you a few of those. Do you know that a fisherman always boards his boat from the right for good luck? And fishermen always lash three boats together when leaving a harbor — because it's bad luck to be on the third boat out! If they didn't do that, no more than two boats would set out! But if change a boat's name, you can change its luck."

"Should we keep this boat's name or change it?" asked Mick.

"It's not ours to name or rename," replied Rosie.

"What other beliefs did the fisherman have?" asked Sarsfield. "For it was only farmers around my townland."

"Men who make their living out on the fickle wave of the Atlantic don't like to take chances. And you cannot blame them — can you? I know that the fishermen never keep the first salmon of the season. No, they do not. And, some of the catch is always left on board.

"In August sometimes we used see big shoals of herring — shoals so thick you could walk across Killary Harbor on the backs of the fishes! Well, whenever that happened, the people said we would have a plentiful harvest."

"Fish can foretell the weather as well," said Rosie. "When porpoises swim near the shore or when lobsters and crabs sit up on the rocks, then stormy weather is on its way. Same when you see any sea-birds flying in toward the land."

"Were you born during the day or at night, Sarsfield?" Seamus asked.

"In the morning, I think."

"That's why you are unable to see the good people."

"He can't see them because they are not there," rasped Tom.

"They are there, indeed, even if you don't believe in them," Rosie snapped.

"People born before noon cannot see spirits or the good people, but those born at night can, so they say."

"Were you born at night, Mr. Logan?" Sarsfield wondered.

"I believe I was."

"Maybe that's why you saw the abandoned village come to life!"

"Could be! That could very well be! I supposed it is a gift of some kind, although it caused me plenty of distress as I came to settle in Connemara."

The lull in the conversation in their corner of the steerage compartment gave the creaks of the boat and the snoring of a napping older man a chance to be speak up. The ladder amidships allowed more light to descend 'tween decks than usual. The sun must have come out above.

"Oh!" Sarsfield exclaimed, sitting up. "I know one! Did you ever hear any superstitions about cats?"

"One or two, I think."

"In my home place, they say if a cat strays into a house, you should try hard as you can to make it stay. But, if a family moves, you leave the cat behind. We did so when we left our house."

"I never heard those before, Sarasfield, *a gradh*, but I did hear something about taming a wild horse," Seamus replied.

"What is it?"

"To tame a wild horse, you whisper the creed into his left ear every Wednesday and into his right ear each Friday until the animal is calmed."

"Why do you teach the lad such nonsense?" Tom called out. "Horses learning the Apostle's Creed! You'll have sheep reciting the Lord's Prayer next."

"I'm just repeating the practices taught to me. I can't vouch for their effectiveness. You know, Sarsfield, the good people always have their revenge. I heard that people are strayed at night, often on the unseen path between earthen forts. It's bad luck to build on a path between forts. You can be strayed on a road you know as well as the back of your hand — even in your own field in sight of your own house whether you offend them knowingly or not — and you'll wander around all night. But, if you turn your coat inside out, it won't happen."

"Put your trousers on backward," Tom cracked. "And you'll be avoided by the living and the dead!"

"Such language, Tom!" admonished Rosie.

"Aye, Tom," added Kevin. "Remember the ladies."

Seamus continued.

"Speaking of wandering at night, Sarsfield, when I was walking the roads of Mayo in the dark, especially when I could hear water gurgling, I couldn't help but recall — much as I tried not to think about him — the specter who strolled the surface of Clew Bay with a lantern in his hand to warn of the approach of heavy rains and gale winds or the fairy with hands longer than a man is tall who could reach out and seize you with no warning but the sudden, cold clamminess on the back of your neck."

"Fairies with hands longer than a man is tall! Is that the way you'd be entertaining the poor fatherless boy and his mother too sick and weak to raise her hand? Why is it you don't tell him a story that is real and not be fooling him with a lot of nonsense of fairies and ghosts that do not exist except in your own fancy?"

"Well, you know, *mo bhuachaill*, in this crowded place we must meet all kinds, all the world's believers as well as the doubters thrown into the belly of the boat like Jonah into the belly of the whale and he trying to run away from the Lord. So, c'mere 'til I tell you the tale of the Donegal Doubter.

"One day this man with a very doubting temperament moved himself into a house that everyone in Donegal town knew to be haunted. It was an old relic by the River Eske with slates missing from its roof and graying whitewash, which no one for generations would live in nor go near. On most days, the high grass and neglected bushes and hawthorn trees kept the place hidden from any who did not already know it was there. On other days, the fog and mist from the river made it impossible to find altogether.

"And, if the appearance of the place were not foreboding enough, many of the locals warned the ornery old fish that the house was haunted and not a fit dwelling place for men of this world.

"'Oh, no,' says he. 'I haven't time for any such nonsense. The only spirits haunting this house will be those in *mo cruiskeen lan*.'

"While he was mending the slates and making other repairs before moving into the house, the women of the town stood outside his door night and day and prayed the rosary for him. They called upon every saint they knew — and these were women who knew litanies upon litanies of saints — to intercede for the arrogant man. But he was so overweening in his love for his own self and his own puny knowledge gleaned through the limited experience of his own senses that he cursed at these holy women, not even fearing the wrath of the Almighty God Who created him. He told them to hie from his home and not to trouble him nor the Good Lord with their superstitious orisons.

"The first night in the hidden house by the river, the conceited man was having a wee sup by the fire. Everything was silent except the distant rush of the water down below and the occasional whisper of the wind in the leaves of the trees.

"The stubborn man took up his pitcher of water and poured a drop into his whiskey. He took a long draught from his cup and sighed with satisfaction.

"'Those fools! Avoiding this place because of silly stories and this a fine peaceful house with nothing to frighten a man atall!'

"The man laughed out loud and took another sip of his drink.

"Then, all of a sudden, he saw one of his boots jump from one spot to another. He was gobsmacked! Then the other boot did the same. He dropped his glass and saw it shatter on the floor. The great horror was on him as he watched the two boots move one after the other across the floor! They were moving as if some invisible being were walking in them. After a time, they tramped into the kitchen and he, thunderstruck, sat in his chair and heard them thumping round the bedrooms. In a moment he had had enough. He caught them in his room and scolded them for making all the noise.

"'What is all this racket ye boots are making?' he said without realizing what he was saying. 'This is my house and I'll have none of this nonsense! You might frighten the old women of the town but you'll not scare me! I won't stand for such mischief from my own shoes in my own home!'"

"Well, you know what happened next? One boot rose up and hit him. Then the other took flight and kicked him right in his rear end. Then the other and the other again. The boots hit him so many times that the poor devil had to run out of his house to escape them! He tripped over some roots and got tangled in the underbrush. Sure, that was the only thing that kept the old brute from flopping like a trout into the River Eske!

"And ever since that night, throughout the hills and glens of *Tir Chonaill* the word went out, and you will hear it to this very day, how the Donegal Doubter was kicked out of his new home by his own boots!

"So, don't be too proud to believe in the fairies and the good people of the spirit world. There are many things in this life that our puny minds cannot understand.

"And, besides, these stories — though you may think they are nothing but malarkey — are the truth I'm tellin' yih, the truth of my own life and wanderings."

. . .

Riding shotgun, Paul noticed the schoolyard of P.S. 20, the Anna Silver School, and the high fence along two-way trafficked Houston Street. He saw himself on the other side of a similar fence, looking out from Saint Colman's onto Lancaster Avenue.

There was a stiff chill in the air and a bracing wind. The sun offered no warmth but shone bright and clear. It was what Paul and the other boys liked to call, "Football weather."

Paul's Miami Dolphins' jacket was perfectly suited for these conditions. Undefeated aqua covered his chest, shoulders, and torso, while unbeaten orange wrapped his arms in glowing synthetic hide. The wool hat on his head sported the same colors.

Witt had the plastic pee-wee football. Yellow with fake red laces, the ball was just bigger than the sixth grader's hand and bore the scuff marks and scratches of many landings and tumblings on asphalt. The assembled sixth graders fired the ball around their area as two captains chose sides.

A touch football game commenced. The two teams arrayed themselves on opposite sides of the portion of macadam that was their field. Chuckie hurled the plastic yellow missile. It sailed through the late-winter air and arced down toward the dense crowd of opponents, eager to find its strategic spot.

As when a herd of impalas, started by the appearance of cheetah, gallops across the plain with horned heads bobbing and hooves thundering, so the defending sixth graders, as soon as the ball left Chuckie's hand, raced in a wide line downfield, their coatsleeves woosh-wooshing against their coats and their earth shoes thudding on the yellow-striped schoolyard. The pee-wee football skidded and somersaulted across the asphalt and Witt, of the long feet and big hands, stooped to pick it up. His teammates ran forward to form a bulwark against the rushing tide of opponents. Protected by the phalanx of his teammates, Witt charged forward and a great din mingled shouts of encouragement for him and for his pursuers. Dark battalions densely packed with players charged across the asphalt toward one another to join the dangerous struggle. Like wolves the two sides rushed at one another, the progress of the boy with the ball and its surcease their antithetical aims.

Flouting the recess regulations of Saint Colman's School, which bound them to remain in their designated area, a pack of eighth graders came tramping around the basketball court and between the gyring jumpropes. The sixth graders did not expect them to come onto their field and so were taken by surprise. Just as a cat, seeing a small bird engrossed in its hunt for worms on a dewy front lawn creeps up on the bird, determined not to be noticed but intent on overcoming its prey, so the eighth graders came down upon the sixth graders who were focused on the first plays of their game.

As Witt got up to ten Mississippi, Mark heaved a spiral that climbed into the blue and descended toward the outstretched hands of Jimmy, who had gone long. It looked like a sure touchdown.

But Trelin, a small, wide eighth grader, stepped between Jimmy and the touchdown pass. He plucked his prize out of the air and, a cruel grin spreading across his face, ran with it outside of the yellow-painted boundaries of the younger boys' game.

Unafraid, Paul Logan abandoned the crossing pattern he had been running and sprinted after the thief. With clouds of condensation streaming from his clenched teeth, galloping Logan tore across the schoolyard, his classmates joining in the chase.

The touch football game was no more. The boys were now engaged in a game of Keep Away.

The eighth graders formed a wall behind Trelin as he ran away from the younger boys. Secure in their size and in their advantage in age, the usurpers laughed like so many Goliaths in Catholic school shirts and ties.

As a snowplow pushes aside piles of snow left on a suburban street after a blizzard, so Paul Logan shouldered and shoved the bigger boys out of his way. In his zeal to reach Trelin, Paul hit a long-haired uncoordinated eighth grader. Surprised by the force of Paul's blow, the gangly upperclassman lost his balance and, like a stately poplar that has grown up in a broad meadow beside a marsh, fell to the ground out of the younger boy's path. Another eighth grader wrapped his arms around Paul's shoulders but Paul shrugged him off. Just as he was about to reach Trelin, favored of Hermes, the eighth grader chucked the ball to someone else. But Paul could not stop himself; he crashed into Trelin, knocking him to the hard and gravelly asphalt. Without pausing to look down at his angry victim, Paul headed toward Trelin's receiver, waving his arms like a basketball player frustrating a passer. But the boy got the ball off to a nearby classmate. Paul, still charging, lowered his shoulder and dropped the classmate on the asphalt, vinyl parka and corduroys hissing all around him, before the older boy fumbled the ball like the bully and coward that he was.

Paul grabbed the pee-wee football with both hands and ran out of the pack of boys scrambling for the loose ball.

"Logan! Logan!" a couple of nearby sixth graders shouted, running back toward their touch football "field" with their hands raised to signal for his pass.

Paul ran right while his attackers rushed left. His classmates tried to block for him but Trelin in his fury at being knocked down, started tackling sixth graders regardless of whether they had the ball or not. He shoved Witt, of the long feet and big hands, in the back, knocking the boy to the macadam and tearing a hole in his trousers. And the dark blood flowed from the wound to his kneecap. The other eighth graders, seeing this, began to laugh and do the same.

Paul, spotting the green tunic and white sleeves of Mark's jacket, lateraled the ball to his brother in bravery, over whose heart a blazoned white eagle spread its wings and bore in its talons a white football. The two jogged easily and had a casual catch. The sixth graders were regaining their breath as the eighth graders began to take a greater interest in inflicting pain than in getting the ball.

The Ερισ, or Strife, of the Keep-Away game had been pee-wee-sized when the sixth graders' ball had first been seized from them. The sixth graders had looked upon the theft lightly, as if it were little more than a break in their lunchtime routine. But, as the hits were exchanged and as many elbows and knees were scraped, Strife grew taller and taller until she outstood the steeple of Saint Colman's Church, her ponytail sweeping the clouds and her saddle shoes skipping across the playground. And, the Keep-Away game seesawed back and forth.

Chuckie, bobbling the ball as he dodged through groups of uniformed girls practicing cheerleading and Chinese jumprope, fumbled it when he was hit. Szalla, of the denim jacket with faux wool overflowing from his collar and sleeves, recovered the ball. The eighth grader then made a sloppy pass, which was intercepted by Mark. Mark tore off with the ball until the swarming eighth graders nearly overwhelmed him. He flipped it over to Paul, who, harried by the blows of the frustrated trespassers, had made his way over to help his classmate. Trelin, the short one of the cruel smile, was hot on Paul's heels but the stouthearted sixth grader sidearmed the ball to Witt as he got shouldered from the side. He stumbled but did not fall. Wary of his pursuers, Witt ran three steps this way and three steps that before dumping the ball off to Chuckie on his left. Szalla, the tallest of the eighth graders, hit Chuckie and the ball came loose. Mark recovered it and tried to escape from the harrowing grip of the attackers, but was grabbed and fell, his Eagles jacket and pants scraping along the asphalt. The ball skittered across the gravelly, yellow-striped lot.

Trelin of the cruel smile scooped it up at a full run. He scrambled toward the gym amidst jumpropes and tiny primary-grade pupils, giving them hardly a glance. Now a considerable distance from his pursuers, he began to taunt them. He pump-faked passes, thumping the yellow pee-wee football against the palm of his left hand.

"Come and get it, faggots! It's your ball — isn't it?!"

Szalla took up a position parallel to Trelin and the two lobbed the ball back and forth. Paul Logan, of the great stamina, vainly followed the ball from one receiver to the other. The eighth graders let their lone pursuer come near, as was his wont, but each time they threw the ball high over his head before he could get to them. Soon, the number of defenders grew and, as the ball sailed among them, Paul Logan continued his vain chase.

Just as a trout when it has taken a fly races this way and that fruitlessly trying to loose himself from the hook and line that is drawing him toward the fisherman's creel, so Paul ran back and forth among the eighth graders to no avail. Every time Paul got close to the ball, the entire pack of the invaders moved away, guffawing, until they were in eighth grade territory, where piety would have kept them from the start. A small usurper, cocky in the midst of the large number of his fellows, laughed in Paul's face. The broad-shouldered Logan swatted him away as if he were a low-hanging branch. He soon stood face-to-face with thieving Trelin. Paul lunged toward the shorter, wider boy. Trelin dodged him like bullfighter, leaving Paul with nothing but the late-winter air in his hands. He looked up to see that the eighth graders had formed a circle around him.

Mocking Paul's plight, Szalla shouted, "Hey, Trelin, if he really wants it so bad, let's give it to him!"

"Yeah! If Logan really wants it, he can have it!"

Trelin tossed the ball up and caught it as he marched at the center of an array of upperclassmen approaching Paul who stood firm, hands on his hips, clouds of steam puffing from his mouth, and a scowl upon his face. The eighth graders chanted.

"Logan! Logan! Logan! Logan!"

Themis putting his courage in place, Paul held his ground. He was not intimidated. He intended to show them this, and more.

Sneering, Trelin walked over toward Paul and extended the ball toward him.

Paul advanced toward him. The other eighth graders closed in.

"You want the ball back? Take it!"

Paul, cognizant that this was neither a gift nor a prize, lunged at the ball and ripped it from Trelin's hand. He put his head down like a running back charging into a pile of defenders and punished many with the blows of his mighty shoulders. Some even fell to the ground. But Paul's advantage was fleeting. In a moment, their superior numbers gave the eighth graders control.

Paul fell prostrate on the ground, with a trio of eighth graders on his back. Some of the thieves tried to reach between Paul's chest and the ground to pull the ball away. But, Paul would not let it go. More older boys bounded on top of him. Yet Paul would not yield. Strong enemy arms tried to rob him of the miniature plastic football. Still, he held firm. Some of his teammates, faithful lads all, came to the fore. They fought the impious brutes who surrounded Paul and kicked at his prostrate body like a pride of lions around a fallen wildebeest.

Paul felt the blows of the eighth-grade feet. His lungs and chest strained under the weight of the bigger older bodies. The muscles of his legs tightened as Trelin stepped and walked upon them. He couldn't see his classmates but he could hear them and he sensed the struggle going on around and above him. He heard Mark's voice call his name. Looking up with difficulty, he glimpsed Mark's shoes, legs, and his outstretched hands. Paul squirmed to pull the ball from under him. He tried to hand the ball to his comrade but eighth grade hands prevented him.

Szalla yelled, "Yo, Leighton! Whaddaya think yore doin'?"

And tried to push him out of the way. But Mark shoved him back. Losing his balance, Szalla tripped over one of his own classmates in the pile-up, and fell in disgraceful defeat on his back, on the hard, cold ground

With an opening now clear, Paul handed Mark the ball and the valiant sixth grader, broad-shouldered Paul's brother in bravery, galloped away from the once haughty pack of barbarians who now seemed more like a scatter of carrion left after a battle by Ares, the bloody destroyer of cities, than like a pride of lions.

After a number of final kicks and several loud curses, the eighth graders abandoned the prone Paul Logan, favored of Themis, and gave chase to Mark and John who passed the ball back and forth, making sport of the angered, oldest boys in the school, the former cocks of the walk.

Strife spurred the upperclassmen on and presently they stood in the faces of Mark and John. Mark made a wobbly pass to big-footed Witt. The yellow pee-wee football hit his long-fingered hands and fell rolling and bounding on the asphalt. The ball was scooped up by one of Trelin's cronies and underhanded to him of the cruel smile.

Trelin dropped back to pass like an NFL quarterback and provided his own play by play for his actions.

"Staubach from the shotgun … he sees Szalla downfield … and throws a 'Hail Mary Pass'!"

Clear across the yard, over the heads of the little ones, Trelin threw a high, prideful pass.

"No one can intercept that!" he boasted.

From nowhere he came! From nowhere! The one from the bottom of the pileup who had been discounted came from nowhere! And he sped toward the pee-wee football arcing through the crisp air.

As the yellow ball spiraled into the hands of Szalla, Paul's shoulder struck him a crushing blow and the tall boy fell like a tower. There seemed to be no time between Paul's hit and the eighth grader's landing on the ground.

With the pleasure of victory and the taste of just revenge on his lips, the sixth-grade Logan, favored of Eusebia, reached down and with his strong right arm and one hand, ripped the ball from the ignoble and defeated arms of the sacked older boy.

No celebration came from Paul Logan. His eyes were fierce with the lust of battle, with avenging wrongs but without undue malice toward his persecutors, with confidence in his strength and fidelity in the just outcome that the Son of Chronos was surely arranging for those unjust invaders.

Then as Paul loped back toward the sixth-grade area, Zeus saw fit that the lunch period time should run out, and bade Themis strike the bell to summon the children back into school.

His classmates slapped Paul on the back and gave him great praise. They looked upon him with amazement, and gratitude, and with admiration. For Paul Logan of the great stamina, though winded, scraped, and drenched in sweat, stood bloodied but unbowed, beaten and bruised but unvanquished.

From that day forward in the schoolyard not only the sixth graders but pupils from younger and older grades as well spoke of the day when Paul Logan was set upon by superior numbers of a superior grade, how he was kicked and pounced upon, how the backs of his legs were used as pedestrian ways, how broad-shouldered Paul never abandoned the field, and how in the end he held onto the ball. No matter how they pounced on him, Paul Logan held onto the ball. No matter how many attacked him, Paul Logan held onto the ball. Paul Logan held onto the ball.

...

During Mom's wake, I lost all sense of time. So many conversations took place in quick succession — some people trying to comfort but coming across like alien transmissions intercepted by a satellite, others knowing enough to say very little — that it felt like hours had passed. But, when I asked Kitty, she told me it had been only twenty minutes. She couldn't believe it, either. Many of Mom's old friends had come by, people from Saint Francis de Sales and West Catholic and lots from Saint Colman's as well. I kept filing these encounters away in order to tell her later.

"Mom, you'll never guess who I ran into — Aunt Dotty!"

"Mom, I saw Mr. Dugan. He looks great! He said...."

Only to realize how foolish that impulse was.

A lot of my friends came, too, including many whom I had been in touch with and a few I had not seen in years. There were some I had not seen since the Saint Colman's schoolyard, and others I had not spoken to since I moved to New York. They kept telling me everything about Ardmore and asked very little about life in Hell's Kitchen.

Some of them remembered me from the Rusty Nail and from The Bothy Club and asked me about my guitar playing and my writing. I had to tell them the truth — that I was not doing much. I had gone to some open mics in the Village — but those outings had turned into little more than beer-guzzling Monday nights and hungover Tuesday mornings. And, besides, the old folkie Speakeasy had turned into a Thai restaurant.

Toward the end of the wake, Joe McHugh appeared at the front of the line. He and I had gone to Saint Colman's together and attended both The Prep and Saint Joe's. He had always been around, always part of the crowd when we were kids, though we were never close. Still, it was good to see him and good of him to come. He said he now lived in New York, working as a broker for Morgan Stanley down on Water Street — the street no one could direct me to when I first moved here because of my Philadelphia accent. Mom used to laugh at that story.

Like many others he said:

— If you need anything ... If there is anything I can do ...

And shook hands with Kitty and Dad and disappeared into the crowd.

One Thursday a few weeks later I went to the lunchtime Brahms on Broadway at Trinity Church. Although I hadn't eaten first, I got to the concert late. I didn't care. It was free anyway. I chose a pew in the middle of the church. Swept along by the piano and strings echoing among the thick walls and pointed ceiling of the old church, I admired the elaborate marble altar piece, scanned the musicians' bios in the program, and stared into space. It was relaxing to be away from Susskind Software and any expectation of being able to concentrate, low as that might be these days.

I enjoyed a few movements and joined in the applause at the end of the piece. When the program was over, I proceeded onto sunny Broadway with the greying collection of audience members, and, not wanting to share the same piece of earth as she, stepped around the star marking the spot where Queen Elizabeth had stood.

My mind said to go uptown but my feet took me downtown. There was no particular reason. But, there was nothing compelling me to return to 11 Park Place, either. Myrna Rosenberg was not in. Perhaps I was simply drawn toward the saltwater.

The world was full of summer and sun but my head was full of clouds. For me a fog had filled the narrow streets with mist and ghosts and indistinctness. Mental melodies of German Romanticism repeated and faded as I passed Wall Street and the dreary churchyard. In the TV movie about my life, the sight of tombstones would have been underscored by eerie minor chords on violin and piano, perhaps even blatant organ. But it didn't happen that way. My eyes looked on the blurring tombstones as they did on the bricks and the windows of the buildings and on the Starbuck's cup and Utz potato chip bag on the sidewalk, numb to their potential significance or melodrama.

In the distance, long tree branches fanned Battery Park with pallid green leaves and beckoned me onward. A trio of heavyset ladies stepped out of TGI Friday's right in front of me. They ambled downtown like they had all day and all the sidewalk was theirs. I had to swerve into

Broadway to pass them. Tourists in cargo shorts and motley t-shirts took pictures with the bull. A pair of petite Asian girls on either side of the menacing horns smiled with tilted heads and made peace signs. As they moved away, others came forward and posed with their mouths open and their tongues hanging out. How wild we were with the bull in New York! As if the exact same photos of the exact same poses were not taken there all day every day.

A tall Latino kid stopped next to me as I waited to cross the street. Tinny drumbeats from his headphones drove me away from him. I leaned against the wall of Number One Broadway. When the traffic slowed or stopped, I could hear someone singing and playing guitar in Bowling Green. The jaunty rhythm was jarring at first — not anything like Brahms. But it had a nautical flavor, which, when I thought about it, did suit my surroundings: the rivers on either side, the great harbor dead ahead.

"No more on the docks I'll be seen.
Tell me old shipmates
I'm takin' a trip, mates … "

Of course, it was a favorite of Mom's. I couldn't help moving my lips and hearing her voice joining in. Was this why I had the impulse to walk downtown instead of up? Did she want me to hear that song?

"Brahms on Broadway, my eye! As much as you try to forget, remember."

Maybe she lured me down here to help out with the chorus.

An old sailor's song seemed about right. The busker knew what he was doing, though I imagine it was lost on most of his audience. So much shipping out and disembarking, loading and unloading in this vicinity. You can almost see where they wore out the cobblestones. Great-granddad was one of them. Did he whistle a sea chanty as he passed Bowling Green? The mural downstairs in the subway shows the ragged greenhorns getting off of the boats and the dockworkers unloading the cargo … all the hustle and bustle and work. No sign of leisurely lunchers and grinning tourists. Above me hung mosaic shields of the world's port cities. Other New Yorks in other worlds: Hamburg, Antwerp, Adelaide, Naples, Rio De Janeiro, Paris, Buenos Aires, Genoa, Liverpool, and the one with the shamrocks on it still labeled Queenstown, though it is not called that annie moore. Parallel metropoleis. Were they likewise filled with full-bellied amblers, cheerful takers of holiday snaps, and a fog-brained guy all at sea, leaning against a wall? Or were they living wholly different lives based on wholly different choices?

Suddenly I heard a voice from long ago:

— Paul?

Crossing Broadway from Bowling Green was Joe McHugh. Was this why she had led me down here?

— I thought that was you. I was on my way to get a burger and I heard that Irish tune and stopped to listen.

— Me, too.

— Sure, 'tis in your blood, Paul, he fakebrogued. And there's no denying it.

Little did he know how right he was.

— Djeat yet?

— Haven't had a chance. I went to one of those free concerts at Trinity Church.

— C'mon. He pointed uptown with his head and started to move in the same direction. I'll show you a place with a great burger and fries.

Joe maneuvered through the pedestrians coming down Broadway, and I hustled to keep up with him.

— Have you been to the Irish Punt?

— No, but I've spent a few ... on Guinness.

— They have that there, too.

Moments later we were heading down the narrow alleyway of Exchange Place, chatting about nothing really. I tried to sound halfway intelligent about the concert I had attended, though very little of it had made an impression. We got inside and the Irish waitress in a green, collared polo shirt and black slacks hustled us to a table. The burgers arrived almost before we ordered them. And, Joe was right. They were delicious — with cheddar cheese, sautéed onions, mushrooms, and an Irish rasher on top.

Joe did most of the talking during lunch, which was a relief. I had no energy or inclination to provide the entertainment, as I often have to do when eating with guys.

I admired the mural of Queen Maeve by the front door, an enlargement of the illustration on the Irish Pound. Despite the dim lighting, I could make out the old black-and-white and color photos taken in Connacht, the province she once ruled. There was the Poulnabrone dolmen in Clare, Ben Bulben in Sligo, and a stream among the mountains of Connemara. There were a couple of slanes and hurleys on the walls along with some fly-fishing rods and creels.

— I like this place. It has a nice atmosphere.

And I meant it. Being in this Irish place transported me a bit and took me out of myself and away from my brooding. And Joe was pretty good company.

He told me about his job as a broker. People were good to him though there were some ultracompetitive assholes.

— No one as kind and generous as the people we grew up with, he said.

And, putting down my half-finished burger, I had to agree with him.

Joe liked to come here for lunch to get away from the fluorescent lights and the pressure. His financial talk made me realize why I had lost touch with him. We had been friends as kids and at The Prep. But in college, I took one path toward English while he took another toward business.

Both of our burgers had disappeared and the fries along with them. The waitress came by to check on us a couple of times. She had lovely blue eyes that shone through her tiredness. She was back with the check in a flash.

Joe said he liked to come here after work — especially on Fridays.

Before I realized what I was doing I was agreeing to meet him there after work the next day. I found myself shaking his hand, thanking him for the burger, which he really didn't have to pay for, and promising that the first round of pints was on me.

The next day I hustled down Broadway to Exchange Place with more energy than I had shown all day or all week. Making sure not to step on any cracks, I dodged around streetclogs of slow-walkers, finding daylight wherever I could and rushing toward it. Whatever happened, I wondered, to the fast pace of New York? There is something about meeting friends at a bar at the end of the workweek that puts a spring in your step and scenes full of wisecracks in your head.

I got there first and ordered two pints. I felt lucky to get a standing spot at the bar. As I waited for the pints, my mood was more upbeat than it had been in a while. I was ready for a few laughs. I tapped a coaster on the bar to the beat of the Van Morrison and imagined a sailboat rolling over the waves and beyond the horizon. One TV showed a round table of ex-jocks in suits talking baseball. The other showed a guy yacking excitedly about the stock market. When Joe got there, I shook his hand and handed him his ruby-red settling pint.

He did that gesture with his head again.

— Why don't we hang out over here?

He led me to a wooden counter that ran along the window. I figured we'd have a nice view of the Wall Street women rushing to the subway. So, I didn't care.

After a few minutes of the same type of catching up we had done at lunch, Joe turned to me and said conspiratorially.

— I have a story to tell you. Somethin' you'll be happy to hear ...

— Oh, really? I replied. What?

— Well, you remember when we were at Saint Colman's ... and my dad got laid off from Penn Fruit?

— Yeah, yeah, I remember that. He was out of work for a long time.

I could see that this conversation would not be featuring the wise-cracking I had imagined.

— He never really got back to work at the same level again. It was hard for our whole family.

— Sorry to hear that. I never knew. I really wasn't aware of that kind of stuff back then.

— Don't worry about it. We were just kids. And nobody understood. Except your mom. She knew our whole family was hurtin'. But she made sure it wasn't obvious to anyone else. She was always feedin' me. Even if I wasn't hungry.

— She was like that. She never liked to see anyone in her house without some food or something to drink.

— Yeah, she was great. And, she had me around her house all the time, makin' excuses to my mom on the phone so I could stay for dinner.

— Yeah, I remember you staying for dinner a lot in those days.

The jukebox blared an old song about friends reminiscing ("reminisce," one of mom's favorite words) about their high school years, and Joe smiled. He paused and pretended to look at the mute TVs. An outfielder raced over astroturf to the wall only to watch the ball fly over it.

— Your mom was always generous. Even more so than most people around Saint Colman's. I remember one time somebody said it was because her husband had money but I am sure she was the same way in West Philly.

— Absolutely. They say she was like that even as a little girl. Whenever she had some candy, she would give a piece to everyone in the house.

— I don't know if you knew but a few times before my father died, she would slip money in my pocket when everyone was going to the movies and I was saying I didn't want to go.

— No, I had no idea.

— Well, that was only the beginning. After my father died, she did even more. One night, when we were juniors at The Prep, I knocked up for you but you had already gone out. She told me to come in, anyway, that you would be back soon. It was chilly outside and I could see your dad had the Phillies game on — a playoff game. So I came in and chatted with him.

— Not the world's greatest conversationalist.

— Oh, he can be. When he wants to be.

— Exactly. It has to be on his terms.

Joe nodded and took a sip from his pint.

— But, the whole time your mom is trying to force food or drink on me. Hot chocolate ... a cup of tea ... a piece of pound cake ... some Peanut Chews ... I really didn't want anything. Finally I agree to have a soda. Just to satisfy her. She says, "Why don't you come into the kitchen and take

185

what you want? You're big enough and ugly enough to get it yourself." So, I go into the kitchen where she had a book open on the table and a glass of white wine. I found a can of Black Cherry Wishniak in the refrigerator.

— "Is it Frank's"?

— "Thanks!"

— I'm surprised she didn't know how much I loved that stuff. Anyway, she starts asking me about The Prep and what subjects I liked and what I might want to study in college ... She asked about my family and my sister and all that. I could tell she had been talking to my mom. She already seemed to know all the answers to her questions.

— Those two were always on the phone.

— Yeah, I think she helped my mom out a lot at that time. At any rate, remember the little cookie jar that used to be in your kitchen — with the all frogs on it and the toadstool handle on the lid?

— Defintely! It's still there!

— Well, completely out of the blue, she leans over to me and says, "Lissen, hon, you see that cookie jar? If you are ever over here and the other boys are going out and you don't have money — I know you give most of your money to your mother — I'll tell you to have a cookie. You help yourself to a little spending money." I said, "I can't do that, Mrs. Logan. That's very generous of you but I'm OK." She says, "Nonsense. You just wait for my signal and take what you need from the cookie jar." Before I had a chance to say anything else, your dad came in for some ice for his drink. Your mom sent me into the living room with him to watch the game and when it was over, I walked back home. But for a couple of years, as much as I tried to object, she was true to her word. She kept up that system. She would ask me, "Why don't you have a cookie before you go?" Sometimes she would even sing, "There's whiskey in the jar ... or even Whack fol the daddy-o." Her signals got pretty subtle.

I didn't know what to say. All I came up with was a pragmatic query.

— How long did this go on for?

— For years. At least until I was well into Saint Joe's and was making decent money as a waiter.

— I had no clue.

I stared up at the baseball highlights which were nothing but pretty colors, frenetic movement, and balls arcing through the air. What I could see clearly was Mom's kitchen and her frog cookie jar. Less clear were her secrets: her secret money hidden in the jar, her secret signals, and the secret generosity of her heart.

— She didn't want you to know. She didn't want anybody to know. That's why I kept quiet 'til now.

— Wow. Thanks. Thanks for tellin' me.

— You look like you need another pint.

And Joe was off to the bar.

…

Aunt Kitty, Aunt Nora, and Janey gathered around the pad-covered table on the wooden chairs squeezed into the dining room of the old Logan family home. Fine china cups and saucers were set before the women but in front of young Paul lay a tall glass of milk and a hamburger on white bread.

Janey did not think it ideal to have Paul present for such a serious conversation but she knew he would not disturb the group. He was a quiet child usually off in his own world even in a crowded room, and he had loved Father Sarsfield.

Jimmy and his nephew, James, had gone out to run some errands and talk to the Jesuits. The women met to discuss preparations, but there really weren't many to make.

"It would be nice if those Jevvies left something for us to do," sighed Aunt Kitty, as she placed a pot of tea at the center of the table.

"I know," agreed Nora. "You feel like you have to do *something*."

The viewing of Reverend Sarsfield Logan, S.J.'s body would be held the following evening at Manresa Hall, the Jesuit nursing home at Saint Joseph's College.

"It'll be funny to go to Saint Joe's for a wake. I'm so used to McConaghy's," Nora said.

"It'll be less crowded for one thing. A little more dignified, I guess."

"It seems the Jesuits like to keep control of everything," added Kitty, taking a seat at the head of the table. "They do things their own way for their own."

To Paul the two swirls of wood on top of the china closet looked like tidal waves about to crash into a giant piece of fruit. He always pictured it but it never happened.

"At least we can pick the hymns for the funeral. That gives us something to do."

"You're right, Janey. I've been trying to remember the hymns that Sarsfield liked. I know he always loved 'Faith of Our Fathers.' We have to have that one."

"Here, let me write that down."

Janey rummaged through her purse for a pad and pen. She hummed the melody.

Paul liked that song, too. For a church song it filled his mind with dark and adventurous images.

> *... In spite of dungeon, fire, and sword ...*

He could see people chained to prison walls of dark dripping stone but not giving up their beliefs.

> *Faith of our Fathers, Holy Faith!*
> *We will be true to thee 'til death.*

How about, "The Battle Hymn of the Republic?"

"Yeah, he liked that one. But that was more his father's song".

> *Glory glory hallelujah*
> *Glory glory hallelujah*
> *His truth is marching on.*

In Paul's mind the song always conjured images of a colossal stone face of Abraham Lincoln, buildings on fire before a dark sky, blue and grey hats, the sounds of marching feet, and the sniffling of Aunt Kitty mixed with organ music. She always cried when she heard that song.

> *He has sounded forth the trumpet that shall never call retreat.*
> *He is sifting out the hearts of men before His judgment-seat.*

"It will be beautiful to have his funeral mass at Saint Colman's," Aunt Kitty said.

"It will be. At least we will have the mass in his home parish."

"We need some more peaceful songs. Something that reflects Sarsfield's gentle personality. I think Uncle Sarsfield was more like Saint Francis:

> *"'Whatsoever you do to the least of my brothers*
> *That you do unto me.'"*

"That's a good one. 'The Prayer of Saint Francis.' 'Make me a channel of your peace.' Sounds more like him."

"That's what Jimmy always said about him — such a peaceful gentle soul. Where is Jimmy, anyway?"

"He went over to the church with James. He should be back soon. He said he would be ..."

"Yeah, let's pick, 'The Prayer of Saint Francis.' Janey, write that one down. It's true he was very gentle. He was also conservative and very academic, especially as a young priest."

"Yes, what an educated man Sarsfield was, too!" Nora exclaimed. "And such a logical man ... He had such a way with words, really knew how to express himself."

"Glory be to God, the man had a mind on him!" concurred Aunt Kitty. "Like a steel trap! The professors at Xavier and at Fordham used to marvel at his memory. He studied so many subjects, too. Four years at the Prep. Fifteen years of training in the Jesuits. 3 years philosophy. 3 years theology. He never stopped learning, really."

"People like that usually don't stop educating themselves," added Janey. "The love of learning doesn't end when you leave school."

"And he had such a command of all that knowledge!" Nora said. "He could give a lecture for hours at a stretch and never look at a note. Even as an old man, he was able to help the kids with their homework — in subjects he hadn't studied in years!"

"And the French he spoke! It was flawless, so they say."

"He always claimed he spoke French with a Philadelphia accent," smiled Jane. "But it always sounded beautiful to me!"

"He was always so humble about all his learning and accomplishments."

"It was his father who instilled the importance of education in Sarsfield when he was very young," said Kitty. "'Get an education.' Father used to say. 'It's something they can never take away from you.' I don't know how he figured that out so fast, being from the old sod and all, but he did."

"He was right, too. An education sure makes a difference. It makes a real difference," added Nora. "It's is the key to getting ahead. That's what Granddad figured out. Some of the Irish figured it out right away, I guess, like the Jews. Not like some of these other jackasses. Think they're so smart. Too cool to study. Never open a book in their lives and end up digging ditches. End up with a broken back. That's real cool — isn't it? No, they say Uncle Sarsfield always knew the difference. He figured it out at an early age. They can take your home away from you. They can take your freedom away from you. They can take money away from you. They can take your health away from you. But they can never take away your education."

"Mother used to say he would come home and hit the books right away. He never had to be pushed into it. He never made a fuss about wanting to be outside playing ball. Not that he was a sissy or anything like that. He was a good athlete and a real boy. He was an excellent handball player and played baseball at the Prep. The other kids always wanted him out there playing but he loved his books and he knew the value of an education. So, he stuck to his guns, and, even though the kids in Moyamensing didn't always understand, they always respected and they admired him in the long run."

"And they always asked about him. All the fellows he grew up with.

"'How's Sarsfield?'

"'How's ee doin' up 'ere in New York?'

"'How's 'ee like 'at Big Apple?'"

"Where are Jimmy and James? That's a long time to be talking to the priest."

"They must have stopped somewhere."

"Talking to a bartender, I bet."

"James better not be out drinking or I'll brain him!"

"If I know my husband," Nora said. "Your James was not the instigator."

"Well, let's not jump to conclusions. The boys'll be home soon. More tea?"

"Sure. That would be nice."

"I'll put the kettle on."

Kitty stood and stepped into the kitchen.

Looking down into her near-empty cup, Janey lamented.

"What a shame that Father Sarsfield's gone. The world needs more intelligent, kind, educated men like him."

"Well, he has gone to a better place, the place he prepared for his whole life."

"True. Of course, that's true. It's just hard on those he left behind."

"You're certainly right about that, Janey," interjected Kitty standing in the dining room threshold. "Even though I didn't see him that often, it feels lonely to think that he's not up there at Xavier … to think that he's not sitting down to write me one of his letters. No matter how far away he was, he was always my rock."

"I'm sorry, Aunt Kitty," Janey said.

"His letters were so beautifully written. A little over my head sometimes, but-"

"He gave you a lot of credit!" Nora laughed.

"More than I deserved! There were many times when I didn't know what in the world he was talking about."

"The more recent ones seemed disordered. As if his mind were wandering …."

Hearing the kettle whistle, Kitty rushed into the kitchen and reappeared with a full tea pot.

Janey said, "I hadn't seen him much since the wedding. Christmas times, mostly. I never thought he looked poorly. He always seemed so energetic."

"It must have been lonely for Uncle Sarsfield — they always wondered where he got that name, 'Sarsfield,' but Father never explained — up there in New York. I'm sure it wasn't always easy for the poor old man to be on his own up there. You know, those New Yorkers can be cold."

"He had his Jesuit community," said Janey. She took a sip from her cup of tea and placed it back in her saucer. "They say there's a special camaraderie there with the other priests. And they can have their meals together, I suppose, and talk about things that we wouldn't know about or understand."

"Yeah, I'm sure he had his happy moments and happy times. It must be a fine life as a Jesuit and he was well respected and cared for. And he had his books and his studies to keep him occupied. But I don't care what you say. It must have been lonely sometimes. I think even Mother used to think so, though she never let on much. But I remember her saying that was why he was so good about keeping in touch, sending those beautiful letters home all the time."

"You're right. His letters were always beautiful but at one point they took an unusual turn. He became very concerned about labor unions, things like that. Unusual for a priest of his time. He used to get in trouble with the bishops, even the Jevvies sometimes. As a Jesuit, he had to take a vow of poverty, of course, but he seemed to take it to an extreme. Jimmy even accused him of being anti-business."

"He said all that social justice was Church teaching."

"*Rerum Novarum.*"

"That's right," smiled Kitty. "*Rerum Novarum* was what he always mentioned."

"But it was unusual. Ahead of his time a little bit. You didn't hear many priests talking about it the way he did."

"Something must have happened to him in New York that inspired him."

"He told some funny stories about his students, too — didn't he? I'll never forget the one about his early days as a teacher, the one kid saying, 'That sounds like great assignment for the weekend, Father, and I can't wait to get started on it. But the big game is on Saturday … I really don't know if I can devote to this assignment all of the attention it deserves.'"

The women laughed and, seeing Paul chuckle, they let out a second burst of laughter, which gradually faded into a series wistful, tuneful sighs.

"They say he never let those young men slack off. I'm sure they didn't like it, but they learned from him, boy, I'll tell you. Maybe they complained at the time. I know some of the fellows used to call him, 'Father Chuckles' because he seemed so serious in the classroom. But in the long run they thanked him. He taught them to think."

"You can't put an old head on young shoulders. No siree, bub. He'd hand those papers right back to them and say, 'Write it again! That is not a strong argument, young man, and you do no back up way you say.' He never missed a trick."

The screendoor clattered shut and the voices of Jimmy and James could be heard from the closed-in porch. One started shushing the other. As the pair entered the living room, James tripped over a leg of the sofa, stumbled and regained his balance.

"Where were you two?" Kitty demanded.

"As if we didn't know," Janey muttered.

Jimmy took James's trenchcoat from him and laid it on the couch.

"It was a bit of an ordeal handling all the funeral issues, and so we stopped for a drink on the way home."

"We stopped at a French place," James added. "Very classy. *'Roachee and obrien's'* I think it was called!"

"Very funny, James Logan!" Janey marched into the living room. "You should be ashamed of yourself! Father Sarsfield passes away and you go out to celebrate?!"

"He's not celebrating," Jimmy said. "He's upset. We both are. People have different ways of-"

"Father Sarsfield was a very holy man," James announced, raising himself with some effort to his full height. "A great teacher and scholar. I'm very proud to have him as my uncle. And now he's gone …"

Janey's advance lost neither momentum nor spirit.

"You, James Logan, have a son to take care of! You are no longer a bachelor! You cannot act like this anymore …"

…

Janey sighed.

From her favorite lilypad-print patio chair, she saw the moving truck arrive and her heart fluttered. It marked the end of a rare period of solitude: Paul was in kindergarten for the morning and her mother had taken Kitty so that she would not be underfoot. (This got her mother out of the way as well.) Lisa had to work until 5. So, Janey had decided to enjoy a long, last rest on her West Philly porch. She had to get up to direct the movers a couple of times — it didn't feel right to sit while they worked so hard. But, once the boys fell into a rhythm, she made herself sit down.

Janey had argued with James about the move. She had been a West Philly girl all of her life. Why should she give that up for the suburbs? Ardmore was lovely and she understood that the home and Saint Colman's represented the history and family tradition of the Logans. They were so familiar with the church and its buildings that they often referred to it simply as 11 Simpson Road. And, why not? The Logans had built half the place. Still, it was not her history nor her family tradition.

Her history was here in Saint Francis de Sales, this world of porches and awnings where she had grown up with her brothers and her sister, Lisa, where she had gone to grade school, where on that very pavement she had jumped rope and played hopscotch, where she'd imagined the three-storey houses with conical roofs and battlements were castles, where she'd anticipated the sudden appearance of Heathcliff or Mr. Rochester or Fitzwilliam Darcy from behind a hedge or rosebush, where she had walked to and from West Philadelphia Catholic High School for Girls, where snowstorms made everything seem cleaner and the neighborhood cozier, and where people gathered in her parents' house for music sessions that lasted from Saturday night through to Sunday mass at the leaky-domed Byzantine-Revival church.

Through the bare tree branches and beyond Baltimore Avenue, Janey could make out the large dome with its alternating mosaics of crosses and stars of David. At Franny de Sales, she had received every sacrament from Baptism through Holy Matrimony. She had walked under that dome to receive her First Holy Communion, her Confirmation, and to hear mass every Sunday, listening to the largest organ in the city of Philadelphia after the one in Wanamaker's. Janey had gone to confession every Saturday in the devoted years of her early teens. She didn't confess often now, but she enjoyed examining her conscience using the Seven Deadly Sins and the feeling of being shriven. She liked walking home afterward, protected under the ever-watchful dome. The familiar sound of the trolleys shuttling along Baltimore Avenue would signal her return to the world. Back here on 44th Street, Mom would be making dinner and Dad would be setting up a circle of chairs in which the musicians would sit. Too bad Dad wasn't around to see her big move to Ardmore. It would have given him something to brag about.

Her two children, baptized under the church's mosaics with the names of the twelve apostles and their symbols, would have Sisters of Saint Joseph instead of IHM nuns. Janey had been glad to get away from those uptight biddies when she had gone to West, and she'd be glad to get away from them again.

James was asking her to leave her past behind her. She knew the move made logical sense; yet it was hard. The suburbs would be better for the kids. The neighborhood was changing no doubt. It was not as friendly and clean as it used to be. People didn't sit out as much. They stayed inside watching TV, ever since all the assassinations. The houses were not kept up as they once were. It was certainly not as safe now with all the colored people moving in and the long-haired Penn kids with their protests and crazy concerts at the Arena. A lot of her old friends had moved to the suburbs. Most of them raved about the advantages and comforts they now had. Kids play in backyards with grass and tall trees. There is more space and fresher air. You don't have to worry so much.

But who do the children play with? There couldn't be as many kids in Ardmore as there are in this street of twin houses. Soon a line of them would be walking home from school. In Ardmore, there wasn't a lot you could walk to — Janey would have to do more driving. Would there be neighbors to sit on the porch with and gossip?

Janey laughed to think that the seeds of her leaving home had been planted on her neighbor's front porch.

"The gospel accordion to John."

The movers were drawing the attention of passing drivers and pedestrians. Janey caught some curtains moving in the Ricciardi's second-floor bay window and on the Larkins' third-floor. Well, it should be a big deal, she thought, when Janey Dougherty Logan leaves the parish and neighborhood of her birth.

"I guess Janey Dougherty made out pretty good."

"Yeah, she marries the boss and moves out to a beauteeful house in the suburbs."

"No flies on her."

Well, they could all go pound sand. What did they know about falling in love? About doing what's best for your children? These ignoramuses who have never been anywhere except Wildwood? How could they understand?

In Ardmore, Kitty and Paul would grow up surrounded by a better class of people. She loved most of her neighbors and friends from Franny de Sales but some of them could be quite common. All the deezers and dozers, the men so tough they couldn't tell the difference between toilet and sand paper, and the uneducated and ill-mannered women could not be a good influence on Kitty and Paul in the long run. Maybe the kids would become soft by West Philly standards but they would speak properly, have impeccable manners, and have some culture. Instead of hanging around on street corners, her kids could invite their friends over to a rec room in the basement to play ping pong and have chips and soda. They would have more chores to do when they got older, too. They'd have a bigger lawn to cut, leaves to rake, a driveway to shovel, carpets to vacuum. But this was not a bad thing. In fact, it could keep them out of trouble.

The movers had started to load furniture into the truck. Janey followed them and stood by the curb, issuing commands and worried hisses.

"Don't worry, Mrs. Logan," the guy with the tattoo on his arm said. "We do 'iss alla time."

The aroma of Tom Dugan's pipesmoke! Janey recognized it and turned to find Tom standing next to her. He was more stooped than she had ever known him. But, he was still as sharp as ever.

"So today's the big day — huh, Janey?"

"Yes, it is, Mr. Dugan."

"Lots to do. Lots to worry about. But lots to be excited about, too."

"There is," agreed Janey. "I'm startin' to feel excited about it. Now that it's real and in progress."

Janey smiled to see one of the hulking movers wheeling Paul's knee-high bike on training wheels into the trailer. The bicycle was covered with orange **Re-elect Rizzo** bumper stickers. Clearly, Paul had repented of his decision to festoon his bike this way: white spots revealed where he had tried to claw the stubborn stickers off. She wondered what the young boys of Ardmore would think of the bike's decoration. Did Ardmore have a mayor?

"Sure, it's not like it's that far off," Mr. Dugan said.

Janey watched the cloud of pipesmoke rise and spin.

"A short train ride or a 20-minute drive."

"It's not like it's to Istanbul you're going."

Strange, thought Janey, that Paul was not a bit concerned about missing his little friends. Maybe that was his Logan blood. James is so independent. Much like his grandfather, they say. Came here from Ireland as a young man and never went back. Father Sarsfield, too. He left everything he knew and moved to New York City. Called by God to do so, he'd say, but likely a part of his nature all along.

"It's not," Janey replied. "It's only a couple of miles from City Line. But it will be nice for the kids to have a yard to play in. Paul is all excited about havin' his own swingset. He keeps askin' if it's true, if he will really have one in his backyard."

"Sure," Tom puffed. "It's always good to have a bit of land, some grass, trees," and puffing again. "Perhaps a wee garden."

Janey breathed in the aroma of Mr. Dugan's tobacco and watched the tendrils of smoke shimmy upward into nothingness.

"He's asking for his own basketball court, too."

"Sport is always a good thing for a boy. There are far worse things they can get up to, to be sure."

"Yes, there are, Mr. Dugan. Yes, there are."

Kitty was too young to really understand what was happening. Likely, she would have no memories of 44th Street and would grow up a suburban girl. Janey wondered if it would make a difference in the children's later lives. Would Kitty develop a distaste for the city? Would Paul be influenced by shadowy memories of his urban childhood?

"Well, best of luck to you, Janey girl. And to James. Bring the little ones to see us now and then. You know where to find us."

Mr. Dugan patted Janey on the elbow, shuffled across the street, re-lit his pipe, and sauntered up the hill toward Larchwood, as she had so often seen him do.

Would she see it again?

Janey would have to make a point of bringing the kids In Town on a regular basis. They could come in and visit their father a few times a year. Certainly at Christmas time. They could see the Light Show and the Enchanted Village. And, when they did go In Town it would not be on that filthy rattle-trap El but on a civilized train gliding into Suburban Station.

But when would she come back here to Franny de Sales?

Saint Colman's was a lovely church, too. Like the Logan Construction Company, it was founded by an Irish immigrant. Father Carton. Janey had heard all the stories! She had attended beautiful masses there and liked Monsignor Graham.

And, the Logans certainly had a lot of history at Saint Colman's. James's grandfather was involved in building the church and school around the time of the company's 25th anniversary. He donated the stained-glass window of the resurrection in the back of the church. In the 1920s, James's father, Jimmy, helped make the new grey-stoned Gothic church look more like one in Ireland. Now James is making plans to help with a more modern rectory. It made sense for the head of the Logan Construction Company to live in Saint Colman's. It was perfectly logical and sensible. And James loved it. But it was not hers. It was not home.

Still, even when she was arguing against it, she could admit to herself that, along with a sense of loss, there was a certain thrill to moving out. The dawn of a new day! She would be joining a set that her parents had never been part of. Certainly, none of her friends had made it to the Main Line. Her children's lives would be better than hers — and isn't that what every mother wanted? Let the gossips say she was benefitting from marrying her boss. If it was good for the children, it was good for her. Kitty and Paul might miss out on some things that she had taken for granted, but how can they miss what they never had?

It was clear this was not just a move out but a move up. She would have a lot of fancy neighbors on the Main Line, smart people from Saint Joe's, Villanova, Haverford, Swarthmore, Bryn Mawr, people with old money, businessmen and country club ladies.

Janey sighed.

. . .

Too bad we are so full of dumplings or we could stop for a knish at Shimmel's or for some lox, caviar, and bagels. Run by generations of Russes and Daughters. Only a few such places left. Years ago this area teeming with Jews. Some of them Greenhorns in caftans, beards, and shaggy hair under Russian hats. Others seasoned, clean shaven and close cropped, with American clothes and American dash. Judaica and matzoh factories. Let my people go! Get a corned beef at Katz's, the only place still open. And a few blocks back the 2nd Avenue deli. Yiddish Walk of Fame.

And the time is chosen and the curtain time arrives … and the kings and the prophets, never taken away … and all the words and tales carried across the sands and snows over the seas to strut the Bowery boards … The National and The Thalia … And their glory is not of the past but of the moment and of the future ... And their light brightening the darkening stage … and celebrated on today's mosaic lightposts … brought long lines to the sidewalks and great crowds rushing breathless to see the shows of those whom no one wanted …and the muted heartache moan of the clarinet drifts over the time, nearly regardless of it ... And the fingertip-tapped teks and spirited kas rattle round and round awaiting, anticipating the next doum's fall … And the poet-king strums his lyre and the diademed dancer's feet praise the Lord on the riverbank of freedom … And the past is not the past but the everpresent … forever aflame but never consumed … And the audience is not the pogrom-haunted hunted herd, the sound of shattered glass and screams in its ears, scattered from the ancient home, sojourning among the settled nations only to be blown away again over the sea … survivors of riots, pogroms … girls on overseas voyages alone, supporting the men and boys of their family with their toil but Prophetic and Royal and Holy … but the heroes of the moment … and of the past … let my people go … and those of the heroes and prophets of the future let all the Lord's people go … And you can feel it … And you can consume it … and you can digest it … because it was for you …

Finding the Way from the Lower East Side to the FDR

To find your way to the FDR:

1. Continue on Houston Street from Attorney Street
2. Progress past Avenues C and D of Alphabet City
3. Approach the threshold of the ramp to the FDR

Vertical neon letters spelled out, "Parkside," a bar and grill whose lights were still lit. Like Parkside Lounge in Overbrook but not really. South of Houston it was Pitt Street but north of Houston it was Avenue C.

— Hey, I almost got a job at that bar. It's a music place. Kinda like the Orange Crush. Different music every night, cool pool table and all.

— I went to this Charlie Parker jazz festival not far from here. Somebody handed me a flier saying that Bird used to hang out there.

Mira! You saw that Mistah Logan? They call that street "Loisaida." You gotta know some Spanish when you come down here, boy. Or at least some Spanglish! Word! They ain't playin' down here.

— When I went there for the interview? There was this guy with an earring? He wanted to tell me the whole history of the place. He told me there is an old tunnel from the basement all the way to the East River.

— His way of recruiting bartenders?

— I was like, whatever. Your place is too far from any subway.

The light turned red on Avenue D. So close to the entrance to the easy-drive FDR. So close yet not quite there.

Leading her through this Jewish world and another Puerto Rican one. Never imagined this. Dreamed of leading her through ancient Egypt at the Met. Why? Because the famine became severe throughout the world.

I am taking her through gallery after gallery and she is following, though I never thought of myself as a great interpreter of Egyptian art. I had spoken to her about the Islamic Calligraphy exhibit. Could that be the connection?

As we wander through the museum, she's absorbed by every detail I point out, every observation I make, every insight I share. Like never in real life. And she's laughing at my jokes and bopping her shoulder against mine.

— Look! This estate manager was buried with beer! I exclaim, stopping in front of a large gallery sign. They thought of everything for the afterlife! The Egyptians invented beer, y'know.

— And this guy invented the toilet, Laura cracks, pointing to a stolid blocky pharaoh seated on a throne.

We bend down together to examine a scorpion amulet and an ancient miniature galley filled with dark men and women and their cargo of fish and game. We peer through fiberglass at some turquoise-colored ankhs and at a fantastic faience falcon with its right wing fully extended.

— The falcon is the symbol, I say as if I know what I'm talking about, of order, of proper obedience to the gods.

Is that even true? I don't know but the statues nod their heads in approval.

— The deadliest scorpion was from North Africa, I say like an expert, and the pharaohs wanted to be known for their deadly sting!

— Wow! I never knew that! Scorpions just make my skin crawl.

— When you get stung, you'll feel more than that.

Next I draw her attention to the extraordinary shades of green and blue in the tiled wall decoration and to the Roman mosaic of Isis, not even in that section of the museum.

— How awesome is this place! Laura exclaims.

We stop to look at the statue of an Egyptian couple, Memi and Sabu. Memi's hand reaches over Sabu's shoulder and cops a feel of Sabu's breast. I jokingly put my arm over her shoulder and she pushes me away laughing. She is wearing the same blue hoodie and tie-dye shirt she has on now.

A seated bare-breasted Isis offers her nipple to her absent son, Osiris, her hand cupping her left breast. A bare-chested Egyptian man with arms locked at his sides strides over to take a look.

Now some Rodin sculptures appear among the Egyptian artworks. *Orpheus and Eurydice* prepare to cross the threshold of the Underworld back to this world. *Cupid and Psyche* share a passionate kiss. A naked couple make out in *Eternal Spring* but, unlike Memi, the man leaves the shapely breasts untouched.

— I can tell you used to be a teacher, says she. You explain all of this stuff so well. I understand it so much better.

I give her a kiss on the cheek. But my lips slide toward hers. The corners of our lips touch accidentally on purpose. Like this whole museum trip and the long wandering gallery to gallery is accidentally on purpose.

Memi and Sabu smile and turn to look at each another.

— It's like I'm being introduced to a whole new world. And having so much fun!

Then she lets out this sexy moan and leans into me for a real kiss.

Memi and Sabu kiss, too.

Laura wriggles her hips like she can't get her body close enough to mine. I am pressing her up against the fiberglass display window but no security guard comes near. Indeed, there are no more people in the museum.

The statues notice us, however. Laura and I make out in Perneb's Tomb and the engraved pharaohs nod in approval. Their queens wink. We kiss and grope each other all through the long halls of galleries with statues and decorative arts. Laura plops her ass down on a mummy case and I slide my hand between her blue-jeaned thighs. The mummy seems uncomfortable but the colorful slender girl bearing a duck in her hand and a basket on her head, smiles. Greek statues of Icarus, Phaethon, and Arachne peek through gallery entrances. We tongue-kiss and caress each other — my fingers are running through her hair and I can feel her heat beating, her large tie-dye heart — as we stumble past the friezes of pharoahs and hieroglyphics, treasures of this life and illustrations of the afterlife. The *Wounded Amazon* towers in the threshold to the temple of Dendur. Practically topless, she starts to fondle her one fully exposed breast. The Kouros boy, arms firmly at his sides, turns his whole body to look.

I am tempted to lay her down on one of the cases holding the elaborate mummy coffins. But a female face of the dead disapproves and a staring turquoise-and-green-eye amulet freaks me out. Laura and I continue our passionate stumbling into the wide and high gallery housing the Temple of Dendur.

Before the Temple of Dendur, we undress, tossing our clothes into a pile to make a bed on the marble floor. Statues from Egypt, Greece and Rome, Italy, Africa, and Oceania in various stages of undress and nudity surround us. And they urge us on. I massage Laura's breasts and the female statues start to do the same with their own and each other's. Square-jawed *Zeus Ammon* plants a kiss on the reclining *Mexican Girl Dying* who hitches up her grass skirt. Golden *Diana* drops her bow and caresses gently the mysterious *Mourning Victory*.

— Look at what has happened, Paul? All because of you! There is no one so discerning and wise as you. You are an artist who inspires artworks!

Then we are locked in a long kiss. And I cannot wait any longer. I enter her. She moans and so do I. The male statues start to stroke the female statues and their own members, even though many of them had been cut off. *Evening*, a sensual nude with hands in her hair permits the caresses of the *Two Natures of Man*. *Aphrodite Anadyomene* presents her nipples to the mouth of seated *Cleopatra*.

And Laura says:

— I love art! I love the way you teach me, Paul! I love it!

And I am thrusting and thrusting and we are moaning on the marble floor before the Temple of Dendur and the sky-high windows exposing dark Central Park's fanning leafless tree branches in the streetlight. The waves in the fountain where *La Belle Irlandais* has abandoned her picture frame to wade in the nude, rise and fall with our movements. Sculptures of lion-headed and dog-headed gods and goddesses rut all around us. Pygmalian and Galatea do more than kiss and Tahitian women in vivid red and blue-and-yellow pareus recline languidly, awaiting the descent unto them of Prometheus of Rockefeller Center.

— You fill me up so much, she says. Oh! My heart and my brain! ... Oh! ... Much more than Charles.

And it just goes on and on. I thrust and thrust. A recumbent sphinx starts licking a goddess with no head nor shoulders. One Egyptian woman brushes another's hair but soon their fingers are in one another's mouths and they forget the small baby with them and everything but their desire for one another. And I thrust harder and harder and the waves from the fountains splash against the slanting windows onto Central Park. Yet, there is no climax. We get distracted now and then by the statue orgy. A headless *Diadoumenos* is being pleasured by Sakhmet, the powerful one. The Libyan Sibyl takes into her mouth the toe of Caesar. And Asian tourists are taking pictures of the temple without noticing the Bacchantic scene in front of them. We change positions and it just continues. I get no closer to orgasm. A striding jackal-headed god with his hands before him like begging dog's paws comes over.

— That's Anubis, who brings people to the Underworld.

— You have such a head for knowing, Laura says.

Anubis takes Laura's tie-dyed-heart t-shirt from under her head with his snout and drops it on a scale, while a relief of Persephone runs her hand between his ears. And still I cannot climax. A chamber group plays in the balcony over the Great Hall. Islamic designs from the Damascus Room appear and still we go on and on with no orgasm for me. Then she is on top and I am looking up at her and at the *Bacchante and Infant Faun* and there is intensity and pleasure and she is happy but I get no satisfaction.

And the conductor throws a giant Christmas tree over the balcony and it lands in a medieval gallery and knocks over a statue of a bishop. The orchestra doesn't know what to do and starts playing screeching tones all out of time. And still I keep humping and Laura keeps taking her pleasure and complimenting me and I grow no closer to climax.

...

Janey remembered that when she was planning the wedding reception, she fell in love with the Warwick Hotel immediately. Janey loved the Warwick because of its Old World charm. Although it was built in the 1920s, it hearkened back to earlier days. It could have been lifted from a plot of land in Europe and deposited intact alongside Philadelphia's Rittenhouse square. It was also in a perfect Center City location: a short walk from any number of respected shops, fine restaurants, and prestigious office buildings. The entrance to the hotel alone was enough to take Janey's breath away. From Rittenhouse Square, you could see its wide, grand stairs between large white urns planted with manicured shrubs. Above the entrance to the lobby, the middle of the hotel itself was recessed so that the rooms were at a remove from the noisy streets below. She loved the arching bow windows that bathed the lobby with sunlight by day and the grand chandelier — bigger than she was even in her bridal gown — that lit the luxurious space by night. She could imagine her guests strolling to and fro, stretching their legs by the balconies that looked onto the lobby from above.

Mr. Logan, who, going against tradition, had vociferously declared that he would help pay for the reception, was also pleased with the Warwick. To Janey, Mr. Logan's generosity provided the final confirmation of the outsized affection he had shown her since the day James had introduced her to the Logan patriarch. Mr. Logan remembered when the hotel was first built and had taken a keen interest in its rise. He was pleased that the Warwick had played host to the elites of Philadelphia society and that it overlooked the city's most prominent residential district, the world-renowned Rittenhouse Square. He envisioned the dignified entrances that would be made by his high-placed friends and business associates — those whom he would invite or exclude based on the loyalty they had displayed over the years. Truly, only Santa Claus or Saint Peter pored over their lists with more assiduity than Mr. Logan. He loved the gigantic star-spangled banners which draped elegantly down on the either side of the entrance. Though it had been years since he'd served in the military, when he saw these monstrous flags, he had the urge to salute. He could hear himself telling his old army stories. Privately, he yearned to see depending from one of those poles the flag of a true 32-County Irish Republic. He had no use for that banner of quislings, the one that represented the partitioned Free State. He was working on getting stories in the *Inquirer* and the *Bulletin* about the wedding, as well. He hoped that the Gowens, the Protestant rivals who had blackballed his father when he had first come to this country, would read them and have an apoplexy. Maybe he'd mail them copies — C.O.D.

James Logan, the groom, was just happy that both his bride to be and his, at times, overbearing father were content: they chattered away about the wedding night and day. He thought it was neat that the Warwick was at 17th and Walnut whereas his *alma mater*, The Prep, was at 17th and Stiles. He imagined all the laughs his school chums would have, joking about how he had finally been snared, the one they'd always imagined would never be caught. He knew they'd be grouped around the bar, neglecting their dates, telling well-rehearsed tales of their days at The Prep, and, once lubricated enough, launching into the school fight song. He could hear it echoing in the hall already:

> *Swing on along with the crimson!*
> *Swing on along with the gray!*

It would certainly be wonderful for Janey to walk into such a lovely place as the bride of James Logan. She would be entering into an enviable, even glamorous life and leaving behind her the gossip over James's previous engagement, the office whispers of those who would slander their love for one another. People can be so tiresome. Do they have so little to concern themselves with? Two people running into each other at the Automat? Really! But, on June 2, 1962, Janey and James Logan would be married, officially together, for all the world to see.

Reverend Sarsfield Logan. S.J., or, as James and Janey knew him, "Father Sarsfield" was pleased, for the same reason as James was, to see the hotel's 17th Street address, as much as he disapproved of the ostentation and materialism that the choice of venue represented to him.

"So, you want me to eat in that den of Republicans — eh?" he'd ask with a smile.

Alas, he would not spend much time at the hotel, as everyone knew but would try their best to prevent. This would not be for partisan reasons: he would leave any party early. He would give a blessing to the couple, lead everyone in the Grace Before Meals, drink a toast, eat, and leave quickly, only saying "goodbye" to those he happened to encounter as he made his escape. No one would be offended, however; they'd only laugh at this well-known eccentricity of old Father Logan's.

Mr. Logan would not be so indulgent with his ordained elder brother as most others were. He had a good mind to warn his brother not to offend with one of his infamous rude exits the constellation of Philadelphia's business and political stars that would be assembled in the reception hall. He most certainly would speak to Father Sarsfield. But, it would do no good, he knew. His highly impractical brother had no respect for such concerns. Besides, the poor man was in his 70s, though you would hardly have known it to look at him.

Father Sarsfield said a wonderful mass. During the wedding ceremony, Janey could not keep a few tears from dropping from her eyes. Walking up the aisle through all the family and friends wishing the couple well and cheering them for the first time as Mr. and Mrs. Logan was so exhilarating Janey nearly cried again. She remembered the photographer snapping them as they got into the limo, struggling to get the Byzantine dome of Saint Francis de Sales in the frame. That picture turned out so nice. He got some rice in mid-air just over their shoulders, a big, laughing smile on James's face.

Anyway, after all that, it was a relief to ride in the limousine and have a few quiet moments with James — who was still waving to people minutes after the couple had surely disappeared from sight. Janey breathed a sigh of satisfaction and sat back. She watched the familiar rows of Queen-Anne-style houses go by and gazed wistfully at Cedar Park. She said a silent goodbye to the statue of Charles Dickens seated in his thinking-writer pose and his creation, Little Nell, leaning on a cement block looking up at her creator. When they passed Spruce Hill, she threw her head back — carefully because of the veil — and stared at the sun sifting through the aged tree branches. James kissed her and then he sat back, too, and rested his head on the top of the seat cushion. The champagne tickled her nostrils as she saw the Schuylkill go by beneath them and the 30th Street station gleaming white on the other side. Janey began to feel exhilarated again. Soon they would be arriving at the Warwick! The limousine would pull up in front of the grand entrance and her new husband and she would step out and make their way through the excited, parting crowds.

But first they had to stop at the Azalea Garden, a place becoming so popular for wedding photos that James wondered if we had to call ahead to reserve a bush. He was so funny when they were planning the wedding. But, he got impatient with the photographer at the Azalea Garden. He was so anxious to get to the hotel and celebrate that he hated the delay. That the stop was so close to the hotel, he said later, made it that much more frustrating. (Of course, he was well aware of the plan ahead of time, but he doesn't pay attention to such things.)

The limo did pull up in front of the entryway that Mr. Logan and Janey both admired. And indeed there were crowds waiting for them. Flashbulbs popped on either side of Janey. Subsequently she learned that they belonged not only to their photographer but also to reporters from the *Inquirer* and the *Bulletin*. Janey was blinded for a second. She felt rather than saw some commotion on the pavement to her left. Casting her eyes downward, she saw a pair of ill-shod feet — with toes sticking out of the front of their shoes — going backwards. Awful body odor came to her nostrils and she felt sick to her stomach. She heard a voice that sounded like a Negro's.

"I just lookin' for somepin' to eat! Just lookin' for somepin' to eat!"

Then she saw clearly that a policeman was dragging the hungry man away from them. And Janey began to feel even sicker. All at once, she became aware of herself and what she was doing. She had been so delighted to fulfill her girlish daydreams, God forgive her, in the wealthiest block in the Delaware Valley and this poor soul being dragged away from her was out scrounging for a scrap of food to eat. She wished she could cancel the whole reception, which suddenly appeared to be pure folly, and send everyone home — or to a soup kitchen. Janey's heart went out to the poor man, and at the same instant, as if sensing this, he called out.

"What a beautiful bride! Congratulations! Congratulations!"

Janey heard the driver close the limo door and the policeman slam the Paddy wagon tailgate. The two sounds formed a dissonant chord.

Inside the hotel, Janey could feel Lisa's elbowing her. But, when she turned to her sister, Lisa was greeting someone. Her Maid of Honor looked so lovely in her sunshine-yellow, silk-and-taffeta finery that she seemed to be strolling through a fairy tale. She raised one of her sheer, full-bishop sleeves and elbowed Janey again. In the reverberating hall, Janey tilted her ear toward Lisa's lips:

"Can you believe that crazy nigger tryin' to mess up your wedding?"

5. Sloth & Diligence

Carrying the same walking stick and portmanteau he had taken across the Atlantic, Seamus Logan boarded the Hoboken ferry at Barclay Street, in order to get the train that would take him to Philadelphia. It was one of winter's first short days. The sky had darkened and the air had cooled all at once. Nevertheless, Seamus stood at the stern, tracing with his eyes the tall masts and taller buildings arrayed up and down the west side of Manhattan, the spires of Saint Paul's Chapel and Trinity Church dwarfing poor Saint Peter's in whose bursting basement he'd just made a visit, and a one-, two-, three-layered slice of Castle Clinton at Battery Park. Taller than everything else, on the far side of the island, loomed like a colossal ogham stone the tower of the Brooklyn Bridge, already joined by undulating wires to its twin on the Brooklyn side of the East River. Was Seamus leaving something unfinished? He couldn't be certain that he was not. But he had no interest in seeing the bridge completed if Queen Famine would celebrate her birthday on it. Not enough that she drove his people out of their homes with hunger. Now she had to witness how they lost their lives to connect two cities of wealth and plenty building this so-called, "Eighth wonder of the world."

Seamus sighed.

New York did provide a beautiful prospect from this vantage point. Manhattan suited Seamus in some ways. With its great and steady push toward the future and its little regard for the past, Manhattan embodied ambition itself. It was a sort of in-between place, a doorway between worlds. Janus, the two-faced god of doorways, should be its tutelary deity: it looks out toward the great sprawling continent of America while gazing back over Neptune's depths to Europe, Africa, and the Orient. Janus could have been Seamus's patron saint as well.

Still, Manhattan is not part of either world. Though the Old World is imported through its gates each day and recreated wherever possible, it is truly not the Old World. As an amalgamation of immigrant customs, it was, likewise, not the New World. It was surely not the wide-open, limitless continent that people abroad dream about. Rather it was a narrow island overrun by foreigners, a dirty and dangerous world unto itself, which never ceased regarding itself. Perhaps another Greek myth applied better: Manhattan the brick-and-mortar Narcissus admiring its reflection in the harbor.

A disheveled tramp dragged his left leg onto the ferry and limped in Seamus's direction. Seamus was surprised the fellow had the price of the crossing on him. He wore a hat so battered and squashed it appeared to be on sideways. His shoes and shoulders were dusted with a light powder, possibly cement. He stopped next to Seamus, gazed up at the view of Manhattan island, and lit an odiferous two-for-a-penny clay pipe. How could he stomach such awful smelling stuff, wondered Seamus. It probably was a good distraction from the stink of his own body. The tramp had a light in his eye that told Seamus he would be seeking conversation, but Seamus had no patience to suffer his company. He picked up his portmanteau and moved close to the paddlewheels at the boat's center, still looking back at the island from which he was departing. Barclay Street was littered with barrels, baskets, and boxes, making it hard for people to pass through. The salesman and loafers accosting the pedestrians must like it that way.

Seamus rejoiced to get away from New York's crowds and noise, the constant rushing, the confusion and disorder, the myriad struggles, the poor souls, like that pipe-puffing Bend refugee, habituated to daily suffering. Philadelphia was a big, bustling, and growing city — so his friend Dennis had oft written him — but one in which you can breathe. Dennis assured Seamus he could live there in more comfort and greater safety than on the Lower East Side. Some workers he knew owned their own homes. Philadelphia could provide a more stable foundation on which to build his life in the New World. Buildings were springing up everywhere, said Dennis: rows of houses, Catholic churches and schools, and even homes in new suburbs from which people could travel by train into town. These were logical reasons offered by Dennis, and they were indeed valid. But it was really the restlessness in his bones that made him go, that same restlessness which had guided him from Bunowen to Connemara, Galway City to Cork, Queenstown to New York.

Seamus looked at the stars in the sky and the gas lamps in the hundreds of windows and wondered how the city would appear the next time he saw it. Perhaps he would not see it again but some descendant of his would ride a ferry like this in the opposite direction, when the city was more than half begun. Ferries might not even be needed then. The gaslights might be replaced by electric lights. Maybe there would not be so many sails on the horizon. Now on the North River there floated some steamships, some sailboats, and some that relied on a combination of steam and wind, as if the navigational world had not fully committed to a means of propulsion. Seamus would miss the changes in this rough-and-tumble island, the second rough place that offered him a home. People did marry and put down roots in New York City but Seamus could not imagine doing so.

A chain rattled against the ferry's steel deck. The gates creaked to a close. No one else would be boarding. The weighed anchor clanked and the boat bobbed on waves stirred by the traffic of vessels. A couple of girls squealed and took hold of the railing. One blue-eyed lass with blonde hair slipping out from under her bonnet looked Seamus right in the eye as she righted herself. And Seamus smiled. New York City had many beautiful women, that was certain. He hoped Philadelphia would, too.

The horn blew, the engine exhaled a black stream heavenward, and the ferry began rising and dipping on the man-made swells.

Unmoored from Manhattan, his gaze turned upward, Seamus prayed.

"Dear Lord, please lead me toward the right place to settle. If Philadelphia be that place, let me find a home and a wife there. If I am to take root in some other place, Thy will be done."

Seamus shoved his walking stick into his oxter and opened his newspaper. He always searched for news of home first. And here it was: a caricature of Oscar Wilde posed with exaggerated delicacy, a personified sunflower gawking down on him. **OSCAR WILDE IN YORKVILLE** said the headline. The Irishman had lectured at Parepa Hall dressed in "a black velvet coat with profuse ruffles, knee breeches, and low shoes. He wore silk stockings" as he spoke "On the Practical Application of the Principles of Home Decoration, with Observations on Personal Dress and Ornament."

Out in the harbor, two Staten Island Ferries, their wide bodies crowned by pilothouses and twice-tall scape pipes, passed each other under the eyes of the Statue of Liberty. Seamus watched them come and go and turned back to the news.

Under **IRISH POLITICAL AFFAIRS**, he found stories about frustrated rebellions, informers, and special police powers. The English were implementing Section 16 of the Coercion Act, subjecting suspects:

> ...to extensive interrogations without charge or trial in their effort to
> identify the murderers of Irish Chief Secretary Lord Frederick
> Cavendish and his Deputy Thomas Henry Burke in Dublin's
> Phoenix Park in May. Police believe the Phoenix Park murders

were an act of revenge for the police shootings in Mayo the
previous day. Dublin bricklayer James Carey, one of the group of
'Invincibles' suspected of involvement, is under questioning.

Seamus sighed and lowered the paper. They would grant themselves whatever power they need to get what they want. He'd read no more of it.

On the New Jersey side of the river, smokestacks let loose blacker clouds than those above them. Compared to what he left behind him, the hills and grey cliffs to the north seemed forlorn and empty. This was the first time Seamus had been aboard a ship since he had crossed the Atlantic and, recalling that, he was glad that he would be disembarking in a matter of minutes. How sweet it had been to walk on *terra firma* after the horror of that voyage! Seamus could not help but remember the night he had rowed across Killary Harbor from one county to another in the boat placed there for him by Providence. Somehow as a boy John Cardinal McCloskey had managed to row from Brooklyn to Manhattan to hear mass on this very street. How had he secured the boat? Seamus still thought it strange that incurious Connemara had never questioned him about the rowboat he himself had borrowed.

How much quieter that crossing was than this! Ferry horns' blowing, steam engines' running, paddlewheels' splashing, and sailors' shouts filled the air. Tugboats shouldered barges up the North River. Other ferries crisscrossed the waters separating one state from the other. Men hurried about the various vessels, their arms and legs busy with their labors. It felt strange to be still and idle. His muscles even felt relaxed and disused: he hadn't worked in a couple of days since punching out Agins, his old foreman. For the time being, he was free!

This was surely the land of the free tongue, Seamus smiled to think. At Fulton Fish Market, the witty hawkers and fish mongers were never at a loss for words, never without a joke or an insult if it seemed warranted, in a way in which you could never do at home: you might be insulting your distant cousin or your friend's. And those fish mongers at the market and the vegetable sellers with their street carts never tired and never ceased performing. Their daily lives were spent before the eyes of the passing multitudes, a perpetual, ever-renewing audience.

Then there was the Five Points. A couple of times Seamus had allowed himself to be dragged to that district, not far from Jane McElroy's boarding house. He had often heard that the neighborhood was much better than it used to be, that the worst slums and streets had been demolished. But, the Bend still had an odor that did not seem to come from this world. Animal waste and human waste and garbage combined to create a stink that could knock a man right over. How could those people live like that? He supposed they were used to it. Maybe their noses had just given up, considering it too much effort to carry that stench to the brain. People could get used to anything that necessity forced them to accept, Seamus mused. These people had survived the famine and the coffin ships and they would survive the worst of the slums, too. But to see a people used to green fields and fresh air forced to live in such squalor by the misrule of a foreign queen made Seamus sick to his stomach! It would not be forgotten.

For all of the disgust it aroused, the Five Points also held a certain fascination. What an admixture of people it housed! Whole families on the floor of one room — and taking in boarders. But that overcrowded district roared with energy! The music and dancing and the drunks ... The banjos ringing out from the basement bars into the overcrowded streets … the stomping and tapping of feet … Like nothing he'd ever heard! Even the threat of sudden violence gave the place an air of excitement.

He would not miss those disgusting bars and shops, though. Five Points had grocery stores everywhere selling grog at all hours of the day or night. People who had ruined themselves through drink stumbled along the shitsmelling streets swallowing whatever cheap liquor they could get. Some of them were mere children — not only fetching growlers of beer for their parents but getting drunk themselves! Was it for this that these families had crossed the ocean? It was certainly not why Seamus had. He had come here for a reason. In Ireland, if you had a dog as useless as those parents, you'd take him out back and shoot him. Still, these poor souls were runaways like him, likely running away from something worse than broken female promises. As the man said, "If you lived in this place, would you ask for milk?"

The worst were the stale-beer dives hidden in alleyways and basements, where degraded men — and women! — drink leftover beer put back in a keg. What desperation those people must feel to spend their time in such lightless, hopeless dungeons, walls covered with filth and crawling with insects in order to drink drafts of bane from tomato cans! Handing over the coins they had begged to aproned hags who must have lost her souls to accept such custom in such Plutonian pits! Some of the denizens even spent the night in these holes. Two-cent restaurants, they called them, where drunks could pass out at picnic tables. Jail must be a relief to them when the dives get raided!

But, those scenes of horror were behind him now, Seamus hoped. For tonight at least, he had no one to answer to. And that suited him well. He didn't like to associate with those who gave orders and insisted that theirs was the "way things were supposed to be done!" They reminded him of where he had come from.

Doubtless there were pitfalls to avoid in this country, especially in that city that was bouncing away into the distance, but there were plenty of Americans who had overcome them — like the sailors moving so nimbly among the decks and masts of the ships around him. How strong and agile they were! It delighted Seamus to watch them. They seemed personifications of his new country and harbingers of his new life!

Now he was on his own, he could go at his own pace. He was free to admire how light from another state could play on the surface of the water at his feet, to follow the white reflections on the tiny waves flittering like leaves in the wind, to listen to the water's lapping and splashing, to watch the breakers churned up by the ferry and detect a faint smell of the sea. No one expected anything of him, except Dennis who would be waiting at Philadelphia's Broad Street station. As he headed down the gangplank in Hoboken, he thought that his bold pushing onward had served him well in the past and prayed that it would continue to do so into the future.

Seamus boarded the train and took a seat facing a gentleman with a top hat resting on the seat next to him. He smiled at the stranger who nodded and returned to his *Harper's Weekly*. Seamus slid into the seat by the window across from the top hat. As the train headed south, he watched the dark swampland turn to firmer soil and he realized he was moving farther away from the sea, farther inland into his new country. An anxious feeling arose in his stomach: he didn't like being far from the sea. In New York, you could sometimes forget the sea was nearby but then a bracing wind or summer breeze would remind you. Back in Bunowen, amid the smells of the land, the turf fires, and the manure, the air always bore a hint of salt from Clew Bay and you could often hear its music, *an ceol na mara*.

Yes, Seamus was moving one more step away from home, from his wronged country that had wronged him, and from the Cause. He would not be a jester for the Protestants in England and America like Wilde. He would defeat those who would hold him down, those who would hold *them* down, by being a hard-working gentleman. He had read an article or two in a discarded *Harper's Weekly* himself — though he would never buy a rag that published Thomas Nast's cartoons insulting the Church and the Irish. Seamus refused to live of life of dependence, a life in which his hard work did nothing more than keep hunger from his door. At the same time, he would not forget his countrymen still in chains nor the ghosts of the starved.

Seamus would miss the way an Irishman is immediately welcome in New York City. So many New Yorkers were born in the ould sod that an Irishman received a *Cead Mile Failte* like no other. You'd think New York were an Irish county. Even its name harkens back across the sea — to the homeplace of Seamus of York, the *Seamus an Chaca* who fled to France when things got rough at the Boyne and exposed the Catholics' necks to the yoke of the Penal Laws. At Saint James's Church, Seamus had joined the lads from the AOH talking revolution. Their conversations had a different ring to them than similar chat at home. They made his heart beat more quickly. For in their words there was true possibility: something could arise from the defeat at the Boyne, the butchery of Ballinamuck, and the humiliation of the Great Hunger!

The gentleman across from Seamus turned the page of his magazine and folded it over. Seamus noticed the headline of an article:

THE PROBLEM OF LIVING IN NEW YORK

He smiled. He wanted to read more but didn't want to make it obvious. He turned his head back to the window and watched the dark flatness of New Jersey chug past. Seamus had only traveled a few miles since crossing the North River and already he felt that he was in a different land, a land closer to that sought after by the newcomers.

He peeked over the top of his newspaper to catch a few more words of the article.

"In no considerable, thoroughly settled city on the civilized globe is material living attended with so many difficulties as New York. The average New-Yorker ... has no expectation of a home ... the most he dares to hope for is a sojourning place for six months, or a year or two at furthest."

Seamus chuckled to himself. He'd take it as an omen.

In Philadelphia, there were plenty of Irish. He had heard about Irish Brigades from Pennsylvania who had fought in Gettysburg. New York had its anti-Irish bigotry but it was probably worse in Philadelphia. He had read about how Know Nothings who had burned down convents and churches there, which had not happened in New York. But that was years ago, during Famine times. Still, wasn't it only five years ago that they had hanged all those Irish coal miners in Pennsylvania? But Dennis said it was safer and healthier in Philadelphia. He says the Nativists are afraid of going near Irish neighborhoods like Devil's Pocket. Seamus himself had no intentions of kowtowing to any bigots. And he had no doubt that there would be some Irishmen in his new city who would stand up with him.

Seamus knew that there were AOH divisions in Philadelphia. The National Convention of Hibernians took place there recently. He could get a letter of introduction from the Saint James lads. Maybe he could help them organize their divisions and get them on a sure footing.

Seamus leaned his head against the window as the rocking of the train lulled him. Images of his various futures danced in the darkness, as Seamus Logan gave into sleep.

...

Laura reached the end of Houston Street and took the ramp that curved down onto the northbound Franklin D. Roosevelt East River Drive. Dark dirt infields stood empty on the right while red-brick Lillian Wald housing projects loomed over the left. Now that they were on the long-sought FDR, it was easy giving her directions.

Taking the FDR to Midtown

To take the FDR to Midtown:

1. Take the 42nd Street exit.
2. Head west on 42nd Street.

Watching a pedestrian bridge pass overhead, Paul felt relieved that the directions and the driving would be easy for a while.

would love to lay my head back let her drive the highway just stare at the river take me to my bathroom but gotta make conversation don't let this chance go by

— I can't believe you never get drunk, Laura said, resting one hand on the wheel and letting her shoulders drop. No matter how much we drink, you stay the same … Wait, except for that one time we went to Stagecoach.

Laura filled the quiet car with a gleeful riff of giggles, her head rocking forward and her torso shaking. Paul liked the way she really let herself go when she laughed.

— Remember that?

so she now has a story to tell and the energy to talk cool

— Sort of.

Stagecoach lay by the West Side Highway — on the exact opposite side of town. When the bartender and some customers had started doing the limbo one Thursday, the bar had felt like a remote western outpost of the world. The barmaids' western hats and boots didn't discourage the impression, nor did the flannel shirts tied over their exposed midriffs nor the shortshort cutoffs. The hot young women also jumped on the bar to dance when the spirit moved them.

— That was one night when you seemed totally drunk. Do you remember what you said?

He wasn't sure and, besides, he liked to hear her tell it.

— No. What?

— They took your hat and danced around with it for a while. Then another girl came up and took your glasses. A few minutes later, you came up to me and said, "Where're my glasses? I can't see. This isn't funny anymore!"

Her hands flew around her bedraggled blonde head and her lips seemed redder and more kissable as she told the story. She really got a kick out of it.

— It's all kind of a blur, I have to admit!

— You were so funny at that place! But then you seemed to sober up after that.

Laura's rattle-trap machine zoomed by the Jacob Riis Houses. *How the Other Half Lives.* A blinding flash down the dark tenement stairwell of memory. The other world just on the other side of the highway and an elevator ride away. And Laura blissfully unaware of it. Her BMW passed under another pedestrian bridge. A quartet of Con Ed smokestacks came into view. In the backseat, Charles's head hung forward, practically parallel with the floor of the car. The English kid was a real lightweight. Poised enough to be able to sleep while this crazy blonde is at the wheel, though.

Ours is not to reason why.

— I can't believe I still have a paper to write, Laura remarked …

— When's it due?

— Not until next week … But, you know … until it's done it's always at the back of your mind …

— I know exactly what you mean! It's one reason I don't miss being in school. What's it on?

— Oh, it's just a response paper about some short stories we read. Not a big deal, but it's just a pain.

— I remember having lots of papers to write — for just about every subject.

For the theology paper due in the morning, Paul had scribbled only a few rough pages along with some notes and ideas in the margins of xeroxed articles. He had nothing typed. Paul sighed and tried to untie the knots forming in his stomach. It was clear that before this night was over, he would have to compose at the typewriter. And, he was not a good enough typist to do that. Maybe he should write more of the draft by hand before he plugged in the typewriter. Whatever his strategy, Paul needed to get started if he wanted to sleep at all tonight.

But the dull ache in his stomach was a distraction. First, he needed to eat.

His mom had left some meatballs and sauce in a CorningWare casserole dish in the refrigerator. He could microwave those and put them on one of the Kaiser rolls resting on the counter in a plastic bag.

Paul removed the CorningWare dish from the refrigerator and, taking off its lid, placed it in the microwave with a paper towel on top of it. He stood watching the dish of meatballs spin around and around, the cornflower pattern on the white casserole dish appearing and disappearing, the sauce steaming up the paper towel, like sweat coming through a dress shirt on a humid Center City day.

Surely, there were more interesting things to watch.

He stepped over to the black-and-white TV set on the windowsill and pulled its half-inch knob. Familiar voices sent straight lines and zingers across the Logans' kitchen table: the characters from M*A*S*H* 4077th.

WORLDS

— Oh, this is a funny one! Paul said to himself.

He plopped down at the head of the table, laying his chin in the palm of his hand, and stared at the colorless images from the cathode ray tube. He knew most of the dialog by heart. Still, a few of the show's jokes made him smile. The microwave beeped. Paul ignored it. A couple of wisecracks got him to laugh. The beeping continued. As the commercials came on, the persistent tone goaded him from the kitchen chair.

Taking the meatballs from the microwave, he realized he had not opened a roll for his sandwich. He hadn't even gotten out a knife or a plate. Paul put down the dish and took a plate from the cabinet and a steak knife from the drawer. He cut the Kaiser roll open and placed its yawning maw on the plate.

The show came back on.

— Henry, isn't that your desk?

Paul slumped in the chair until the conclusion of the episode. Without taking his eyes off of the screen, he reached over and stuck his finger in the casserole dish. The meatballs and sauce were still warm. Paul could not reach the paper towel from where he was sitting. So, he put his finger in his mouth and sucked from it the tangy, warm sauce.

During the commercial break, he looked around the kitchen. The sandwich was still unmade, the typewriter remained unplugged, and all the typing paper still lay in its clear plastic wrap.

— Oh, well, let's eat. First, we need a thingy.

With a soupspoon he retrieved from the drawer, Paul scooped some meatballs and sauce from the dish onto the bottom of the roll's mouth and fell back into his seat. The sandwich was sloppy; as he bit into the roll, pieces of meatball and globs of sauce fell onto the plate and his hands. But he had never gotten himself a napkin or paper towel. So, Paul licked his fingers. A piece of meatball fell on the floor with a squishy sound. He saw the red blob between his feet. He'd clean it up later.

The first few plucked notes of the guitar accompaniment to "Suicide is Painless" came from the TV speakers. On screen, doctors and nurses in olive fatigues rushed toward helicopters. He better not watch. He needed to get to work on that paper.

He flipped open his Logan-Construction-Company steno pad to the introductory paragraphs he had written and skimmed them. But half the sandwich still slumped in front of him.

— Well ... just while I eat ...

Thirty minutes later Paul had a full stomach and a collection of dirty dishes, but he could not move until he heard his favorite line.

214

— You could say all of us together made up Captain Tuttle.

Now it was finally time to get to work. But, he better clean up before starting to type: he didn't want to get spaghetti sauce on his theology paper.

As he rinsed the dishes, he heard pseudo-dramatic synthesized horns and plunking keyboard chords. He turned toward the screen. Capital yellow-orange letters spelled out:

LIVE FROM DEARBORN, MICHIGAN

An excited mustachioed host was lisping:

—... a worldwide two-hour television event. Sixty years ago at the height of the roaring 20s, this estate, called Fair Lane, after the birthplace in County Cork, Ireland of his adoptive grandfather, belonged to of one of the richest and most famous men of his time, Henry Ford, an individual who literally changed the world — revolutionizing the way Americans travel, transforming the traditional factory into worlds of energy and productivity, and altering the American landscape itself. Our familiar milieu of malls, shopping centers, freeways, and drive-thrus would not have existed without his innovations. But, sadly, Henry Ford's legacy is not all positive. Later in life, he sullied his own reputation with anti-Semitic publications and pronouncements — even influencing members of Germany's Nazi party.

Closing the dishwasher door, Paul shook his head and laughed.

— Ridiculous! he exclaimed, as he slid back into his seat.

— After Mr. Ford's death, the estate became a museum and landmark — with some of its property turned over to my *alma mater*, the University of Michigan. Earlier this month, an archeologist from that school found a secret chamber underneath the outbuilding behind me. There is evidence to suggest that this massive concrete chamber harkens back to the Motor City's heyday of Model Ts and the rise to wealth and fame of this son of an orphan immigrant, Henry Ford.

Paul plugged the typewriter into the same outlet as the TV and pulled out a fresh sheet of typing paper. He guided it into the machine with his right hand, turning the platen knob with his left.

— Often bygone days hold impenetrable secrets but tonight we will play urban archeologist and uncover them, peeling back layer after layer of the past ... of an estate, an industrial city, a country ... What, if anything, that chamber contains, we don't know. What secrets can be found inside? What great Unknown lies buried beneath the concrete, under these very streets and under the floor on which I am now walking? We will find out tonight on live television.

Paul put his fingers on the indented plastic typewriter keys to begin work but noticed that the typing paper was crooked. He'd have to take it out and reinsert it. His hands fell back onto the table.

The breathless TV host continued:

— Together you and I are going to step back into history, which the owner of these grounds once famously declared is bunk! One way or another, this mystery will be solved tonight on:

THE MYSTERY OF HENRY FORD'S SECRET UNDERGROUND CHAMBER

When the commercials played, Paul removed the sheet of paper from the typewriter. Holding the page upside down as it reclined on the machine's paper table, he looked left and right along the sheet's bottom to see if it was straight. When it seemed properly aligned, he rotated the platen knobs until a half inch of the paper rose above the type guide. It was slanted, but, good enough.

Paul turned down the volume on the TV set. He knew he really should turn it off but figured he could keep the show on while he typed up what he had drafted. He could do the cover page, and get that out of the way at least. He would definitely shut the television off when he had to write new material.

Through the spaces left by the clatter of the typebars against the page, the would-be dramatic keyboard chords and fake horn notes crept back into the kitchen. On the screen the title of the show reappeared in yellow, shadowed, block letters before an aerial shot of Henry Ford's mansion. The host walked among dusty, rocky basement debris and jabbered away but Paul only gave him half of his attention. In the center of his page, he underlined the words requiring it in the title, "Contrasting Weltanschauung: Nietzsche's Will to Power and the Prophets of the Old Testament." In the bottom right corner, Paul added his name, class, and tomorrow's date. He had completed the cover page.

As Paul turned the platen knob to remove the sheet of paper, the voice of the TV host filled the kitchen:

— Henry Ford, founder of the Ford Motor Company and innovator of the assembly line technique of mass production, became one of the richest and most powerful industrialists that American ever produced, but his childhood was modest. He was born on his father's farm in what is now Dearborn, Michigan on July 30, 1863. His father, William, had been born in County Cork, Ireland and adopted by Patrick Ahern ...

— Ireland? asked Paul. He was Irish?

There was some sauce on Paul's plate but his knife and fork were already in the sink. Anyway, Paul did not expect anyone to come into the kitchen. They were down the basement. He lifted the plate up to his face and cleaned it off with his tongue.

...

Father Logan recited the opening prayers hurriedly and from memory. The altar boy was standing there with the book and so, for appearances' sake, the priest raised his limp arms and pretended to read. He allowed the Latin words to run into one another, which was probably the way they spoke the language on the streets of ancient Rome, anyway. His words echoed through the large, domed nave of the Roman-Basilica-style Saint Francis Xavier Church over the buzzing of the industrial-sized fans and the faint street noise that came in through the open bottoms of the stained-glass windows, which did not tell stories but resembled mosaics of blue, green, red, gold, and lavender. He had noticed that the congregation was smaller than usual. Father Logan surmised that many parishioners had fled the heat of the city.

Well, if they are hot in their suits and dresses, the priest thought, they should try these vestments on their piano.

Father Logan knew the readings well. He had preached on them many times ... manna in the desert ... fleshpots of Egypt … *ollas carnium Aegypti* … God's plan etc. Plus, he knew he was good at speaking *ex tempore* when he needed to.

He never did ascertain what was causing it, but all week Father Logan had been sapped of energy and bereft of zeal. Perhaps he could blame that on the heat as well. He supposed that it had had its effect, much as he liked to think that he could overcome the weaknesses and temptations of nature. It might have been the lighter schedule of the summer months. When he had less to do, he often felt less energetic than when he was busy. He didn't know.

Normally, he took pride in his homilies and spent hours on Fridays and Saturdays, if not earlier in the week, studying the readings and preparing what he would say on Sunday. But this week, whenever he sat down to go over the scriptural passages, he would end up looking out the window at the rooftop water towers and listening to the quieter sounds of the city in summer, unmotivated, uninspired.

He was reminded of his changing approach to grading papers. As a young teacher, he had put a great deal of effort into marking each collected assignment. He had been dedicated to writing comments and correcting every grammatical error — even the accents grave and acute. Now he had reduced his efforts to writing large letter grades at the tops of the papers. Familiarity, he supposed, does breed contempt. Was that the whole story? It was hard to say.

Nevertheless, here he was on the altar with the Liturgy of the Word for the Eighteenth Sunday in Ordinary Time passing by like the cars of a train rolling by above Sixth Avenue.

The lector was reading Psalm 78:

Quanta audivimus et cognovimus ea et patres nostri narraverunt nobis.
Non sunt occultata a filiis eorum in generationem alteram...

All the great stories have been handed down generation after generation, simultaneously passing the time and teaching the children. The psalm has to do with bread and the water from the rock. What was the theme? Was it the impatience of Moses — his lack of faith? No, no, this is all about the greatness of God. He would latch onto something when he read the English. *Il est temps*.

The second letter of Saint Paul to the Ephesians was next. The gospel would be about Jesus's preaching about bread at Capernaum.

All the readings seem to focus on bread, on manna, on the Lord's mercy in the desert. He could talk about faith and hardship, but the people out there among the Greek columns and Roman arches looked like they'd heard it all before. Maybe he could pass on some background information, have the people feel like they walked out of her with some new piece of knowledge today.

Before he knew it, the *Alleluia* was being sung and the people were rising in their pews. Father Logan strode to the center of the altar, turned and genuflected before the tabernacle, and stepped into the low pulpit. He took his time turning the gilt-edged pages of the large Book of the Gospels and finding the designated passage marked by a red silk ribbon. He adjusted his glasses and began.

With his thumb, Father Logan made the sign of the cross on his forehead, on his lips, and over his heart. The congregation gestured along with him but finished before the priest did. He read the Gospel in Latin and then re-read the three chosen passages for the Eighteenth Sunday in Ordinary Time in English.

The selection from the *Gospel According to John* told how Jesus criticized the people for seeking the bread of this world. As he read, Father Logan tried to home in on an idea or phrase that might provide the crux of his sermon. One verse seemed like it might do and that is what he would start with:

"Do not work for food that goes bad but for food that endures for eternal life."

He languidly blessed himself saying, "We begin in the name of the Father and of the Son and of the Holy Ghost."

The congregation followed suit and uttered "Amen" along with the priest.

"Working for bread," Father Logan said. "Is what the gospel addresses for us this week. Working for bread, of course, is necessary. We all must work in order to eat. Some are born with more and have more than others. Some men continue to have more bread to eat than others for their entire lives. Others have little. Whether they worked for it or not. Is this justice? It doesn't seem so. Is this the Lord's justice? It is hard for a mere mortal to say."

Father Logan heard coughing and saw movement in the pews. People were fidgeting. Well, what did they expect in the middle of the summer, a priest to do a song and dance? Clearly, he had spoiled them.

"The bread of the prophets, like that distributed by the great prophet, Moses, was given in the desert when the people complained that they had left behind the fleshpots of Egypt for this hard freedom in the wilderness.

"The phrase 'fleshpots of Egypt,' by the way, has nothing to do with human flesh. This is a common misconception. Rather, the pots contained the flesh of animals — meat — for the nourishment of the Hebrew slaves.

"Another common misconception is associated with the phrase, 'eye of the needle' as in 'It is harder for a rich man to enter the Kingdom of God than for a camel to pass through the eye of the needle.' People assume the needle in question was one used for sewing and that, therefore, it is impossible to fit a camel through it. Yet, in actuality, 'the eye of the needle' was the name of one of the gates used to enter the walled city of Jerusalem. The gate was so low and narrow that camels laden with goods and supplies had to be stripped of their burdens in order to squeeze through it. And so Our Lord, who in many ways was a poet, uses a very apt metaphor to show how attachment to worldly goods can get in the way of our salvation.

"In today's reading from the *Book of Exodus*, the Israelites in the desert complained about the lack of meat and received instead manna or bread. Likewise, Jesus says not to work for the bead of this world but to substitute for it the bread of heaven, the bread that lasts. That is what we should work for.

"The bread of this world can get in the way, just like the bundles on the camel can get in his way. The rich man can have too much bread and be self-satisfied and complacent and the poor man who doesn't have enough envies and resents him."

Father Logan noticed a man in a gray suit sitting in the congregation next to his veiled wife and a row of well-dressed and well-groomed children descending in height from right to left. Such a good-looking family with well-behaved children, he thought. But then to his dismay, he saw the man lean back and yawn! The man covered his mouth but otherwise made no effort to conceal his drowsiness.

What was he thinking? Where did he get his nerve?! In Father Logan's time, people had respect for their priests!

"And people wrongly give credit to Moses for the manna in the wilderness. This is another misconception. The manna in the desert came from Our Lord, God the Heavenly Father, and Jesus is the Bread of Life. And it was not the unleavened bread or matzoh — that was what the Israelites ate before they escaped from bondage. So, it is important and necessary, my brothers and sisters in Christ, to clear up these misconceptions and to refrain from crying out in the wilderness because God's plan is not immediately reconcilable with what we want, with our tastes and desires, or with the comforts we are accustomed to."

Was it his imagination or were people coughing and fidgeting more? His homily had begun to wander like the Jews in the desert. But who were these people to grow impatient with him?! After all, he had been a priest before many of them were even born, before people forgot how to behave in church!

He took a deep breath and turned his gaze right and left on the small, listless assemblage in the pews. Clearly, it was time to move on.

"So I ask you to join me in celebrating the Eucharist, bringing the unleavened bread of this world to the altar in the offertory procession so that it might become, through transubstantiation, the body and blood of Our Lord, Jesus Christ."

Father Logan concluded by blessing himself. The congregation did as he did, but the sound of the laconic "Amen" that murmured up from the pews made Father Logan feel weak. Had they had gotten anything out of his words at all?

How had he allowed this to happen? He had had an opportunity to preach some of the most significant and beautiful truths of the Gospel and what had he done?

He had babbled like a fool.

As Father Logan stepped down from the pulpit, his cheeks grew hot with shame.

He vowed that he would never again ascend those steps so unprepared.

...

"Thanks be to God it didn't take me long to settle in Connemara, though it was dirty miserable work at the start. As Swifty had, I found an old Paudeen to welcome me and this hospitable man introduced me to an old widower named Daly whose stables needed looking after. Though they called round to the house now and then, his oldest son was too full of himself and his married daughters were too busy with families of their own to be useful to him. Sometimes in the morning after stuffing myself with the generous breakfast the old fellow would give me, the stench of the manure would hit my nostrils and my stomach would do a backflip. I'd have to rush back outside for a bit of fresh air. But, sure, I got used to it in the end, as we can get used to anything at all if the Lord provides enough of it."

Seamus glanced down at young Sarsfield who appeared to be neither listening nor getting any better. He hated to see the lad looking so poorly. So, Seamus gazed at the tumbling and twirling motes in the shafts of light falling through the hatch, and plowed ahead with his story.

"No questions were asked about what brought me tramping through the hills to his door. Sure, in Connemara if you ask what time it is, they ask why you want to know. Every sojourner in those parts had his reasons for coming and it was best not to be too curious about them. There was plenty of talk, surely, but precious little exchange of information.

"From Leenaune, I could look across the harbour and see my home county. And the sight of it was both a comfort and a curse to me. At times, I turned my back to it to keep me from thinking about home. I looked at the manure in my shovel and thought it less sickening than what I'd left behind in Bunowen.

"At other times, I would remember the little hovels in the gleneen back home with turf smoke coming out of them. I'd remember the red flowers that looked like bells on the bushes in summer, the buttercups and odd clutches of daisies adding bright color to the grasses as I walked the paths, my feet crunching on the gravel.

"I also thought of my parents and brothers and sisters … my old schoolmaster and friends …. I would think often of Swifty, the hero of '98 and the tales of his exploits.

"But mainly it was just the memory of little things, unimportant things."

Seamus sighed at the empty bunkspace where Rosie had lain, thinking how she would have appreciated this part of his tale.

"The grass standing tall in the middle of the roads, black tiny fists of sheep droppings on the ground, bits of sheep wool clinging to branches and gate posts, and cows staring at me from just over the stone walls.

"The tall hedgerows on the side of the *botharins*, once were useful for hiding behind with Mar-

"The walls along the *botharins* were also high enough so that no one could see can see you cry.

"Then the thought of her and what had happened would make it all whining for the fleshpots of Egypt. And my anger would throw me into my work. Before long those stables were the cleanest in the West of Ireland, and Daly never knew the reason why.

"My hands were getting calloused from the handling of shovels and spades and brooms on soft days and the odd sunny one. I spent more time outdoors than I had in Bunowen. So my face began to turn red from the harbor breeze and the summer sun.

"It was the first time I ever lived on my own and supported myself with the work of my own hands. Though the work was dreadful, it meant my freedom and for that I could endure nausea and disgust. I had sunk to the bottom but I was truly me own man for the first time. And, isn't the bottom the only place to start from if want a clear idea of how high you've climbed?"

Sarsfield's breathing grew heavy. Seamus adjusted the old blanket on top of the boy. The sleep might do him good.

"Work meant money, food, shelter … But it was also where I could let all the pent up energy flow out of me, the way the deep waters of Killary Bay flow out to sea at low tide and leave stretches of rocks and sand and blankets of kelp exposed, filling the air with a briny salt odor. *Maise*, I had plenty to avoid thinking about. So, throwing myself into work is what I did. My hurt, my pain, my rage, even my former desire for a wife and family all went into the labor I was engaged to do. The energy I once devoted to love, I now poured in to work. The ability to work, truly work, with a purpose, like your work really means something, not just to feed your body but to feed your soul was what I learned in those early days in Connemara. It was the same type of industry that took me over and helped me build the company when I became my own boss.

"Before long, Daly had me do a bit of farming for him, digging hills of potatoes and taking care of the cattle. One time I was up all night with him and a calving cow. I cared for her and her offspring as if they were my own animals. And Daly seemed to understand this, though we never discussed it.

"After a few months, Mr. Daly needed someone to clean up in the pub. So I started sweeping floors and cleaning glasses. Before long I had settled into a regular sort of life in Leenaune, working mostly indoors and away from the elements. I kept myself very busy and led a quiet life. My memories of that time all surround stables, fields, dirty floors in the pub. But it didn't take long for me to save a biteen of money.

"I did become friendly with some sound lads who were good craic. On occasion I went to the pub with them and drank my share. We had some good laughs. We also attended some meetings that helped quiet the ghosts I had heard up in the hills. And, it made me angry to see how these Men of the West were forced to live. The masters of our people seemed to say, 'Here is your bit of land: a tiny patch of rocks and bog with a stone wall around it. Go and live on it, raise your family on it, eke out whatever living you can on the land of your fathers.'

"It was the equivalent of raising a middle finger to their faces.

"So, I met with some men who still had pikes and old swords from '98 hidden in the straw of their barns. We were able to add a rifle or two to this arsenal, but most of what occurred in those days was talk, dreams, schemes, and more talk.

"I met a young woman as well. When I was helping get the hay in one afternoon, she called out to me.

"'Is that all you do is work?' she said.

"She was a pretty lass crossing the fields with a strong wind blowing her thick dark hair about. She had lovely blue eyes and a turned up nose with freckles scattered across it. She was a fine healthy figure of a woman, too, with broad shoulders and hips and an ample bosom. I had seen her passing before but I only knew her to see.

"'That's what your man pays me for.'

"'Sure, but there's a time for work and a time for rest.'

"I saw her in the town a couple of times. We traded barbs and jokes now and again. We discussed the weather and the crops. Her name was Nancy. I suppose she fancied me a bit and wondered why I did not go out of my way to be friendly to her the way the other lads did. I must have been a bit of mystery to her. Maybe she thought I had a dark past like some of the others. She was surely beautiful and I enjoyed her lively chatting and sense of humor. Maybe, I started to think, I could be happy here with her.

"I was contented with my life in Connemara and pleased with my prospects there. Each evening, when my work was finished, I would drag my sweaty body into the cool night air and revel in the satisfaction of work and freedom – which I now perceived as two sides of the same coin. I was starting to think of the place as a home.

"One day Daly took me aside from the others — mostly Irish-speaking lads and a few of them dangerous and desperate-looking characters. He said, 'Anyone who works as hard as you do deserves a better job than this.' Perhaps Daly had a future in mind for me in Connemara as well. This made my heart beat a little faster.

"Yet, at the same time -— I don't know how to explain it exactly —as satisfied as I was and as comfortable as I felt, there was this great restlessness within me, this notion that I was just stopping in Connemara for a time. In the evening, when I would smoke my pipe and gaze at the blue-edged mountains holding Killary Harbor in a motherly embrace stretching down to the sea, I would feel a love for the wee place that had embraced me, too. But, I would also hear a voice within me saying, 'No. No, this is not your final stop. No, this is not where you will make a home. No, this is not your destiny. *Tá tú deorai.*'

"Perhaps the view across the harbor was responsible for this. Home was far away, over the water, but also too close: it was just over there. Just across the bay."

Mick turned his back and tuned the strings of his fiddle one by one. But the sounds didn't disturb young Sarsfield.

"But, I had to ask myself, 'What about the girl?' Feelings had been growing between the two of us. There was no use in denying it. Still, the more I began to think of lovely Nancy, the more vehement grew my restlessness. I feared to get entangled with any situation that would keep me in Leenaune indefinitely. Perhaps I was still too heartbroken over Mary and her parents' treachery. I knew that my future did not lay with Nancy and Leenaune, painful as it was to realize this.

"So I did my best to save my coppers. One day a man came into the pub and we got to talking about passage to America. And I thought maybe the disquiet I felt was the call of the New World. Maybe there I could find a way to make things better here, I thought. So I decided to head west to the land of the setting sun.

"In the end the impatience of my bones proved stronger than the beauty of the mountains reflecting in the harbor, the blossoming affection for a lovely girl, and the welcome, respect, and prospects I had had in Connemara. I now knew that I could work and get ahead in the world and I did not have to settle in my first place of sojourn.

"I had proven myself. I could move on. And, I did.

"Now that's an end to my stories. Mick, play us a tune on the fiddle, or someone give us a song."

...

The black-and-white television summarized Henry Ford's biography with narration over static-marked footage and interviews with old-timers recalling the days before the Model-T.

Paul removed another sheet of typing paper from the plastic wrap. He rested it against the typewriter's paper table and tried to roll it in straight. But, it wound up all cockeyed again — even worse than his first attempt at the cover page.

— In 1879, Ford disappointed his father by leaving the family farm and heading to Detroit to work as a machinist. Young Henry said the only thing he loved about the farm was that his deceased mother, Mary, had lived there.

Paul rolled the paper until an inch of it rose above the type guide. He squinted at the handwritten paragraphs in his steno pad and typed:

An ancient Israelite prophet, as depicted in the Old Testament or "the Law and the prophets" was a person who was called by God to communicate His message to His nation. However, "the prophets," as they are often called, were not a monolithic institution. Prophets came from a variety of backgrounds, spoke to different audiences, possessed idiosyncratic styles, and used assorted methods. In terms of responsibility, their primary function in their society was to communicate a particular message to the people of Israel.

Friedrich Nietzsche was a 19th-century German existentialist philosopher who mocked the language and the tropes of the prophetic books of the Old Testament in works, such as <u>Also Sprach Zarathustra</u>, filled with pseudo-religious aphorisms and who, like the profits of old — described himself as having come down from great mountain heights to deliver the startling pronouncement to the world that, "God is dead."

It is the purpose of this paper to compare and contrast the role of Nietzsche as a spokesman of man-centered, subjective existentialism rejecting the a priori *values of the Judeo-Christian society of his origin with the deeply religious and frequently disruptive role of the prophets of ancient Israel who believed their missions and messages to be divinely inspired to exhort the Chosen People to return to their traditional path.*

The TV host stood surrounded by men in hard hats, drilling. The crew was removing cement and old bricks and mortar and the host was shouting:

— Our guys are hard at work trying to discover what might have been buried by the mechanical genius and millionaire, Henry Ford. I wanna show you how much work we did in preparation for tonight's broadcast. We have dug up several layers. We bounced sound waves inside the chamber. We have explosives prepared to remove some of the final obstacles of our live televised treasure hunt.

Paul flipped over a couple of pages of the steno book. He had worked his way through a good portion of what he had already written. It amounted to less than a page. There was one Nietzsche quote he liked and could work in somewhere to take up space.

> And do you know what "the world" is to me? Shall I show it to you
> in my mirror? This world: a monster of energy, without beginning,
> without end; a firm, iron magnitude of force that does not grow
> bigger or smaller, that does not expend itself but only transforms
> itself ...

This was going to take hours. He needed some caffeine.

Paul picked up the kettle and ran some water from the sink into its spout. He could have taken the lid off of the top but this way he could add water and use only one hand. He placed the pot on the closest electric burner and turned on the heat.

On the small screen, Model T cars rolled off of an assembly line, out of the factory, and onto the street.

— By 1914, the assembly process for Henry's Ford's Model T became so efficient that it only took 93 minutes to assemble one.

— Man! In the time I have been hanging around this kitchen, Paul said to the watched pot. I could have built a car.

— In that year, the Ford Motor Company produced more cars than all other automakers combined. Ford's industry and initiative made him what the people of the time called a great man.

He was not only rich and successful but had a lasting impact on the lives of his employees. Henry Ford created his own minimum wage for his workers, promised not to fire them until they had been given second chances, and guaranteed them a fixed amount of his profits. It was true that he wanted his workers to be able to buy his cars but he also seemed to want to use his largesse, in these days before labor unions, to retain them as happy employees of his world-famous motor company.

Paul sat and read over the first page of his paper. There was a typographical error in the paragraph about Nietzsche. He sighed and lay back in the chair, his arms dangling at his sides. The teapot started to grumble. Did he have to retype the whole page? Maybe he could fix it with whiteout. It would look sloppy, especially since it was the first page, but retyping the whole page would take time. Paul reached for the bottle of whiteout.

The host stood by a Model T outside of a nightclub, surrounded by a group of partiers in 1920s clothes. The women shaking their fringe dresses and twirling their long strings of pearls looked thrilled to be on TV. Men in striped suitjackets and white pants and shoes mugged for the camera. They were having a party to celebrate the uncovering of the underground chamber.

— People with too much time on their hands, said Paul.

— What do you think we'll find in Henry Ford's secret chamber?

One man with a floppy motoring cap grunted into the host's microphone:

— Money!

— Diamonds, squeaked a woman with a tall feather protruding from her headband.

— Stocks and bonds, murmured another, fingering the gold chain of her pendant.

Another guy in a straw boater guessed:

— Bootleg liquor!

The crowd behind him cheered and raised an assortment of glasses.

The host took over.

— Well, there are lots of ideas of what could be inside. It inspires the imagination. Could it be bonds, cash, jewelry, designs of cars not yet made, papers from Henry Ford's airline, copies of his anti-Semitic publications ...?

— Everything but hope, Paul responded.

— ... Who knows what we will find? Agents from the Internal Revenue Service are standing by, just in case. More after this.

Paul lowered the volume of the TV set. The teapot gurgled and shook and would start to whistle presently. But, Paul had just inserted his second page into the typewriter.

Although there were many differences in terms of origins, techniques, and reception among the prophets of the Old Testament, there were some characteristics shared among all of them that made their ministries "prophetic." To obtain a full understanding of the role of the Old Testament prophet, it is important to examine these shared characteristics.

The host was now pacing the grounds of the spacious Michigan estate. Paul increased the volume but continued typing.

— Henry Ford built this estate, Fair Lane, in 1909. Although there were other architects who worked on the project, Frank Lloyd Wright was the original visionary. Believe it or not, compared to the homes of the wealthy elite of his time, Fair Lane was not very large. He did, however, install some luxuries. Mr. Ford had both a pool and a bowling alley. Today the pool has been transformed into a restaurant.

The kettle started its cry with a low whistle, which soon rose in volume and pitch to a shrill scream. Annoyed, Paul leaned on the table and got himself up, his eyes still on the small TV screen. With two fingers, he lifted a teabag from a yellow box in the cabinet and straddled it over the lip of his cup. He poured boiling water over the bag and proceeded with the teacup back to the kitchen table and his seat.

The Israelites frequently forgot about the covenant they had made with God, lost their resolve, and slipped into living like the Gentiles around them. It was the prophet's duty to reenergize their communities: to remind the people of their duties and of the great things God had done for them. The exercise of this duty was not always welcomed by the Israelites, however. In fact, prophets were often met with persecution. The prophet Jeremiah was famously cast into a well, much like the Patriarch Joseph was before him.

With an orange helmet on his own head, the host was in the basement with the hard hats again.

— Can you guess what we have planned for that wall? When we come back from this commercial break, we're gonna blow it up!

Paul turned down the volume.

Friedrich Wilhelm Nietzsche was born on October 15, 1844 and reared in the small town of Röcken, near Leipzig. Nietzsche's parents, Carl Ludwig Nietzsche, a Lutheran pastor and former teacher, and Franziska Oehler, had married in 1843. Like Ford, Nietzsche also lost his father as a boy, in 1849, when the philosopher was five years old.

Perhaps this death-filled and peripatetic childhood, like the wanderings of Abram and the covenant marked in the flesh of his descendants, influenced Nietszche's revolt against his father's Lutheranism, and Christianity in general, his refusing to go into his father's business, his refusal to be sacrificed on the altar constructed by his father, so to speak.

Would Nietzsche criticize Isaac for submitting to his father and the God of his father Who had conspired to murder him? Or did he think what didn't kill Isaac made him stronger? The firm obedience of Abram/Abraham and the constancy of his son, grandson, and great-grandson contrast sharply with the disobedient son who sought to outrage society and rebel against Christianity and its Jewish God.

Paul stood up to get a cigarette from his jacket pocket. Before moving, he took a sip of tea and noticed that a guy in an orange hardhat was showing the host the t-shaped plunger of a detonator. Paul turned up the volume.

— We're going to blast down this wall on live TV. Ready?! Fire in the hole!

The whole crew counted down:

— 5 .... 4 ... 3 ... 2 ...1!

The basement filled with smoke and dust. When it cleared, it was plain that the wall had come down, only to reveal another wall.

— I don't know how to tell you this, the host said. But, at eight minutes to the hour, we ran into a wall. We talked to some interesting people and heard some good stories but what we found was not a lot. It seems we have struck out. I am disappointed, as I know you are. We chased a rainbow with no pot of gold. What can I say but, "I'm sorry"? See you soon.

The host stepped out of the shot and the credits ran.

Paul switched off the TV and examined his own progress: only two pages. Returning to his chair, he stepped on something soft. There was a red viscous mess on his shoe and the floor: the meatball he had dropped a couple of hours ago.

...

The bricklayers had all gone to Boyle's almost two hours ago. It was almost five o'clock. By now they were used to Seamus's absences. It was Tuesday and they knew he would join them only on Fridays. Seamus sighed, thinking of those drinking boyos. He almost envied them and their contentment with their station in life. It must have been pleasant and reassuring to fall into the routine and to spare yourself extra work and premature grey hairs. But he couldn't really be one of them. They wanted to go no further than where they were. They didn't want to take any extra steps. But this attitude did not suit Seamus's hectoring bones.

Besides, Nora didn't like him smelling like the pub at the dinner table.

The hanger rattled on the back of McCann's door as the long coat was removed.

"Stayin' late again, James?"

"For a bit. I have a few letters to finish and I want to look over some others that might need to be recopied."

"All right. But don't work too hard. Your eyesight will be ruined. You need to take care of yourself, James. Doesn't Nora wonder where you are?"

At McCann's Construction Seamus had risen quickly from a hod carrier to a bricklayer. When Dennis first introduced Seamus to Mr. McCann, he had boasted that Seamus could read and write and, as a true credit to his hedge school master in Louisburgh, was a wizard of mental arithmetic. McCann had answered that he might require help with the pen and the adding and subtracting sometimes — you never knew — but for now he needed him to carry a hod. A couple of years later, the need did arise and Seamus started splitting his time between bricklaying and working in the office.

McCann exited, the door closing behind him with the jingle of a bell. Seamus finished the letter he was writing and put the pen back in its inkwell. He blotted the ink and reread the letter from beginning to end. Finding no errors, he folded it in three and inserted it into an envelope, which he then addressed. Seamus then turned to a short stack of files on his desk to find the next client in alphabetical order.

Analyzing the course of jobs from contract to conclusions, Seamus noticed cost overruns and tried to infer the reasons for them. Some increases were unavoidable. Materials turned out to be costlier than anticipated. There were delays caused by weather. Other increases were downright crooked. Workmen deliberately slowed their progress. And Seamus knew that materials were stolen.

Later the following afternoon, Seamus went to talk to McCann. He passed men in overalls coated in mortar residue and stepped around a tall stack of brown boxes with fading labels of perfect penmanship.

With knitted brow, McCann leaned forward in his four-wheeled chair, sifting through the piles of white and yellow papers on his desk, taking care not to upset his cup of tea nor to push anything into his pen and inkwell. His satchel was open on the floor next to him. He appeared to be packing up for the day.

"Have a seat, James," he muttered without looking at him. "What's on your mind?"

Sliding into a worn, wooden chair, the younger man said, "I have a proposition for you."

"Sure. Just a minute, though. Where in hell did I put that damned letter?"

Seamus gazed as he had done many times at the formally posed portrait of McCann's wife and children in a fanciful yet dusty frame on the desk, next to his pad of Western Union telegram blanks. He enjoyed the relative quiet: the secretary who had been clattering away on her typewriter all afternoon had gone home. Near the corner of the paneled wall behind the boss hung a portrait of the risen Jesus with a pierced left hand pulling back his cloak to reveal His Sacred Heart encircled with thorns and crowned with flames and a cross. Closer to the desk was a calendar whose colorful sketch had recently been changed from Independence Hall to Elfreth's Alley. Tacked up right behind McCann's head was an early version of the now ubiquitous sign emblazoned with the slogan, "If anyone can build it, McCann can!"

"Ah, here it is! Sorry about that James. Had to find this before I can go home. Now I'm all ears. What is it you are proposing?"

"Well, … as you know, I've been spending some time looking through the company's correspondence. And I've noticed something … There appears to be a consistent and quite large discrepancy between the estimates we give our clients and the final cost to them."

McCann chuckled and linked his hands behind his head.

"There certainly is, James. There certainly is. That's the way the construction business is, me boy. An estimate is an estimate. It's not a promise or a contract. And customers understand that."

Seamus forced a smile.

"Yes, I understand that's the usual practice and everyone is quite accustomed to it. But what I'm thinking of is a way to be different from the competition … If we can figure out how to keep costs in line with estimates — perhaps with bonuses for gangs staying closest to the quotes — we could win more business than companies using the same old practices."

"They can complain all they want but once the work is done, it's done. If the price is more than they expected to pay, then too bad. They have to pay."

"True, the customers have to pay once the work is done. That's only fair. But what I am suggesting is that we try to stand out from the pack. Let people know that all we are interested in is a fair day's pay for a fair day's work. If we change our practices, we can build a reputation for being different … for saying what we mean and meaning what we say. The company might make less in the short term but we would build a better reputation. And, with a better reputation we could get more and bigger jobs ... and make larger profits in the long term."

"Look, this is all very interesting to speculate about, but when my stomach is growling, it seems like so much dreaming to me. I got to go home to the little woman. And you should think about getting home yourself. Doesn't Nora wonder where you are? And what about your little boy, Stanislaus?"

"Sarsfield."

"Oh, that's right. Of course, Sarsfield, hero of the Siege of Limerick. See? I can't think when I'm hungry."

McCann rose and stretched his arms over his head.

"No bother atall, Mr. McCann. No bother. How about if we give it some thought … I'll work on my ideas a bit … then we can talk again tomorrow?"

"That sounds grand, James, me boy. Grand, indeed. Get home to your wife and wee one. A family is much nicer to spend an evening with than a bunch of oul' letters."

On Wednesday afternoon, Seamus entered McCann's office again, arriving a bit earlier so that the boss would be more focused. He would make another attempt to get his suggestion across to the older man.

"I have been thinking about my idea," he began. "Trying to clarify it in me own mind if for no other purpose. You are very right in saying that construction companies always exceed the estimates they give to customers and that customers are quite accustomed to this. But what I am thinking of is a surprise for our customers. Imagine if customers hear that our estimates are accurate estimates, honest estimates! Think about your slogan, 'If anyone can build it, McCann can!' We can add, 'Count on our estimates? At McCann, you can!'"

"People act like they have money to burn these days," the boss replied. "I don't think people are worried about the question of estimates. Construction is a one-time business, anyway. It's not like men are coming back to us a week later wantin' another house."

"True. We're not runnin' a pub, dependin' on regulars. But I'm thinkin' instead of takin' longer to build a single house, we could build many houses. It is so easy to get more contracts with the ground rents people pay — with no mortgages needed. If one man is happy with a house we build, he can recommend us to his cousin or brother-in-law or friend. We can build houses for extended families, for whole neighborhoods, whole new sections of the city!"

"You'll have me workin' me men to death! They're content with the work they have. If I ask men to throw up house after house, there'll be ructions!"

"If we have more work, then we can bring on more workers, keep growing. The city is expanding north and east along the Delaware River."

Seamus pointed to the map on the wall behind McCann.

"The City of Philadelphia keeps growing. And if the city is growing, why not McCann Construction?"

"Like I said, James, no one is concerned about this. Aside from the predictable griping of cheapskates, no one complains about our prices. As a Yank friend of mine says, 'If ain't broke, don't fix it.'"

And like the day before, McCann got to his feet. Clearly, the boss considered the subject closed.

On Thursday evening, Seamus heard the familiar rattle of the hanger on the back of the door. Without slowing his progress toward the street, McCann asked, "Still here?"

"I am. But going home soon."

"Have a good night."

Maybe McCann didn't like Seamus's staying late anymore. Had Seamus gotten too big for his britches? It is McCann's name over the door after all.

Seamus had other ideas that he hadn't mentioned to his boss. If he hadn't liked the simple estimate suggestion, what would he think of the others?

> *The men are content.*
>
> *The customers are used to things as they are.*

It was hard for Seamus to sit still. He finished reading the file he had in his hand and put it down. He stared at the letters on his desk but was not reading them.

Maybe it was time for Seamus to make his own decisions, to do things his way. How much time and energy was he to waste on selling ideas to a welcoming but closed-minded man, a boss with no eye for the possibilities?

McCann had been very kind to Seamus but it pained the young bricklayer that his employer had not given a more serious hearing to his ideas. There was nothing rash or unreasonable about them. The old man was just set in his ways. He only saw, "This is the way it has always been done" and sought to enjoy his comfortable life. Seamus had encountered his type before — in Mayo, in Galway, in Manhattan, and now in Philadelphia. And as it had before, that familiar restlessness, that need to move on from what had and could be accomplished in a place, began to overtake Seamus.

The office was silent. McCann was well and truly gone. Seamus took his jacket from the hook on the wall.

Could he go into business for himself? He could talk to Feeney about that. Sitting in his back booth at Boyle's — he was even independent as a drinker — Feeney was always saying how easy it was to become your own contractor.

"Logan," he said. "You'll be diligent morning, noon, and night — when it is your own name over the door. It changes your commitment to your work. It rewrites your schedule. Sure, when your name is over the door, it's a different thing altogether."

McCann probably thought Seamus was trying to run the company his way. Maybe he thought Seamus was trying to take it over. Seamus felt a ball hardening in the pit of his stomach. Could he be wearing out his welcome? He probably shouldn't be the last one to leave every night.

The awnings of the Italian Market on Ninth Street were drawn in for their night, the tarpaulins taken down. Yet, there were a still a couple of fires burning in metal barrels. A tall man wearing a stained apron around his stout belly stood in the street talking to a much smaller man in another dirty apron. There were wet papers and bits of straw strewn about the asphalt. A grey cat glided from one sidewalk to the other. But the street was quiet. The Italians were not out hooting all night like his neighbors in Moyamensing. Some of them did have grapevines growing in the alleys behind their houses, though. Seamus tried to imagine them drinking their own wine in the privacy of their homes, but he had trouble picturing it. What kind of lives did these newcomers lead behind these rowhouse facades?

If he were to go out on his own, could Seamus hire some Italians to work for him? They would work cheaply and add artistic touches that the Paddies had no clue about. Seamus had seen some of their masonry work, the fancy details adorning parish churches and schools. Still, Seamus knew there would be difficulties in working with them. They had little English and put an incomprehensible amount of effort into their meals. They complained a lot and took long breaks. But their work was lovely. No denying that.

The Italians could also be his customers. Like the New York Irish hoarding their pennies to get out of Five Points, these Italians would not stay in Southwark forever.

Seamus's heartbeat quickened. He could present this idea to McCann: hire more Italians, win their loyalty, and build their new homes!

But the old man would not listen. He would have some excuse for not pursuing this opportunity. McCann had been out here in America for so long that he took it all for granted. He didn't see the opportunities anymore, nor look for them.

Old men are forever arranging our lives for us, thought Seamus. They disregard our ideas and let us do all the work while they take all the profits and live in big houses with lawns front and back.

Seamus saw the lights of Boyle's down the block. Feeney would be at his table.

Would it be an act of disloyalty to the man who had given him his start in the City of Brotherly Love? Men did it all the time, according to Feeney. And what if Seamus did spend the rest of his life with McCann, keeping silent, following orders, collecting his pay, and handing it over to the publican? Wouldn't that be a betrayal of his own nature? Wouldn't he be selling himself short, turning his back on a greater destiny? Seamus felt he must remain loyal to his spirit of independence.

His feet had taken him to the front step of Boyle's. Indeed, they had been carrying him to that threshold all along.

"The only thing McCann has is 'McCann can'! All he is is a slogan."

"Well, he can keep his slogan."

Seamus entered Boyle's and marched straight back to Feeney's table.

...

When I look out my window, I see little more than brick and mortar. True, it is dawn but I would see the same if it were high noon. For the wall nearly smothers the window. And, there is my old childhood friend, Brick Man, multiplied through the wall's pattern of bricks and cross joints intersecting bed joints. Brick Man wears a hat with a two-brick brim topped by a single-brick crown. His head is a single brick and he has two bricks for arms and one for a torso. The torso of one brick man provides the crown for the hat of the Brick Man below him. I remember pointing out Brick Man to Father when I was a boy, and the roar of his laughter. Indeed, whenever I look at brickwork, I think of Father. Thoughts of the dead at the dawning of the day.

I know he worked construction during his Greenhorn days here in New York, but he never mentioned where. His labor of the last century could, quite literally, be supporting my labor and that of the boys in my charge. I wish I could ask him. He must have worked in Lower Manhattan. There probably wasn't much call for Irish bricklayers this far uptown when Father was in New York, which was in the 1870s, I believe. No, I always thought of this part of town as the Teddy Roosevelt district. It's as though I can see TR's face etched in its architecture.

Now that I think of it, Father was likely still an apprentice when he was here. He must have become a journeyman in Philadelphia. I would love to be able to ask him. From a framed photo he stares at me — eyes intense, hands folded on that oak roll-top desk he loved, correspondence at his elbow, a map on the wall showing the bend of the rivers enveloping South Philly, the old "Neck." He wants to appear stern but his joviality twinkles to spite him. Indeed, I wish I could talk to him about anything at all.

I have been hearing my own floor and the one above me creaking. The men of my community have been getting ready to head down to breakfast, say the Grace Before Meals and our other morning prayers, and begin another school day. Some of their feet are even thumping down the stairs as I write. They have more energy than I do, that's certain. They probably have been sleeping soundly until now: unlike an old man like me who wakes up and can't get back to sleep.

At any rate, their noise signals the start of my day of "*ora et labora*." When Kitty was just a schoolgirl, she knotted and hitched a macramé wall hanging whose red letters, outlined in white on a field of blue, read, "*Ora et Labora*". It hung in our basement for ages. It strikes me that that phrase might be the summation of Father's life.

Father was a man of such Faith that his prayer life guided him through all of his times of trouble and, more impressively, through his years of great success. It is important to work, to make the most of what we are given, like the Useful Servant in Our Lord's Parable of the Talents. Father certainly lived that. He made the most of what had been given him and never let even the smallest opportunity pass him by, like a frog that catches every fly that dares buzz near him. He was always ready to learn and to adapt. But, when James Logan set his mind to something, neither the strongest winds nor the stormiest sea could keep him from it. No one who knew him would say otherwise.

And, as has often been told, when Father came to this country with pennies in his pocket, he made sure his first stop was a church. Which one was it? Again, he is not here to answer. Even if he had been, he mightn't have talked about it. Father was so tightlipped — so unwilling to stop and look back. He was too busy spreading out like the miles of mortar his men troweled over the years or like bricks in a stretching course measuring the Delaware Valley. With the army of men he attracted to him, laying brick after brick, joining house after house, forming row after row, creating neighborhood after neighborhood and parish after parish, James Logan expanded like a building Alexander with nearly endless lands to conquer. And in white and green his shamrocked signs marked the outposts of his empire:

"You can have your slogans. I'm building with Logan!"

He prayed and worked, worked and prayed. He not only spread out across the land, but he transformed it. Father was a priest of construction turning country into city.

The morning appears dim. I can now make out more bricks and more white window casements. But, my instinct tells me it should be brighter by now than it is, maybe because I have already been up for a time. The dimness reminds me of the early days of the war when Times Square and other buildings were darkened and there were no when night games at the Polo Grounds and Ebbet's Field. Nothing ever happened in New York City, though, until this past summer when that B-25 bomber crashed into the Empire State Building. Eleven people killed at the National Catholic Welfare Conference. I must remember to pray for them.

There were times, sad to say, when I saw Father's work life become more important than his prayer life. At mass he would yawn or fidget or struggle to keep his eyes open. I was shocked the first time I saw this. On other Sundays he would anxiously try to catch the eye of a business connection in a distant pew. It was important for him to be seen at church. For a few years, he volunteered as an usher at Saint Colman's. I remember feeling proud and amused to see him coming up the aisle with the long-handled wicker collection basket, looking so well groomed and well dressed. (If only the parishioners had seen what I had seen on those mornings: himself shaving in his undershirt and boxer shorts!) True, he wanted to serve the church but I knew he also wanted to be recognized as an upstanding member of the community. I felt it in in my bones. I remember many mornings standing on the steps of Saint Colman's, going from one foot to the other, restless to get home and change into my play clothes, while Father was blathering away with some crony of his he would insist was "important for the business." Knowing full well even as a child that we do not hear mass for business purposes, I would seethe. "It is written, 'My house shall be called a house of prayer,'" I wanted to remind him. But, I didn't dare say a word or, instead of enjoying an afternoon on the ball field, I'd be spending my Sunday in my room sitting on a sore bottom.

As he grew older, his devotion to his faith appeared to decline, and this troubled me. I wrote to him about it a few times from the seminary. Of course, he told me there was nothing to worry about, that his faith was as strong as it was in his youth. These days he needed to devote the bulk of his energy toward earning a living for his family and building his business for his sons. That was all.

As he entered his dotage, his devotions became more important than ever. Though I wasn't surprised, I was glad to see it.

Truth be told (to use one of Father's expressions), my enthusiasm for my devotions ebbs at times, also. In fact, I am not anxious to go downstairs and start my day of prayer and teaching right now.

Joe just knocked on my door.

"Sarsfield?! Breakfast!" he cried with the fervor of a young priest.

I told him I would be down in a minute but I am not going to rush.

The illumining sky tells me I can't delay much longer, however. The sun won't let me forget the duties of my vocation.

Sometimes Father was so caught up in his business that he overlooked his wife and family. We children would want to play ball with him but he would be too tired or distracted by meetings and possibilities and plans. As an immigrant, he had little knowledge of baseball or football, but we didn't understand that at the time. We didn't understand much about him, really. The Lord knew his heart. Of that, I have no doubt. But, his heart was kept bricked up from us children, and from even my mother, his wife.

One summer day, Father promised to take me to the Baker Bowl to see the Phillies. It was to be a whole day at the ball park for just the two of us. It might have been the first season they played at the stadium. It was one of the first, anyway. I looked forward to it all week. I waited for him to come home from work and take me to 15th and Huntingdon. All day I walked up and down our block of rowhouses peering down the street and through the clumps of adults to spy his approach. I could always spot him from a mile away. His walk was distinctive. Something about it indicated that he was just passing through: this neighborhood was not his final destination. He was not hanging about here like the loafers and low characters and the rest.

I fretted to see the South Philly sky darkening, just as I am now dreading the Chelsea sky's brightening. As the day wore on without a sign of him, I was patient and kept my hopes up. I really believed he would come, that he was delayed but that we could still make it. Somehow he would get us there for at least part of the game. He was called the strongest man in Moyamensing, after all. I at least wanted to see Jack Clements come up to bat or maybe see him catch. He was my favorite. Maybe I'd see him throw out a base runner trying to steal. It was so rare to have a lefty as a catcher; there are none around these days. I knew Clements was born in Philadelphia and had always played for Philadelphia teams. They say he was the first catcher to use a chest protector. No dunce was Jack Clements. But much as I tried to maintain hope, it soon became pointless. When darkness had fallen almost completely over Moyamensing, I knew that I would not see my hero, and I grew profoundly disappointed in the man who was my idol above all mortals, my father.

When he did come home, he had some story about a business meeting he had been unable to reschedule or avoid. He would take me to another game, he said.

Father handed me a cigarette card with a photograph of Jack Clements on it, standing tall by the plate, catching a throw with his bare hands. It's strange to think of it now: the picture showed no glove nor protection of any kind.

"Here's a photo of that *citeog* you think so highly of."

He said he had found it in an abandoned pack of cigarettes in the bushes, though the pack and the card both looked clean and brand new.

I forgave him, even though his reason and his motives were mysterious to me. After all, how many packets of cigarettes had he had to examine before he found the one with Clements in it? Still, I could not be talkative as we walked into the house together. I remained sullen against his Irish charm.

Mother told me to offer it up. I'm sure I did.

Nevertheless, no matter what Father's faults and lapses, we can know him, like the Lord Himself, through his works. What has he wrought? With my mother he created and kept a comfortable home for all of us and gave all of his children a Catholic education. He left behind a thriving business for my brother to inherit and to pass on for his son after him. Today and in times to come, countless people up and down and east and west along the streets of Philadelphia will be able to trace the origins of their homes and schools and churches back to him. And it all sprang out of his passion for his family, his business, and for the City of Brotherly Love.

He really did love Philadelphia. He used to take tremendous constitutionals all over Moyamensing, Center City, Northern Liberties, and East Falls. People noticed his love for walking and tried to get him to hike in the woods or up the mountains. But he always refused. He said he had had his fill of hill walking at Home.

The sun continues to rise. It is spreading its light behind the black water towers on the rooftops. I imagine I can hear the trains arriving and departing more frequently, though the Elevated was torn down before the war. The New York day is getting started in earnest. Soon it will be time to put down my pen, leave the refuge of my little room. join the community, and meet the new school day full of teenage boys.

When I think of my Father now, gone from us for so many years, I start to see a pattern in his life. I could barely see it when I first sat up to write but the gradual dawn has made clearer its outlines. His whole life was hillwalking, onward and upward. Rising all the time, never content to stay at one level, building not just out but up, course by course, to the rooftops of houses, churches, and schools to the top of Philadelphia society. What spurs a man on like that? Often it is some wound from the past.

Perhaps his passion for rising even included his ardent efforts to get into Heaven.

"Why not?" I can hear him say. "Wasn't I born at the bottom?"

. . .

Paul, James, Kitty, and her boyfriend, Kenny, parked the car in the middle of the village of Lisdoonvarna and piled out, stretching and oscillating away from the car and one another. Their car's headlights pointed right at The Traveller's Rest.

— Hey, look, said James. A pub. Let's go.

And he headed straight for the front door of the licensed premises with Kitty and Kenny a couple of yards behind him each.

— But, Dad, called Paul. Let me check-

— Ah, this place is fine, James replied over his shoulder. It might even have music.

Paul followed them in, feeling for his guidebook in the right pocket of his windbreaker. The pub was bright and clean and spacious. The group had been driving all day in the tiny rented Nissan Micra with a couple of bags in their laps, which didn't fit with the golf bags in the trunk. They were happy to be in a dry and warm space where they could spread out. Paul, however, had his suspicions.

He didn't like to keep insisting that they find pubs with traditional music: it might remind Dad too much about Mom. Kitty had even taken Paul aside and asked him to knock it off. They had taken this trip to cheer their father up, after all.

But, they were in Clare and if they were going to a pub, anyway …

Some instrument cases lay on the floor of a small playing area at the end of the room. So, Paul relaxed a little. Still, he had a nagging feeling in his bones. Once the party got a couple of pints into them, they would become comfortable and hard to move. When the young barman passed, Paul couldn't help asking:

— Excuse me. Is there music here tonight?

He said:

— Yes, we've music 'ere. Should be ge'in' stahted soon.

The accent sounded British.

— *Traditional* music? Paul asked.

— Yes, traditional music, he said.

Right. The accent was as British as Charles's.

Paul pulled the guidebook from his pocket and began searching for a more likely spot for trad.

— There he goes, looking in his bible again, James said.

— We're in Clare, the capital of Irish music. We should at least find a place with some tunes.

— Just like your mother. She always loved that stuff. I never got into it.

— Can't you just relax, Paul? Kitty said. We don't always have to find the very best pub in each town. This place is nice.

— 'Nice'? Paul snapped. I didn't come 3,000 miles across the ocean for 'nice'. 'All men desire to know.'

Paul lowered the guidebook.

— I wonder, Kitty shot back, which pub was Aristotle's favorite.

— Not this one.

A pair of musicians lumbered past carrying amplifiers and microphones. Paul's jaw dropped.

He knocked back a quarter pint of Guinness and put the glass down on a wooden ledge. He'd have to find a better place on his own. But, his way to the door was blocked by a file of Nordic-looking seniors just off a tour bus. Navigating through the group, Paul saw that they were all wearing different-colored versions of the same windbreaker. The experience to be had in this Lisdoonvarna pub would surely not be *Echt*.

So out Paul went, stopping by the door to see what the guidebook said. There was a place called the Roadside Tavern around the corner. He jogged in its direction.

Staying up late talking. The week of Mom's funeral. Every night. Hearing the bird's chirping at the dawn. Light starting to glow on the horizon behind the Ardmore houses and trees.

— No, once Mom got out here to the suburbs and started taking care of us brats she never had much time for the city. For the old neighborhood. She met Dad, there, though. So, it must have had some sentimental attachment for her — aside from growing up there, I mean.

— I remember tales of the Irish music sessions they used to have. They had lots of musicians in her house on the weekends. Playing jigs, reels, and hornpipes all night and into the next morning. Grandmom would make them bacon and eggs and toast and tea and send them off to mass at Saint Francis de Sales. Sometimes they'd come back and play some more. The Doughertys always loved the music.

— But she only listened to it when Dad was not home.

— He didn't have much patience for it. "Only on Saint Patrick's Day" was his motto. More of a jazz guy, Dad. And even when he wasn't home she didn't put on the music very often.

— She didn't play and never really encouraged us to play, either. Ironic that there was a whole renaissance going on with the music and she hardly paid attention.

— I guess as she grew older she enjoyed quieter pastimes. Always with those fat romance novels.

— Or sitting in front of a black-and-white movie.

The Roadside Tavern was an old low-slung building that lived up to its name — slouching just off of the main road. Paul entered the place and could see very little at first because of the low light and the smoke. It had worn plank flooring and wooden columns. Its shelves were filled with old brick-a-brack, those cast-iron pitchers of decreasing sizes they'd seen all over Ireland, and the plastic black-and-white Scotty dogs they used to have in their basement in Ardmore. Colorful music posters hung on the walls. This place looked immediately more promising.

A group of fiddlers, accordion players, and a guitarist concluded a set of reels. Shouting over the low-ceilinged room's chatter, a small round man commanded everyone to be quiet for the singer, and the word went 'round the pub, repeated until it's goal was achieved:

— Quiet for the singer! Quiet for the singer!

A chubby-cheeked girl wearing a waitress's white button-down blouse and black skirt rose from her seat on the window sill.

Oh yes, this was more like what we are looking for, Paul thought.

He loved to see this respect for song. For him it was an encounter with something ancient that had persisted despite all the invasions of armies, languages, customs, and modern contrivances.

In the silence of the crowded pub, the girl, who didn't look old enough to be there, sang a slow air Paul had never heard. Her soprano voice penetrated the smoke and brought the seated people to their feet. When she finished, the pub rang with applause.

Paul ducked out and ran back around the corner to the touristy pub where the Nordic punters were now sampling comical-looking half-pints of Guinness.

It was not hard to talk the group into leaving but getting everyone "off of the elevator," as Laura called it, of varying levels of drink proved more difficult.

Once they got to the Roadside Tavern, everyone liked it. Though Kitty had some complaints about the smoke, they all said they were happy they had moved. Jigs and reels rollicked and roared from the musicians while the crowd chatted away. Now and then another miraculous song came from the young waitress and other singers, with silence strictly enforced.

During one of the sets of jigs, James leaned against a paneled wall near the bar. Paul was trying to read a poster on the wall about a concert by Sharon Shannon.

A man in a jeff cap approached James and pointed at the blue Nittany Lion on his grey sweatshirt.

— Who went to Penn State? he asked in an American accent.

— My daughter went to the main campus.

— Oh yeah? My sister went there, too?

— Really? What's her name?

— Patty Meehan.

Kitty joined in the conversation.

She knew Patty; they'd been friends through all four years of college.

The guy lived in Havertown. But, he had grown up in Saint Francis de Sales. He introduced himself as Dr. Halloran, an orthodontist.

Kitty recognized the name and told him that he had had our cousins, the Doughertys, as patients.

Unreal, they all agreed.

— I knew the Doughertys back in West Philly. Their aunt and uncle used to have Irish music at their house all the time.

— Those are my in-laws! My wife grew up listening to that music. She used to love it-

— Is she-

— She passed away six months ago, said Kitty.

— I'm sorry to hear that.

— Thanks. I appreciate it.

— She came from a great family. Everyone loved their parties. They were so hospitable.

— Yes, they were.

The young waitress stood to sing again and the talkers were silenced. She announced that the title of her song was, "The Blacksmith." When she finished, the traditional tunes and the conversations resumed.

— How long are you here for?

— Two weeks altogether. We have about a week left.

Saying they had a week left calmed the uneasy feeling that their time in Ireland was slipping away.

— How do you like it?

— We love it! Everybody's been so friendly! It's so beautiful ...

— Do you have relatives over here?

— Not that we know of. My grandfather came from somewhere in Mayo. He never talked about it.

— They never do — do they?

— We took a beautiful drive yesterday. From Westport.

— Dje go to Matt Malloy's?

— Yes, we squeezed in there for a little while. Paul insisted. He knew his mother wouldn't have missed it.

— Then we drove from Westport down to Connemara. Route 335 — wasn't that it, Paul? It didn't seem big enough to have its own route number. We saw some goats wandering around on the road before we got to Connemara. What was the name of that town, Paul?

— Leenaune.

— We passed by some beautiful lakes on the way, added Kitty.

— There's a great fly-fishing resort near there, too. Delphi, I think it was called. I wouldn't mind staying there sometime.

— How did you end up in this place?

— We were around the corner but my son read about it in his book.

— Our guidebook says it's one of the best in County Clare. We drove all the way from our B&B Ennistimon to get here.

He raised his pint of Carlsberg.

— Glad you made the extra effort to find the real thing. *Slainte*!

— *Slainte*! How else would we run into our neighbors?

Another young woman in a waitress uniform stepped in front of the musicians.

— Quiet for the singer! Quiet for the singer!

And she began:

— *Tá mo chleamhnas déanta ó athrú aréir …*

…

Once James and Janey had lived alone on an "island of love." But now that was no more than a distant memory.

She supposed bringing the children into their lives was at the root of it. Children's crying can spoil any illusion of an island of love. But, she could never blame the children nor ever regret having a family. And they brought into their home a different and quite powerful manifestation of love.

It got so that she would look at couples in an old movie — she still had a weakness for those black-and-white flicks *The Late Show* loved to broadcast — and see them eating and laughing together … looking out for each other's feelings … and she would catch herself scoffing at it.

This, of course, made her wonder about herself. How warped or cold-hearted had she become? To find a movie plot preposterous simply because a couple in it liked each other?! Maybe it was her own married life that needed re-examination. Surely, there must be some happy couples — men and women who have spent years together and yet retain some warmth in their relations, some affection for one another.

None came to mind, however.

Dispassionate. That was the word for what she was. What they were. How had they gotten that way? How had two people whose loving togetherness had cut them off from all others, who had caused a scandal at the office of James's family business, who had created strife between father and son, and who had broken up an engagement approved of by two successful families become merely a man and woman living under the same roof, mostly in different rooms? Janey didn't have an answer. Their marriage just remained in motion.

Marital inertia: bodies in marriage will stay in marriage.

It was taking her forever to get out of bed. The kids were up already. She could hear them in the kitchen. Were they making breakfast themselves? She looked at the clock. She was late enough. They must be hungry.

From downstairs came the clatter of utensils on the table, and then on the floor.

Holy Mother of God! They must be making a mess! She better get down there.

"Paaaaauuuuul!" whined Kitty, as she always did, followed by Paul's calmer rebuke, "Take it easy. Don't be such a spaz!"

She threw on her fuzzy pink robe, took her green pack of Salems and her lighter from the nightstand, and, after a couple of attempts, lit one. The lighter was running out of fluid. Could she just stay and smoke, just finish this one cigarette in peace? Was that possible? Just five minutes?

A plastic bowl hit the linoleum kitchen floor. Janey heard it bounce once, roll across the floor, spin — wobble wobble wobble wobble — and then stop, silent.

"God, bless my life!"

Shrinking cigarette in her lips, Janey tied the pink sash around her waist and shuffled downstairs.

No, it is not possible to have even one minute's peace.

"Mom, Paul knocked my cereal bowl on the floor."

"It was an *accident*. I *told* you that."

"But now it's all dirty."

"Knock it off, the both of you. Here, Kitty. Here's a new bowl. I can wash the other one. I'm going to have to run the dishwasher, anyway."

Janey plunked a bottle of milk on the table, flopped into a chair, and stubbed out her cigarette in the emerald glass ashtray.

"Can you pour it for me, Mommy?"

"You're big enough and ugly enough to do it yourself."

"But it's heeeaaaavy."

"Oh, all right! But no whining! I told you about that. Talk in your normal voice or I won't listen to you. And, you better hurry up or you'll be late for school."

While she was up, Janey spooned Sanka crystals into a cup and put the kettle on. She leaned against the Formica counter, looked at her kids shoveling wet cereal and milk into their mouths and let out a heavy sigh. She wanted to light another Salem but decided to wait until the kids were gone. She really needed to cut down but lately she couldn't find the will power.

The kids ate quietly, except for the thunking of spoons against bowls. At what age would they start to care about manners? Couldn't the time come sooner?

To speed up the process, Janey got the kids' coats from the closet.

"Put your dishes in the sink and I'll take care of them."

As Kitty returned from the sink, Janey helped her on with her coat. Then she did the same for Paul. She figured she might as well. She pulled up Kitty's hood and tied a loose bow knot for her. Paul put on his wool Miami Dolphins hat. They'd need them on this grey winter's day on which the sun didn't feel like making an appearance.

The kettle whistled and Janey removed it from the burner, which she switched off.

"Don't forget your schoolbags and your lunches."

They both ambled out with everything they needed and Janey, finally, finally, closed the door behind them.

Janey knew she should fill up the dishwasher and run it, but all she wanted was bed. She grabbed the emerald ashtray and wandered into the living room. She lay down on the couch and slid the ashtray to the middle of the coffee table. Funny, she thought, how she never turned on the TV during the day. It never even tempted her.

Last night, Janey had made hot dogs and macaroni and cheese for dinner. It was something different. And it was easy.

Halfway through the meal, James, who never complained about anything she served, put down his fork, and sat staring at his plate.

"What is this?" he finally said.

Everybody at the table stopped.

"I work hard all day. And I don't ask for much. But, when I come home, I at least expect a decent meal. This isn't a meal. This is a snack you'd get at a ballpark."

He was right, of course. Yesterday, she had not been able to bring herself to conceive of a worthwhile dinner idea and implement it.

What was wrong with her? With them?

She and James shared the same house, even the same bed, with hardly anything to do with each other. They had each gotten into solitary habits in which the other had no interest. She figured that was natural enough; you couldn't expect two people to have the exact same interests for their entire lives, especially people of opposite sexes and different classes. A person has to have her own interests, her own identity — and it is understandable that one might not enjoy what the other found compelling. However, the habits had gotten so engrained as to lead them to neglect their marriage, almost to forget about it, sad to say. You could never tell from their example that marriage requires such a thing as effort.

It had become a mere habit, filled with numerous smaller habits. Janey would read her big, fat Victorian novels, sometimes something as far back as the Romantics — the Bronte sisters, of course, and George Elliott. Now and then she would pick up a book by Charles Dickens or Jane Austen. James would read the papers or watch the Phillies in the other room: he was courteous enough not to disturb Janey's reading. It had begun as a courtesy, at any rate. But after several months of this, it started to mean something else, to symbolize their separate lives. When he was ready to retire, James would give her the usual kiss on the forehead before tramping up the steps of the worn-carpeted staircase, creaking despite the carpet (which she had long since stopped bothering to complain about). Janey would stay downstairs for a long while with her books. Sometimes she would turn the TV to channel 6 for the *Million Dollar Movie*.

Why was it that every marriage seemed to consist of one night person and one morning person?

Janey felt in the pockets of her robe for her cigarette and lighter.

"Ugghh!"

She had left them upstairs. Maybe she would go up and lie down in bed for a bit ... in a minute.

Some nights when James would return from an evening at a business dinner or a handball game at the club, Janey would already be in bed. Often in half sleep, Janey would hear the heavy door slam and know he would be creaking up the stairs and collapsing into bed next to her. Other times it would be his fall into the bed that would awaken her. But it never really bothered her, except for the smell of scotch on his breath: she never could abide the sour odor. He would be very affectionate on such occasions, throwing his rough arm over her, tickling her with his hairy chest and legs, nuzzling the back of her neck, giving silly kisses to her shoulders and back. Janey would giggle and return his affection in her half sleep. But she would always try to get back to her dreams before James start to snore, as he did when he drank.

However, some nights she would hear the car door slam, listen to the creaks in the staircase, and expect his silly affection — only for it not to come. Maybe he was holding a grudge over some secret infraction and thought to punish her. Maybe he had had way too much to drink. Maybe he felt guilty about coming in so late. Janey never gave it much thought. It wasn't worth the energy. She was glad not to be fully awakened and to be able to return to her deep sleep.

This marriage is nothing but a world of apathy.

Her craving for a cigarette —manifested in her watering mouth and the restive veins of her forearms —had grown too strong to ignore. It drove her from the living room couch to the stairs.

Janey supposed James had had affairs over the years. She had neither proof nor strong evidence. But there had been times when the tales of his nocturnal adventures seemed implausible or hastily thrown together. She did not attribute her marital inertia to these suspected dalliances. They did not cause the rift, if they had occurred. They were, rather, a symptom of it.

Even if Janey felt fairly certain that James had strayed — though when or with whom she knew not — she herself had remained faithful, physically, at any rate. Her mind, on the other hand, had for years been awash in stories of love and adultery and broken hearts. Perhaps while reading old tomes or watching her favorite old movies or in her reveries, she had committed some sort of mental infidelity.

The Salems and lighter sat where she had left them on the nightstand. She sank onto the bed and selected a cigarette from the pack.

Now and then a flesh and blood man would become like one of those heroes in her stories. And there had been some friendships with men that had made her heart race. Sometimes, Tommy, her friend's husband, made her laugh so much at a party that she found herself thinking about him the next day, giving his face to Mr. Farebrother or some other 19th century character as she read.

Janey tried to light her smoke but the lighter only produced small sparks. She tried twice, three times. No good. Maybe she should give it a minute.

Of course, there were little flirtations — eye contact lasting a bit long with store clerks, inside jokes with men she had known throughout her married life, or before it. So, if she really examined her conscience strictly, she might have been guilty of a few minor affairs of the heart. This cost her some guilt, of course, but mostly she felt that it spiced her life with a dash of romance.

But as for James's possible affairs, Janey would have to transform herself into a detective and then a prosecuting attorney to do anything about it. She grew tired and frustrated just thinking about it.

She tried the lighter again. Hardly a spark left. Maybe James had one. Sometimes he kept a spare one in his drawer.

Janey shambled over to James's bureau. She pulled his sock drawer halfway out and felt around inside it looking out at the dull day. No lighter. She tried the underwear drawer with a slight increase in anxiety. Her fingers felt nothing but the soft thick fabric of his boxer shorts. Didn't he keep a lighter or matches around here somewhere? She pulled the drawer out farther and reached toward the back. There was that old cigarette case with his initials. Then the tips of her fingers encountered the jagged edge of a paper bag, some sort of gift. But her birthday wasn't until July. Janey pulled the drawer out even farther and removed the bag. Inside was a jewelry box and a note.

Inside the box, Janey found a string of pearls — real ones.

She unfolded the note.

> Dear Brittany,
>   Enclosed please find some rocks I spotted at 8th and Walnut and miraculously made disappear from the store window.

He never was much of a poet — was he?

I hope they remind you of that magical evening at the garden party at Overbrook, an evening on which you were the most beautiful flower dancing in the breeze of the country club garden, an evening I will never forget.

All right, Janey thought. He's getting a little better.

Where we danced by the stone walls around the garden like the jetties down the shore ... And we stopped for a nightcap at the strangely quiet McCloskey's ...

McCloskey's? It's a wonder Joe didn't say something. But then these men always stick together.

... where we found a back booth with some old black-and-white photos of the West of Ireland, the mountains reaching down to the sea, the sea crashing into the rocks ... and our lips meeting for the first time ... during that fleeting August respite from reality when the families are away in Ocean City ...

So this is what he does while I'm away watching his children down the shore?

It was a night to be remembered for me and I hope you remember me by these shiny rocks from the sea.

Janey had suspected. Truth be told, she had known it in her bones for years. And he had been so careless about hiding it. If you're going to try to deceive me at least be clever about it. Maybe he was drunk or maybe he just didn't care. At any rate, she now had her proof in hard cold stones and words in his own handwriting.

She could throw this in his face. Spending his money on some floozy. Brittany! Must be a classy broad!. When was the last time he bought her a precious stone or tried even the shortest poetic phrase on Janey — the mother of his children?!

But would it stop him from doing it again the next time she was away? Even if he promised not to? For all of the effort and anxiety, what would she gain? Nothing but nastiness and pain. James still provided for her and the children. He was kind and understanding toward her. Would some kind of prosecution and admission of guilt bring them back to the island of love?

Janey really needed a cigarette now but she still had no light.

She could go down and light it on the stove. She still needed to run the dishwasher, anyway

6. Greed & Charity

Having read so much in his brother James's frequent and detailed letters about his new, stately, and, it would seem, coveted home, Reverend Sarsfield J. Logan, S.J., took the opportunity afforded him by his summer break to board a train at New York's Pennsylvania Station, bound for his native city of Philadelphia. Although he felt some nostalgia for the fresh air and the North River waves' slapping against the ferry (and the thought of his mother and father at the end of the journey), he had to admit that being able to get on the train without leaving the island was an improvement over the old way of traveling home. He admired the design of the Pennsylvania Station as well, architecture being an avocation of his. From the outside, the structure's sheer height made it stand out among the four-storey buildings around 34th Street. He also appreciated the arched windows extending high above the avenue. Inside, he relished the vastness of the concourse with its Roman arches and its myriad people rushing around the iron columns, which appeared so light, like the graceful legs of *La Tour Eiffel*. That this was all created for the common man to catch his train made Father Logan love it even more. He delighted in the Roman-numeraled clock suspended from a chain, the Corinthian columns in the main waiting room, and the marble stairs. Father Logan loved to dawdle along the wrought iron railings as he descended the steep two-leveled staircase down to the track. It almost made him not want to get on the train. It was true that he visited his hometown less frequently since the decease of his parents, but this was not intentional.

Rocked by the train's chugging under the Hudson, Father Logan relaxed with his copy of *Hard Times*, taking breaks from the novel now and then to enjoy the novelty of the flat open spaces, the grass and trees of New Jersey, and to say some of the prayers of his Daily Office. Before long, he looked up to see Trenton fading away from him and realized that he was crossing the broad, rippling Delaware to his home state. The trains had gotten faster since he was younger.

As had happened many times before — though infrequently enough to enable him to forget that events had unfolded in precisely the same way the previous time — when Father Logan's train left North Philadelphia and neared Broad Street Station, his mind began to draft narratives to be shared with his family: the lessons he had taught to and learned from his students, the characters he encountered on the faculty and in the rectory, and some of the interesting and unusual scenes and events he had witnessed on the streets of New York City's Greenwich Village, Chelsea, and Grammercy Park. These mental preparations occurred as a matter of course, as if Father Logan were expected to give a sermon or lecture or to narrate adventures as a traveler of old might, though it would soon become clear, once again, that no such expectation existed.

Instead of the audience his mind always anticipated, he found — and discovering this immediately brought back memories of identical experiences from past visits — that people were bursting to fill him in on every event that had occurred since he had boarded his last New-York-bound train. His long absences from home, moreover, provided his brother with voluminous amounts of news and anecdotes to regale him with about upwardly mobile suburban life. He had barely disembarked — with hardly a chance to look westward along the station's "Chinese Wall" viaduct toward the Schuylkill — and reached for his luggage, the carrying of which would in no way be permitted, before his brother began his loquacious monologue about the exploits of his children: their classroom successes and academic proclivities, their schoolyard shenanigans and ball-field prowess — young Jim was a centerfielder with a graceful swing — and their humorous and pithy observations about the world around them, their school, and their Faith. Hot on the heels of these remarks would flow praises for the virtues of his new home, its many bedrooms, acres of land, well-tended gardens, manicured lawns, energetic fountains (imported in pieces from Italy and reassembled in Gladwyne, Pa by immigrants from its native land), the obsession his wife had with flowers and, indeed, how she should be granted an honorary degree in horticulture so much time did she spend learning about plants and shrubs (particularly the expensive ones, which he enumerated with keen interest) so that she could give detailed instructions to the gardener. Interspersed among his expounding on his two main themes were updates on former schoolmates Father Logan had not thought of in a decade.

Occasionally, when James needed to catch his breath, he would huff or puff a question to Father Logan about how things were in the Big Apple. Father Logan had hardly spoken since his arrival, but, as he answered, he felt winded himself.

Though he considered such feelings uncharitable and ungrateful to his sibling and host, Father Logan had to admit that after the quiet time of reading and prayer on the train, it was staggering to step into this torrent of talk. Preoccupied with being polite — with listening closely and responding appropriately when he seemed called upon to do so — he hardly noticed, let alone appreciated, Broad Street Station's typical Frank Furness Gothic spires and arched windows, which were rounded without pointed chancels. Before he knew it, his luggage was in the trunk and he was installed in the backseat of his brother's new Packard, being forced to decide whether or not he wished to make use of the plump cushion armrest that his brother pulled down for him.

"We gotta take the Parkway, Sarsfield! I know you haven't had much chance to ride on it. You'll like some of the new buildings."

James turned the wheel this way and that, maneuvering through a couple of streets built for horses.

"Yes, I have been reading about some of the new struc-"

"I tell yih, people are havin' a hard time gettin' useta all these one-way streets. You gotta keep your wits about you these days driving In Town."

"Well, thank you for picking me up. I apprec-"

"No! No! Don't mention it, Sarsfield. That's not why I brought it up. It's just that Old Philadelphia is changing before our very eyes. Streets are gettin' wider, buildings gettin' taller, more churches and schools — all of which is good for the business, of course — the buildings gettin' electric. Must look pretty different — huh?"

"It does."

James made another turn and the brothers emerged from the puzzle of narrow streets onto the spacious Benjamin Franklin Parkway. Sarsfield admired the windowless Palladian façade and the copious Italian Renaissance dome of the Cathedral Basilica of Saints Peter and Paul.

"I don't remember this fountain."

Across the street from the basilica three unclad bronze figures luxuriated on their backs while holding atop their heads two swans and a fish whose mouths spouted and sprayed jubilant arches of water.

"No, I guess you didn't spend much time In Town last time — when you were here for the funeral. 'Fountain of Three Rivers,' they call it. Three naked goddesses — one for the Schuylkill, one for the Delaware, and one for the Wissahickon."

"I've crossed two rivers already today."

"Well, now you're in Logan Circle! Do you feel at home? "

"Remember Father telling people his grandpa had been friends with William Penn?"

"And they believed him! 'You're one of the Logans of Logan Circle?!'"

"Some people are just gullible, I suppose."

"And don't know an Irish brogue when they hear one! And can't figure that a guy from an old Philadelphia family doesn't lay bricks."

"See the new library? They finally finished it."

Sarsfield sat up to take a closer look at the gleaming white building with Greek columns, arched windows, and two sloping roofs with front-facing triangular pediments. In black capital letters, it proclaimed itself, "THE FREE LIBRARY."

"Greek Revival? … Or maybe Beaux Arts?"

"They've been fighting about it forever — since before the war, even. But now it's finished. Looks good, too. They're talkin' about puttin' a statue of Shakespeare over there or something. They got a couple for Civil War Vet'rans right there."

"We Philadelphians like to memorialize," Father Logan mused, staring up at the twin bright pylons. "And remember, I suppose."

As James's Packard rolled along the expansive boulevard modeled after the Champs Elysees not a decade ago, Father Logan noticed green grass and empty space on both sides, bisected by pavements, which looked untrodden. There were green lots on the right-hand side, standing empty at the moment, but Father Logan surmised they would not remain so for long.

"Sarsfield, it's like the whole city is one big construction site! Look! At the end of the Parkway, they're building a museum!"

Father Logan leaned forward and saw what looked like the sides of two Greek temples facing each other. In between, there were large accumulations of stone and rough scaffolding. He supposed it was for the edifice that would link the two smaller constructions of columns and pediments.

"More Greek revival, it appears."

"Of course, you would recognize that right away! I always say for a French teacher, you know an awful lot about architecture. But this museum, it's gonna be like a Philly Parthenon. Our City of Brotherly Love is gettin' to be a classy place, lemme tell yih. New buildings are going up everywhere. Not just museums and libraries but houses, too. And stadiums! Down in The Neck they built that Municipal Stadium.

Sarsfield noted how his brother stressed the third syllable of the stadium's name.

"Where Gentleman Jim beat Jack Dempsey."

"That's right. Dempsey never should have fired his manager. And how 'bout Franklin Field? Dja hear they wanna add an upper deck to it?! Everybody's got a project, a blueprint, and a work crew. And that keeps the money flowing into Logan Construction!"

"I can see that. It's like visiting a farm in early summer. Things sprouting everywhere you look."

"I hope things keep sproutin' — and bring us a big harvest."

Father Logan cleared his throat. A quote from Montaigne came to mind.

"*Il n'est pas la faute*," the essayist wrote. "*Mais plutôt l'abondance qui crée l'avidité.*"

James descended a slope and Father Logan bounced toward his brother as the Packard went around a curve.

"Here's your third river of the day."

Father Logan looked across the Schuylkill River at the Fairmount Waterworks. A collection of Greco-Roman style buildings, the whiteness of their pediments faded, the surfaces of their columns worn, spread across the top of a grey stone wall, and everything reflected in brown water so calm one would never know it had just now come rushing over the wide falls. Of the three rivers of Father Logan's day, this one offered the most magnificent prospect.

"There is so much Greek Revival architecture around here, the tourists might think we are pagans!"

"Hey, why not? Our name is Greek!"

The row of boathouses, some Tudor style, others in various American styles rolled by on the other side of the river.

"I half expect to see Kelly out there in his green hat."

"He's got other races on his mind these days."

The road curved westward and the trees grew taller. Soon the river and its bridges could only be seen in glimpses. As the brothers neared the city limits, James's talk turned more and more to the beauty and luxury afforded by his new dwelling. Though Father Logan endeavored to remain polite, his attention flagged. When he noticed City Avenue, he succeeded in squeezing in a sentence or two about his wanting to see the new tower at Saint Joseph's College and to visit the Jesuit community at 54th and City Line.

"Sure, sure," replied James. "I'll give you a ride. Or you can borrow the car — that is, if you remember how to drive one?"

"It's been a while."

"Have you ever driven a Packard? Ha-ha! Ask the man who owns one."

...

Taking the FDR to Midtown (revised)

To find the way home to Hell's Kitchen:

1. Exit the FDR at 42nd Street.
2. Proceed along East 42nd Street past Grand Central Terminal.
3. Turn right on Madison Avenue.
4. Turn left onto 47th Street.

It was strange and pleasant to see the FDR so empty. They rolled up the highway with no fear of any traffic jams and little fear of getting lost. And, suburban Laura, now on familiar driving terrain, seemed relaxed behind the wheel. Charles hadn't spoken in a while. Likely, he had fallen asleep again.

A few lights sparkled and bobbed on the waves of the East River, but mostly it was dark and flat — and broad, which was novel to Paul's urban eyes. As they passed 23rd Street, the old world of downtown faded away in the rearview mirror and the buildings before them grew taller, grabbing at the sky for more and more square feet.

say something say something now you have an opportunity talk about the skyline about the potholes about charles baudelaire the rain stopping driving on a highway veronicas veil the relics of the true cross c'mon c'mon the revolution will not be televised

The Empire State Building looked grey and stately in its sleep as the FDR rose and curved. Then it disappeared behind some projects. In an eyeblink, it reappeared, looking solitary, as if all the other buildings had stood aside for it, parting a giant brick-and-mortar curtain for the star to accept its adoration.

workers finished it in a year and a month guys like great granddad sitting up there on the beams having their lunch smoking laughing staring at death at posterity in defiance such magnificent aplomb did their forbears lunch so casually upon the stones they rowed and rolled to newgrange or the clifftop of dun aengus the empire state the true great granddaddy of them all rivets and girders mortar and bricks with half the straw thrown up so fast so al smith could cut the ribbon but what was the hurry that great rushing that tremendous energy of the city people love that but always suspected it comes from the people working their spirits to a drone all that perpetual motion all that twinkling blinking glittering fueled by the souls people give in exchange

For?

As the BMW sped around the bend of Kips Bay, the highway turned toward the city. The Water Club approached on Paul's side and across the river in a giant red script, there curled and sloped the words, "Pepsi Cola."

Symbol of a generation? We have not turned out to be the Peppers they wanted us to be. Sell-out generation.

Ahead, and over the East River, the lights of the 59th Street Bridge were strung like giant luminescent pearls.

say something be a poet offer her a string of marvels that can stretch across a river from where the sun was born and light up its waves

Seeing a green, white-lettered sign for 34th Street and The Queens Midtown Tunnel, Paul sat up.

— Better get over to the right lane. You have to get off soon.

ain't poetic exactly but need to warn her in advance or end up in the bronx

She maneuvered into the right lane. Presently the signs for the 42nd Street exit appeared.

A couple of yachts nodded off to sleep at the dock.

do they dive from those boats for pearls of light do they sail up to hunts point for cuchifritos or some of that crack can you imagine

— There's the exit for 42nd Street.

She took the ramp, which immediately began lifting them above the highway. The FDR dove down and away from them. The ramp was wide and flat with cracked cement and there were no roadsigns to confirm that they were going the right way.

— Is this right? We're going up!

— I think so. The sign said 42nd Street ...

At the top of the ramp, the road turned sharply left, changing the car's heading so that it seemed precipitated right at midtown Manhattan's wall of skyscrapers. They looked so quiet and peaceful at this hour and from this distance, though their hallmark was workaday and workanight frenzy.

almost there no real need to piss remember when the city was an incomprehensible maze of unknown streets uncountable undifferentiated infernal hordes hurrying now the shades of former days surround me proofreading ads crisscrossing midtown for lunches with kathy the saint philomena guidance counselor getting an order of irresponsible french fries to go with my packed meatloaf sandwich i wanted to buy my lunch damn it at least let me buy some fries to go with the brown bag scrimping bread cold meat eaten under the circle of columns in the park across from tommy makem's cheap bitch didn't know how to enjoy life

The majesty and power of it all still made Paul's heart beat a little faster. Those breathtaking towers of business and storefronts full of treasures. It excited him despite himself. In those old midtown days, he would deliberately walk across town on 57th Street just to breathe it in and marvel at the things for sale: Tiffany jewelry and Steinway pianos, sculptures from ancient Greece right there in the windows, clothes from renowned designers and famous stores — he remembered for the first time in his life looking at shirts and ties and jackets in the window and wanting to buy them for himself.

sitting by fountains for lunch near where kathy had that costly company christmas party glitzy they called it buzzwords joking about how the pigeons took off from their skyscraper ledges all at once such entertainment now i can afford expensive lunchspots for my little friend here take her someplace in tribeca to nobu or montrachet if i can get this mistress of the night out in the daytime pigeons conquering the air conquering gravity conquering the heights of those piles of wealth that out of town visitors loved to see rockefeller trump carnegie written on them was so enamored with that glorious skyline couldn't take my eyes off it still can't

— I can't imagine myself ever working in an office …

— Really? Why not?

— I don't know. Doin' the whole nine-to-five thing … sitting in some stuffy cubicle all day …

— Ah, you never know. It's not so bad. You could probably do it. Some offices are not as stuffy as you think.

— Still, it's hard to imagine — isn't it? Me being all corporate? Good morning, Mr. Paul. Morning!

— It is, Paul chuckled. Yeah, that is hard to imagine!

Despite the time, the Chrysler Building still looked ultra bright, shining floodlights on itself, lights upon arrows of light on narrowing arches pyramiding upward.

Should be called the Avis building. It tries harder.

Yellow cabs, vans, trucks, buses, and cars still flowed east and west along on 42nd Street. The traffic was far lighter than it would be at most hours of the day and night but it was steady enough.

> *Where the underworld can meet the elite,*
> *Forty-Second Street.*

— But nowadays offices are not all that conservative. Most people don't wear suits. Even in the financial places. And some offices are really casual — especially these Internet startups.

— Yeah, I miss that a little.

— What?

— Guys in suits.

Laura's beaten BMW glided past the familiar wideness of Second Avenue.

kathy afterwork at murphys jamesons clancys fond memory brings the light but dim as the early morning glow wavelengths of the same intensity yet one was waning while the other just beginning kissing her was so easy the first time when she almost stumbled into the bleecker street gutter outside the back fence holding kathy's hand walking to the subway had a big awkward hard on going through the turnstile at west 4th

But why dwell on the past? Why spend time thinking about an outmoded ex-girlfriend who's no longer around? When you can have the new prestigious deluxe, high-quality, model sitting next to you today! Act now. Reach out and touch the ultimate driver. Limited time only. A hand on the driver's seat will put you in the revolution. Make you Hertz. Offer good while supplies last. Order today. Better just do it. Gutsy is job one. Between love and madness, have it your way. When it absolutely, positively has to be done overnight. Have a poke and a smile. Look, Ma, no timidity! The push that refreshes. When I.M. Horny talks, people listen.

C'mon! Don't let it die down. She started it up. Now keep it going. You know it doesn't really matter that much what you say. *Daily News* building's arching entryway. It's later than you think. You never told Carmen how you felt and she vanished from our lives. Why is it always the men who have to be the pursuers? Women have no idea how hard it is. Say something. Keep it moving forward.

At Third Avenue, a red light stopped them. Above them shone the steel and glass of the Grand Hyatt Hotel and for a half a block there ran a transparent awning to protect wealthy heads waiting for hailed cabs. Opposite was a castle flying a flag emblazoned with, "Cipriani" and a faceless bartender in mid-cocktail-shake. Across 42nd Street arched the Park Avenue Viaduct. The MetLife Building puffed out its chest and lowered its eyes toward the Roman-numeraled clock of the Grand Central Terminal. Hercules sat on one side of the clock, looking up and asking Mercury, "Where else do you want to go today?" while Minerva, on the other side, checked the train schedule.

— What's going on here? Laura complained.

She jerked herself toward the steering wheel and squinted with knit brows through the drop-specked windshield.

— The light is green but nobody's moving.

Horns began to honk.

— It's all cabs. Must be dropping people off. See if you can get over to the left lane. Hold on. Not yet … not yet.

Laura let the car roll and then hit the brake, pushed the gas pedal slightly, and then hit the brakes again.

— Not yet … OK. You can get over. Go around these cabs and get ready to make a right on Madison Avenue.

Laura stuck the nose of her car into the other lane and slowly pulled into it. Under the Viaduct, old-Great-White-Way letters shouted: PERSHING SQUARE. They went under the Park Avenue Viaduct and past Vanderbilt Avenue.

— Better get over to the right lane.

Time is running out. Why delay? Each item sold separately. Will Charles lean forward and say please don't squeeze the charmer? You only have one life. Live it up with this blonde. Some assembly required; some restrictions may apply. Pussy: the fabric of our lives. Batteries not included. Time to make the overtures. The right relationship is everything you always wanted. And less.

— This is where you used to work — right, Paul?! Your old days as an ad man?

—That's right. Madison Avenue! But I didn't stay in that business very long.

— You didn't like it.

— Not really.

— You had more important things to write.

Paul shot a wide-eyed glance at Laura's bedraggled profile. Her eyes were fixed on Madison Avenue. Paul smirked and then licked his lips.

madison avenue like a straight seam running up this strange island off the coast of america when creative put on a display of the years work even proofreaders could gawk above it all we were telling america what it wanted al above depeynted in a tour saugh i conquest sittynge in greet honour even greater than that hertz edifice of washington the breathtaking capitol dome don't those clowns have to come here for help here where we legislate needs and desires play on insecurities lusts all the seven deadlies

Does she still want it or doesn't she? An amazing once-in-a-lifetime offer of this miracle product. New York, New York 10017. Hey! How about a nice Philadelphian kiss? Every kiss begins with "Hey!" No risk, no obligation, no down payment, no purchase necessary. I've fallen *mo cuisle* and I can't get up. Magically bodacious. They're g-r-r-eat! Real and spectacular. Pardon me, do you have any great hard on? Like a rock. Quality, value, performance. Pussy-lickin' good!

Cunnilingus comes standard. Manly yes, but I like it, too. Blowing is job one. Mama mia, that spicy meatball is the quicker pecker upper. Fill it to the rim, her quim. Hey, Charles ... she likes it!

— Here's Madison. Make a right here.

Laura turned right and headed uptown along this narrow street of skyscrapers, banks, and shoe and clothing stores. There wasn't much to look at, thought Paul, but there were plenty of places to get money and spend it. He looked out at the scaffolding and down at the worn spots in the white lines on the street.

— But you never know what kind of crazy characters you'll meet in these offices, Paul said. One of the first managers I had when I moved to New York — right near here — was this Gothic punk rocker, with spiked bracelets. In the building where I work there's a guy who comes in dressed like a cowboy every day.

— See? Now, being a cowboy every day is kinda easy. You wear the same kinda thing every day.

— Yeah, but how do you pick your everyday look?

— I don't know. That's the hard part. If I had to get dressed up every morning, it would take me forever. I'd be late, like, every day!

— Who knows? Maybe they'll come out with tie-die office wear.

Laura threw her head back and laughed. Paul smiled at her but then turned his eyes quickly back to the streets. It felt good to connect with her like this. Yet it was she who made the conversation. It always works when she wants it to.

— If you had an office job, you could sleep at night and work days. It would be easier for you to finish up school at night. And once you finish school, you can-

— Make more money, that's for sure! I bet a lot of advertising guys are rich.

writers illustrators photographers designers selling their talents to whatever cookie manufacturer or light beer brewer walks through the door so proud of it look at all that we have done talents not buried in the ground but filling times square with flashes the air waves with noise to sell stuff for what a pile of money to sit in a bank a steak instead of a hamburger a glass of scotch instead of a bottle of bud should be a red light district calgon take me away

On 43rd Street Paul saw the tall arching windows of Grand Central, like something you'd see in a church, but dark, no saints for the light to shine through. And on the corner, by the portal to the Terminal, for the commuters thirsty for a pint before catching their trains bound for tunnels leading out of the City, was the pub, Annie Moore's.

There's a statue of her on Ellis Island, the first immigrant to set foot there, and an identical statue in Cobh — saw it there that miserable rainy day — where the ship left, the emigrants looking back the pinnacle of Saint Colman's last bit of Ireland to disappear into the sea. For an English major, she said, you know an awful lot about history. Time to put an end to the Irish history, Paul — is it not?

What if nothing comes between her and her Charles? If she wants the limey in her tank? Don't be fooled by imitations. Don't fall for scams, rip-offs, gyps, con games, come ons. Man tested. Woman approved. What if Laura is bullshit on America? Side effects could include confusion, swindling, misunderstanding, pyramid schemes, hornswaggling, fraud, humiliation. What if there are no refunds, returns, or exchanges? If that's not what she meant at all?

On an old tower of brick and mortar glowed a set of jaunty, stylish white letters, whose N and Y and K flaunted devil-may-care flourishes, spelled out in the dark sky: *New York*. It made Paul think of Westchester ladies in the old days in fur coats getting off the train at Grand Central — maybe a stop at the husband's office — to do some shopping along these avenues, maybe clutching *New York* magazines in their oxters, for something to page through on the train. Laura's mother? Not bloody likely.

—Better get over to the left lane.

— Left lane?

— Yeah, you're gonna have to turn soon.

All sales are final. Caveat emptor. That virus is forever. What's in *your* wallet? Because so much is riding on your rubbers. You could bring good things to life. Allow nine months for delivery. Mileage may vary. Hospitality, friendly service, name brands, easy terms, low low prices. If it seems too good to be true …

Laura slowed down and slapped her turn signal at 45th Street.

— No, not here. At 47th.

They approached a red-brick colonial style building bearing a sign with red Chinese characters and black Roman letters: Bank of China.

A good spot for them to rake in all that American dough. Their stock exchange probably hopping now as New York takes its fitful nap.

Plus, tonight you've been a king of beers and offer is good only while supplies last. We love to drink and it shows. Good to the last drop. Leave the drinking to us. Try the new wonder drug, Viagra. Better fucking through chemistry. So nice to fool Mother Nature. Is it live or is it Memorex? Real and spectacular? Miracle or hoax?

— Make a left here.

…

"Look at that rug!" Janey thought.

She clenched her teeth and scowled at the obvious signs of wear. They were right at the lips of the lower steps where Paul and Kitty used to slide down on their behinds. Maybe they still did. Janey had forbidden them to many times but they didn't listen.

The stairs really needed a new carpet. There were so many things around here to be upgraded or repaired. Sometimes she found flaws everywhere she looked. The drapes were a thousand years old. The bushes in front of the house cried out for the serious attention of a landscaper. Grass grew tall through the fissures in the front walk.

She would love to finish the basement and turn it into a paneled game room where the kids could have their friends over. They could have a pool table and a ping pong table, maybe even air hockey.

But it was tough to ask James for the money. He worked so hard and was under a lot of pressure to pay tuition for two private schools. Janey wished she had her own job and her own money as she did in the days before she was married.

What could she do? Maybe she could work with children. She missed having little ones around.

Janey opened the car door and got in.

It was best to get away from the house. The more she looked at it, the more she could find things that required money to fix — money she didn't have. Better to get away from flaws she could not remedy.

Besides, she needed to find the right pair of shoes to go with her dress for James's party Saturday night. She had decided to wear her powder blue dress but her shoes that matched it were getting worn out.

Janey drove away from the house without even looking at it. Though it was the wrong way to go to the shopping center, she looped down Simpson Road and took the backstreets to Ardmore and then Lancaster Avenues.

She parked in the Suburban Square lot and went to Kinney's first. Some of the shoes on display could match her dress but none excited her. She tried on two pair and they fit well enough. But they left her feeling uninspired.

Janey left the store and walked around the center, nodding and smiling at a few people she recognized, not able to make up her mind about anything. Should she buy a new pair of shoes or stick to the worn numbers at home that she knew were suitable for a long evening?

Then in the window of Florsheim's she spotted an elegant pair of electric-blue shoes with stiletto heels and upper and lower straps. They looked sexy and yet easy to wear for a night out.

And the color seemed just right. She knew they were expensive without having to look at the price tag. But, it wouldn't do any harm to try them on.

Janey entered without noticing the bell jingling behind her or anyone in the store. She headed right for those blue heels.

"Hi, Janey!"

She stopped and turned. It was the mother of Paul's friend, Joe McHugh. Ellen. Ellen McHugh.

"Hi, Ellen!"

Ellen wore a name tag. She was working at Florsheim's.

Jeez, times must be tougher for the McHughs than I thought.

"How are you? I didn't know you were working here."

"Yeah, I just started last month. I can walk to work and bring in a little extra money. Those tuition bills aren't getting any cheaper."

"No, they aren't! That's for sure."

Please, Lord, remind me to ask James if he can offer a job to Ellen's husband.

"How does Joe like it down at the Prep?"

"Oh, he loves it!"

"Have you ever known a boy who doesn't?"

"No, it must be something they put in the air conditioning."

"Really."

"So, can I help you with somethin'? Is there a pair of shoes you'd like to try on?"

"Well, I have this thing to go to with James on Saturday night. And I looked around at home and at Kinney's and haven't found anything that's just right. I was passing the window and those electric-blue pumps caught my eye. I know they must be expensive but I couldn't resist at least coming in to take a look."

"Sure! I know just the pair you're talkin' about and I don't blame yih. I bet they would look great on you. What size?"

"7."

"Have a seat. I'll see what we have."

Ellen turned and strode toward the back room. Janey sat down on the bench.

There was no way Janey could buy those shoes. It was an extravagant idea to begin with, but now! There was no way. There was just no way.

Ellen hurried back to Janey, taking the lid off of the shoe box and placing it by Janey's feet.

"Here yih go. I can't wait to see how they look on you!"

Janey kicked off her low black heels. She unwrapped the shoes from the white paper and slipped her feet into the blue stilettos.

Ellen dragged the shoe-fitting stool over and squatted on it.

"This is crazy," Janey said, placing one foot and then the other on the stool's foot rest. "But I just couldn't help myself."

Ellen bent over and buckled both straps of each shoe for her. Janey's cheeks burned.

"How do they feel?"

"Great. They seem like a good fit."

"Stand up and try walkin' in 'em. There's a mirror over there."

"Wow! They feel just right."

The fit was indeed more comfortable than Janey had expected and they were a breeze to walk in.

"What color dress are you gonna wear Saturdee night?"

"It's blue. Powder blue."

"Oh, these would be perfect with that! Really, perfect!"

Ellen was right. The color of the shoes would make a lovely match for her dress.

Janey turned this way and that before the mirror. She stood still with her fingers over her lips and tilted and turned each foot side to side.

They were perfect. Absolutely perfect. But there was no way. There was just no way.

She slinked back to the bench.

"They are really great but I can't even think about them. I just came in here on a lark. Leave it to me to spot the most expensive pair of shoes in the store."

"Are you sure? They really look beautiful on you."

"Yes, I'm sure. It's just too extravagant for some construction company event."

Ellen leaned forward and winked.

"Talk to James about them. Maybe he'll like 'em."

"I will."

Janey put her old shoes on and Ellen wrapped the pumps in their paper and placed them back in the box.

"I really have to get going," Janey said. "I need to pick up Paul from his guitar lesson."

"Really? How's he doing with 'at?"

Ellen rose and put the lid on the box.

"Pretty well. He doesn't practice as much as he should, though."

"I hear yih. Seems like these kids just expect teachers to open up their skulls and pour the knowledge in."

"True. Kitty can be like that, too, though most of the time she is a hard worker."

"That's good. Well, give them my best."

"I will. Give my best to Joe and the kids."

"And if you change your mind, these'll still be here," Ellen said shaking the shoe box.

Janey hurried over to the A&P and cashed a check. After she picked up Paul from the guitar lesson, she went straight to the kitchen and deposited the cash in the cookie jar, singing to herself:

"Whack fol the daddy oh
There's whiskey in the jar."

...

At Jimmy Logan's Gladwyne mansion, the talk around the Thanksgiving table centered on the stock market crash and the economy. This frustrated Father Sarsfield.

"Remember Cholly Porter from Wynnewood? He went to Carroll …"

"Wasn't he in the service with Jimmy?"

"Yeah, that's the guy."

"His family had a grocery store — right?"

"That's right. They owned the A&P in Ardmore. And the son did really well in the supermarket business. He opened up a couple stores around the Main Line and in Manoa. He was doing great. I remember that Cadillac he drove, boy. That was one helluva car. You see that thing drivin' toward you ... you think it's the President of the United States coming down the street. And that house of his in Rosemont? Beautiful place. Huge! Like a mansion."

"The grocery business is a good one — people always need to go food shoppin'. They might not need new buildings but they will always buy food," Jimmy added.

"If they have money," Father Logan said.

"Kind of like funeral homes — never run out of customers."

"Maybe people'll start buildin' supermarkets and funeral homes."

During the mass, he had said at Saint Colman's that morning, Father Logan had spoken about how men on Wall Street, not far from his home at Saint Francis Xavier High School in Manhattan, had attached themselves to the goods of this world and had been crushed by the loss of the wealth they had spent their lives earning.

"Think about that for a moment," he had urged the congregation of his home parish. "These men had spent much of their lives sweating to obtain mere things, things that fall apart and become useless, things that float away and vanish like bubbles, things that could be taken away in the blink of an eye. And they weren't just disappointed. They were crushed — *suicidal*! These men had so identified with the accumulation of wealth, with the piling up of inanimate objects that they considered the loss of these things worth the loss of the precious gift of life! The amassing of the treasures of this world had become the very center, the very purpose of their lives. And when they lost those objects, as it is inevitable for all of us to lose even our most precious possessions, they saw no purpose in life. They considered jumping out of their office windows the only recourse available to them. How sad it is and how blind these poor souls must have been to allow the possession of temporal things to become more important than the precious gift of life Our Lord had given them. Can you imagine such foolishness?! It seems unthinkable when you look at it from the right perspective. And yet we can imagine it — can't we? We are all of us guilty of this to one degree or another."

Father Logan had thought the sermon had been well received.

"Can you pass the stuffing?" Mariellen said. "I can't get enough of it! You really outdid yourself this year, Kitty."

"Well, clearly Cholly Porter should have stuck to the food business. He'd be in much better shape now," declared Jimmy, passing the stuffing.

"Y'know, I ran into Eddie DiGregorio the other day at the shopping center and he said Rick De Vries declared bankruptcy. Lost a big chunk of change in the markets."

"That's a shame."

"Before the crash, we were too focused on material things," Father Logan had preached. "Surely the Church is not against work and private enterprise and no one wishes for people to suffer from poverty and privation. However, this recent economic crash is a clear example of how the Lord giveth and taketh away. It offers us a lesson about the folly and, more importantly, the danger to our immortal souls of putting too much faith in the perishable things of this world. Such misplaced faith distracts us from the state of our eternal souls and from our relationship with Our Lord, Who has no beginning and no end. It is my fervent prayer that this Depression will cause us and anyone who has been perverted by their delight and pursuit of glittering gold to examine their consciences, to remember what should come first in their lives and to store up for themselves 'treasures in heaven, where neither moth nor rust destroys, and where thieves do not break in and steal.' For material wealth could all be gone tomorrow."

"How about old Joe O'Leary? Dja hear about him? No flies on that guy, I tell yih," Jackie said.

"What's he up to?" asked Kit.

"Well, one of his buddies down the Knights of Columbus had a connection and got him a government job. He's working for the City now. Just before the market went belly up, he landed safely in the department of Sanitation with the City of Philadelphia. Everyone else is out looking for work and he's bringing in a fat steady paycheck."

"Smart man," Jimmy said. "People will never run out of garbage, either."

"A lucky man, too," Jackie replied.

"Good for him," Kitty added. "I always thought he was a good guy. All the O'Learys are nice people."

"You know the government is not going to stop spending," Jimmy said.

"Yes," Father Logan interjected. "When businesses and ordinary people stop spending, the government has to step in. Otherwise, everything would freeze."

Father Logan had not wanted to disturb his congregation with too vivid reminders of the Depression. So, he had concluded with thoughts about the holiday.

"Since it is Thanksgiving, let us be thankful for the little things, the simple pleasures of life. Let us be thankful for the basic and important gifts: that we have life itself ... that we have food to eat ... that we have family with whom we can gather around a table ... that we have our Faith that saves us and sustains us in periods of straitened circumstances ... and let us remember those less fortunate than we ... that we have a duty to help them no matter how difficult our own circumstances might be ... Above all, let us use this holiday of Thanksgiving in this troubled year as an occasion to renew our commitment to the values of the gospel — faith, hope, and love — 'and the greatest of these is love.'"

"I guess I can accept that in a state of emergency like this," Jimmy said, spearing a slice of white meat with the oversized silver serving fork. "But, in general, I prefer it when the bureaucrats leave business to the businessmen."

"There were some British statesmen in the last century who had a similar attitude when people were starving."

"Please, let's not turn this into a political discussion," cried Kitty.

"I won't, Kit. *Ça ne fait rien.* I know there are not many Republicans who are willing to listen to reason, anyway. They are like the stony soil in Our Lord's parable."

"Sarsfield!"

"Well, someone has to speak up," Jimmy declared. "Before the Democrats spend the whole country into the Poor House!"

"Don't forget," Jackie said. "Some of that Democratic spending is helping to keep our company operating. Without that, we'd have a lot less work and have to let more men go."

"True," Jimmy agreed. "Hey, if the government is the only one spending money, I don't see why some of it shouldn't come our way."

"A man of great principles, I see," Sarsfield chuckled.

Everyone at the table laughed, including Jimmy.

"My principal need right now," he said. "Is for more potatoes. So, do you mind sharing the wealth?"

Chuckling, Father Logan passed his brother the potatoes.

"You said it yourself, Sarsfield. In times like these, the government has to spend to keep businesses alive and keep people working. I mean, if it's good for the men-"

"Now you sound like Father," Kitty said. "Doesn't he, Sarsfield? 'I'm interested in what's good for the men!' That's what Father always used to say. Word for word. He really did care about them — didn't he?"

"He did, indeed," Father Logan said. "We can credit his great Faith for that."

"And his upbringing. You know how the Irish always looked out for one another."

"Sometimes, when I think about how much he cared for his employees," Father Logan continued. "I think it is a wonder he became a success at all."

"It is a wonder," Jimmy agreed. "I don't know how he did it. He was a very impractical businessman in many ways. Just giving money away ..."

"People loved him," Kitty cried. "He loved the men and they loved him. His customers loved him. The police and fireman, the politicians loved him ..."

"He had an unusual way at looking at things, alright. And some peculiar business practices. Yet, he was still successful."

Still impassioned, Kitty continued:

"He loved to give money to support Saint Colman's and the Prep — he paid for a few of the marble columns as well as a few boys' tuition costs ... He gave to Catholic Charities, the cause in Ireland ... He was a Giver. And all the love and generosity he gave out, came back to him!'

"People looked out for each other in those days," Jackie said.

"It was a different time," Jimmy repeated.

Father Logan sat up straight, lifted his scotch, and took a long slow slip.

"I remember one famous example of his unusual business practices," Father Logan began. "It started in the very early days of the Logan Construction Company, not long after Father first went out on his own as a contractor. He was struck by how his men, who spent most of their days building houses for other people, were trapped in tiny apartments and cramped tenements down in South Philadelphia."

"I remember this story," Kit said.

"It always bothered him. One day he was chatting with one of the bricklayers at the end of the day. The man was about to get married and was worried how much room his miniscule apartment would have for a wife and family. He complained that he would love to start his new life with a decent home but with paying rent, sending money back to Ireland, and his other expenses it was hard to save for a down payment. So, Father says right there on the spot, 'The Logan Construction Company will lend you the down payment. How much do you need?'"

"Yeah," Jimmy laughed. "He agreed to pay it before he even knew how much it was! And he charged no interest. He just said, 'Pay it back when you can'!"

"*Absolument*! '*Petit a petit, l'oiseau fait son nid*' — 'Little by little, the bird makes its nest,'" Father Logan exclaimed. "And that became his standard practice. Whenever one of the men was in the market for a house, he would lend him the down payment. No interest and no deadline."

"And the men paid him! Every one of them!" Kitty said. "They probably paid him back faster than they would have a bank. They were so grateful to him."

"And they became so loyal," Jimmy added.

"True, they never wanted to work for anyone else. The Logan Construction Company was the place to work — because of Mr. Logan!"

"You can have your slogans …"

…

— Paul, you used to work in advertising — didn't you?

— Yeah, I did. I was a proofreader. I also did a little bit of copywriting.

Paul had told Laura the story of his advertising days in fits and starts, fighting interruptions from other customers, from friends, or from the power chords of live bands. It was never the way he imagined it: the way he would have told it in a memoir of his more youthful days:

Working as a proofreader on Madison Avenue was cool for a while. It felt like a step up from being a teacher. The money was your average entry-level salary for the corporate world but after teaching in Catholic schools, I felt rich. Plus, I was working in the media, which I knew in my bones was the center of the world I had grown up in.

Still, despite the better pay and the prestige of working in a shining Madison Avenue skyscraper, I felt this nagging discomfort that I could not shake.

I used to proofread the ads for crackers and cookies, local telephone directories, and credit card companies. I even proofread ads for cigarettes, which people made a moral stand about. In those days, that was a thing to make a moral stand about.

"My grandmother died from lung cancer. So, I-"

But the issue I had with the whole enterprise — the general prostitution of talent going on throughout the Creative Department, on all of the company's floors, up and down Madison Avenue, and all over the country? Nobody took a stand about that. In fact, everybody was so busy haggling over how much their souls could bring on the open market that no one even saw what troubled me. They were all hellbent on exchanging whatever talents they had for the stuff ballyhooed in the latest catalogs, magazines, and TV and radio spots, for a big bursting house in Connecticut in which to reproduce, and then buy the Game Boys, Super Soakers, and Tickle Me Elmos hawked to their offspring. They would have thought I was crazy.

I kept a low profile and proofread my cookie ads, my cracker posters, the newspaper ads for banks … And at lunchtime I wrote in my journal. I always had an LCC steno pad with me. Hell, after pestering Carmen and the other kids at Saint Philomena's to write in theirs all the time, I could hardly neglect my own, especially now that I had no papers to grade.

Sometimes when there wasn't much to do, I even wrote in the journal at work: ideas still lingered in my head after lunch and I didn't want to forget them. I'm not sure if anyone ever saw me scribbling on company time, but it was possible.

One time when I was waiting for the elevator to the lobby, this copywriter named Tim, a tall thin guy with a dark, curly head of hair and a mustache, asked me what the steno pad was for. I told him it was a journal I liked to write down ideas in, that I wrote poems, and sometimes short stories.

— Gotten anything published?

His question struck a nerve, as it always did. Whenever you reveal your identity as a writer, people ask that question. It's natural enough, I guess. But your average person has no idea how difficult it is to get something published these days nor how that question makes a writer wince. And, I was so hungry for it then — just to have something in print! I had had stories and poems in literary magazines at the Prep and at Saint Joe's. But not yet as an adult, as a professional. Doug at Saint Philomena's used to tell me that once you get the first thing published, it is much easier to get other pieces in print. The key was that first publication. And I was still looking for it.

— Not yet, I said.

At home I had the current *Writer's Market*, the fat annual publication that became quickly outdated as each year flew by. Maybe you'd buy the new copy in March. You'd type and mail the stories and poems — no choice but to use a typewriter back then — to literary magazines whose requirements seemed to match your submission. And then you'd wait. Before you'd know it, it was November or December and the little form rejection slips and, occasionally, the full-fledged form letters would arrive in the mail. And by that time, the notices in the *Writer's Market* were outdated: it had to have been a year since the requirements had been written, after all. You might as well wait for the new edition to come out in January, which, unless you got it for Christmas — and from whom? — you probably wouldn't get around to buying until March.

— Do you submit things?

— Yeah. When I get a chance.

— Keep at it, said Tim. You'll get there.

I often wondered what I would do with the first money I made with my writing. I imagined I would take myself to a bar that had Guinness on tap and have a nice creamy pint. (Budweiser was more appropriate for my bank account in those days.) I pictured myself alone with my thoughts, drinking in the moment of victory.

It was kind of Tim to encourage me. He seemed like a cool guy. But he was under a lot of pressure, you could tell. A couple of times I had to stay late and look over his revisions to a series of banking ads and walk them over to him. The whole floor was quiet, practically empty. He had his own office, which was dark except for the light from the desk lamp. Through his office window, I could see the still substantial traffic following Madison Avenue's pocked and faded white lines past windows where mannequins held their noses in the air. I liked it in Tim's office. It seemed respectable: he had his own space to be a writer. A Clio on his desk. And a good salary to go with it, I assumed.

He probably saw me checking everything out.

— Ever think of doing this — copywriting? Tim asked. You enjoy writing ...

— I wouldn't mind giving it a try.

I had no ambitions in that area, really, though my father often urged me to head in that direction. Still, I wasn't completely against the idea.

But clearly I had given Tim the wrong answer. It appeared to him to reflect a lack of ambition, though ambitious I certainly was. Just not in a way that Madison Avenue and my dad understood it. I guess I was expected to salivate all over the floor at the prospect he had offered to me, to hunger as the others did, not to differ in desire.

— Give it a try?! It's not so easy, he exclaimed. Man, everyone here is looking to get into Creative!

He wasn't lying. The traffic people, the various hottie assistants, the freelancers coming in with their storyboards in big flat black cases, the receptionist, probably the janitor, too, all wanted to be copywriters or permanent graphic "artists" in the multi-million-dollar business of advertising. They all wanted to use their imaginations, their creativity to tantalize the global appetite, to push the levers of real power. And the levers of the cash register, too, of course.

— I thought, Tim continued, that since you like to write so much-

I realized I should change tack. I didn't want to be rude, and, like I said, I was hungry to be published, to be recognized. I didn't want to just write anonymously in steno pads. I wanted an audience.

— I do. I just never wrote that kind of thing before.

It was true I didn't know much about advertising. I had been an English major and a teacher in Catholic schools. What did I know about the world of creating ads? They didn't start their day with a prayer here. It was true that I had read one book on advertising by a Scotsman, David Ogilvy, "the father of advertising," which gave me a good grounding in the fundamentals, but I'm sure those principles were considered old-fashioned by now. I had, after all, learned them from a book.

About a week later I had to stay late again to proofread Tim's work. I had kept up the journal writing and the submissions to literary magazines, but, while I was pursuing my literary ambitions, some advertising part of my mind must have been working subconsciously. For, when I went to bring him my corrections to his ad, I found myself making a writing suggestion.

— Instead of "Bowery Defeats Other Banks," why not "beats other banks"? It's only one syllable, fits the layout better, and has alliteration.

Tim eyed me strangely.

— I thought you weren't really interested in this type of work.

He mouthed silently the words he had written and those I had suggested.

— But that's good. That's a big help. I think I'll use it.

— Really? Wow! That's great!

— How 'bout that? A word you wrote will be in the *New York Times* tomorrow.

— That will be incredible!

— Hey, and maybe when some new assignment comes in and I don't have time to work on it, you can help me write a rough draft. I'm not promising anything but who knows? It could be the beginning of something for you. And, more money, too.

— That would be great, Tim! Thanks! I appreciate it.

I couldn't believe it as I packed up my things that night. A word of mine would be in the *New York Times*! No one would know about it, but it would be something, a real, if minor, victory. But what about promoting a bank I knew nothing about and cared about even less? That did not sit well with me. But a word I wrote would be in print! That would be a small feather in my cap, and perhaps just the first one.

So, as I rode the subway home, feelings of excitement and nausea jousted within my gut. By the time I got home, nausea was winning. I tried to put the whole thing out of my mind as I did laundry and half-watched the Yankees. But, the next morning when I was getting ready for work, excitement regained the upper hand.

On my way to the subway, I grabbed a copy of the *Times* from the newsstand and stood there in people's way, paging though it. There it was, the simple word I'd added — for all the world to see! Despite being smooshed against the door of a crowded train, I managed to keep the paper open and to stare at the ad all the way to 59th Street. No one could tell that I had written it. There was no byline and no way I could prove that it was my contribution, but I knew it. And that gave me enough to enjoy a private triumph on the rush-hour 4 train.

But nausea quickly made a comeback. As I fought my way out of the train, I spotted discarded copies of the *New York Times* on a broken-down subway bench. Before I began the steep, stale-aired, and sweaty ascent of the escalator, which was always broken, I saw copies of the other local papers — *The Daily News*, *The New York Post*, and *New York Newsday* — on the platform, on the tracks, and in the overstuffed trashcans. I almost slipped on newspapers discarded on the escalator stairs. It seemed that my glory was not only fleeting, but quite disposable.

Nausea began to dominate as I hustled through the lobby of my office building surrounded by mobs of people hurrying, just like me, dressed in business attire, just like me, and taken in by ambition and the rat race, just like me. I looked around the elevator at the faces of the others crammed inside. They looked weary and jaded but, at the same time, anxious. They all looked hungry for the very kind of chance that I had gotten and exploited and been sickened by. In their faces I saw fatigue and frustration, but also a resolve to get upstairs, to get started, to get going, to get done what needed to get done, to get over with what needed getting over with, to get closer to some goal grasped at but barely remembered and hardly delineated, some golden day of wealth and glory.

So when Tim came over to congratulate me, I had to force a smile and pretend excitement. I think he knew it. There was a feeling of *déjà vu* to the whole exchange: it reminded me of talking to my dad, for some reason. I knew my dad would have been very excited about this opportunity. He had never understood my majoring in English nor my not joining the Logan Construction Company. He was always imagining ways that my skills could prove worthy of exchange in the marketplace. But, the whole idea made me restless for some reason. Whenever my mind dwelt upon it, I couldn't sit still.

That afternoon Tim approached me about drafting a couple of concise paragraphs about gum that refreshes your breath. But, the bad taste in my mouth was too strong.

— Thanks, Tim, but I'd rather not.

— You'd rather not?! What do you mean?

— Yeah. I think I should just stick to proofreading.

— But why turn down this chance? It could lead to a better job.

— I know. I appreciate it but-

He leaned forward like he couldn't believe what he was hearing or what he felt compelled to stage-whisper.

— It'll mean more money!

— I know. I know. But I'd rather not- It's not what I want to write. It's not what I want to do.

— Are you kiddin' me? You know how many people would give their right arm for a chance like this?

Now he was really sounding like my father.

But this was not what I had given up the comforts of home and a place in the family business for. It was not what I had saved and sacrificed to come to New York for. It was not what I meant to do with my life. It was not how I intended to use whatever talent I had been given in this world.

— Thanks. But it's just not for me. Sorry.

Needless to say I didn't last long in advertising. Word got around that I was not serious enough. Or maybe their guts told them what some others had learned about me, that I was, in actuality, too serious: more interested in jotting lines of poetry in a steno pad than in brainstorming cookie slogans. Anyway, they soon found an excuse; it didn't matter what. And I was out of that job and away from Madison Avenue for good.

Laura thought I was crazy when I got to the end of the story. But I think she admired it, too. It might have been part of what made her go around telling people I would be famous someday.

— Watch out for that cab. He's coming over whether you want him to or not.

— Yeah, you never know what these guys are gonna do.

...

Dearest Kit,

All through my childhood, along with my milk and oatmeal, I was fed with the inviolability of two faiths. The first was that taught and mystically embodied by the Holy Roman Catholic and Apostolic Church, in the service of which I have dedicated my life. The second was that preached by America itself: cheered and wept over in every theatre and movie house, consumed at every dinner table from the humblest to the mightiest, and breathed into the lungs of every back-woods, back-alley, or back-yard American boy and girl, that through hard work anyone can rise *ex nihilo* to the upper echelons of society. As you well know, Kit, Father preached the truth of both of these faiths through his words and through his vigorous and clear example.

I do recall that in one of your recent letters you objected to all of my philosophizing in my correspondence with you. You are "just a simple woman," you say and not a scholar. Well, I believe you are more capable of serious discussion than you give yourself credit for and that is the reason why I enjoy expressing my thoughts to you. However, out of respect for your wishes, I will not go on too long or in too much depth.

The first, the "Faith of our Fathers" you might say, has steeled me through all of my trials from childhood through adulthood and led me to fulfilling my priestly vocation in a strange city among strangers with backgrounds quite different from our own. I believe the Faith steeled Father as well, as he navigated the business world, closing his ears at times to siren songs of opportunities immoral. Of course, like anyone living a life of faith, I have had my moments of doubt. Years ago, I even suffered through a short Dark Night of the Soul. Yet, this crisis did not last long and my faith was all the stronger for it. Throughout my life, I am grateful to say that my faith in God and in Holy Mother the Church has always been present to me as a source of strength, life, and growth. It flows through me like sap through a tree.

The second faith, however, in improving one's lot through hard work, contains tenets about which I am starting to harbor some lasting doubts. I cannot help but see that the immigrants living in the vicinity of Xavier High School — mostly from Italy and Russia — do not seem to be advancing as immigrants once did. Of course, these new immigrants carry the added burden of having to learn the language of their adopted country. Clearly this makes it more difficult to improve their circumstances. It is true that some Irish people did come here speaking their own language. (Remember how Father's stories were often spiced with words and expressions from the old language? We had some good laughs at his expense, poor fellow, when we were too young to know any better.) Recently, I have been pleased to read that there are major efforts underway to revive the Gaelic tongue. However, with regard to emigration to this country, the Irish knowledge of English, has to be considered a benefit bestowed upon us by the conquerors of our ancestral land. Yet, fluency in English is not the only difference between the older generation of immigrants and today's. I walk around the Italian and Jewish slums and see the workers and their families not progressing at all. Rather, they are struggling to avoid sliding backwards. Could my faith in betterment through industry be unfounded?

From what I have learned from Esther Rosenfeld, these newer immigrants are more likely to return to their homelands than those of the Emerald Isle. I can hear Father's voice now as I write,

"Sure, maybe 'tis because they have a homeland to go to." But this might not be the only reason they want to go back: there must be something they feel is unsatisfying about the New World.

When I see how the progress of the immigrant around Greenwich Village appears to be stagnating, I marvel more than ever at the swiftness of Father's rise from an immigrant in steerage to the proprietor of a successful business and the owner of a home on the Main Line. Doubtless Father was an exceptional man. Perhaps we never realized how exceptional he was. Perhaps his life story was a rare one, in which came true the myths we ingest through melodrama and popular fiction, and the tales of those scratching to survive in the slums are the norm.

Nevertheless, I can't help thinking that the chances of achieving what Father did have changed, that perhaps there are underlying conditions that we have not examined that are making it difficult for even an extra-ordinary individual to rise. The pamphlet that Esther gave me makes a good case for this. Immigrants who come to this country in search of their fortunes today find that they are just cogs in the wheel spinning more gold for men who live in a beautiful upper world of expansive marble buildings full of comfort, beautiful views, and servants at their beck and call.

Sometimes, I take the Broadway local uptown and walk through Riverside Park to get some fresh air and to enjoy the shade of the trees in summer, the colorful foliage in autumn, and, always, the prospect of the Hudson River. It is a welcome and healthy break from the narrow odiferous streets of Lower Manhattan. As I admire the handiwork of the Lord, I also take note of the fine work of the artisans in the homes posing so luxuriantly along the rising and falling slopes of the park. To walk along the Riverside Drive is a pleasure for anyone with an eye for architecture, craftsmanship, and beauty. There are carved images of Green Men and seashells, delightful filigree on the faces of the buildings, medieval towers and gargoyles, walls that curve around street corners, marble Ionic and Doric and Corinthian columns — a whole panoply of architectural details and styles. But, when I think of the men who live inside, who are the proprietors of these domiciles, my reveries and aesthetic pleasures come to an abrupt end. For, at moments like these, I recall that the owners of these dwellings are the same men who run the factories overstuffed with ill-paid immigrants downtown. For them, this is not an occasional escape from the noisome streets. Each day, they collect the money made by the hard and often dangerous work of their immigrant laborers and return home to clean air, lovely scenery, and luxuriously designed houses fronted with classical ornamentation.

Nevertheless, the classical adornments on these dwellings cannot conceal the lack of classical wisdom inside. The workers these men employ, like Esther, support with their efforts and meager recompense whole families crammed into tiny tenement apartments with absurd windows placed in the middle of their living rooms to comply with the letter of the law. I often wonder how men with any shame can spend such money and energy on creating the fancy externals while doing such shoddy work on the internal. Surely, propagating such conditions would not jibe at all with the words and deeds of Pericles or with the philosophy of Socrates. Amassing such wealth and filling your homes with treasures while one's fellow citizens remain so poor and their homes so empty does not correspond with any classical sense of harmony or balance, with any sense of the Golden Mean. But then, maybe I am being naïve. Perhaps, when they had columns installed in their homes and classical *motiven* to their walls, they were not thinking of Athens of the fourth century Before Christ but of Rome in first century *Anno Domini*, those days of avarice, gluttony, lust, bread and circuses, and feeding Christians to the lions.

Some of these men even send their sons to our school, perhaps thinking that the teachers at Xavier can introduce to their boys a sense of morality that their lifelong examples counterpose. Or perhaps they only send their sons to our school so that they can ease their consciences — make a contribution to the Church and to the Society of Jesus to atone for their mistreatment of their workers. Perhaps they enroll them so that the boys can learn the skills needed to count up the profits made by the labor of the virtual slaves in their fathers' employ. Maybe it is for status alone.

How do I reach such young men? How do I instruct them so that they understand how privileged they are? Sometimes I have half a mind to march these spoiled students over to Mulberry Bend or to East 4th Street and show them how others live. For some of them, that would be the only thing that would awaken their consciences.

Some of them are sensitive souls, however, despite the luxury in which they have been raised. It is not their faults, after all, what their fathers do for a living.

I suppose we were fortunate to develop a sense of charity, despite the success and wealth of our father. We never lorded it over our peers as I recall — although I remember with some shame announcing haughtily to my classmates that my father was a business owner — without ever mentioning that the business comprised the labor of placing brick upon brick.

Though he was known as a demanding boss, he was good to his workers. Father helped many of them to buy their first homes. He employed many immigrants at Logan Construction Company (though they say he never felt at ease with the Italians) but they never appeared mistreated or abused like some of the workers I see and hear about. Was I just young and blind to it? Perhaps. But most owned their own homes — houses rather than apartments, and they all were grateful toward Father, never resentful or bitter. The number of employees who paid their respects at the wake and funeral attests to what a generous employer he was.

I also remember being confused as a young boy by how much money Father gave away. It seemed to exemplify the opposite of what he taught. He gave large donations to and was always at the center of fundraisers at Saint Colman's. He would provide the food and drink for their beef and beer parties. His company helped build Saint Colman's school at no charge to the parish. It did a lot of *pro bono* work for the archdiocese as well. You could say that Logan Construction Company was a big part in building the Catholic school system in the Archdiocese of Philadelphia — one of the first such systems and a model for Catholic education around the world.

All this made no sense to my childish mind. My father worked hard and was trying to get ahead. He consistently stressed the need to save. He did not believe in throwing money around like the many spendthrifts and wastrels he had in his employ who, as soon as they received their paychecks, would rush straight to the bar and drink all their money, acting the big man and buying rounds of drinks for all of the fellows. But here he was giving away the fruit of his labor to the poor, to his workers for medical bills or for buying a home, to the Catholic Youth Organization, to the hungry of India, and to the church for a new stained-glass window. Were his actions contradicting his words?

As I matured, I understood. What I was witnessing was an unending combat of champions between Father's two Faiths. While he spoke more about his faith in the American Dream, it was the One True Faith that was wordlessly motivating him. As much as he loved America and took pride in his success, his Old World Catholicism would never be unhorsed from its fine white charger.

...

When Seamus Logan, founder of the Logan construction company, passed away, people gathered from all around the Delaware Valley, and his son, the Reverend Sarsfield Logan, S.J., traveled from New York to mourn with his siblings James, Catherine, Michael, and Anna and to celebrate the funeral mass. Friends Seamus had made over the many years he had spent in the Philadelphia area since coming to this country from his native Ireland streamed to the McConaghy Funeral Home in Ardmore for the viewing and to Saint Colman's Church for the Mass of Christian Burial. These were joined by many of his former employees who had fond memories and sincere gratitude toward their generous benefactor for his munificence and by a good number of his customers who never forgot that it was the Logan Construction Company with the local savings and loans that erected the first homes they ever owned. Seamus Logan was also remembered for his generosity to his church, to Saint Joseph's Preparatory School, to famine relief in India and Africa, and to the cause of Irish freedom. Officers from Philadelphia *Clan na Gael* paid their respects at the viewing, as Mr. Logan was a great supporter of Ireland's War of Independence. There was some talk of notifying his relatives in Ireland but no one knew how to reach them or, indeed, if there was anyone to be contacted. He talked so little about his childhood and his homeland that the only thing people knew was that he had been born in County Mayo and that he had happy memories of Connemara. The obituary stated simply, "James Logan was born in Ireland. He left his native country as a young man and never returned." However, he kept it always in his heart contributing to many Irish charities and organizations, causes, and, of course, The Cause.

When James Logan's eldest son, the Reverend Sarsfield Logan, S.J., arrived at the family home in Ardmore, he noticed that, in addition to the grief he had expected, there was an air of tension and secrecy in the old house. He wasn't sure what could be the cause of it and his brothers and sisters took pains to conceal whatever the issue was. There were times when he heard murmuring and whispering that stopped immediately when he entered the room.

One morning, when he was breakfasting at the head of the dining room table and reading his Lauds from the Divine Office, his sister, Catherine, came in and took a seat. Waiting for him to finish, she began to pray herself, whispering "Hail Mary" after "Hail Mary" and running her thumb and forefinger over the old, black rosary beads she always carried. When Sarsfield concluded his Lauds, she placed the beads down on the table and, just after her Jesuit brother did, made the sign of the cross.

"Good morning, Kit. Sorry to keep you waiting. Going to join me?"

"No, Sarsfield, thank you. I had a nibble earlier. You know I never eat much in the morning. I don't want to disturb you but there's something I need to discuss."

"No problem at all. Why don't you at least have a cup of tea?"

Sarsfield did not mind being disturbed by his youngest sister. Catherine had always been a pet of his: she was so gentle and sweet. When they had been children, he had always feared that she would get trampled on in the schoolyard of Saint Colman's, and later, he worried about how she would make out in the schoolyard of life. When he could, he tried to protect her from his more assertive siblings, whom he always thought would run roughshod over her, given half a chance.

"No, thank you," said Kitty. "You enjoy your breakfast. I just want to talk."

Sarsfield lifted his china cup from its saucer and sipped a few drops of the hot tea, slurping just a little. He placed the cup back in its saucer and shot his sister a sidelong glance. Kit had not taken the opportunity he had given her to speak.

"What is it?" he asked.

"It has to do with Father's passing and his will."

He sipped his tea. Something about the way he did it made her want to smile.

"It is very sad for all of us — and a very difficult time," Father Logan sighed. "I keep having this irrational impulse to climb the stairs and tell Father about all of his friends that I have seen. As if he had just been unable to attend the party."

It was true. Some part of his mind repeatedly forgot that old Seamus was not just absent from the gatherings but truly gone.

"But we all must die, as Our Lord did, so that we can enter fully and truly into His kingdom."

"Yes, that is true. I'm sure Father died in Faith and has gone to his eternal rest."

He held the teacup in front of his lips, pausing before a second sip. Remarkable, thought Kit: the mannerisms were Father's. Father Sarsfield picked up his knife and reached for the butter dish.

"It's buttered, Sars."

"What?"

"The toast. It's already buttered."

"Oh. Oh, I see. Thank you!"

Sarsfield squinted at his sister. He couldn't make her out. She seemed at once determined and hesitant to get to her point.

"What I have to tell you is very difficult, even perhaps … a little shameful," she suddenly stated. "I'm not sure if you are aware of all that has gone on … You've been away and your life- The life you lead with your community is very different, very removed from our day-to-day struggles…"

"There is nothing you can tell me that will be shocking or unfamiliar to me. It is my duty to understand the virtues and the sins of human nature. I have spent years studying them, and counseling people."

Father Logan picked up his toast and thought he'd inject a little joviality.

"Besides, I spend my days teaching teenage boys! What could surprise me?"

His sister laughed quietly and didn't know where to look. Sarsfield dipped his toast into the yolk of his fried egg, took a bite, and started to break off and scoop up bits of the egg white with his fork.

"Well, maybe I should just get right to the point. Father has left a great deal behind. He was a very successful man. It is incredible what he accomplished, and the wealth and collection of treasures he accumulated."

"He was quite a success. To think that he came to this country as a penniless-"

Afraid her brother would take the conversation off track, Catherine blurted what had been worrying her.

"Our brothers and sisters have been going through Father's room! His attic, the basement …

Taking some things for themselves …"

"That's understandable," Sarsfield replied, taking up his cup of tea. "I suppose it is natural for people to want to take mementoes of Father, now that he is gone."

"But that is just the problem!"

"What do you mean?"

Taking another triangular piece of buttered toast from his plate, Sarsfield paused.

"Well, they started before you came home!"

He took a bite of the toast and laid it on his plate.

"That is a little unseemly but I don't mind, really. I have no desire for anything for myself."

"But not only before you got here, but before Father-"

"Do you mean-?!"

He put the teacup down.

"Yes, it shames me to say it but they started going though Father's things before he passed away. I urged them to wait for you so that you could give us some moral guidance. I urged them to have some decency, to let Father live out the rest of his life before they started to ransack through his worldly goods. I believe, and I am convinced that you believe, that this is immoral."

"I do. I think it is shocking! Not only indecent and ungrateful but … heartless!"

Sarsfield glared at the mess of eggs on his plate.

"The man — their father who sacrificed everything for them — was lying suffering on his death bed and they are more concerned for what they could get for themselves than for the poor dying man?!"

He reached for the tea cup again.

"That's what I thought — and tried to warn them about — but I am not as eloquent or as strong as you are. I was really appalled by their behavior."

"I don't blame you. I am appalled to hear about it. I only wish I had been here to prevent it."

"Yes, but you are here now, thank God!"

Father Logan sipped, paused, sipped again, before replacing the cup in its saucer.

"I am. I can prevent any further disrespect to Father's memory."

With his fork, he swept a few more small pieces of egg white into his mouth.

"True. That is very good of you."

"Don't mention it. It's the least I could do to protect Father's good name."

"But what are you going to do about the damage that has already been done?"

He dipped his toast into the egg yolk and cleaned up the rest of it.

"There doesn't seem to be anything I can do. I mean, what's done is done — isn't it? I have no intention of squabbling over who took what and what meaningless object should not have been taken."

"Oh, but I thought you would do more … you know … to help to return things as they should have been at the beginning."

"But I don't see what I can do, Kit. What do you have in mind?"

"It's just that it is all so brazen … I thought you would want to rectify the situation ... You could tell them to give everything back so that we could start again."

"They can go to their confessors about that. I don't want to set myself up as some kind of estate judge."

He picked up his cup of tea, took a sip, and then held it before his lips. Her son, now that she thought of it, drank his morning coffee the exact same way.

"It just seems that what they have done is so immoral … so ungrateful, as you say … But not only immoral. It's also … I don't know …"

"What? What is it?"

"It's also … well … unfair!"

Father Sarsfield Logan, S.J., placed his teacup down into its saucer and let go of its handle. His eyes grew wide as he realized what his youngest sister intended.

…

"I tell yih, Kitty, I don't like Paul working in that bad neighborhood up there or living in that dangerous place. I just don't understand it."

Janey took a sip of chardonnay from her glass.

"He's teaching young women who need help. I think it's great."

Kitty filled her mother's glass and topped off her own.

"But I don't understand what he is doing up there in the Bronx? He had a nice life here in Ardmore. His own air-conditioned room. Meals cooked for him. Wash done for him. Why did he have to run off to a place with cockroaches and mice, graffiti, and dangerous characters roamin' the streets? Might as well move to Beirut."

"I don't know. He wanted to be in New York, I guess. He wanted to try and make it in music and writing, and New York is the place to be. Plus, his friends graduated from Fordham and knew the neighborhood."

"But didn't our family work hard to get out of places like that? After all these years, he goes right back to the kinda place everyone is trying to get away from? It makes no sense. His great-grandfather lived in New York City, but got the hell out."

Janey took a large sip of her white wine.

"I don't really understand it, either. I wouldn't want to live there but that's where he can afford to live. Maybe he doesn't want to make sense. He says his graduation speaker said to make decisions people around you won't understand."

"Great! All that tuition money to teach him to do things that don't make sense!"

Raising her glass, Kitty offered, "I coulda taught him that for free. Cheers!"

"Cheers, Kitty!"

They put their glasses down on the kitchen table and Kitty gazed unseeing at the jack o'lantern in the living room. It was just the two women in the quiet house. James had gone out with some client or other and was still not home.

"The city is exciting for some young people these days. Not everyone, of course. But you know Paul always liked to hang out in Center City. Maybe he was just not satisfied with the suburbs."

"Not satisfied with the suburbs? Tell me about it! I have not been satisfied with them for years. I used to love being there on 44th Street sitting on the porch and watching the world go by. I guess he has a little bit of me in him after all."

"The other thing is that in places like the Bronx, that's where they need teachers. The students really need him there. There's not as much help needed in Ardmore."

Kitty picked up the bottle and tried to give her mother a smaller portion than before. But Janey pushed her glass forward for more. Kitty filled her own glass.

"There aren't as many stray bullets in Ardmore either!"

The jack o'lantern's candle flickered and its jagged smile remained inert and crazy no matter what subject was discussed. The wind had picked up outside. The nearly naked tree branches were dancing in the yard and tapping now and then against the front window. A cardboard witch and black cat flew her broomstick by a crescent moon on the back of the kitchen door. Plastic pumpkins hunkered down on various counters and tables. It was funny the way Janey persevered in decorating the house as if small children still lived there — with decorations bought when Kitty and Paul had been little.

"He's used to bad neighborhoods from The Prep and Saint Joe's."

"Those Jesuits always hold on to properties in those old neighborhoods. No flies on them."

Janey sighed and pictured Girard Avenue through her car's windshield: brick-and-mortar buildings falling apart, boarded-up windows, Baptist church after Baptist church. South Bronx even worse. Tall tenements with nothing inside. Bricks all over the abandoned lots. The abandoned people.

"But no one in our family even goes to the city anymore … Dad says the animals are running the zoo. It's a mess. The mayor dropping bombs on people …"

Kitty gulped her wine.

"So what's wrong with Ardmore? That's what I say."

"Paul says he took that job in the South Bronx to help people. His girls are memorizing Poe, for Christsake! In one of his letters he says he feels like he's lifting the world onto his shoulders like Atlas at Rockefeller Center. Atlas became his model, trying to take on the burden of freedom. … he says he wanted to start at that bottom and work his way … like Great-Grandad ..."

"What the hell does all that mean? Why should he have to start over again? He had a good job all set up for him here. A company built by his family."

"He says the business is not the same as it once was — it's not serving the working man anymore. It's a rich company building houses for people who have plenty of money. Dad even eats lunch at the Union League."

"Who does Paul think he is — some kind of Francis of Assisi?"

Kitty took a sleeve of Ritz crackers from the box on the counter, poured half of the crackers onto a plate, which she put beside her mother's glass.

"I don't know. Like I say, I don't think it is anything I would want to do. All I know is what Paul wrote in his letters. (And I don't know why he thinks I can understand all the deep stuff he writes to me.) But, he says he wants to lift society up from the bottom — working with Black and Hispanic *girls* in the poorest zip code in America."

"Maybe it is his way of being rebellious, though I don't know what he would be rebelling against," Janey began, filling her wine glass and ignoring the crackers. "But he is not rebelling at all. He is not the first one to move to New York in this family. And he is not the first one to become a New York teacher. His Granduncle, Father Sarsfield, did both — after graduating from The Prep and The College, too. I'll have to point that out to him next time I see him. Chap his behind. The rebel who follows family tradition!"

"But Father Sarsfield educated the rich, the middle class at any rate. Manhattan Catholics who had made it up a rung or two."

"The Jesuits always know which side their bread is buttered on and how to get more from the buttered classes. But they have their reasons. The rich sons must be educated to help the poor. They don't own anything but they live comfortably, believe you me."

"They are great teachers, though. No doubt about it. Men for others — isn't that what they teach them? For most, those are just words you see on a wall on your way to class or something to be studied for a test. But to Paul they actually meant something."

"That's true. He always took Religion class seriously. I don't know why. The other kids were so cavalier about it ... I remember when he used to go to mass every day, doing the spiritual bouquets he gave us all for Christmas. I thought he might have a vocation to the priesthood. But maybe that would have been too much like Father Sarsfield. But he ended up being a teacher just like he was, anyway."

"He didn't plan on teaching. I remember when he was at Saint Joe's and people would always say to him. 'English major? So you wanna be a teacher?' And he'd always snap at them, 'No!' But when Saint Philomena's extended him an offer on a hot August afternoon to be a man for others, he took the contract in his hand — with his guitar in the other, to hear him tell it. He was on his way to the Philadelphia Folk Festival for the weekend. He likes to tell this story after he has few beers."

Kitty chuckled and swirled her wine.

"I don't like him drinking so much."

"Either do I. I worry about that sometimes, too."

"That's a family tradition he *should* rebel against!"

"And when was the last time he played the guitar? He says he hasn't touched it much since he started teaching."

"It's probably in its case, collecting dust under the bed."

Kitty looked toward the front room again. There was still no sign of Dad.

"I hope he doesn't give that up."

"Me, too."

"I'm sure he'll come back to it when he is ready. But he's doing good work now. We should be proud of him."

"I am proud. It's not everyone who could make a success of that job."

"I guess we'll hear all about it at Thanksgiving."

"Gobble gobble."

They clinked glasses.

"Gobble gobble."

...

Finding the Way to Hell's Kitchen

To find the way home to Hell's Kitchen:

1. Cross Fifth Avenue and enter the Diamond District.
2. Proceed through the Diamond District.
3. Proceed along 47th Street through the Theatre District.
4. Continue west to 8th Avenue.

Laura piloted the BMW from the East Side to the West Side. Among all of the white zebra stripes at the crosswalks and crisscrossing in the middle of the intersection into lozenge shapes like an element from the carpet-page of some unimaginative monk, the Green Line from the 237th New York Saint Patrick's Day Parade had remained. It had faded surely but not vanished. Paul's mother had always dreamed of seeing the NYC parade. He stretched his legs toward the other side of the car and looked uptown toward twin spires of Saint Patrick's Cathedral, the grand church that Dagger John built.

thousands upon thousands of drums war pipes uniforms marching see our numbers don't' fuck with us right after that friday the 13th maybe bad luck maybe good.

Standing sentinel on the uptown and downtown corners of 47th Street were two diamond sculptures illuminated radium green and held aloft by steel bars representing diamond pavilions, girdles, and bezels of ascending size. Laura, Paul, and Charles crossed through the portal to the Diamond District.

JEWELERS ON FIFTH cried large letters on the building to the southwest corner. Part of our name is part of our address. Down the block marked off with remarkable piles of garbage, Paul could see NATIONAL JEWELERS EXCHANGE in pink neon. Timeless Diamonds LLC? They've been popular for what — half a century or so? World's largest marketplace for those shiny rocks right here on this street. Gemological Appraisal Lab of America, yes, make it sound scientific.

The jewel carriageway. Close to the end of the ride, Chief, and you haven't gotten rid of the English chef in the backseat. You vowed to kiss those lips again. Before the cock crows. But how will that happen with him around?

He had walked with her when the spring air was full of potential, when she had first stumbled toward the curb and by reflex he had put his arm around her, and she had removed it and taken his hand.

skin against skin first touch leading to first kiss though you didn't dare dream it we walked hand in hand down broadway

O, that ferry ride! *Mon beau navire*! That first kiss came to an end and her head fell on his shoulder. Her wet hair was cool and soft on the side of his neck. In his hands, her ribcage worked up and down slowly, in a rhythm strong and steady. Her cheek dragged along his shoulder, and, she was looking up at him again, with widening eyes and a small befuddled smile. He fell toward her this time. They kissed long: and there was nothing but the peristaltic motion of their lips and jaws, the short, shy probing of their tongues. Suddenly, the ferryboat John F. Kennedy was there: the gangways' rattling and creaking down onto its upper deck, the gate's scraping upon the lower deck, opening for the crowds moving along the walkways along the side of the grates over the sloshing slate waves.

Laura led him by the hand toward the lower deck, ducking under the keel of the suspended orange rowboat. Seizing the first available seat, the long bench facing the windows, she slid her bluejeans along the chocolate wood scarred with initials and put her Amstel bottle on the floor by the orange wall. He put his Guinness bottle by his feet in front of the baby blue sign with the white-stenciled words, "Life Preserver." Removing his hand from hers, he threw his arm over her shoulder. Water slapped the side of the boat. Through the opened back doors and the half-open blue-framed window came the mingled smells — stronger now — of salt water and fuel exhaust. He cocked his head and locked his lips to hers again. The gates clattered against the studded metal floor and clanked closed. Now they were inside. And the lower deck was almost empty. Freely, he ran his hand along her curving hips and along her side and back finger brushing against the bra strap he had seen from his barstool as she had bent over her Baudelaire. Deep now, their tongues brushed one another hard.

When the ferry reached other side, Laura ran off to catch a bus. Paul floated back to Lower Manhattan alone.

— Oooh! Laura purred. Wouldn't it be great if all these jewelry stores were open and we could roam around inside? And just try them all on with no one trying to sell you something? It would be so much fun to, like, fall backwards into a big pile of them?

Hmmm, maybe the art book in my bag was not the ideal gift for her after all. Every kiss begins with K. A lot of nonsense, really. It begins with her.

— What's so special about diamonds anyway?

AA Pearls & Gems Co., Inc. Hey! Hey! We got pearls here, too.

— I don't know. A diamond is forever. They're romantic.

— I mean as opposed to other kinds of jewels … Aren't they're just a bunch of carbon atoms arranged a certain way?

— Aren't we all?

— I guess so!

Vertically arranged letters shouted the approach of the NY JEWELRY CENTER.

— Plus, they have all these different facets you can look at from all different angles. And, they use them for all kinds of drills and scientific tools. They can cut glass. You wouldn't have stained-glass windows without them.

An English accent joked from the back seat:

— A girl's best friend, I s'pose.

Paul and Laura laughed

— I think a lot of it is marketing and advertising, said Paul.

He recalled a *Times* article about the early ads. A woman picking a diamond off of a tree. Jewel of knowledge of good and evil.

— Maybe, it's a bit silly, but they are so shiny and bright ... And just think of all of the engagements that started on this street.

poor sap has to come scuttling down this street to spend two months salary on a rock all because she wants it shes been convinced it is necessary i have to have a premium this 57 varieties of that i need this new kitchen this designer dress because im worth it this specific kind of stone from an african mine to prove that im loved say it with money the men who would be happy to live in a shack with some tube that shows sports and some means of keeping the beers cold they go out and get it for them cause they care enough to steal the very best

— I imagine the African miners don't find them so romantic, Charles said.

It was probably his ancestors who first sent them down there.

— Yeah, Laura replied. Those mine owners are so greedy … All they think about is their profits.

they always say that if women ran the world there would be no war nor any of the cruelty and stupidity that men wreak everyone nods his head knowingly including me but arent the ladies the ones stoking the engine of materialism i want i want i want i love to shop i love to shop to satisfy them men compete with each other fight start wars stack brick upon brick up to the sky dig down under rivers to support monsters of steel stretching from bank to bank end up in all kinds of brutal situations they never would have asked for but they want that pussy betcha can't eat just one so they will give into the girlies greed make themselves miserable monsters bringing back from the jungle or the battlefield whatever pearls of great price the bitches want they think they are so innocent of the bloody state of the place well girls are a diamond dealers best friend

Paul recognized the passageway to 48th on the right and Berger's Deli, home of yet another great corned beef sandwich on his left.

I wonder if Berger knows Katz. Like "Tiffany! Cartier!" Family businesses. And in a Philadelphia accent, "Robins 8ᵗʰ and Walnut." His dad's old refrain: I remember as a kid looking at bums on the street, at guys who used to be bigshots trying to sell apples for pennies and nickels and thinking to myself, "Thank God! Thank God that I was born into a family with the foresight and work ethic to build a solid business where I can work and never become like that!"

Upon shiny rocks, they have built their district. More power to them. But time is running out for the business for which you have waited and watched this night.

Laura's car nosed out into the Avenue of the Americas.

...

James Logan and Father Sarsfield Logan, S.J. cruised along a serpentine road with leafy embankments that made it rare to see a house let alone a resident.

They don't even want to see signs of their neighbors' existences, thought Father Logan. Who is my neighbor, indeed?

"Beautiful downtown Gladwyne! The name sounds Welsh but I don't know what it means in English. I know what it means in numbers, though. A lot of simoleons."

As people got wealthier — in contrast to the chummy swarms of the Village or East Side poor — they wanted more distance between themselves and others. The more they possessed, Father Logan reflected, the more they became alone. How foolish to pile onto the camel's back more obstacles to fitting through the Eye of the Needle!

Presently, they turned from the road onto James's long driveway. Thin trees, still young enough to allow a partial view of the house, arrayed themselves along either side of the brothers' route.

At the end of the driveway sprawled the broad, stone-faced house his brother had moved his family into. Father Logan had read and heard so much about it, he felt as if he had visited it before. The size of it impressed him, nevertheless: it looked two city blocks wide. "Why would five people need a house of such dimensions?" he wondered.

"Well, here we are," said James. "Be it ever so humble..."

In front of the house, there was a jocund fountain with two stone bowls, the higher one smaller than the lower. It was a remnant of the Old World that stood out in these newly constructed surroundings.

Father Logan thought that that must be the fountain James had been telling him about when, sure enough, James turned and said, "See?! There it is — the fountain I was tellin' you about. Isn't she a beauty?!"

On the lower bowl was carved a figure that resembled Pluto seated on a throne.

"I was just noticing it. My goodness, it looks like something that should be in front of Saint Peter's in Rome!"

"It *is* from Italy. Moved over here brick by brick, which seems kind of fitting — doesn't it? Mariellen says it's depressing. But I say, 'No! Look! Here's the goddess of spring!' See the seeds and the plants?"

"Indeed," replied Father Logan. "That appears to be Persephone planting and producing the abundance of springtime."

Father Logan heard the scrape of saddle shoes across gravel. He turned to see skipping toward him a little girl in a cream-colored dress with a lace collar and pockets in front. Her brown, braided pigtails fell past her waist. Bright blue eyes shone from her freckled face and her wide smile revealed a couple of missing teeth. She was accompanied by a cocker spaniel whose coat matched her dress and whose tail was wagging so hard the poor creature could hardly walk.

"Hello, Father Sarsfield!" Nora sang out as she skipped toward the elderly priest.

She broke into a sprint, then stopped before him and jumped up and down.

"Is this Nora?!"

She practically leapt into his arms and Father Logan, though his back was a little sore from the trip, was able to lift and embrace her.

"How are you, *mon petite*? Almost too big for old Father Sarsfield to lift!"

A lanky, hunched-over figure, hands deep in the front pockets of his pants, followed his long legs and big feet out the front door, his gaze intent on the gravel his shoes were shunting before him. He struck Father Logan as a rather serious, proud young fellow. In sharp contrast to his sister's jubilant salutation, Young James simply offered a firm handshake and muttered in a voice surprisingly deep, "Hi, Father Sersfld."

"How's the ball playing, Mike?! I hear you're quite the centerfielder."

"He plays for the Prep. They just beat Roman the other day," interjected James, as he wandered over toward the fountain.

"Xavier has a decent team this year," Father Logan said. "How's The Prep's?"

"Pretty good," Michael muttered.

"They're leading the Catholic League," said his father, as if addressing his words to the fountain.

Mariellen Logan waited with a gentle smile as Father Logan turned to greet her and the infant she held in her arms. Mariellen was a beauty of chiseled features and an alabaster complexion set off by an ample mass of wavy, jet-black hair. Her eyes, nearly as pale blue as turquoise, glimmered with delight as she leaned toward Father Sarsfield and gave him a kiss on the cheek.

"Hello, Father Sarsfield, long time no see."

"Mariellen! You're looking well. And, how is this little fellow?"

Mariellen beamed down at her child and back up at the cleric.

"He's doing fine. Fine. He just had a lovely nap and isn't quite awake yet. Is he? Is he?"

The dog stood on his hind legs and put his two front paws on Sarsfield's pants.

"Get down from there, Laddy!" James shouted. "Down boy!"

"Oh, he's all right," Sarsfield said, bending over slightly and patting the spaniel on the head. "Hi, there, fella."

James dragged the dog away by its collar.

The baby gurgled and squirmed, his arms and legs dancing in the air.

"I haven't seen your youngest since the christening. I can't get over how big he has gotten."

"Mommy?" Nora cried.

"Incredible — isn't it? You're changing their diapers one day, you blink your eyes, and they're asking you for the keys to the car."

"Mommy?"

Nora tugged on her mother's skirt.

Everything in his native city seemed to have matured while he'd been away.

"What, Nora!?"

"Mommy, what kind of name is Sarsfield? It sounds funny."

"Don't be disrespectful. There's nothing funny about it. Sarsfield is a very distinguished name."

Mariellen looked up at Father Sarsfield.

"A hero's name."

"Nothing to worry about, Mariellen. Nora is just being curious. Reminds me of her namesake. '*Les petits ruisseaux font les grandes rivières,*' as the French say. 'Rivers of knowledge start with a trickle of questions.'"

"You speak such beautiful French," Mariellen said.

"Well, he oughtta!" James cried. "He's been teachin' kids the lingo for years!"

"Enough so that they could pronounce," Sarsfield murmured. "The names of the fields on which they died."

Mariellen was crouched down by her daughter.

"Let me tell you about Sarsfield, the hero, Nora. Sarsfield was, I guess you could say, the

Paul Revere of Ireland. You know about Paul Revere — don't you?"

"Uh huh," the girl nodded.

"Well, like Paul Revere, he rode through the countryside on his horse telling people about the war with the British and urging them to fight for Ireland and their Catholic Faith."

"So he was a messenger?"

"Nora! Bite your tongue!"

"No, he was a cavalryman, a soldier. Patrick Sarsfield was a brave general who loved his country and tried to help the people even when the situation looked hopeless."

"But you're a priest, not a soldier! Why did grandpa name you that?"

"My parents did not know that God would call me to the priesthood. That all happened later."

"Oh," replied Nora, putting her first two fingers in her mouth and walking away.

Mariellen rolled her eyes at Father Logan, who grinned back at her.

"No one knows why my father chose it. It doesn't seem to be in the family, as far as anyone knows."

James came up behind Father Logan and shook his brother's shoulder.

"C'mon, Sarsfield! Don't dilly dally around the driveway. Let's go inside. I'll give you the grand tour."

James held the front door open for Father Logan and then slipped around in front of the priest. He dropped Father Logan's suitcase on the floor and with his elbows bent and his hands upraised spun around to show his delight at the width and height of the foyer. Sarsfield smiled. His brother was clearly proud of his new home, which was quite capacious. The vestibule alone was big enough to contain Sarsfield's room at the Xavier Rectory twice over.

Where was the Ardmore of his father's twin house and the horses and buggies delivering milk? He was glad that Kitty was keeping the house in the family.

To oblige his brother, Father Logan tilted his head back onto his shoulders and remarked on how high the ceiling was and how impressive the glittering chandelier.

He was finishing some humorous remark about how Mariellen had picked out the brown-and-yellow floor tile. Father Logan smiled, nodded, and followed the echoing voice of his brother.

"Looks like your bag," James said, examining the cracks and creases in the leather and the flimsy attachment its handle had to the suitcase. "Has seen better days."

"It holds my things on the rare occasion that I leave the rectory. That's all I ask of it."

James snorted and shook his head.

"Mike, take Father Sarsfield's bag up to the guest room — will you? That's a good boy."

The boy grunted and shuffled toward the stairs with the suitcase.

"Make him do something to earn his keep around here — right, Sarsfield? We spoil these kids rotten."

"I find that praising a boy can encour-"

"And here's the living room. I don't know where we are going to get all the wood for this fireplace. But it is beautiful — isn't it?"

"Certainly."

The fireplace was carved in medieval *motiven*. Above the mantel, appeared lords in soft hats and ladies in conical henins with veils depending from them. Toward the center of the relief there charged from opposite directions two mounted knights armored, with lances couched.

James slapped his hand on the stone mantel.

"I love it," he said with another slap. "I just love it!"

"It reminds me of something you would see in a manor house in England."

"Well, this one's in the suburbs of Philadelphia, the Cradle of Liberty — and it's owned by an Irishman! I tell yih, we've really come up in the world, Sarsfield."

"We might even have a Catholic president soon."

"That would be somethin' — wouldn't it? He could bring you in as his chaplain. You know a Catholic president would have to have a Jesuit! Plus, he'd like a fellow New Yorker. Why not you?"

"I'm a schoolteacher, James. I'm not worthy to advise a head of state."

"Always the humility routine with you! C'mon, let's finish the tour. We can come back and have a drink by the fire when we're done. So, here's the dining room. Those tables and chairs are made of yew wood."

James knocked on the table with his right fist.

"Late Regency style. I think it has real character. Plus, it comes with extensions in case we have a lotta people over."

He always had to touch things, Sarsfield remembered. As a young boy, he was forever fingering candle holders and playing with salt and pepper shakers.

"In the hutch, we have Waterford crystal Mariellen got from the old sod. Some Irish china and linen, too. We hardly use it. We never use this room, actually. We eat in the kitchen. You know how it is."

Sarsfield estimated that this room used only for special occasions could host all the priests from his rectory.

"Out in the back we have Mariellen's garden. She loves all those plants. Nothing practical like a vegetable but lots of flowers and shrubs. A couple of unusual trees. Personally, I've grown really fond of that Japanese maple. It's probably my favorite."

"It's very pretty."

Father Logan leaned closer to the window to see if any birds were taking advantage of the simple concrete birdbath. He saw none.

"Let's head upstairs. I'll show you the bedrooms and my study. And your room."

"That would be fine. Fine."

As the two brothers climbed the stairs, James turned to Sarsfield.

"So whaddaya think?" he asked.

"What do you mean?"

"You don't have much to say for yourself."

"It's a lovely home, James."

"It is — isn't it?"

"It seems very comfortable, a fine home."

James grew sullen and didn't speak as he led Father Logan along the second-floor hallway. Father Logan felt sorry that he had disappointed his brother.

"So these are the bedrooms," he prompted. "How many are there?"

"We have five, one for each of the kids, and one for Mariellen and me. And the guest room. Here's the master bedroom."

James gestured into the room but Father Logan perceived that his brother's heart had gone out of the tourguiding. He could still see the boy in the man his little brother had become.

"I suppose Mariellen picked out the canopy bed."

"Yes," some emotion, exasperation, was returning to his voice. "She picked out this one — and one for Nora, too. The boy's room is a mess: I'll spare you that. But let me show you my pride and joy — my study."

James directed Sarsfield down the hall toward the front of the house, to a room overlooking the Italian fountain, the broad flatness of the front yard, the winding driveway, and the young trees. Along all of the room's walls, from the floor to ceiling were solid mahogany bookshelves, filled with orderly rows of leather-bound volumes.

"This is my study!" proclaimed James.

"Very impressive!" said Father Logan. "Quite masculine. No frilly canopies in here!"

"No, this is the one room that is truly mine. My inner *sanctum*."

"Is that Father's stick?!" exclaimed Father Logan.

He rushed toward a worn piece of a bog oak, leaning in the corner.

"Yeah, I found it in the old house. Didn't know where else to put it."

"How marvelous! Father's walking stick!" Father Logan held the stick in both hands admiring it. "I can't believe you have this, James! I never thought I'd see it again."

James leaned back and saw through the kitchen door that Sarsfield was seated in the living room with his scotch, peacefully lost in thought.

"I'm showing him all of this beautiful, expensive stuff," he whispered to Mariellen. "Imported furniture. Exquisite materials and workmanship. Objects that took years to pick out and collect. And he hardly breathes a word about any of it."

"Well, you know your brother, James. He's just not interest-"

"'Very comfortable,' says he, 'A fine home'! Probably never been inside a house half this luxurious in his entire life. Then the only thing he shows excitement about — that stupid old walking stick Father picked up offa the ground somewhere. You'd think a man with all his learning — a man who has dedicated his life to education — might have looked at one of the books. But, no! He gets worked up over an old stick."

"It belonged to his dad, James, and yours," Mariellen said, checking the number of crackers on the tray against the amount of cheese. "It must have brought back memories for him."

"Ahhh, he's just too pigheaded to admit he appreciates all this. Always has to be Saint Sarsfield, the anti-materialist! Especially if he can put down what I've achieved."

"That's your brother you're talking about, James — and a priest! A priest forever in the order of Melchizedek!"

"If he's my brother, then I should know what I'm talking about — shouldn't I?"

James and Mariellen came into the living room to find Sarsfield sipping his scotch, an enigmatic smile playing across his lips.

He couldn't have heard what they'd said — could he?

Then again, as a teacher, Father Logan's ears were attuned to the sound of whispering.

7. Anger & Forgiveness

Last week marked the third Thursday night when Paul arrived at the Orange Crush at 7 (and did not pay at the door).

Why did Walter have to give him that look? The five bucks meant nothing to him. He could pay or not pay.

don't worry let him sit at the door and see for himself whats miraculous and what isn't

Paul thought this time he could finally succeed in taking Laura around Tribeca. But, right after he came in the door, she began prattling about how she totally wanted to hear this Santana cover band, *Bruja.*

A ripple of irritation spread within Paul, but, before the waves could swell into annoyance, he closed his eyes and bit his lip. Dropping the shoulders of his leather jacket onto the back of a bar stool, he said:

— O.K.

Laura zipped over to the Guinness tap.

Paul had tried and failed at getting Laura out of the Orange Crush enough times to remain unsurprised. He had heard this fiery band before and he knew its appearances were like a full moon. Frustrating as the situation was, Paul knew the evening would be a wild ride.

The Orange Crush had changed the paintings on its walls since the previous Thursday. One above the bar portrayed a TV screen inside of which shouted the words:

TUNE IN TOMORROW

FOR RERUNS

FROM YESTERDAY

How deeply deep. At least Walter supported local artists, such as they were.

Bruja brought in its equipment and set up as Paul sipped his first bitter pint: Laura still hadn't learned to build a Guinness. He took a seat under the dusty orbs glowing down on the beaten, reddish-brown bar. While Laura finished all her cash-counting business, Paul glanced around at the other new artworks.

A crescent moon with a black cat sitting on its lower tip. Tail hanging down. Two tall crumbling towers of a castle. A ruin, really. Eerie dark-blue background. Three *naif* fat women lounging naked in the foreground.

Weird sisters? Wearing nothing but veils over their mouths. Muzzled witches? Womyn silenced by the patriarchy. But not missing any meals, evidently.

A homeless black man standing on a streetcorner, his mouth opened wide in song. No one near him. Just a few pigeons searching the sidewalk for crumbs. The song appears to come from deep within him.

But the drawing! Brother, can you spare a line? An idea? … A notion? … A concept? Anything you can contribute would be most appreciated. God bless you.

The band started playing just as Laura came out from behind the bar. She picked up her Amstel on the rocks and gave Paul a look, pointing to the stage with her head, and waved him along.

Things were not all bad.

Paul followed her under the large brass chandelier of red-orange lights, depending from the ceiling between the jukebox and the pool table. When they got closer to the stage, it became clear that *Bruja* had brought its share of followers. All of the chairs were taken — except one. Paul grabbed it with his free hand and placed it in front of Laura. She lowered a single denim cheek onto the seat and turned to say something to Paul. He bent his ear down to her mouth and her high-pitched voice broke through the raucous band's evil ways.

— We can share, she said. And she slid over in the seat.

Why not?

Paul squeezed onto the old wooden seat. Soft at first then firm, Laura's flanks leaned against his. Her supple thigh was warm. He liked it when her bare arm brushed against his dress shirt. Was this a miracle or hoax? Suddenly Laura was willing to touch and be touched by him in front of her coworkers and customers, not just on the furtive bottom deck of a ferryboat. She didn't care if she was watched by the Port Authority workers concluding their happy hour after crossing another day off of their calendars at the Twin Towers. She didn't mind if she was seen by the band's hirsute and tattooed crowd. For the moment, in the constant, horn-butting competition in the Orange Crush, Paul was the winner. Maybe he would get her out of the bar after *Bruja's* set.

Bruja's wild jamming and rolling insistent beat transformed the Orange Crush into a place more primitive and passionate. A voice within him urged him to capitalize on the situation he found himself in.

put your arm around her make a move dont be the dorky business man among the rockers she shared her seat with you now answer

But, maybe it was best to wait. When the time came for a move, it would be clear. Now it was anything but. Laura kept leaning forward onto her thighs, sitting up and bending down again without warning. He didn't want to put his arm around a shoulder that wasn't there.

When the right time came it would be clear, just as it had been as they had stood among the rectangular columns under the ramp of the ferry terminal with the salt air and the water lapping against Manhattan's nether shore. His day would come again.

tiocfadh ar la holde hire harde by the haunches no ful politesse he was

In general, he took a bookish approach with Laura. She seemed to like his writerly persona: she often introduced him as a poet. So, a couple of times, Paul sneaked out of the office to see her in the afternoon, finding her practically alone. It was a gentler atmosphere at that time of day … when the golden sun slanted through the high windows streaked with Lower Manhattan dust … when the only customers were occasional clusters of construction workers … when the jukebox sang low about the girl with– well, you know what kinda eyes she got … when Laura appeared pretty instead of hot … vulnerable rather than cool ...

Laura spoke to him about the classes she took on Saturdays, how she was trying to finish her degree. Sometimes she gave into temptation and went out on Friday, only to awaken too hungover for class the next morning. One time she told him of her dream of being lost in a series of marble halls; Paul said she is still trying to find her way in life.

— You gotta finish your education, Paul admonished. That's something they can never take away from you.

look at you playing the teacher again did she axe you for advice mistah logan do you keep on comin heah to teach huh or to date huh as if butter wouldn't melt in your mouth shades of carmen every time you want a girl you come on with the books and lectures what if she knew how you fucked kathy after every schoolday so insatiable her pussy cried no mas and she had to satisfy you by hand

Paul felt delighted that she loved art and did well in her drawing classes. It was even more exciting to find out that, when she had time, she liked to read.

— I just bought this book, she said a couple of weeks ago.

Seated on the stool next to Paul's, Laura reached down to backpack and retrieved a fat, fluorescent-green volume.

— It's the best short stories of 1997. I was walking around the neighborhood — I was really early the other day — and I thought I would take a look around. It's pretty cool around here — y'know?

— Yes, I know.

— I saw this over at that big bookstore at the World Trade Center, and I thought, y'know, I've always liked short stories. So, I bought it. I just finished it. You can borrow it, if you want.

— Thanks!

these collections are all about people misunderstood in the woods or the prairie and always feature a character named naomi

— I should bring in some of my short stories and show them to you, Paul offered.

— Yeah. That would be cool. I'd like to check them out.

On another afternoon, Laura again came around the bar and sat on the stool next to Paul's. She wanted to show him a French novel whose title and author's name she wildly mispronounced. The two bent over the bar to look at a passage that she liked, bumping shoulders. He told her about Zola's *Nana* and von Sternberg's *Die Blaue Ängel*.

But tonight they could only converse by shouting. Now and then Laura would lean back to tell him something. The feel of her soft, thick lips breathing words into his ear made him feel vital. Through the din of reptilian guitars, fiery organ, rumbling bass, and polyrhythmic percussion, he was able to make out most of what she said. He smiled and nodded even if he did not. Not understanding her made him feel old.

Bruja had fallen into a solid groove, guitars and keyboards trading squealing notes in an extended jam. Paul went to the bar, squeezed in next to regulars Sean and Bill, and ordered another Guinness and Amstel on the rocks. Jeanette filled a pint glass with ice in what resembled a single motion but took her time pouring his stout. It pleased Paul that she made the effort to pour it properly but, truth be told, punctiliousness was not the only reason for the delay. While she put the pint aside to settle, she got distracted by a Wall Street guy in a grey-striped suit. Leaning on the bar and playing with her dark ponytail, she kept her exposed olive-skinned back to the pint, the unopened bottle of beer, the glass of rocks, and Paul. Though he appreciated the view of her petite figure in tight jeans, Paul grew impatient. He wanted to get back to the blonde in the narrow chair. But before he got the drinks, the song faded, the set concluded with a drum flourish and symbol crash, and Laura was standing beside him.

— Here you go, said Jeannette. Another round for the Gruesome Twosome.

Laura quickly retorted.

— Hey! What about Sean and Bill? Don't leave them out!

Sean and Bill looked bemused.

Jeannette liked Paul, liked "them." Paul considered her a witness to the miracle.

Laura startled Paul with a squeal.

— Oh my God! she cried. Stacey, you made it!

To Paul's left was a young woman with short blonde hair. She was cute and well-coiffed, but seemed ill at ease in the downtown bar: a whiff of suburbia clung to her.

Laura threw her arms around the woman and gave her a big squeeze.

— Paul this is Stacey, my friend from Port Chester. This is Paul. He's a poet!

Paul handed Laura her drink and shook Stacey's hand.

— Would you like a drink?

— Sure! Stacey replied. She stood on her toes to survey the beer taps. What do they have here? How about a Yuengling?

Jeannette delivered the pint and sauntered back to the grey suit. Before Stacey took a sip of her lager, Laura declared:

— We need some shots!

And she flitted around the bar, flinging various ingredients into a cocktail shaker, which she raised to her right ear with both arms and rattled up and down.

Stacey told Paul about her train problems, how she had gotten off at the 6 train at City Hall Park and walked toward a statue of Ben Franklin, not realizing that she had gone the wrong way until she saw the towers and cables of the Brooklyn Bridge. She knew Laura's bar was not across the river!

Laura filled three shot glasses with what looked like cherry juice. She had some left over and so, what the hell, gave some to Sean and Bill, too.

— What's in it? Stacey wondered.

— I don't know. Something I just made up!

The band started their second set but Laura, Stacey, and Paul remained at the bar.

Why didn't Laura mention that Stacey was coming?

When the set was finished, the next band came in and *Bruja* decided to hang around. While all the guitars and drums and wires were being carted in and out, Laura got into a game of pool with Sean. Then Paul and Stacey played. Laura chatted with the sullen guys from *Bruja*, who didn't have much to say for themselves. She made more fruity shots, and, before long, Jeanette was buying them all a round of Jameson.

Then Laura and Stacey realized it was late and Stacey took out her train schedule. But, wait, Laura had her car! She totally had her car!

The three of them piled into Laura's BMW and bumped along the potholed West Side Highway. Laura's driving was unsteady. How many Amstels and shots had she drunk? But, she showed more confidence on the highway. Instead of directing her to Hell's Kitchen, Paul had her drop him off by the Car Wash at 47th Street. She swerved a little too hard toward the curb.

— I can walk from here. Are you sure you're all right? Paul asked as he got out of the back seat.

— She's fine, Stacey said. Laura's a pro.

— Be careful, Paul said to Laura.

— Thanks, I had a wonderful evening, said she, as if they had just come from the ballet or something.

He watched the BMW rattle up toward the Henry Hudson Parkway.

— Better luck next Thursday, Paul sighed.

…

"C'mere, Sarsfield, *a gradh*, 'til I relate to you the exploits of the brave men of '98, in my home County of Mayo. You remind me of myself when I was a *garsun* and my neighbor, a stouthearted old fellow we called 'Swifty,' would tell us children stories to divert us when we were upset or needed something to occupy us on a rainy day. How many days when our bellies were empty in hungry July or when the rain and darkness of November had us huddled indoors did he keep us children diverted with his narrations, God bless him? Sure, and he taught us a great deal, so he did. 'Twas he who first taught me to read and write as we stood in his little hedge school in Louisburgh and 'twas he who drilled the mental arithmetic into me. 'Twas he who taught me the exploits of the great Irish heroes, Finn mac Cumhaill and Cuchullain and Queen Maeve and of the Old Testament patriarchs and prophets and warriors, the Greeks and Romans, as well. The rage of

Achilles over his feud with Agamemnon! And real-life heroes, too, the O'Neills and the O'Donnells who resisted English rule and the great rebels Wolfe Tone and Henry Joy McCracken and Robert Emmet who tried to overthrow our oppressors and unite our country. 'Twas he who first told me tales of Connemara where I found freedom, welcome, employment, and a respite from my cares.

"In my eyes, he was a great warrior, gallant Ireland's bravest and best. He was a hero in our village of Bunowen, my own home that I'll never see again. And, sure, no one will ever know the like of Swifty, though I can picture his face, *mo bhuachaill*, clearer than anything before me in this dungeon the English call 'steerage clahhss.' 'Twas a narrow face he had on him and a thin nose. Whenever he taught us of the feats of Hannibal or Ajax or Samson or Xerxes — I would envision that hero with the face of Swifty. For he was out in '98 to join with the French and the United Irishmen. And didn't he lose his right eye for his trouble? It makes my blood boil to think that these Strangers who had taken so much from us took an eye from this brave and learned man."

Seamus rose from his seachest and almost bumped his head on the low 'tween-deck ceiling. He crouched down and continued.

"How could I ever forget the blind cruelty of the Sassenach … when I could see every day that Swifty had but one eye with which to take in the world that God created? … when I could witness daily how, despite what they had done, Swifty could see much farther, higher, and deeper than they? I have always remembered. And, I always will."

Seamus sighed, sat back down, and then looked up.

"Well, Sarsfield, I am not the great *seanchai* that he was but I will try to play his part and tell you some tales that he oft told me.

"During the spring and summer of the *Bliain na bhFrancach*, 'the Year of the French,' the British soldiers knew the people were going to rise. So the yeomanry went round with money to tempt people into informing. And if that didn't work, they had pitchcaps to torture information out of them. The Redcoats would pour hot tar or pitch — the black liquid people use to keep torches burning — into a linen cap and stick it to a Croppie's head. The monsters would wait for it to cool and then tear it off, taking part of the man's hair and scalp with it! Sure they were worse than the bloody savages scalping men in the New World! And they claimed to be bringing civilization to their colonies! The yeomanry were allowed to take whomever they wanted into the guardhouse and pitchcap them like this. There was nothing and no one to stop them. When they were finished their work, they would loose the poor victim — suffering and often blinded by the hot pitch that had rolled into his eyes — to stumble about the town while they laughed and made sport of him. My neighbor, Thomas Lavelle, was pitchcapped and you can be sure that everyone who knew him or heard the tale in Bunowen or Louisburgh volunteered to be out in '98."

A few wretched boys and girls and a couple of gaunt-looking adults were now sitting up and paying attention to Seamus's story. They inched closer to him along the steerage compartment floor.

"Come on, gather around, ye who would like to hear," Seamus said to them, playing with a bit of straw that had fallen from one of the berths. "Come as close as you want to hear my *seanchas*, though there isn't much space between us anyway.

"And, sure, along with the pitchcapping, the yeomanry had other means of learning what they wanted. They would rub moist gunpowder into a man's hair and set it ablaze! They would cut off a man's ears or his nose! But despite what the Bloodybacks might have already learned —and there wasn't much you can be sure of that —the lads were determined to rise with the bold United Men. Indeed, the more the Redcoats tortured the people, the more the people grew enraged! No man will argue that it was not their brutality before the rising that made more men want to be out chasing the Redcoats to the sea!"

"In August, the word went 'round that the French would land near Killala. And Swifty started making his way to them. General Humbert and his second in command, General Sarrazin, landed at Kilcommin, at a spot called *Leac A'Chaonaigh*, and the French and Irish armies chased the Bloodybacks out of Killala! There, Swifty and hundreds of others joined the Mayomen and United Irishmen, Henry O'Keon and Niall Kerrigan, at their new headquarters — the palace of the Church of Ireland archbishop!

"The French army and this raggle-taggle group of Irish farmers with pikes made more Redcoats turn tail and run on their way to Ballina. A couple of days later, they marched south along the Moy and then east on the Ballinahaglish road, past the old cemetery and Castlegore Wood to Knockfree, near Lough Conn. For they knew that Foxford contained a large British garrison."

In the dust between his feet Seamus used his bog oak stick to draw a rough map of Lough Conn and Foxford, Crossmolina, and Castlebar.

"Can everyone see that?" he asked. "They couldn't go this way because of the large number of British soldiers stationed here in Foxford. So they had to march 'round the lough.

"How joyful it must have been to march through those winding roads overhanging with summer growth and lined with yellow celandine and high green grasses — and know that for once they, and not the Strangers, were masters of them!

"They had good weather for marching from the time the French landed until they reached the Windy Gap. When they arrived at Lahardaun, the French and the United Irishmen were greeted by a fierce rainstorm. But the rebels were able to have a wee rest and, Father Conroy, the parish priest, and the good local people, fed them. When the rising was over, poor Father Conroy was judicially murdered at the hanging tree in Castlebar's Mall. He gave his life for his Lord, his country, and for the people, God rest him."

Seamus bowed his head and blessed himself. Several of his ragged fellows —adults and children — did the same.

"Then the Bold United Men followed Captain Mangan, a native of Castlebar, through the rough and hilly terrain of the Windy Gap, through miles and miles of bog and mountain most would have considered impracticable: past Bofeenaun by Levally Lough and Barnageeha, with the undulating mountain peaks always before them and to their west, past more bogland and wild countryside around Croaghmoyle Mountain to Burren and Sarnaght. I heard Swifty tell it so often, it's as if I had been there myself."

Seamus traced their route with his stick and then looked at each member of the growing audience for his story.

"Sure, it must have been tough going along those narrow roads and rough fields, especially in the dark. I often thought of these men's travails as I took my lonely march through similar country on my way from Bunowen to Connemara.

"But, an hour or two before dawn, the fatigued rebels came upon a sight worthy of Xenophon himself — the County Seat of Mayo, the town of Castlebar.

"As the sun rose, the Redcoats saw the approach of the rebels and fired their canons at them. *Maise*, many a brave man died at the dawning of that glorious day! The rebels made two charges, which accomplished nothing more than the slaughter of their own men. But General Sarrazin found some covered terrain directly in front of the British artillery in which they could charge."

Seamus shouted and gestured as if holding a pike.

"The French shouted, '*Allons*' and pointed their bayonets and the Irish shouted, '*Abu*!' and raised their pikes and the two armies rushed the English cannons!"

A couple of the men in steerage lifted their arms and gestured with Seamus.

"Their charge surprised General Lake and his troops, who fled the battlefield and abandoned their artillery. The United Irishmen and their French allies sped down Staball Hill and took Thomas Street and Castlebar's marketplace. And, there was great excitement in it, believe me. But the real thrill came when the Bloodybacks, there to protect the County Seat, broke ranks and ran in all directions. Can you believe it, *mo chairde*? 'The Races of Castlebar,' they called it. All those Redcoats fleeing like hares!

"And my neighbor, Swifty, excelled in running down the cowardly troops, a swift-footed Achilles he was, using his pike to redden the roads and the fields with the blood of his fleeing enemies. He caught many of the cowards as they stopped to plunder the homes of the people. Rebel or loyalist, they took no notice!"

Seamus shook his head and cast his eyes in the floor of the steerage compartment.

"I used to imagine all the fuchsia flowers on the sides of the roads around Bunowen were drops of blood shed by Swifty.

"But, 'twas a great victory and the United Men were delirious with joy! Can you imagine how exhilarating it was — I don't think the English language has a word for it — for those men who had spent their lives under the heel of the Sassenach to take an Irish town with their pikes and to raise over it in place of that bloody English rag their own flag of green with a golden harp?! Humbert had landed on Wednesday evening and by midday on Monday the County Seat was theirs! Hundreds more volunteers flowed in from the surrounding countryside and from as far away as Longford and Kilkenny! General Humbert declared a Republic of Connaught and made John Moore our president! The United Irishmen were on the march!"

Sarsfield clapped his weak hands and the other tattered listeners started to cheer! Even the grumpy people in the bunks opposite forgot the churning sea and began to applaud and shout.

"The French were happy, too, but Swifty said they were odd fellows in some ways. The United Men, according to him, were vehement to fight for both the Dark Rosaleen and the Virgin Mary. The Stranger had tried to snuff out our Faith, and he could never be allowed to succeed! Wasn't it our Faith that had kept the fires lit in our hearts and fortified us against our troubles? These French fellows were Catholic, too, of course. Disturbed yet moved, they attended the masses at the *carraigh an aifrinn* or the cemetery at dawn with the boyos keeping watch to see were the English coming. But, in general, they did not show the love of their Faith (or the love of the cause for that matter) that our lads did. Often, according to Swifty, they seemed to be there for francs from the French Directorate only.

"They looked down on our lads as poorly disciplined soldiers, which they were. They hadn't many guns and those they had must have seemed antique. Many United Men were armed with mere pikes and pitchforks. And devil the training they had!

"Of course, the British looked upon the two groups differently as well. As became clear later …

"But in those stirring days of victory, for the United men, the excitement and celebration — and there were a few drams drunk the night they chased the Redcoats from old Castlebar, make no mistake — were tempered by a need for a greater state of alertness. They knew well that their victory was only over a biteen of land and that whatever number of troops had run away and left Castlebar in their hands, there were many more to replace them. They had taken the beast by surprise but it would soon be able to gather its strength and strike back at them. Once Surprise comes out of hiding, her power dissipates quickly.

"Two weeks later, the United Irishmen and General Humbert's French army had found their way across the Moy and the Shannon, up through Leitrim and down into Longford, where they ran into General Cornwallis and General Lake at Ballinamuck. There, sadly, the bold adventure was to end for many.

"They say if Humbert had landed six months earlier, the rising would have turned out much differently, and Ireland might have been liberated. Indeed, there mightn't have been any need for us to leave our native land at all."

"Poor old Ireland," murmured Tom.

"God save Ireland," said young Kevin.

Seamus sighed and went on.

"Cornwallis had 15,000 troops and Lake 14,000. Sarrazin was overwhelmed from the rear in no time and had to surrender. Humbert held out longer, but for only an hour.

"The French surrender was accepted by the British. But the Irish were slaughtered. The British massacred 2,000 United Irishmen and hanged priests like Father Conroy and Father Manus Sweeney of Newport who had helped them.

"Swifty lost his eye at Ballinauck from but got away with his life and his limbs. Only for the speed of his legs he might never have lived to tell about it.

"With no more army to fight, the Redcoat forces rampaged through the countryside. They butchered without mercy anyone they suspected of having a part in the rising. The high sheriff of Mayo, Denis Browne, hanged so many men in Claremorris that the people named him, '*Donnchadh an Rópa*,' 'Denis of the Rope.'

"A fortnight later at Killala where a few French and United Irishmen still stood strong, the British acted as they had at Ballinamuck — accepting the French as prisoners of war and murdering the Irish. The little road to Killala became known as '*Casán an Áir*,' 'the Pathway of the Slaughter.'

"Swifty would tremble with rage years later thinking what they had done to the homes of the people, even the innocent ones. He was in Claremorris the day they hanged his friend. And after all of this cruelty he burned for the rest of his life to take revenge and to see his homeland free of such people. He always said that the loss of his eye helped him see more clearly who was at fault for our country's woes.

"'They will be repaid when we rise again!' Swifty said. 'You can be sure of it! Ballinamuck will not be forgotten! Indeed, the true rising, the rising that will free the living and vindicate the dead, will begin in Ballinamuck, the Valley of the Black Pig!'"

A hush fell over Seamus's audience at the utterance of this prophecy. Then, one sickly man reclining some distance away spoke up.

"May it come soon!" said he.

And the steerage passengers applauded and cheered.

"The nation we are sailing to, the United States, sent the Redcoats packing last century. We can learn something from the people there and drive them from our shores as well. There are single-minded men working to make it happen."

...

You set your alarm so you could get up before everyone in the house and drive away. While they were still lost in their dreams, you prepared to ensnare others in yours.

— Who do you think you are? That car doesn't belong to you!

Mom looked at Dad, angry herself but a little afraid of his temper.

— If we tell you to come home by a certain time, she said, then you bring that car home by that time! Driving a car is not a right. It's a privilege!

You lifted the hatch off of the back of the car, the hinges long since broken, and put the Peavey T-60 guitar and amplifier into the orange AMC Hornet. You halfsat in the driver's seat, leaving one blue-jeaned leg hanging out of the car, turned the ignition key partway, and put it into Neutral.

— What are you doing out so late with the car, anyway?

— I'm sure he's not saying his prayers.

— I don't want you getting behind the wheel of a car after you've been drinking.

Leaving the door open and with one hand on the steering wheel, you stood up and pushed the car backward. It took some effort to get that first roll. After a moment, you got the wheels to rotate a few times, despite slipping on the gravel. You went around to the front of the car and pushed on the hood. The Orange Hornet picked up speed. You jumped in. When there was enough distance between you and your parents' bedroom, you hit the brakes, shifted into Park, and turned the ignition.

This was stupid, you felt, but it was the way it had to be. You could not hitchhike with a guitar and amp.

— You can't respect our rules about your use of the car. So now you don't have a car to drive.

— How am I supposed to get to school?

— Take the P&W. Buy your own car. See what I care.

— James!

—I need to bring my electric guitar to school on Friday.

— You shoulda thought of that before you deliberately and repeatedly disobeyed our rules!

The punishment was impossible to abide by. It was a rejection of sense and ambition, pride and fate. It was a cloud obscuring the dawn of a musical career, a sin against the Spirit of Music itself. Unveil your songs before the complacent college nimrods in the Campion Student Center! Wake the alligator-shirted dead! Without music, life would be a mistake. No foolish law nor ridiculous prohibition from parental overlords was going to keep you from performing and perfecting your art.

Didn't her friends tell stories about how "Janey used to sneak out of her room at night and climb back in the window"? And old James Logan, I bet his teenage years were not the model of purity.

You went left on Simpson, in the opposite direction of where you needed to go. Only then did you slam the door shut.

What would happen when you got back?

— How dare you take that car when you were expressly forbidden to?

— Is that car yours? Did you pay for it? No, you didn't pay for anything. You don't know the value of a dollar.

But nothing was going to change Paul Logan's mind once it was made up. You'd have to listen to a lot more nonsense. But you would put up with it. It was for Music!

And what became of all your stubborn grand theft auto, anyway? What about musical history? Destiny? Career? Laura doesn't care about it. All it got from your peers was mockery or indifference, from Mom and Dad nothing but fights.

But those arguments only presaged the larger recurring one. One time late at night he wanted me to stop watching TV and get to bed.

— Keep turning out lights and closing doors, I said. That's right. Keep turning out lights and closing doors!

what a pretentious fuck you were back when you knew everything

And this segued into the usual argument.

— So what are you going on? Just a bunch of dreams!

— But your grandfather had a dream! And he followed it. Aren't you the one who always told us those stories?

— Yes, and because he fulfilled his dream we have the family business! You can continue to build on that.

— But that was *his* dream. I have a dream of my own that I have to follow

— You *have to*? You *have to* chase after a dream instead of building on something with a solid foundation? Why?

— I have to chase this dream. Not someone else's. My dream.

—You got a solid future, on solid ground, based on a past of solid hard work. What the hell good are dreams? How do you know they will get you anywhere?

— I know.

— How do you know?

— I just know.

— That means you don't know.

— Well, then I'll find out, Paul said.

— Why give up something you do know?

— I have to.

— I was born during the Depression and I grew up when people were happy just to get a job, any job. I was damn glad to know that my dad and granddad had built a business that would provide me with a position, an important position when I finished my education. Then the War came and afterwards the G.I. Bill and the business boomed. It offered me not only security but success like none of us could have imagined when we were young. I remember as a kid looking at bums on the street begging for money or something to eat … at guys who used to be bigshots trying to sell apples for pennies and nickels and thinking to myself, "Thank God! Thank God that I was born into a family with the foresight and work ethic to build a solid business where I can work and never become like that!" But I always made sure that I gave those guys something, more than they expected, because there for the grace of God go I! I with secure ground under my feet because of the vision and sweat of my dad and granddad. And you, the poet laureate?! You want to turn your back on all this and move to the Bronx?! Because you've had a couple of ideas for poems?! I can't comprehend that.

— Why is it so hard to understand? Didn't your grandfather leave his country to start his own life?

— That was different. He wasn't born in the land of opportun-

— Didn't he take a chance going out there on his own?

— Yeah, but he built something. Hell, he built half the city of Philadelphia. And it wasn't with similes and metaphors, lemee tell yih. How are you going to eat while writing poetry? Or does starving give you inspiration? My grandfather left an impoverished country, where there was famine and oppression. He had no security there. The boat he sailed away on had more stability than the land he'd grown up on.

— I should have known better than to try to explain.

Well, it was they who sent me here ... locking me out of the house ... throwing me into the cistern of those college years … with no light cascading down. Wanting me to wallow in the cement mix, to dig holes in the ground, to lay bricks higher than anyone ... How high can you go? Only as far as Billy Penn's feet. Tried to force me into it. Then it was into the wilderness of El Bronx.

Oh, diploma. Free at last. Deliver me unto the land of bondage. Any day now … Any day now … I shall be … Bring me your tired, your poor, those yearning to drink free. My brothers, those brothers of love who threw me down and sold me. For an accountant to be named later. No, they did not follow me.

dreamt that a dog was chasing me down an upper darby alley loud deep fearsome barking nothing but fences barbed wire my jeans get caught the dog keeps coming look back at what i left behind glad it hasn't followed me

Laura doesn't care about your music but she is impressed that you write poetry. Where's the latest poem, though? With your brain cells and a stringless tennis racket in the back of a beaten-up BMW.

> For all that I've written
> I might as well be
> Where the mountains of Mourne ...

...

Then one day, James returned. I heard his voice answering the greetings from the row of secretaries outside the offices.

"Good morning, Mr. Logan."

"Good morning, Mr. Logan."

"Good morning, Mr. Logan."

I was busy, of course, and pretending to be much busier. My face felt flushed. I hoped I was not blushing. I knew there was no chance of my going out of my way to acknowledge him. All during the dark period of his absence, I had trained my neck not to turn in the direction of anything to do with him. I didn't even lift my head to watch his approach.

As he passed my desk, I offered the same greeting as everyone else, and in the same tone.

"Good morning, Mr. Logan."

At least I tried to use the same tone the other girls had. Perhaps he detected more emotion in my voice or perceived an effort to hide my feelings. There was a small hesitation in his step as he passed my desk. Maybe he was trying to get a sense of how I felt — as if he couldn't have guessed.

But in this hesitation, I caught a whiff of remorse … and the scent began to open deep within me a blossom of forgiveness.

And the blossom opened indeed. The reconciliation was quick and complete. We were back to normal so rapidly that I hardly remember the stages we had passed through.

However, there were stages. Of course, I was angry. Hell hath no fury and so forth. But, more to the point, I was hurt. The anger might dissipate quickly but the hurt could not be so easily healed.

I avoided him that morning (along with everyone else, truth be told.) Oh, to the whole office I must have appeared to have quite the work ethic! James seemed to take the same tack. I could hear him talking with the other men and the girls and laughing loudly — extra loudly to my ears — as if bound and determined to make the morning resemble the start of an average workday.

When lunchtime came, I asked Sally to go with me to Horn and Hardart's. How brave I was being — even with my choice of restaurant! In the six days since I had last seen James, I had avoided the Automat like a plague. In fact, if I had had to pass it, like when I made a visit to St. John's a couple of times (a quiet place to pray was a daily necessity), I would walk on the other side of 13th Street or circumvent the place altogether by going up to Market Street and then down 13th. Yes, I really did this! I wouldn't have been able to keep down anything from there, anyway. When Sally told me she couldn't make it, I determined to go there on my own. I'd show him that it didn't matter if I'd first had lunch there with him or if I had gone there for an audience with the Pope. It was my usual spot and I would go there with my nickels whenever the spirit moved me. So I sat on my usual bench using a large icy coke to wash down the driest sandwich in the world, when, of course, himself showed up.

And that was the way it was — he just appeared at my table. I'd had no chance to stop him and couldn't have done so, anyway. It was the Automat after all.

Our eyes met and I might have looked at him as if he were an irritating ghost. He appeared chastised from the very start. I could think of nothing else to do but leave. I coldly placed my sandwich on my plate and rose.

"Janey," he called in a desperate hush. "Don't go!"

Would that I'd had the opportunity to make that request of him.

"And why should I not leave, Mr. Logan?"

"Janey, please … stay here a moment."

"I'm sure you have some important people you need to talk with, people whose need to know your whereabouts is much greater than mine. No sense wasting your time on an underling like me."

"I need to talk to you."

"You have ample opportunity to talk to the secretarial staff at the office. It is up to you to take advantage of the opportunities afforded you."

"Janey, I'm sorry."

"Sorry? For what?"

"Please, sit down. I want to apologize."

I took my seat but kept a firm grip on my purse, ready to storm out at the least provocation.

"I've missed you so much … I was stupid …"

Glib James Logan was suddenly at a loss for words. This well-dressed executive, this immaculately groomed son of privilege, stood cowering and penitent at the Automat. All at once, he was deflated of his power and confidence, a true sight to behold.

Pity for him rose up within me, displacing my anger. It reminded me of when I used to babysit. No matter how irritated an obstreperous child might make me one moment, I could smile and play with him the next. The children were simply too cute to stay mad at. And as he spoke to me from across the Horn and Hardart's table, a multitude of impulses rose up within me and scattered like sparks in a fireplace. In my face, my shoulders, and my arms, I could feel the cold front I was trying to keep up against him. But, other parts of me didn't remember that I was supposed to be mad at him. There were moments — when his head turned a certain way or his face took on a particular expression — when I felt flashes of attraction for him. I already said how he reminded me of a child that needed babysitting and consoling. These maternal sparks found a home in my chest.

"I was so confused," James said. "My father was pressuring me about Linda … He was worried about how it would all look … what people would think … not just about him and his family but about the company. Especially Linda's father. He wanted me to go to Scranton to meet an old supplier — my grandfather had started doing business with them years ago. I fought with him. I refused to go at first. I knew it was a mistake. But, he has a way of putting pressure on me — you know?"

"Yes, I'm very familiar with those kinds of pressures. Still, a phone call-"

"I know, Janey. I know. I should have called," he explained, lost in thought and memory, his eyes roving from the table to the floor to the sandwich windows, "but I was so upset, so angry with my dad and with Logan Construction and the whole situation …"

Deciding on a more direct appeal, he leaned forward, looked straight at me, and widened his eyes.

"I didn't want to take out my frustration on you … and there seemed to be so much to explain. I also needed time to think. And, believe me, there isn't much else to do in Scranton!"

I laughed out loud at this. I couldn't help myself. And neither could James.

I could see it now: James had to go through the pretense of going away to think things over, even though, as he said, his mind was made up.

"There was never any doubt that I could not marry the woman he wanted me to. I don't know why I agreed."

And the blossom of forgiveness was now fully distended. I absolved him in that instant. I knew that I would be his and that our relationship would go back to normal. And I think he saw this in my open gazing eyes.

But, I had no plan to let him know at that point.

"I really don't appreciate being left in the lurch like that. I haven't heard from you in almost a week. I deserve a little more respect-"

"I'm sorry, Janey. You're right. There is no excuse. I should have let you know that I was going to Scranton. I got this boneheaded notion in my head that I needed to get away from everything and everybody. I became John the Baptist all of a sudden."

You weren't feeding on locusts and wild honey— were you?"

"Practically. Take a miracle to find the greatest sandwich in the world up there."

He saw me laugh again. Thinking he had won me over, he reached across the table and put his hand on mine. As much as I wanted to squeeze it, I heard my mother's voice telling me not to be a fool. There was also that lunchtime crowd paying such careful attention and yet pretending to pay us no mind. I pulled my hand away.

"I understand, James. I think I do. But I … uh," I said, leaving my seat. "Have to get back to work."

He followed me a step or two toward the closing door. I had never seen him act like this before. It was strange and exhilarating — perhaps my mother was right— but I also felt a little uncomfortable.

"Dinner tonight?" he muttered so as not to be heard.

I stopped and looked back at him, clutching my purse. In a voice and tone that did not seem my own, I answered him.

"You say your mind is made up and that your little retreat upstate was no more than a formality. Yet I still hear you mention that other woman's name. And I still seem to be playing second fiddle."

Since we were solving problems, why not tackle the biggest one?

"I'll take care of it."

I nodded, stepped across the threshold alone, and slipped into the lunch-hour crush.

By the next night, James had broken off his engagement — in a manila folder of letters that needed to be answered, he had included a handwritten note that said, "To my first and only fiddler" — and I was sitting across from him at D'Orazio's in Overbrook, our old spot. His wooly hand was on his scotch on the rocks and his head was thrown back in laughter. My fingers were on the stem of my chardonnay glass and my head was shaking over the wax-covered Chianti-bottle sconce. Just like always. And if anyone had told me a week earlier that this is where I would be and how we would be, I would have said he was crazy. As James leaned back with his uproarious laugh, I saw that he was wearing the tie clip I had gotten him, the one I had gotten so angry with myself for buying. It was beyond belief. A dream. A fairy tale. At the same time, I wondered how I ever could have doubted that this is how it would end. Now that the noonday sun was shining, had it ever really been dark? If so, the darkness never seemed so distant.

Yet it had lasted until lunchtime the day before.

Are such miracles possible? Well, we are the proof.

...

— Paul, Laura said, why don't you tell Charles about your friend, the cook?

— It's funny how we don't think of certain people as major characters in our lives but they keep reappearing. Almost miraculously. One guy like that was an old buddy from the Prep, John Lafferty. He was in my homeroom freshman year, 1H with Father Kelly. I don't remember much about him from those days except that he was tall and kind of quiet. He was a gentle sort of soul, not a great student or a bad one, not outstanding in anyway, really. But after freshman year, like a number of others, he didn't return to the Prep.

like carmen at saint philomena's end of her sophomore year end of my freshman year as a teacher those blackbutton eyes bronzegold hair her name in gold script dangling from that girlish brown neck ahmma miss you mistah logan

— In the beginning of my sophomore year, I signed up for the cross-country team. I was impressed the first time I went to a meet at Belmont Plateau where hundreds of high-school boys lined up in school colors like troops arrayed for an ancient battle. And in the middle of all that, who did I see but John Lafferty, in an Archbishop Dougherty jersey and shorts? He said "hello" to me and was quite friendly. We chatted before the race. He had transferred to Dougherty, the largest Catholic high school in the country at the time, probably for financial reasons. Or maybe his grades were not good enough for his parents. Anyway, he seemed the same happy guy. I think I might have run into him once or twice at other races but I don't recall much about those encounters.

— A few years later — during the summer between freshman and sophomore year of college — I was working at the Logan Company's Center City office, purging boxes of old files. I was standing by 16ᵗʰ and Chestnut, watching a Jimmy Hendrix marionette humping his amplifier to the tune of "All Along the Watchtower," when there he was again — John Lafferty. We had lunch around the corner at Oscar's Tavern and he told me his crazy tale.

— He had gone to La Salle College for a semester, commuting from his parents' house and, when he wasn't in class, cooking in a greasy spoon in Fishtown, a small dive near K&A that let him whip up simple dishes. I think it was a seafood joint, which would have been fitting, given his story. He sweated over the stove for a couple of months until one day, he got in an argument with his manager. He was so exhausted from school and work and his parents' giving him shit all the time that he couldn't control his tongue. He cursed out his boss and stormed out.

— He didn't know what to do. So he just kept walking south in the general direction of Center City, along the waterfront. He passed by Penn Treaty Park, where William Penn made a peace agreement with the Delaware Indians. He also went by a neighborhood called Northern Liberties and came near the Olde City. Bright, tall Philadelphia stood to his right; dark, hunched Camden squatted to his left; and in between the Delaware River flowed flee. The sight of the water calmed him down. So he continued to walk alongside it. Not far from Penn's Landing, he ran into a group of Irishmen who were standing around looking nonplussed.

— You love your fancy words, doncha, Paul, Laura teased.

— Sorry, was that too much for you? They were confused. How about that? They were standing around like they didn't know what to do next. Is that explanation more amenable to you?

— That's fine. A fine explanation. What was it that you called the regulars at the bar — the dwellers of the Orange Crush?

— The denizens. Denizens of the Orange Crush. Is that so strange?

— A good word for them, I'd say.

— Thanks, Charles! At least some people from England can speak English.

— So tell him what happened with your friend and the Irish guys.

— OK, so my friend, John, who had been walking quite a distance at this point, sat down on a bench and lit a cigarette. One of the Irish guys came over and asked him for a light. John gives it to him and, in a better mood at this point, started chatting with the Irishman and his friends.

— Eventually, the Irish guys asked John what had brought him out to the waterfront at that time of night.

— John told him he had been walking and walking trying to calm down, that he had just lost his job and had been really pissed off.

— So, John asked the Irishmen a similar question: "What are you guys doing out here?"

— "We're the crew of this tall ship," he jerked his thumb back toward an old-19th-century vessel with high masts and sails and riggings, like down at the South Street Seaport. "We were due to set sail for Ireland this evenin' but we've not been able to."

— "Why not?" asks John.

— "Our cook is just after quittin' on us."

— John's jaw almost hit the ground. It was like a miracle.

— "Well," he said, taking a puff of his cigarette. "You'll never guess what I do. I'm a cook and I'm looking for a job."

— The Irish sailors couldn't believe the coincidence. Next thing John knew he was talking to his parents on a payphone, telling them he'd signed on with these Harps as cook. And, yeah, he did it. He set off for the Emerald Isle that night.

— He said he got used to the nautical life very quickly: he only got a little seasick in the beginning. The Irish guys liked his cooking and they taught him all about riggings and sails and knots and even a little about navigation. He showed me pictures of himself sitting on one of the yardarms where they hang the big sails and taking it easy on one of those rope ladders the sailors use. "A shroud," John called it.

— The shroud of Turin! laughed Laura. I'm tellin' you you should totally write about it.

— You should write this cook's tale, too, added Charles. Sounds like quite the adventure!

— It was, said Paul. Once he got to Ireland, John found that working on a tall ship was not exactly a lifelong career. But he also realized that he liked living in the old sod. He went out to visit his grandmother in Donegal and was able to survive on a bunch of odd jobs. He cleaned stables. He worked at a pony trekking place taking fat tourists horseback riding on the beach. He helped out in a local pub.

also told me he joined a couple of lads on a dangerous mission to paint brits out on the side of some cliffs but that story is best left for another audience

— What about his family back here? Charles asked.

— His parents were pissed at the way he had disappeared on them but they calmed down eventually. His mom was happy that he was spending time with his granny. So, crazy as it seemed, it all kinda worked out …

— So, what was he doing back in Philadelphia when you saw him? Laura wondered.

— When the tall ship made its next crossing, the sailors asked John to come along and cook for them. So, he had a chance to go back home, see his parents, hang out in his hometown a bit … That day when I ran into him by the Jimi Hendrix puppet, he said he was heading back to Ireland when the ship set sail again. He had a chance to work for a pirate radio station over there. He had substituted for some Donegal DJs a couple of times and they liked him. The Irish enjoyed hearing a Philadelphia guy introducing their rock records. And the girls liked his accent.

…

Janey had done yeoman's work cleaning up after the party, but the Logan house was still a mess. She opened the screen door to see if the back porch needed to be redded up. She thought she might have left her wine glass out there. And, there it was on the table, where Mr. Logan and James were seated with their glasses of scotch. Catching the door behind her so it wouldn't slam, Janey breezed over, picked up the goblet, and turned to go back inside.

Mr. Logan's voice stopped her.

"The dishes can wait, Janey. Siddown and have a nightcap with us."

The air was close and warm but there was a breeze, a cool breeze that had an early taste of autumn in it. It was only eight o'clock. Yet over their heads it was pitch black.

"I really should help. There is still so much to do."

"You've done enough — more than enough! Have a seat!" Mr. Logan said, pointing with his chin at the empty chair next to James. "It's better to arrive at the end of a fray and drink at the end a feast. That's Shakespeare!"

"Yeah, Joe Shakespeare," interjected James. "He was one of our best bricklayers. Tremendous worker."

"Really, Mr. Logan, I would feel more relaxed once everything is cleaned up."

James stood and disappeared into the house. Janey felt like she was being pulled into another maelstrom — this time by two Logan men. She had to put up a fight.

"I can't leave Mrs. Logan in there doing everything. It's a sin."

"Ah, she's just supervising! The real work is being done by her nieces."

James pulled the cork out of the half-empty bottle of chardonnay he'd fetched from inside. He smiled and took the wine glass from her hand.

"Allow me," Mr. Logan said to his son. "C'mere, Janey. Sit down."

There seemed to be no way to win this argument. Janey took a seat and reclined against the rattan backrest.

Mr. Logan took the bottle and tilted its neck over her goblet. By the time he finished, the white wine reached almost to the brim: it was a real Logan pour. He handed her the chardonnay saying, "We didn't invite you here to do manual labor, Janey Dougherty."

"Thank you, Mr. Logan."

If she drank all the wine in her glass, she wouldn't trust herself washing a single dish in the house.

"You're very welcome! Besides, you can't deny the wish of an old man on his birthday — can you?"

"Where's the old man?" she asked. "I don't see any."

Mr. Logan chuckled and settled back into his chair. As Janey sipped her chardonnay, the clouds proceeded across the heavens with grace and majesty, now covering up the waxing moon and now revealing it. A white Adirondack chair, which had served as a throne for Mr. Logan as the party had sung for him, now sat empty, its long thin feet sinking into grass that was lush and ankle high. She would have loved to have gone barefoot: it was hard to navigate the yard in heels. There were tall hedges all the way across the backyard so you could not see any neighbors. Janey felt that it was funny that you could hear them sometimes but never see them. They were like ghosts: the phantoms of Ardmore. The old swingset was speckled with chipped paint and rust: she could even tell in the dark. She liked to imagine James and his brothers and sisters playing in the yard, though she could not help thinking how different their childhood was from hers.

"Cheers!" said James, clinking his scotch glass against her goblet. "Janey hath chosen the better part."

She took another sip, the tip of her tongue enjoying the wine's grapey tang.

"What were you boys talking about?"

"Dad was telling me about how his father ended up in Philadelphia," James said.

"Yes, young lady," added Mr. Logan. "And, it'll behoove you to learn something of the history of the crazy family you're about to marry into."

"He started off in New York, I know," Janey offered.

"That's right," Mr. Logan said. "He worked as a bricklayer in New York. He came over from County Mayo sometime in the 1870s. He was there when the finishing touches were being put on the Brooklyn Bridge."

"But he never felt at home in New York — did he?" said James.

"It must have been an awful shock to him," his fiancée added. "Coming from down on the farm to the Big City."

"I'm sure it was a hard adjustment, Janey, but it wasn't just that. He said he liked it in New York in the beginning. I remember him saying it many times. There was plenty of excitement for a young man with energy and more than enough opportunity for a man of ambition."

He looked up as if the Manhattan skyline was spread across the heavens. The moon was slowly being revealed, the clouds parting like a sheet of cotton wool slowly torn in two. He swirled his whiskey and its rattling ice and tilted the drink between pursed lips.

"More than enough of everything if you ask me," Mr. Logan added.

"Too much of everything!" Janey concurred. "I don't blame him for wanting to leave."

"Father Sarsfield doesn't seem to mind all the hustle and bustle," said James.

"Nah, he's been a real New Yorker for years now."

"The Jesuits sent him to New York — right?" Janey said.

"Oh, yeah. They had to send a Philadelphian up 'ere to teach 'em proper French."

Janey almost choked on her wine.

"He sent dad a nice card," said James. "Too bad he couldn't make it in person."

"Sure. Sarsfield is very at home up 'ere. Father liked it for a while, too. He made some friends and enjoyed the camaraderie at the job sites. But despite how much opportunity and fun he had, there was always this restlessness inside him. That's the way he used tell the story, anyway. Do you remember him telling it, James?"

"Vaguely. I've heard the story so many times … I feel like I heard the story from his own lips!"

Janey pictured Mr. Logan's father, Seamus, working out in the middle of the East River, the wind whistling through the ropes and wires, the dark rolling waves adding a hint of salt to the air. Seamus marvels at New York, and yet, as the wind tugs at his hair and his body, a yearning tugs at his heart as well. He must move on. This is just one stage of the journey done. There is another place. And it will be shown to him.

"The City of Brotherly Love was calling him!" James cracked. He took a stout pull from his scotch.

"Silly as it may sound, that's what he believed."

A chorus of crickets sang background from lush obscurity. A couple of individuals hiding closer contributed long solo notes. One was particularly louder than the others but Janey could not figure out where he was.

"And who's to say he was wrong?" said Janey, letting the vanilla of the wine linger in her mouth and watching the drifting clouds.

"He certainly made a great success here," added James.

A mass of dark clouds now veiled the moon, though a few of the clouds glowed grey. Janey raised her goblet and, squinting, aligned the remaining half of her wine over the sky's brightest spot. Closing one eye like an astronomer, she pinpointed the moon's location.

"Sometimes it is important to listen to those inner voices," she said. "Life is not always rational. Especially the big decisions. That restlessness your father felt … It could have been the workings of the Holy Spirit."

"I think Father would have liked that explanation. He probably would have agreed with it."

Mr. Logan nodded and swirled the deteriorating ice cubes in his whiskey.

"In fact, I'm surprised he never offered it himself. He always said it was time to move on … that there were bad omens … friends getting in accidents on the job … a neighbor's little boy who died … rats infesting his building …"

"The entrails offering a dim outlook."

"Now, now, your grandfather took that stuff seriously. As good as he was with business, there was still plenty of superstition in the old man. He worried that all these bad things were happening around him in New York … but he had good steady work … a city constantly under construction …"

"Still not finished!" laughed James.

"But then one day there was the last straw. His friend had a bad back and had missed a few days of work — and in those days, if you didn't work, you didn't get paid. No sick days or unions for those buckos. And the friend still wasn't feeling a hundred percent. In fact, Father thought he looked like he was going to fall off one of the beams. Father grabbed his collar with his left hand one time. Probly saved his life. Now, Father knew that his friend had a wife and a couple of small children. So, he tried to cover for 'im. He slowed down his own pace so that he could keep an eye on 'im, y'know, make it less obvious that his friend was slower than everybody else."

"Yes, the guys still do that today," interjected James.

"Well the foreman, Agins — funny that Father always remembered the foreman's name, 'Agins,' but not the friend's name: I guess he never forgave the guy — so this Agins guy is giving Father's friend the hairy eyeball. He was always ridin' the guy, even on his best day. And then he started glaring at Father, too, as if to accuse him of loafin' on the job. And Father was a proud and powerful man. The strongest man in Moyamensing they usta call him. He would not take kindly to any suggestion that he might not be pullin' his weight. Even when he was an older man and had been the boss for years and years, he felt guilty that he was not out there with the guys carrying loads of bricks in his hod."

James took Janey's hand under the table. His father was now in full flight.

"But it was obvious that Father and his friend were fallin' behind the other teams. Father could not stand the man's deliberate cruelty to his sick friend — or any deliberate cruelty — and when Agins starting givin' him a hard time, he was more than usually sensitive about it. Father said he could feel his response to Agins before the foreman even opened his mouth.

"But, before you know it, Agins is laying into Father's friend.

"'How can you slow everyone up day in and day out?' says he. 'I gotta a problem wit' choo every day it seems. What is wrong wit' choo?'"

"'Leave him alone, Agins,' Father said.

"'You stay out of this, Logan,' Agins shoots back. 'This don't concern you. Or maybe it does… Maybe you *like* an excuse to take it easy. Maybe you're *both* a couple of goldbricks. Well, I don't want no lazy good-for-nothin' loafers slowin' up da works and jeopardizing my project!'

"'Your project — is it?' Father says. 'Precisely what part of this project is yours? It's the likes of us doing all the sweatin' and strainin' on this job, while you whine like a bitch in heat.'

"'All of it is, Logan,' the foreman says. 'All of it. And if you want to keep workin' on *my* project, you better realize that — and the sooner the better.'

"'And what if I don't?! Do you expect me to respect a man who gives the hard word to a man who's feeling poorly?'

"Agins's face grew redder than a stop sign and his mouth started to sputter and spit. Father stepped to within an inch of him and squinted right into his eye. He had run into many tough customers in Connemara and was well able to handle himself.

"'You're nothing but a bully and a coward!' he said.

"Agins never had a chance to respond. Before an intelligible word could come out of his mouth, Father hit him with a left that threw his head back and then a right to the jaw that knocked him on his behind.

"And he quit the job on the spot. He collected the pay that was owed him, and the next day, boarded a train for Philadelphia."

Janey admired the moonlight reflected in her wee remainder of wine and exulted.

"People in that generation really *lived* — didn't they?!" said she. "God bless him!"

"Too bad you never met him, Janey," her fiancée said. "You really woulda liked him."

"No doubt about it," she responded.

"And he would have liked you," added Mr. Logan.

"*Slainte!*"

...

— Should I turn here? Laura asked as she cruised toward the middle of the wide avenue.

— No, no. Keep going across 6th Avenue.

— Does anyone ever call it, "Avenue of the Americas"? Charles asked.

— Only the street signs. Laura, keep going until you get to the bright lights.

They drove by an elegant Indian restaurant, a passageway to 46th Street, and a building labeled U.S. TRUST. In the distance, the lights of Times Square were coming into view through Laura's dirty, rainspotted windshield.

WHO'S WHO

PAUL LOGAN (*Suitor*): Paul is grateful to make it to Broadway in the front seat. He'd like to thank his mother for the love of reading and writing, his father for the stamina and the thrill of the chase, his grand-uncle Sarsfield for moving to New York City to teach, and his great granddad for his persistence in walking away and in climbing up. Favorite roles: Shotgun in *A Used Car Named Desire*, Edmund in *Long Night's Journey into Day*, Stanley Creamer in *Flowers of Evil*, Elvis in *The Dashiki of Many Colors*, and First Immigration Officer in *A View from the Ferry*.

Charles Bellamy (*Third Wheel*): is happy to land on Broadway after a long night, and cannot believe it, it's been such a blur. He'd like to thank U.S. Immigration, Senator George Mitchell, and, as always, Queen Elizabeth II. Favorite productions include: *Guess Who's Coming to Midtown, Brit on a Not Thick Roof, Laurie and Chuckie in the Clair de Lune, and The Cook, the Thief, the Strife, and Two Lovers.*

LAURA (*Driver*): After hours of working and getting lost in the streets of Lower Manhattan, Laura is delighted to make it to Broadway. She'd like to thank her Polish mother for the blonde hair and high cheekbones and her father for the use of the car. Love you, Mom and Dad! Favorite roles include: *A Funny Thing Happened on the Way to Hell's Kitchen, That's a Lot to Live Up To, Beauty and the Barflies*, and *The Drivin' King*.

Beyond the FedEx office, the yellow cab in front of them came to a halt to let its passengers out. Laura hit the brakes. She didn't have the experience or the nerve to go around the cab and Paul said nothing. He slid his hand into his messenger bag: the book was still there.

In the tunnel between 47th and 48th. Girls' shouting. Black and Latina voices reverberating. Paul sat up automatically and a Pavlovian teachers' scowl came over his face. Out of the tunnel and onto 47th Street sashayed two loud Latinas with hips swaying, curves wiggling, forward-turned wrists swinging, feet rising but an inch above the sidewalk … less of a step than a languid glide. They were followed by a gangly African-American girl raising a large hand to slap one of the other girls. She was yelling. What are they doing out at this hour? Probably off from school tomorrow. They were arguing. A fight? No, they're laughing. Our revenge the laughter of our children. The Saint Philomena's girls were so loud sometimes it was hard to tell. If I didn't laugh, I'd cry …

the din could give you a headache the smells of bubble gum of grape nowandlaters of cheap perfumes hairspray sometimes even nail-polish remover all mixed together in the close claustrophobic room 11 was enough to make you sick

The taxi pulled away. After a moment, Laura's BMW followed. The three girls were still laughing and hitting one another as they made their way toward Times Square.

The brightening lights keep going, and going, and going. Times Square, the antidote for civilization. Desire under the lights …

— Laura, which way are you going after I get out?

— Downtown.

— You can drop me off at Broadway then. You can just make a left and I can walk home from there.

Started off on Broadway and here we are again. Is she putting me on? Am I really supposed to get out and leave him here?

drop me off at the corner of sin and depravity

The traffic light at the corner of 47th Street and 7th Avenue turned red. Behind it, lights of all colors were flashing from all directions.

Flashing for Coke. Flashing for *Miss Saigon* and *Ragtime* and *Rent*. For cologne and clothes. Flashing for fast food. Flashing for peep shows and investment banks.

flashing in time … wasted time … uncloaking the corrupt … illumining the squandered … divulging the debauched … exposing the lost …

From there they could see the Morgan Stanley headquarters and the four banners with giant red letters … T … K … T … S … farther along 47th was the Barrymore Theatre *Wait Until Dark*.

Lines of out-of-towners usually here at the TKTS, trying to save money. Bring in da tourists, bring in da money. Oh, but they are spending it. Watch the flashing lights while we pick your pockets. Flashing to part the tourist from his money. Follow the lights with your eyes. Sleight of hand. Phantom of the phantasmagoria.

— Do you get to many Broadway shows, Paul? Laura asked. I mean living so close to them …

Talking like an out-of-towner herself.

— No, I don't. It's all bullshit. When was the last time they put on anything worthwhile? It's all musicals based on sitcoms.

corner of greed and gullibility lighting by hieronymus bosch

Tweedling sitcom characters in search of a tourist. Garbage! Touching off the rage of the poet. One who writes nothing but directions.

Finding the Way to Hell's Kitchen (revised)

To get to Hell's Kitchen:

1. Direct Laura to drive across 7th Avenue to Broadway.

2. Present Laura with the artistic gift.

3. Get out of the car.

4. Walk to Hell's Kitchen.

5. Don't look back.

— Can you believe Eugene O'Neill was born just a few blocks away? Paul asked. Isn't that something? America's greatest playwright born in Times Square … where all that crap is performed every night.

— They should call it O'Neill Square.

— There is a Logan Circle in Philadelphia but no relation to my family. It goes way back to Colonial days. And there is a Logan Airport in Boston. No idea who that's named after. How about you? Anything named after your family? You know, I don't even know your last name. What is it, anyway?

—Maze, my last name is "Maze."

—Ah, but we call it "corn."

—No, not that kind of maise. Maze! M-A-Z-E.

— Your name comes from a puzzle?

— No, it's a prison.

— A prison? You mean-

— You know the Maze Prison in Northern Ireland?

maze unreal maze of h-blocks the men behind the wire maze she had led him through all night maze of all those old streets maze of history

— Yes … Yes, I do.

— That's where my father is from. Maze in Northern Ireland.

Paul could think of nothing to say.

the maze that captured you sound of doors slamming maze prison of your heroes maze of dirty protests should i tell her my nickname at the prep was bobby sands

Laura pulled the car over under the giant Coke bottle stopping in front of the Olive Garden at 47th and Broadway. She slapped the button for the hazard lights.

… limelighting beaming phosphorescing sparking reflecting blinking bouncing ….

Flashes of the future … Flashes of the past … Blinking white lights running in circles and rectangles: Old Great White Way … a broken heart for every- … scrolling slogans phrases … shards of language … zipping all the words fit to crawl … flashing all the news that's fit to flash …

… U.S. SEEKS POL POT FOR TRIAL … CIGARETTE MAKERS QUIT BILL NEGOTIATIONS … LOGAN MUST LEAVE LAURA'S CAR … DESPITE PENDING PRESENTATION OF EASTER GIFT … STUDY: ONE IN EVERY EIGHT PLANT SPECIES IMPERILED … TIME … IS … RUNNING …. OUT

… fading in swiping dissolving wiping cutting zooming fading out …

— Well, thanks, Laura. My place is just a couple of blocks from here.

— See you, Paul! It was a wonderful evening.

strangely formal again funny how she does that

— Here. I got something for you. It's a little Easter present. People don't really give Easter presents but I saw this in the Irish Bookshop and figured what the hell?

A car pulled up behind them and was inching closer. Paul could see the car's headlights in the rear-view mirror.

— It's a Celtic art book. *Ready-to-Use Celtic Designs.* It shows you how to make Celtic designs, how to build your own Celtic artwork … See?

He flipped through a few pages of colorless knots, interlacings, and spirals.

forms geometric biomorphic metamorphic plant and animal to human and human to animal

— You can imitate the little patterns and color each piece however you want. Then you can create a whole picture made up of the little pieces …

Paul handed to Laura the book.

— Your own illuminated manuscript!

— Wow! Thanks, Paul! That's very thoughtful.

well done paul stupid stupid

The driver behind them started beeping.

— I better get moving.

— OK, well, have a happy Easter!

— Happy Easter!

— Have a good one, mate, said Charles.

Paul gathered up his bag and looked around the car to make sure he had everything. Advertising gleams bounced off the damp, dirty windshield, spotlighting the decrepitude of the shell-shocked car.

As Paul stooped in the open front door, Charles got out of the back seat and stood behind him.

where is he going is he leaving too

Stepping back, Paul asked:

— Is Charles headed uptown somewhere?

Charles slid in front of the door in Paul's hand. Paul was unable to see Laura's face.

— No, downtown.

— Downtown?!

Charles settled into the front seat.

— Yeah, Staten Island Ferry Terminal.

It took a moment for this to sink in.

Charles reached out and closed the door. Paul stood on the curb. On either side of him Broadway and 7th Avenue converged. Everything was converging — from the scrolling ticker symbols in the corner of his right eye to the theatres and hotels on his left — narrowing to a five-block-distant point.

He stopped her statement from sinking in before it really hurt.

— Well, I guess you can head all the way down Broadway and take it all the way down to the bottom of Manhattan.

where the island converges to a distant point downtown where we started rivers converging into the harbor waters converging into the sea

The car behind them raged in long beeps.

— I have to go, Laura said.

His lips trembled. His mouth sputtered. He could only mouth the word, "Why?"

She tilted her head toward the wheel to see him better, and added:

— Sorry, Paul. If you only had an accent …

that gallery painting a cordate pattern cut out from the chest of a retro dress somehow had had a chance and lost it was that a joke born in the wrong country a real live nephew of my uncle sam

Paul watched the BMW limp down Broadway.

... spangling glinting irridescing sparkling twinkling bedazzling spotlighting ...

...

After the death of his father, Sarsfield made an effort to travel to Philadelphia more frequently. His sister, Kitty, had moved into the Ardmore home and was taking good care of their mother. However, Sarsfield was concerned about Nora and how she would cope with the loss of her spirited husband.

Nora had the fur coats that Seamus had promised her when they first married and the Cadillac he had managed to buy her after many years of toil. She had her daughter to keep her company. And, her son and wonderful grandson were quite nearby. Still, Sarsfield knew she must have felt alone. She had lost her life's companion, her lover, the father of her children, and the founder of a company whose success had made life comfortable for all of them. For this, of course, she was to be pitied as any widow. But the loss of Nora Logan's husband was different from most. For Seamus had been a force of nature, a dynamo who had transformed much of the Delaware Valley. Such a loss was more than an absence. It was a subtraction.

So, disruptive as it was to his life in the Jesuit community, Sarsfield would hop on the ferry or the train to Philadelphia as often as possible during the months following his father's passing. Though, as a visiting priest in the family, he was welcomed like a prince or Broadway star, he tried to get as much time as he could alone with his mother. He enjoyed drinking tea with her at the kitchen table at which she said the rosary in her charming accent and at which she wrote letters to her friends in upstate Pennsylvania and to her relatives back in Ireland.

Nora had an elaborate process for making tea, a skill lost to her American offspring who were mainly coffee drinkers. After boiling the water, she would scald the pot and tilt into it a precise number of brimming soupspoons of loose leaves. Sarsfield had been accustomed to rambling on about his life in New York City as she performed these rituals, but in these quieter days of her early widowhood, he would fall silent and watch how she poured the steaming water from the kettle into the pot and how she covered the lid with a tea cozy as the brew steeped. Sarsfield felt that he had grown closer to his mother during these visits. Over tea, he even began to confess some of his own troubles to her.

"One aspect of being a teacher that I have always found difficult," Sarsfield began one rainy afternoon, "is controlling my temper. Sometimes the Xavier boys can really get my Irish up. Adolescent boys possess advanced skill at provocation. Once I let a boy out of Jug because he told me he had just started a job making deliveries for the local greengrocer, only to learn quite by chance that the boy had lied."

Nora sat down and poured cups of tea for the both of them. She put a small pitcher of milk on the table, though they both made such little use of it that there was not much point in doing so.

"The Blessed Mother told you," Nora smiled. "She does not like to let children fib."

Sarsfield chuckled.

"I suppose she did. She let you know often enough when we were dishonest. It seemed like we could never get away with anything. I know you never tolerated dishonesty but I recall your being patient with us most of the time."

Sarsfield sip-sipped the hot tea and lowered the cup back onto its saucer.

"But … what surprised me about this incident was the ferocity of my rage when I discovered that the boy had lied. It was like when I learned that Joe Jackson had taken part in the Black Sox scandal. Such a disgusting, disheartening breach of trust! It made me furious! It turned out that the boy had no job whatsoever. In fact, he was seen that very afternoon loafing on a street corner puffing on a cigarette. I gave him a public dressing down in the school corridor and made sure he served not one but two afternoons in Jug. But this still didn't satisfy me."

"That's understandable, Sarsfield." Nora said, pouring a drop of milk into her tea. "What the boy did was very wrong. It's your duty to teach children to be honest. You had every right to be angry."

"Thank you, Mother. I do feel that I was justified in being angry and in punishing the boy. But it was more than that. After discovering his dishonesty, I found myself harboring a grudge against the youth and when I heard him muttering insults behind my back — clever witticisms like, 'baldy' or 'Father Four Eyes' — I wanted to strike him across the face. I could almost feel the sting of smacking his cheek on my palm. I had visions of following him to the Sixth Avenue El and beating him up, as if I were some kind of street tough. I had to tell myself, 'No, Sarsfield! He is just a boy! You can't follow him to the train station!' I was shocked at my own imagination and fury. It must be the Irish temper I inherited from Father."

"Oh, I don't know if you should blame your father entirely. You might have gotten a biteen of that temper from myself as well."

"Really, Mother?" remarked Sarsfield with genuine surprise. "I have always considered you the more patient and forbearing parent."

"Well, I have had my moments of rage and obstreperousness," Nora said. "Did I ever tell you about how I ended up in this country in the first place?"

"No, you never have."

"When I was a young girl in Mallow, there was an oul' fella named Brophy with a farm just outside of the town, who fancied me. My parents fancied him, as well, or more to the point, they fancied the large parcel of land he had just come into."

Nora drank her tea, looked toward the lace-curtained window, and sighed.

"Looking back on it now, I don't suppose I can blame them. Sure, they were only looking after their daughter in the only way they could at the time.

"Anyway, one day they sat down in the snug at O'Malley's with old farmer Brophy. I wasn't allowed go' but half the town was loitering by the window wondering what the verdict would be and what kind of deal would be struck. A long meeting it was, from what I was told, and when the negotiations were finished me ma and da came home to tell me that I was going to marry the man and move into his cottage.

"Well, obedient as I always was to my parents, I had my own ideas about this deal I had no part in making. I threw a fit and refused to have anything to do with that dirty old goat as long as I lived. For days, I raged and stormed about the place refusing to take anything except a wee sup of tea on the sly. I was fit to be tied and swore that they could move Heaven and Hell before they could make me budge a single inch. But me ma and dad were just as stubborn. (After all, where do you think I learned it from?) And the great stalemate continued for several days. It was not the first time I had gone toe to toe with them over some girlish desire of mine and it soon became clear that my parents would not be made budge any more than I. I realized that defiance would never work.

"So, in the end I told them I would agree to the match, while secretly planning a way to take my own advice."

"A *reservatio mentalis*," Sarsfield smiled.

"Yes, indeed it was. I let no one know about my plan."

Nora slid forward in her chair, stirred her tea, and continued in a hushed tone.

"Well, the news went 'round that the match was made and the two families planned a celebration for our engagement. When I was asked what I would like for a present, I demanded a bicycle. I made it quite clear that I would accept nothing else. Knowing my opposition to the marriage and the great stubbornness I had shown in trying to prevent its occurrence, my parents made sure the bicycle would be provided.

She put down her spoon and leaned back.

"There was nothing really suspicious about the request, anyway. I had never had my own bicycle and I even suggested that I could use it to cycle home from the old goat's farm to visit them."

Nora put her forearms on the table and adopted a conspirator's tone again.

"The night before the engagement party, I had me bundle all packed. At the party, I thanked my fiancé warmly and, at first light the next morning, I pedaled off on the Mitchelstown road and cycled all the way to Dublin. In Dublin, I found work cleaning houses through a friend, and, as soon as I had the passage saved, took the first available ship to New York. So, my engagement present freed me from a bad marriage and brought me all the way to the shadow of Lady Liberty!"

...

... blazing dazzling flaming glimmering scintillating flickering incandescing lighting ...

Paul stepped across to the downtown sidewalk of 47th Street. He hung the strap of his messenger bag over his shoulder and just stood there.

read the symbols of this soleil cou coupe nightmare doubts since that first friday the thirteenth can't say it ain't so always get interested in girls who aren't right for me so stubborn heart upside down is a flame

He moved a few paces toward the back of a Celtic cross in Duffy Square.

like a cemetery by the road an ancient cross picks you up says follow me

Paul stopped by the forsaken TKTS. Across 7th Avenue, high above the hubbub of the street, a ghost ad had returned from the dead. Painted on the bricks a century ago, it called:

CARRIAGE MANUFACTORY

REPAIR

Despite all efforts to cover it up, it reappears: the obstreperous past. Long ago, they bought and sold horses here and fixed carriages. Horseman pass by. Did great grandad read that ad? Before he boarded the train to Philadelphia?

CLINTON ... LEWINSKY ... LAWYERS WANT ... CLOSED COURT ... CITICORP-TRAVELERS ... MERGER ... TOO BIG? ... I ... WILL KISS ... THOSE ... LIPS ... AGAIN ... CONSUMER ... GROUPS ... CONCERNED ... IF YOU ... ONLY ... HAD .... AN ACCENT ...

what does she want from me i have a philadelphia accent kicking out brits for over 200 years slan abhaile

Paul found himself behind the Celtic cross. He read each word etched onto its back.

A LIFE OF SERVICE

FOR

GOD AND COUNTRY

SPANISH AMERICAN WAR

NEW YORK NATIONAL GUARD

MEXICAN BORDER

WORLD WAR

Father Duffy must have led the league in last rites. For kids he once baptized.

i taught kids french so that they could pronounce the names of the battlefields they died on

The World War. Funny to read that. War to end all wars. End of the enthusiastic ones, anyway. World to end all wars. Next war to end all worlds. 'Twas the first of a century of war … Send war in our time, O Lord! … War more war and more war … interrupted by periods of exhaustion … continuing through all our stupid, repeated Vietnams.

Lennon's billboard to end all wars. Where was it?

WAR IS OVER!

IF YOU WANT IT.

Yeah, work for peace and they shoot you in the back.

JAPAN SURRENDERS on the zipper. It's all over. The war is over. Grab a blonde and kiss her.

all night chasing after that stupid blonde never accomplishing anything never kissed her never had a moment alone with her only to end up seething work for love and they stab you in the back how much money did i waste better off going to one of those hookers loping around here throbbing bulbs of peep land live girls blinking single neon eye red booths muffle recorded womens moans showtime strong industrial soap sharp in nostrils never wanted to pass saint pats on the depleted walk back cave cave deus videt to the ad agency

And to find out that she's half Belfast prod!

The Union Jacks so thick over the Shankhill you can't see … What flaw of identity? What soul-flaw are they overcompensating for? Just like her. Doesn't know who she is.

Forbidding city of watching … Barrel of the Mona Lisa gunman aims ever in your direction … under the low sky of grey … under the high sky of blue … through the rain and the rainbow both. The Shankhill and the Falls mirroring each other, Mona-Lisa glaring at each other … through rifle scopes …

Limies don't want them. Neither will he after he finishes with her. His heart does not palpitate like mine.

Above the glittering MacDonald's on 7th Avenue shone a triptych advertisement in red. The letters L and a G formed a white face whose single right eye stared down at Paul's left. As white light wiped the display, the face's single left eye reflected in the windows above Broadway stared down at Paul's right.

But back down to the harbor she goes with that cockblocking bloke. Skinny little creep. I could break him in half with my bare hands. Pencil-necked twink! Ears like ladle bowls sticking out from the sides of his head! I'd make it a long Good Friday for him. A broke, sad, weak, derided, and dozing cook. Can't handle his liquor. And a serious impediment in is his reach. Nation of centkeepers. I hope the April showers make him shiver and shake all the way back home. Rule the waves, indeed. Ferryboat the right speed for him.

WELFARE ... TO WORKPLACE ... COMPANIES SAY ... WELFARE ... RECIPIENTS ... GOOD PRODUCTIVE ... EMPLOYEES ... I COULD ... SHOW YOU ... AROUND ... NOT M ... A ... I ... S ... E ... M... A ....Z ....E .... NEVER ... AGAIN ...

Paul sidestepped around the High Cross and stopped next to Father Duffy. The bald warrior-priest held two clenched fists at his trenchcoat beltbuckle.

> *Punchin' babies with me fist*
> *And so I thought I might enlist*
> *And join the British army .*

The cup of noodles advertisement near the top of the Times Tower belched forth a cloud of steam which, rising, covered for a moment the neon digits, 1998.

Some say the divil is dead but I rode with him in a beat-up car all night Holy Thursday. Talks like a faggot, too. Can't stand that. Mom had no time for them. Couldn't stand to hear the accent on TV.

Hope a ghost of a man drowned in the harbor haunts him all the way to that garbage island where he belongs. Filthy thieves think they're better than everybody. Look at any trouble spot in the world and guess who was there drawing lines in the bog, sand, or jungle before they skedaddled back to their Satanic mills? Iraq, South Africa, India, Zimbabwe, Israel ...

Who makes peace by building a wall, anyway? I could put my fist right through it! Only they who can think only what they have thought before, who can try only what they have tried before.

And what a fine conversationalist he is! Nothing to say for himself. Nothing to offer. Never read a book, let alone wrote one. Never watched a movie that didn't have explosions in it. Talk to him about music, he doesn't know "Blackbird" from Black Sabbath.

How dare he think he can take her away from me? With that Brit aplomb, "Bye, mate!" I ain't your mate, pal. Brits Out, buddy. No kidding. Sweep the Saxons from the walls of New York town. Out of my island. Out of my life. Have you got no fuckin' homes of your own? Stuyvesant should have never let the perfidious bastards in.

In a black and white photo, half of Alfred Hitchock's face was hidden behind crumbling brick and mortar with one visible eye looking up toward the slogan, "Think Different." Another one! Damn people coming over here and making themselves rich in Hollywood then taking the money back to their miserable island and its parasite queen.

The queen of ye:

Who invaded our land to help wife-stealer Dermot MacMurrough,

Who tried to crush our religion,

Whose Cromwell sent Catholics to hell or Connacht,

Who planted Protestants on our soil, hoping it would blossom with them,

Who imposed the Penal Laws,

Who tortured and the massacred the United Men in '98,

Who shipped food out of the country while the people starved,

Who executed the heroes of 1916,

Who sent the Black and Tans,

Who partitioned the land with a gerrymandered province that never existed,

Who kept the Six County Catholics from voting,

Who presided over Diplock Courts,

Who watched from the Divis Towers.

Who shot peaceful protestors on Bloody Sunday,

Who colluded with the terrorists to kill Catholics,

Who let the Hunger Strikes die

        ….in the Maze.

Ye that have imprisoned and starved!

Ye as full of hypocrisy as ye are empty of imagination.

Ye who rounded us up in your camps.

Ye whose uniforms we refuse.

Ye that have hated and hurt, see the hatred that burns.

Ye that have tried to douse it only for it to grow.

In your prison of filth, we will spit in your face

The tales of our heroic past

That probe the passage tomb of *Bru na Boinne*: Newgrange, Knowth, and Dowth

That glow from the Gospels of Kells.

... floodlighting shimmering coruscating glittering illuming ...

...

Janey had finished everything except adding the mayonnaise to her potato salad mixture. Was that rain?

She had heard a tap on the window pane, followed by another and another. But, she had been so busy cooking that she had not noticed the change in the weather. There was so much to do. That's why she had sent Paul to the store to get mayonnaise. She didn't like it herself and so she never knew when they were out of it.

Suddenly, the wind picked up. It took hold of the multiplying rain drops, and dashed them against the kitchen window, replacing the solitary taps with a quick, soft rattle.

Janey left the sink and stepped over to the window. It really was raining now; and Paul was not back yet. He should have returned by now: the A&P was just over at Suburban Square. She stared for a moment at the blooming magnolia trees in the backyard. The darkened sky gave their bright blossoms a moody backdrop. She thought of evenings at Saint Francis de Sales, before West Catholic, before Logan Construction Company, before James and the kids ...

The screen door out front clattered shut. Aroused, Janey went to the kitchen doorway. She spied Paul crossing the living room. His hands were empty and the look on his face told her he did not know what to say.

"Where's the mayonnaise?" Janey asked.

"It was in a brown paper bag and I was riding home with it and it started to rain. The bag got wet."

"They gave it to you in a single bag?"

"Yeah, and it got wet and the bag broke. The jar fell in the middle of the street and it smashed."

"Where?"

Paul winced.

"Just down the street ... Simpson Road ... I tried to make it back...."

Paul could still picture the first few speckles of moisture appearing on the paper bag. He had started pedaling harder to get home before it got completely soaked. He kept looking down at the bag draped over his handlebars, getting more and more alarmed at how quickly the raindrops were darkening its shade of brown. He tried to hurry but, it was just too far. The bag split in two and the mayonnaise jar crashed to the asphalt.

"But the bag got too wet."

"Just a single bag? They gave it to a young boy in just a single bag?"

Strangely, she seemed angrier at the store clerk than at Paul. Maybe he would not get in trouble.

"Yeah, it was only one bag and it wasn't that strong when it got wet."

"Get in the car! I'm going over there and tell them a thing or two about sending young boys home with a jar of mayonnaise in a single bag in the rain!"

Without a word, Paul hustled out to the car, ducking his head to avoid the raindrops, and sat himself in the passenger seat.

"Are you just going to leave your bike in the driveway?"

"I thought- … Um … You said-"

"Put it in the garage where it belongs!"

His mother's anger was now branching out in different directions and he didn't want it to contort itself toward him. Paul ran out of the car, toed his kickstand up, and wheeled the bicycle over to the garage. He bent down and grabbed the black door handle and with some effort got it moving upward. Once it had some momentum, it went easily up and over. He put the bike inside and closed the door again. Janey rolled her eyes when it slammed onto the concrete, as Paul hustled back to the car.

Janey started the engine. The radio came on with it. A WFIL announcer blared on about a contest and Janey shut it right off. She did not want anything to disturb or distract her.

They drove in silence through the moody streets overhung with blossoming trees. The sky was dark and the rain was soft but steady. Some tree blossoms were stuck to the street and the sidewalks by the rain. No one was outside in the small front yards. The only sound was the rhythmic whooshing and squeaking of the windshield wipers.

When they got about halfway to the supermarket, Paul spotted the smashed jar in the middle of the street: mayonnaise and broken glass and brown paper all mixed into a disgusting mess. It reminded him of the dead birds he sometimes saw on these same streets as he walked home from school.

"There it is."

"I see it, hon'."

The mess didn't seem to make her feel sad. It seemed only to increase and focus her rage.

They pulled into the Suburban Square lot and parked. Janey shut off the car and pulled the keys from the ignition. She marched directly toward the front door of the A&P. Paul hesitated for a moment and then figured he should probably follow her.

He stepped on the black mat and the door swung open. As he got inside, he could hear his mother shouting at a teenaged cashier

"… the manager," she was saying, as if to someone who couldn't understand English, "I WANT… TO SEE … the MANAGER!"

A small man with an obsequious smile beneath his mustache appeared, trying to appear important and polite at the same time. He was not even able to utter, "How can I help you, ma'am?" before Janey Dougherty Logan turned on him her flamethrower of ire.

"I would like to know what genius put a jar of mayonnaise in a single bag for a young boy to take home on his bike on a rainy day! Whose brilliant idea was that — to give a flimsy little bag to a boy trying to run an errand for his mother on his bike?"

She glared at the cashiers one by one as if she could read the stupidity and meanness on the culprit's face.

"Whatever happened, ma'am, I'm sure we can talk it over in a civil tone."

"Civil tone, my eyeball! You'd like to keep everything in a civil tone, as quiet as can be — wouldn't you? Maybe in your office. Well, I'll tell you, I am a regular customer here and I want everyone to know…"

Her voice grew even louder.

"… I want all the regular customers to know how a young boy running an errand for his mother is treated by the A&P of Ardmore! I asked my son, Paul, …

She pointed toward her boy who stood timidly at the edge of the scene, his hands in his pockets, his eyes on his shoes.

"… to get me a jar of mayonnaise. And one of the Einsteins you have here put the jar into a single bag. Are two bags too much for A&P to afford? Is it too much trouble to double bag a jar of mayonnaise on a rainy day?! The bag got wet in the rain and the jar is now lying smashed in the middle of Simpson Road."

"Well, if something happened on the way home after he left the store-"

"Yeah, something did happen on the way home — the single bag you gave him broke!"

"Come over here, hon'," she said under her breath.

Paul walked over and she put her arm around him. She raised her voice again.

"Do you want to go out and see the single broken bag and jar in the middle of the street right now? I'm prepared to show it to you and anyone else who is interested …"

Customers had stopped in the aisle to listen. A couple of women pushed their shopping carts closer to the checkout lines to see what was going on.

"… if you really want to go to such trouble to defend service so poor and so stingy that you can't even double bag your groceries on a rainy day for a customer obviously too young to drive … if this is what you want me to tell my friends, your customers — that the A&P is too cheap to double bag its groceries, then-"

"Of course not. Of course not, Mrs. Logan. What kind of mayonnaise was it? Charlie, come over here and help Mrs. Logan."

A few minutes later, Janey and Paul walked out of the store with a free jar of mayonnaise, in a double bag.

Paul felt his mother could have gotten a whole order of groceries for free if she had wanted to. But she had fought like a lioness for only a jar of mayonnaise.

And she didn't even like mayonnaise.

…

Tip my hat to Mr. Cohan? Yes. Yes, I should. Fellow link in the songwriters' chain.
Instead of heading home along 47th Street, Paul's feet took him toward the statue.
Did George ever shop on Music Row?

But it is Mary, Mary
Long before the fashions came…

Paul looked back toward 48th Street and then up again at Father Duffy.
What does he have in his hands? A cross? A book. A bible. Only to find Gideon's Bible.

Before the lights of Times Square Paul could see the dark statue of the great song and dance man, assuming a jaunty post while leaning on his cane. In the skybluing light of dawn. In the distance two old time dudes in black relaxing over mugs of beer, one with a cane. Times Square Brewery.

And in the nadir of it all
A recruiting station.

A recruiting station on Fordham Road tipped the scale toward accepting the Saint Philomena's job. You wanted peace.

… HE SAYS HE HAS A REAL JOB … JAPAN ECONOMIC REFORMS -- JAPANESE PRIME MINISTER … RYUTARO HASHIMOTO'S … $30 BILLION TAX CUT PLAN … ANNOUNCED TODAY … RUSSIA'S DISGRUNTLED WORKERS PROTEST … THE KREMLIN'S INABILITY … TO PAY … BACK WAGES …

Just over there …over there … the other world? … Is that where he's looking? *Tá Tír na nÓg ar chúl an tí.*

It's a grand old flag!

Cycle of Times Square history. Used to be able to get a sandwich for a nickel at the automat or watch the progress of the World Series on a giant model …. Then sleazy heart-pounding danger … now becoming Disney …Cycle of Broadway to Broadway …

Manhattan converging at its tip … at the Staten Island Ferry … coming together in a point … everything converging and rising …

Give my regards to Broadway!

A horse with blinders on trudged down Broadway pulling a white carriage with red interior. Paul smiled at a decal on the side of the carriage, which displayed an Irish tricolor and the words, "Made in Skibbereen." Behind the coachman's seat stood a tall bouquet of flowers.

Are they looking for tourists this time of night? Maybe it's a ghost buggy looking for that phantom repairman.

Easter's on its way, don't forget. Hippity hoppity. Easter lilies for sale in bodegas. Wrapped in white. 1-800-Purity. The daffodils who entertain. On the stand across the street a Chinese man sat waiting for a tourist to ask for a caricature. 70 times 7. 70 Times Square 7.

All we are saying … British man of Irish descent. Not for London or for Rome. Walked the silent streets of Ardmore listening to his interviews on the boombox after they shot him. Inspired my first songs. Convergence and rising. Transcending. Beyond the tribal conflicts.

So, the cook ran away with the maid. The dish ran away with the spoon. The prod ran away with the Brit. And the little dog laughed.

We'll be over!
We're coming over
And we won't come back
'Til it's over over there!

You're nuts turning it all into an international historical ethnic national conflict of peoples and countries and tribes. These foreigners come over here taking our hard-earned dollars and high-cheek-boned barmaids!

Charles is a nice kid for the most part. He never did anything to you ... on purpose. He can't help it if she likes him. It's not like he knew what he was doing and brought it about.

> *But soone shal he wepe many a teere*
> *For wommen shal hym bryngen to meschaunce!*

When she turned those half-mast eyes toward you, what did you have to do with it? And he has a lot in common with her. He is closer to her age. Young and footloose like her. No specters of exes on the streetcorners of other days. Both of them are denizens of the night world, cooking food and pouring drinks into the wee hours.

> *And baby goes home to her flat*
> *To sleep all day*

While they're sleeping it off after a night shift, you have to get up, join the straphangers on the 2 or 3, be sober, be professional, contribute to your 401k.

And you, Mr. Savoir Faire, do you think that you handled it all so perfectly? Your idea of seducing her is showing up for your "date" in your best pampooties. Oh, give a girl a chance.

Charles did buy the dumplings in Chinatown. And he pays for a round of drinks now and then. He's just a kid working in a restaurant. He doesn't make the same amount of money that you do and can't afford these Manhattan prices.

DO YOU GET ... TO MANY ... BROADWAY SHOWS ... PAUL ... FUNERAL SERVICES ... WILL BE HELD ... IN NASHVILLE ... FOR COUNTRY SINGER ... TAMMY WYNETTE .... TOBACCO'S FUTURE UNCERTAIN .... A FACE ON IT ... AND IT ... COULD BE ... GOD'S ...

And those Tommies in the Six Counties, most of them were just poor kids doing their jobs. The women on the Falls Road used to make them tea. Then they turned on them. And blamed them for everything. Banging their binlids. Cursing those gun-toting boys with a fury you'd find nowhere else. Hard for those boys to know whom to trust. You wouldn't want to be in their place. Caught between the taigs and the prods. Like our boys in Vietnam. Grandma didn't mind them. Said many of them were nice people. Forgive them for they know not what they do. Government's policy, not their fault. Informers inform, burglars burgle, ... They thought they were going over there to make peace and they have to build a wall to keep the citizens from tearing each other apart. Throw people in jail and they rub their own shit on the walls and live in it. No wonder they thought we were bloody savages at times. Being blamed for everything, even problems caused by ourselves alone.

"Violence brings force more violence." Saint Philomena's Elizabeth Irizarry on *Macbeth*. Is that Alec Baldwin production still running? Would be cool to see that live.

I don't always hate their accents. I love listening to the Royal Shakespeare Company actors. An Oxford tutorial would be like heaven to me. Meeting with a tweedy old professor to discuss works of literature. Watching him carefully select a leather-bound volume from the shelf in a room smelling of pipe smoke and moldering paper. A book chosen specifically for you, for this moment of your education.

— Why not try this work by Thomas Hardy? What about Jane Austen? Or Lord Byron?

you like the mad bad and dangerous to know maybe theres a pattern

Ironically, that kind of teaching seems made for me. You do have a degree in their language and literature, after all.

And their humor. Mom said she never liked it but nothing makes me laugh harder. Cheese shops and silly walks.

History to blame. But to wake up first one must sleep. Manhattan babies never sleep until the dawn.

Good night, baby
Good night, the milkman's on his way

And then there are the Beatles and all the great rock bands. Irish people have lived there for years.

And we won't come back
'Til it's over over there.
Over there!
Over there!

The zipper? Is that where he's looking?

On the front of the Times Square zipper, Paul spotted the word, "Ireland." Was he imagining things?

Paul stood there beside the Cohan Statue and waited for the news to come around again. And this time there was no mistaking the words:

N. IRELAND ... TALKS ... IGNORE ... DEADLINE ... PEACE ... AGREEMENT WITHIN ... GRASP ...

Yes, that is what it said.

Will it really happen? Could he believe it?

... "IT COULD BE ... IN BRIGHT LIGHT," ... OFFICIAL ... SAYS ...

— Is it a miracle? Paul asked himself. Or a hoax?

And walked on.

ABOUT THE AUTHOR

John Kearns is the author of the short-story collection, *Dreams and Dull Realities* and the novel, *The World* and playwright of dramas including *Boann and the Well of Wisdom* and *In the Wilderness*. John's fiction has appeared in publications such as *The Medulla Review* and *The Irish Echo*. His poems have appeared in journals including the *Grey Sparrow Journal* and *The Razor's Wine*. His essay "Bronx Thunder to Riverside Angels" is included in Colin Broderick's *Writing Irish of New York*. John has a Masters Degree in Irish Literature from the Catholic University of America. He lives in New York City.

ABOUT *WORLDS*

Worlds was a finalist in the 2018 William Wisdom - William Faulkner Creative Writing Competition in New Orleans. An early excerpt from *Worlds* was a finalist for the 2002 New Century Writers' Award. Another excerpt was named a finalist for the 2012 James Hearst Poetry Prize and published in the *North American Review*. The *Danse Macabre* online literary magazine has published four additional excerpts from *Worlds*.

In 2016, Malachy McCourt read an excerpt from *Worlds* at "Welcoming Ireland," New York City's celebration of Ireland's 1916 Easter Rising centenary. In 2018, an excerpt from *Worlds* was read at a County Mayo Foundation wreath laying at New York's Irish Hunger Memorial.

ABOUT THE COVER ILLUSTRATOR

Tim O'Brien's illustrations have appeared countless times on the covers of magazines and books and he has illustrated several US Postage Stamps. Tim has received awards and recognitions from the Society of Illustrators, *Graphis*, *Communication Arts*, the Society of Publication Designers, *American Illustration*, *Spectrum*, *Advertising Age* and the Art Directors Club, sweeping bronze, silver and gold in 2019. Tim's paintings are among the collection of the National Portrait Gallery in Washington, DC. Tim is the current president of the Society of Illustrators, NY.